PhD.

(A Time Traveler's Search for Bacon)

David W. Dubé

For Robert

Our son with a PhD. in bacon

Dubé Family

	Married	Spouse
Robert Aditya Dubé Born: May 17, 2002 Syracuse, New York	Married	Spouse
David William Dubé Born: January 27, 1952 Syracuse, New York	August 16, 1997 Syracuse, New York	Maithreyee T. Chavan Born: July 28, 1971 Coimbatore, India
Robert Jean Dubé Born: Sept. 23, 1917 Montmorency Falls, Québec Died: June 6, 1993 Syracuse, New York	June 29, 1946 Schenectady, New York	Jane Elizabeth Hand Born: June 28, 1919 Amsterdam, New York Died: May 23, 1993 Syracuse, New York
David Douglas Dubé Born: April 7, 1872 St-Colomb Sillery, PQ	September 17, 1892 Sillery, PQ	Agnes Daly born: November 15, 1875
Charles Dubé	November 11, 1866 St-Colomb Sillery PQ	Mary Theresa Kerr Born:1842 Greene, NY Died:1910
Mathias Dubé Born: February 25, 1810 Saint Louis, Kamouraska	June 23, 1835 Notre-Dame de Québec Québec City	Theresa Duval Born: 1810 Québec City, PQ

Joseph Augustin Dubé Born : June 12, 1775 Riviere Ouelle PQ Died : July 21, 1845 Notre Dame PQ	January 26, 1807 Riviere Ouelle, PQ	Marie Clémence Rivard Born : April 18, 1773
Joseph Maurice Dubé Born: February 15, 1733 Riviere Ouelle, PQ	January 12, 1761 Riviere Ouelle, PQ	Marie Anne Plourde Born: January 15, 1739 Riviere Ouelle, PQ Died: October 12, 1788
Louis Dubé Born: February 2, 1698 Riviere Ouelle, PQ Died: April 16, 1765 Riviere Ouelle, PQ	January 8, 1721 Riviere Ouelle, PQ	Céline Emond Born: May 11, 1702 Riviere Ouelle, PQ Died: April 1765
Louis Dubé Born: May 25, 1676 Montmagny, PQ Died: March 1, 1747 Montmorency, PQ	January 28, 1696 Riviere Ouelle, PQ	Marie Angélique Boucher Born: October 28, 1676 Died : March 2, 1716 Riviere Ouelle, PQ
Mathurin Dubé Born: 1631 La Chapelle Thémer, Fr Died: December 30, 1695	September 3, 1670 Riviere Ouelle, PQ	Marie Catherine Campion Born: 1654 Rouen, France Died: January 28, 1697

Riviere Ouelle, PQ		Riviere Ouelle, PQ
Jean Dubé	1630 La Chapelle Thémer, France	Renée Suzanne
Born : about 1610		Born : about 1610
La Chapelle-Thémer, France		La Chapelle-Thémer, France

Introduction

This is a novel about my family's history. My reason for writing this is to give our son a better grasp of where my father's side of the family came from. Originally my plan was to construct a concise list about our family and French history. As I learned more about our history and read more about French history I decided to create a story from it

My goal was to be as accurate as possible regarding people and events. I combined Robert's appreciation of science and love of bacon with the information I learned from my cousin Louise and books from the Syracuse University library courtesy of my wife's aunt Charu. The cities, churches historical events and the people involved are as accurate as I could make them. While the people Robert came in contact with i.e.: Louis XVI and the Royal family, Gabrielle etc. existed; those closest to him; Ron, Bernard, Lisette and Herni and Gerard did not.

The Onondaga Indian Reservation (Onondaga Nation or the Nation) was going to play an important role in the story. Having grown up a few miles from the Nation, I wanted to be as accurate as possible with their information as well. I tried contacting members of the Nation but their response was unremarkable. They were semi helpful and my information is therefore semi accurate.

My hope is that this is a story our son can share with his children someday and we can all appreciate what it took for Mathurin and Marie to leave their homes for New France.

ACKNOWLEDGEMENTS

About the same time that I decided to write a story about our family history, I happened to be talking with my cousin Jackie about our plans to visit France that summer and possibly the village where my ancestor had left France for the New World. She mentioned that my cousin, Louise de Foy had done extensive genealogical research and I should contact her.

Very shortly after that, my cousin Louise, whom I hadn't spoken to in fifty years contacted me and shared a lot of helpful information. This was really the basis for much of my story in France.

When I was struggling for ideas about how Robert would power his time machine, my wife's cousins Tejas Rane and Rushil Rane suggested using an U.P.S. as the alternative.

Hanshi Greg Tearney's advice regarding Robert's use of karate was invaluable.

In the middle of conducting research into the Dubé family, two names kept popping up; Linda Dube and Paul Dubé. They were both very helpful and added a lot to the story of Robert's visit to La Chapelle-Thémer and the children's reenactment of the battle against the British behind the Dubé house.

I read partially or entirely about fifty books to gather information for this story. That never would have been possible without my wife's Aunt Charu Chawan, a research librarian at Syracuse University.

My wife, Maithreyee is a genius with computers and helped me remember the many things I forgot about her instructions including indentation etc.;. Preparing this story would have been very difficult without her help.

Contents

THE HAHAMOG'NA

Nearly 1500 years before the birth of Christ, the Tongva people left present day Nevada and journeyed west for hundreds of miles, stopping when their trek ended at the ocean. A branch of their tribe, the Hahamog'na, would eventually settle in hamlets along the banks of the Arroyo Seco among shady sycamores, tall oaks, manzanitas, wild grapes and elderberries.

For more than 3000 years, their lives proceeded fairly unchanged. They began their day when the sun rose over the unnamed hills and mountains in the east and signaled the end of the day as it settled into the ocean in the west. Their dome shaped lodges, thatched and constructed from willow poles, were well suited to the climate.

Food was abundant, consisting of a diet of corn meal, seeds and herbs, venison and small animals. Sometimes they traded with their Tongva cousins who settled on the coast, for ocean fish and soapstone cooking vessels they had obtained from the Tongva who lived on Catalina Island.

Soapstone vessels were sought after because they were heat resistant and could be left on a fire, but to reach Catalina Island the Tongva would navigate across 22 miles of the Gulf of Santa Catalina in their canoes called a ti'at, which were constructed from planks of wood, tied together and caulked with tar.

This life worked well for the Hahamog'na and their Tongva relatives for centuries. What no one could have foreseen was how their culture would collapse rapidly, due to a series of events; beginning with two births, a world away in the early 18th century

Miguel Joseph Serra was born on the island of Majorca; about 175 miles off the coast of Spain in the Mediterranean Sea on November 14, 1713 and Gaspar de Portola entered this world into nobility in the farming community of Os de Balaguer in Catalonia, Spain, in 1716.

Miguel entered the priesthood and in 1730, and in 1749 Father Junípero Serra's duties found him in Mexico City as a Franciscan scholar where he would eventually build 21 missions from Baja to Northern California. Lieutenant Gaspar de Portolá led expeditions into northern California to establish missions and other outposts, accompanied by Father Serra.

In 1770, tired and frustrated from a series of failed expeditions, Lieutenant De Portolá stumbled into the Hahamog'na village and was immediately warmly welcomed by their leader, Tumia'r Hahamongvic, who shared a piece pipe with him.

Father Serra established the Mission San Gabriel and imposed the name Gabrieliños upon the Tongvas, just the beginning of many intrusions.

California became a Mexican territory in 1822 and the fatal intrusion into the Tongva lifestyle became unstoppable. Those Tongva who were converted to Christianity, were not allowed to return to their people to prevent them from reverting to their old religion. The Hahamog'na land along the Arroyo Seco changed hands several times over the years. Mexicans were granted land in that area, provided that they would cultivate it and in the event that they failed to do so, the land was reclaimed by the governor and granted to someone else.

The United States took possession of California following the Mexican-American War and the last Mexican landowner, Manuel Garfias, sold property to the new Anglo settlers. One of them was Benjamin Wilson, who established the Lake Vineyard property and was called Don Benito by the Hahamog'na.

In 1873 Dr. Daniel Berry, a physician from Indiana, purchased land along the Arroyo Seco for his asthma patients and named it the Indiana Colony.

Mail for the Indiana Colony was delivered to the Los Angeles post office, where it would remain until someone from the colony would travel approximately 15 miles to retrieve it. As the colony continued to grow, the residents of the Indiana Colony petitioned the government for their own post office, but the Postmaster General required that they rename their town something that he considered appropriate to their surroundings. The final names submitted were, "Indianola, Granada and Crown of the Valley". The Indian translation of "of the valley" was Pasadena and that name was adopted.

Pasadena rapidly evolved into a resort town, leading to the construction of several great hotels. The Hotel Green in 1888, The Raymond; which was destroyed by fire in 1895, and the Vista de Arroyo, which eventually became home to the Ninth Circuit Court of Appeals.

In 1891, Amos Throop, a local businessman and politician, founded a much needed preparatory and vocational school for the growing community in downtown Pasadena. Throop College attracted many influential scientists, such as George Ellery Hale and the name eventually changed to Caltech in 1921. In spite of its small size, Caltech alumni and faculty have won a total of 33 Nobel prizes and 70 have won the U.S. National Medal of Science or Technology. The only student protest was in January 1968 at NBC Burbank studios in response to rumors that NBC was going to cancel Star Trek.

For millions upon millions of years before the arrival of the Hahamog'na Indians, the sun rose over the unnamed hills in the east and set beyond the Arroyo Seco into the Pacific Ocean. The sun's predictable rhythm was repeated daily for the Tongva and all those who had preceded them.

The movement of water caused by the less predictable rains resulted in swiftly flowing streams, sweeping through the Arroyo Seco, slowly moving one stone, striking another and setting it in motion in addition to sand and leaves and branches.

As this force was carried by the current faster and faster, formerly still water involuntarily moved steadily forward as the result of all this activity.

Like the force of the stream, the movement of people, once the force was applied, led inevitably to the final outcome. Until the moment when this energy was transmitted to those parts which have been unaffected by the downhill flow, they remain stationary and dormant. Stones will rest in their streams or eddies, while a neighboring stream is also still and motionless as it remains from the last storm. But the movement finally arrives when the rushing water reaches them and responding to the ebbs and flows all of these pieces that existed separately, now takes part in the common movement.

Just as the result of the swift complex action of immeasurable volumes of water coursing down the Arroyo Seco is in deep contrast to the slow, regular movement of the sun which indicates the passing of seasons, so too is the result of all the complicated human activities of the Tongva and Europeans.

All the desires and expectations of individuals, as well as the results caused by the collisions of these cultures; drive the slow movement of human history for countless seasons where the sun rises over the San Gabriel Mountains before crossing the San Rafael Hills.

Eventually, its light envelops Pasadena, warming the tops of pine trees and eucalyptus trees which stand above the other plants and pools and fountains, making up the landscape on the campus of Caltech. Manzanita bushes and other various shrubs surrounding the physics laboratory, all receive the sun's gesture that the new day has begun, as sunlight reaches both those who are proceeding toward their destinations and those who are waiting to be awakened

.

PhD.

Sunlight streaming through the window warmed the side of his unshaven face as he heard a door open and then close, followed by the smell of strong coffee.

"It's a great morning," announced a familiar voice.

"What in the world is someone doing in my room?" he pondered, finally succeeding in opening his eyes.

Directly before him, holding two large Starbuck's coffees was his colleague, Ron Maxwell. Ron reached across the desk and placed a cup of Starbuck's near Robert's right hand. "Tall drip as usual. You know Robert, for all the money you spend for your apartment at Avery House, you might consider sleeping there more than in our office."

Realizing that he had once again fallen asleep while reclined in his chair; he raised his feet from the desk and placed them on the floor. As PhD. candidates at Caltech, Ron and Robert were both accustomed to working long hours. Ron seemed best suited to study in his apartment at Avery House, one of eight on campus student houses; while Robert was doomed to work late in the physics laboratory and wake up at his desk. A large number of graduate students and faculty chose to live at Avery House, which was convenient as it was located on campus.

Robert stood nearly 6 feet tall with dark brown eyes, straight black hair and wide shoulders from years of involvement in karate beginning at the age of four, first as a student and then as an instructor.

After spending his first few years of life in the small red cape style house in the Valley section of Syracuse, his parents moved to nearby Camillus, where they felt his educational opportunities would be greater. His mother worked at Syracuse University where he was introduced to scientists where he hoped to one day, pursue his studies in physics. Following completion of his master's degree in physics at Syracuse University, Robert had been accepted into the doctoral program at Caltech, the only program he had applied for.

Ron grew up on West Berks Street in southwest Philadelphia. It was a neighborhood that was held together more by the will of individual families than the community itself. This should have been and once was an excellent place to raise a family. Schools, their church and the Fairmount Athletic Field were all located a few blocks from their home.

However, most of the buildings were in some state of disrepair. Weeds grew freely in long neglected sidewalks in front of row houses separated by barren lots bordered by small wooden fences erected by someone, hoping they would brighten the dismal emptiness where a home once stood. People sat on steps in front of windows and doors covered with sheets of plywood unwilling or afraid to make eye contact with anyone walking past.

When Ron finished elementary school, his father had seen and experienced enough to compel him to move their family to a town near Pittsburg. This community was completely different than his old neighborhood. The area consisted mostly of small single family homes with large yards where Ron was able to concentrate on learning at Upper St. Clair High School among tree covered hills. His new home was located about 15 miles from Carnegie Mellon University where he completed his graduate program in physics.

Ron was much taller than Robert, with very dark skin, short hair, black lustrous eyes and fragile shoulders. They immediately became fast and inseparable friends to the point that despite their differences in appearance; people on campus constantly confused their names.

Other students may have been more gifted academically, but each shared a restless imagination which separated them, questioning and utilizing methods that other in the academic community would never have considered.

They had both begun their research in black holes while they worked toward their master's degrees and became especially interested in the possibility of time travel, enthusiastically deciding to work together; their goal being the construction of a working machine capable of time travel.

"And what have we learned today?" asked Ron with a hint of sarcasm.

Robert flexed his toes on the carpet and took his first sip of coffee. As its aroma and warmth gradually returned him to life, he brushed from their competition and led them to constantly seek answers to his hand across the face of his laptop and the project they were laboring on was projected onto a screen suspended from the ceiling.

"The good news is that I didn't discover any new problems," Robert began, rubbing his face as he sat up in his chair and focused on the information shown on the screen. "However, we still have the same list of items to solve if we are ever going to build a working time machine. First, in theory, we should be able to travel forward in time, but not travel any further back in time than the date of the time machine's creation. Our goal should be to eliminate that barrier if we want to proceed."

"Second, a ring laser will be necessary to change the gravitational field, allowing us to construct a time machine but we still need to find a way to generate more power; in theory."

"Do you realise that we seem to either begin or end sentences with the words, in theory? Is there anything in your laptop that doesn't begin or end that way?" asked Ron sounding slightly annoyed.

"We have this," offered Robert as he opened a file, projecting new content from his latest efforts onto the screen. "If we put these together, I really believe that we can arrive at a solution, well in theory."

As they studied their work on the screen, they heard a knock at the door and turned to see Mrs. Spencer; Dean Fleming's administrative secretary entered their office. "Good Morning Dr. Maxwell and Dr. Dubé. How are we today?" Mrs. Spencer always addressed them as Dr. in private although they had only recently defended their dissertations before committees.

Mrs. Spencer was a woman of medium height, with rosy cheeks, short black hair and shining black eyes. She was known by everyone on campus for her kind heart

"Fine Mrs. Spencer," they answered together, "and you?"

"Just fine thank you," as she paced quickly about their office clearly interested in locating something. Dean Fleming had a predictable habit of forgetting where he had left anything he happened to have in his possession which had been particularly important to him a moment before abandoning it in favor of an item of greater significance which required that Mrs. Spencer conduct a search for the missing item and today was no exception. Mrs. Spencer circumnavigated the office nonchalantly looking for the missing article.

"Have you seen a file marked "Kip Thorne?" she asked. "Dean Fleming seems to have misplaced it again; it contained some papers written by Dr. Thorne."

Robert and Ron looked in her direction together, "Would you like some help looking for this missing file?"

"No, no thank you, I know it's here somewhere. In fact I've just found it," she replied enthusiastically; nearly pouncing upon the missing item. She walked behind the desk and paused, then stopped as she looked closely at the screen through the space between their shoulders. "What are you displaying on your screen, doctors?"

They both pivoted to regard the ceiling screen as Robert explained, using his laptop.

"More theories, Mrs. Spencer," explained Robert. "This first one states that light spreads out like ripples in a pond. As the strings pass each other, they create a closed loop in time and time travel into the past can take place along this loop."

"The second one," Ron continued," states that the future direction of time is determined by how far light has moved from the source. Think about the direction of time as being shaped like a cone and the widening of the cone as the direction of the future."

Mrs. Spencer squinted at the screen. "I believe I understand part of this. It reminds me of my high school physics class. What does that acronym stand for?" she said, pointing to the screen.

"That is LOTART, which stands for Laser Optical Time Machine and Receiver Transmitter. It is sort of like a radio station which transmits a signal that is received by your car radio. Then you, in turn use your car radio to act as the transmitter and the radio station becomes the receiver."

"But would the receiver need to be at the location you want to reach and if so, how do we get it there?" interjected Ron as he leaned against the desk, addressing their problem having forgotten Mrs. Spencer's presence until she spoke again.

"I don't completely understand what you are proposing but sometimes when Mr. Spencer and I are leaving for a trip, we send some of our things on ahead," Mrs. Spencer said with her hands on the shoulders of her two physicists.

"That is too simple", said Robert. "Could we send the receiver ahead by Fed Ex?"

Ron chose this opportunity to rest his feet on the desk and put his hands behind his head, "I knew that."

Ignoring Ron, Robert turned to Mrs. Spencer. "It would have taken us all day to come up with a solution for that. You did that in a matter of seconds. How did you do that?"

Mrs. Spencer was preparing to exit the office with Dean Fleming's file in hand. She paused in the doorway for a moment before stepping into the hallway. "Dr. Dubé, I have raised two children. I have a degree in common sense. Good day to you, Doctors."

Following a lengthy silence Ron looked up to the ceiling. "And what is left on our screen, Dr. Dubé?"

"Well, Dr. Maxwell," Robert began sarcastically, "I feel that this puzzle is the most difficult because even if we figure out how to begin, they mean nothing if the final piece doesn't fit. The reception and transmission of signals to a future time would be made possible by the use of an array of ring lasers. The problem is generating enough power and that is where we've had no success."

That was true. Whether the shape of the ring laser was round, oval or ellipsoid; the results were disappointingly similar. No more power could be generated beyond a certain threshold. Sending more electricity into the array resulted in one of two outcomes, no power gain at all, or destruction of the array itself. The answer once again, came from Mrs. Spencer. Robert and Ron still hovered around their laptops, looking at their computations on the screen, as she returned to their office.

"Excuse me doctors, I have yet another missing file to search for."

"That's fine, Mrs. Spencer," said Robert attempting to sound sympathetic. He remained staring at his laptop but felt compelled to offer assistance and halfheartedly replied, "Do you need some help?"

"No, no thank you, Dr. Dubé; it's actually on your desk." Retrieving Dean Flemings' book, she walked toward the door.

Ron suddenly stood and took a few steps toward her. "Excuse me Mrs. Spencer," he asked abruptly. "If you wanted to generate a stronger gravitational field with a laser array, how would you do it?"

Robert paused for a moment before rolling his eyes toward the ceiling.

"I'm sorry Dr. Maxwell. I truly have no idea how I can help you. However; I can tell you that stacking those laser boxes of yours would make it much easier for the cleaning crew to perform their duties in the evening. They complain about them daily and I have other tasks to attend do, which do not include listening to them. Have a wonderful day"

"It was worth a try anyway," said Ron disappointedly as he returned to his chair.

"No, wait," Robert said as he looked at the array. "Perhaps it isn't a simple matter of the intensity of the power being supplied to the array. We've never tried stacking the arrays and if we were to put them in a corner they would need to be a different shape than what we've been using."

Upon further experimentation, they discovered that when lasers were placed upon each other in a rectangular shape, its gravitational pull was increased. Their significant breakthrough was achieved when they began stacking arrays in a column. As the number of laser arrays increased, the strength of gravitational dragging also increased. When the total length of the arrays reached 20 feet, Robert and Ron felt they could generate sufficient power and were ready to attempt to send matter forward in time.

Their initial test involved sending a pair of Caltech coffee mugs from their machine to the desk in their office two hours into the future. On Tuesday at 11.00 AM they tested their machine and the cup disappeared.

They now had succeeded in sending matter forward in time. If they were correct, this mug could be sent to a specific location where it could then be used as a receiver. Their goal of course was to send a person forward in time who could initiate a return to the present, with their coffee mugs.

However, to proceed further they desperately needed a living subject to be part of the next experiment, so Robert volunteered Ron. "Think of this as an opportunity" Robert said enthusiastically with a mischievous grin.

"I'd prefer to think of it as your opportunity" Ron replied indifferently.

Neither realized it but once again Mrs. Spencer was about to provide a solution. The following day Robert was returning to the physics laboratory from Avery House when he noticed Ron walking toward him. Ron's numerous skills did not include the ability to hide a secret and he looked as if he urgently needed to share something mysterious. "I have something unexpected to show you in the lab", said Ron attempting to suppress a grin.

Robert struggled to decipher what sort of surprise awaited him but Ron was adamant about waiting until they arrived in their office.

He strode through the office door searching for something that appeared new or out of place. The windows were open revealing the tops of the eucalyptus and pine trees waving in the breeze. The lawn sprinklers had been turned off for some time now and the grass below sparkled in the morning sunshine. Everything in the room was unchanged. Then he saw an object resting against the far wall. It was cubed shaped, shiny silver and something inside was moving.

"You surprised me with a dog kennel?" Robert said dryly.

"Not just any dog kennel", Ron whispered.

Robert glanced inside the kennel. "It looks a lot like Mrs. Spencer's Yorkie"

"It is her Yorkie", Ron said excitedly. "Mrs. Spencer had to leave unexpectedly and asked us to watch her for one day two at the most, while she tended to a family matter." Ron suggested that this would benefit both them and Mrs. Spencer as he nodded in the direction of the time machine.

Robert's jaw dropped as his eyes widened. "You want to send her dog forward in time?" he shouted. "Are you insane? It's one thing for the coffee mug to go into the future, but we need to retrieve the dog at some point. How does any of this make sense to you?"

"It will be fine" Ron said assuredly. "We'll send her forward in time by one or two hours, then one of us, preferably you; travels to retrieve her and Mrs. Spencer picks her up tomorrow. What could go wrong"?

Robert was quickly adding up the possibilities of what could actually go wrong, but Ron's confidence caused him to relent. Sonja the Yorkshire terrier, was about to travel forward in time and reappear with one of them holding her next to her kennel, in theory.

Ron entered the coordinates for Sonja's kennel into the laptop computer and carefully placed Sonya inside the laser arrays. Sonya stood on her hind legs, paws resting against the walls of the array and her nose pressed against the glass. With a determined look on his face, Ron energized the field, passed his hand over the laser to activate the machine and Sonya became the world's first time traveler.

Without speaking to each other, they looked at their watches and the unoccupied time machine and then at the space by the window where one of them would return with Sonya, hopefully.

The silence ended abruptly when the phone rang. Robert was the first to react and answered. Ron thought it odd that he spoke louder than was necessary. "Yes, good to hear that. Yes, Ron told me all about it. Fine, we'll see you soon", and turning quickly to look at Ron he said cheerlessly; "That was Mrs. Spencer."

Looking gravely at Ron's blank expression he said, "Mrs. Spencer's family crisis has been resolved. She's at the Presbyterian Church on South Hill Avenue. She'll be here in about 10 minutes."

"What is your solution now?" inquired Robert, looking at his deeply distressed colleague.

"We could try and delay her somehow, "said Ron; throwing his words out in a way that suggested he had no possible solution.

Robert sat scowling at his desk, "One of us needs to go forward in time to meet the dog and bring it back here. If we do this now we should have the dog before Mrs. Spencer arrives." He paced across the floor of their office for a moment and then bent to face Ron. "We haven't returned anything yet. We need a device to initiate our return trip," and produced the key fob to his Toyota. "We'll send this forward with one of us now. Then we can use this as a key to return. The pulse from the key fob will act as a transmitter and the machine will act as the receiver", he paused, "well in theory anyway".

Ron reached into his slacks and produced a quarter. "We'll flip for it", as he looked at Robert. "One of us has to go now", he added apprehensively.

Robert turned and placed the key chain on the desk between them as Ron flipped the coin toward the ceiling. Following the vertical path of the coin, he was vaguely aware of what items were on the opposite wall. Catching it in his left hand, he slapped it on the back of his right. He raised his eyes and then closed them tightly, "We forgot to call heads or tails".

Roberts hand was already grasping the keys. "Enter the coordinates and send me now", he said with urgency in his voice.

"What if it doesn't work?" Ron said.

"You get to explain to Mrs. Spencer for both of us," Robert answered coldly.

Digesting the prospect of a confrontation with Mrs. Spencer and her missing dog, Ron quickly entered the coordinates into the computer, passed his hand over the laser beam to energize the array and Robert vanished.

Ron then began the ordeal of visualizing how all this would conclude. He was in a constant state of restlessness. Sitting at his desk and staring at the ceiling or pacing across the room, attempting to ignore the spot in their office where Robert and Sonya would hopefully soon reappear did little to diminish his apprehension.

He was unavoidably drawn to the spot where their machine stood however, as it had represented both success and salvation. Now that Robert and the dog were at a point in the future, until they returned and Mrs. Spencer left with her dog, that spot represented absolute doom. In his mind, Ron visualized both possibilities in balance on a scale in his mind. The aggravating aspect of this was that he had no control over what would tip the scales; either in his favor or against.

When he heard Mrs. Spencer's cheery greeting, "Good afternoon Dr. Maxwell", he visualized the doom side of the scales crashing upon his head.

Ron jumped from the chair as if launched from it, his mind racing to arrive at a solution. However he had to admit to himself that he had absolutely nothing to offer. He turned quickly and saw Mrs. Spencer standing in the middle of the office floor. The manner in which she smiled at him suggested she was expecting some action on his part.

Attempting to smile, Ron looked at Mrs. Spencer and sounding very foolish asked "So, how many children did you say you've raised?"

"Excuse me? " Mrs. Spencer reacted with a confused expression as her eyes nervously searched the room for her pet.

"What "? Ron's life was flashing before his eyes as Mrs. Spencer's right eye narrowed.

Appearing particularly vexed she said "Dr. Maxwell, what did you just ask me"?

"Oh, that was simply me asking you how many children you have, Mrs. Spencer," Ron clarified as he seriously wondered exactly how much time he could possibly waste with his tactic. He knew he looked like a deer caught in the headlights and his feeling was that it wouldn't be enough.

"I have two children," she answered suspiciously. "Dr. Maxwell" said Mrs. Spencer in complete seriousness, "where is my Sonya?"

"Robert has her", he blurted out, much to his surprise. "He really loves dogs and thought that Sonya would enjoy a walk before going home. He'll return very soon," he said hopefully.

"We may be able to see him from here", walking nervously toward the window so that the time machine was now directly behind them. Mrs. Spencer joined him and gazed down at the campus, glancing at her watch for a moment, continuing to search the landscape for her missing dog and Robert. Their interests seemed to be diverging and converging simultaneously. While Mrs. Spencer explained how the family emergency had ended and was becoming more agitated by the minute, Ron was focusing on distracting Mrs. Spencer until Robert returned with her dog.

They shared the same goal: get Mrs. Spencer and her dog out of the office now.

As Ron attempted to convince Mrs. Spencer that he saw Robert and her dog at a distance for the sixth time, she became more emphatic. Ron's vision of the future was becoming even murkier as Robert's voice broke the silence. "Thanks for letting me watch your dog", he said cheerfully.

Robert stood behind them, smiling and cradling her Yorkie in one arm, while he held a Cal Tech coffee mug in the other, the kennel lying at his right foot.

"But we just saw you there", said Mrs. Spencer as she pointed to a spot on campus, looking more bewildered than ever.

"No, no, we were on the other side of the physics laboratory. She seems like she had a lot of fun, but she looks tired now. She must miss you and her home."

Mrs. Spencer sounded like the definition of perplexed. "Sonya does look a bit tired, but I am certain that I saw you in front of the building".

"We used the side entrance" Robert added quickly, handing the coffee mug to Ron while placing Sonya in Mrs. Spencer's arms and picking up the kennel as Mrs. Spencer looked quizzically at her dog.

"Come, I'll carry the kennel to the car", Robert offered as he waked purposefully to the door.

"Thank you, Dr. Dubé", Mrs. Spencer said, seemingly resigned to the fact that her best course of action was to follow Robert with her dog.

Ron watched as they exited and began to put in order the questions forming in his mind." What were the implications of a practical method of time travel? Who should they inform? What responsibilities should they assume in the future?

TIME TRAVELERS

"What was it like? What did you feel? What went through your mind?" Ron sat on the opposite side of Robert's desk in his apartment at Avery House. His questions came so rapidly that Robert had stopped responding.

An open bottle of Stone IPA sat on the table between them, but only Ron's pint glass was full. Robert took this opportunity to finish the contents of his glass as he listened to Ron's incessant questioning. As he filled his glass again, he lowered his feet from the table to the floor and sat forward in his chair staring intently at Ronald. "Finished?" he said; a sense of finality in his voice.

Ron sat back in his chair as Robert began, "It's not easy to describe at all. It was not anything like I expected. The closest I can compare it to would be like traveling in a car with traffic around you. You step on the accelerator, but instead of passing the car next to you, it feels like you're both slowing down. One moment you see your destination and the next you are there. There were definite sequences of events, but it all happened very rapidly."

Robert put his glass down next to a copy of "Time and Chance". After glancing slowly to his left and right through the apartment windows, he continued.

"Returning was different. It felt as if I was being strongly pulled in a certain direction. Sonya seemed dazed by the experience. She really wanted to get back into her kennel but I needed to distract Mrs. Spencer so I put Sonya in her arms. Fortunately the key fob worked as the transmitter just as we had predicted. I pushed the button fob and the time machine acted like a receiver".

Robert glanced at his key, fumbled with it in his left hand and looked up at Ron. "I think we need to plan a more ambitious trip".

The room was silent as they observed each other, waiting for one of them to speak first. Robert looked at a poster of St. Moritz near the kitchen door. Ron raised his eyebrows, drew a deep breath and said decisively, "I want to go this time. I have already selected a destination and a proposal".

As Robert settled back into his chair, Ron leaned forward and spoke excitedly. "You know that my father and I are huge Chicago White Sox fans. The White Sox played the Cincinnati Reds in the 1919 World Series. I want to see Shoeless Joe Jackson play in the outfield and sit in the sunshine at Comiskey Park and attend one game in particular. That was the year that several of the Chicago White Sox were accused of throwing the game for money. Journalist Hugh Fullerton of the Chicago Herald and Examiner would later write that he was so disgusted that the White Sox had thrown the game "that the Series should never be played again." "I propose to see the last game of that series."

"The key fob you have has traveled forward and back in time," Ron began. "While you were helping Mrs. Spencer with her dog, I thought of this solution. I will take the key fob and travel to Chicago at the date and coordinates which I entered into the computer. I'll walk to the ball park and after the game, I'll use the key as a transmitter and our machine will be the receiver. Tomorrow is the anniversary of that game. I'll be watching baseball history," and he spun his laptop's screen to face Robert.

On the screen were the coordinates for Comiskey Park:

41 degrees 49 minutes 52.08342 seconds north latitude

87 degrees 37 minutes 53.5152 seconds west longitude

Ron's excitement had begun building before Robert returned with Sonya. Now his voice was rising, his face was flushed, his demeanor wildly enthusiastic.

Robert seemed excessively preoccupied with his pen and then spoke as he pointed it in Ron's direction. "So, you'll take the key fob and…..." But he couldn't finish his sentence as Ron was already headed for the door. He stopped with one hand on the doorknob as he put his sandals on.

"And?" he answered.

"And don't forget the key and leave your credit card here before you travel to Chicago. I doubt they will know how to accept a credit card to pay for your ticket."

The following day was enormously exhilarating and hectic for Ron. He utilized a computer in the audio-visual department to print a duplicate ticket from that game in 1919. He planned to arrive on Chicago's West Side on October 9, 1919 for a baseball game at Comiskey Park in an era when the average person didn't have a phone in their home. His dilemma now was currency. How would he exchange currency which was printed in the 21th century for a purchase in the early 20th century? The audio-visual department again provided him with a solution. He was able to print a small amount of currency from that period, which would pass the inspection of the most discerning vendor.

With a combination of excitement and apprehension, Ron and Robert walked hurriedly from Avery House to the office at the physics laboratory. If Ron had second thoughts, he concealed them completely. This was a project he had conceived and now he was taking part in a great adventure. He wasn't certain if an explorer like DeSoto would have felt this way when he was exploring the Mississippi River, but Ron was exhilarated and focused. He was actually surprised that he wasn't breathing deeper.

Robert was focused as well, downloading the co-ordinates of the location and the date that Ron had entered into his laptop, into the time machine's computer. As Ron stood inside the laser array, Roberts's right hand reached the laser beam that would energize the machine. The two students looked at each other for a moment. Robert winked, passed his hand through the laser beam and Ron vanished.

Placing his right hand on the desk to the left of the switch, he felt that his poorest option would be to remain seated at his desk, staring at the laser array, waiting for Ron's return. Robert was contemplating his future as Ron traveled into the past. The outcome of this experiment would have a profound impact on his life regardless of its success or failure. He was approaching his final days as a PhD. candidate at Cal Tech and the possibility of taking a position there hadn't even been raised by Caltech. He had however, been approached by a faculty member at Syracuse University about the offer of a research assistant position at his alma mater and had decided to accept it.

Robert picked up a pen and rested it on his paper. He had intended to write something earlier, but now couldn't imagine it what was and instead focused vacantly on Ron's picture of Frank Thomas in a White Sox uniform which hung next to the door. He decided to go for a walk, left the physics building and slowly walked toward Del Mar Boulevard before recognizing that having no information about Ron's situation was something he couldn't control and his time would be best spent in the laboratory.

Upon entering the office, he sat in his chair and resumed his previous position; feet on desk, eyes on his computer and attempted not to regard the machine.

Suddenly, the laser array energized and Ron reappeared.

Robert's feet landed on the floor and greeted Ron as he stepped from the machine. "How was it?" he said, immediately concerned with his friend's dour look.

Ron spoke with a dark and gloomy aspect. "Great."

"I'm sorry, but you don't sound very convincing," observed Robert.

"I was supposed to arrive in Chicago on October 9, 1919," he yelled. "You sent me to Chicago on October 9, 1871; the date of the Great Chicago Fire! I arrived 24 hours after the fire began. Three hundred people died and over 100,000 were left homeless and you put me in the middle of it all!"

There was not one facet of Ron's demeanor which wasn't confrontational on a grand scale. This was definitely a situation requiring both of them to quickly put their emotions aside to provide answers to a myriad of questions. He had never seen Ron in such a state as this. His head was tilted toward his left shoulder with eyes that glanced at Robert, displaying a vacancy he hadn't seen before. His clothes were a mess and Ron looked like someone who had a great deal to say, but wasn't exactly certain where to begin.

"The information was entered correctly," Robert said quietly; pointing to his laptop. "Look, here are the latitude and longitude coordinates of the ball park, as well as the date. You should have appeared directly in front of Comiskey Park in 1919." Robert rotated the laptop to face Ron.

It was true. The information displayed was absolutely correct. As Ron looked away from the screen, his hand brushed sweat and ash across his forehead; he took a deep breath, exhaling slowly and sat in a chair next to the screen and looked across the table with an inquisitive expression.

"That is interesting. Why would it be very accurate traveling into the future, but so random when traveling into the past?" questioned Robert, glancing through their office window before turning to face Ron.

"I had some time to consider that as I watched Chicago burn," said Ron "In theory the shape of the cone that represents time travel is the widest part when traveling back in time. Is it possible that it becomes less stable as you approach the horizon?"

"Oddly enough, I have a theory," he added with a sooty grin.

Having a theory about their problem was one matter. The fact remained that they needed a method to resolve it. It seemed to them that the most logical method was through the use of their machine again. Over the next several months they took turns traveling back in time. A world map was hung on the wall and Robert and Ron tossed darts at it from their chairs until an interesting site was hit and then they made plans to travel there.

Each made several attempts to travel to an event with a specific time and date in history. Robert chose to witness the signing of the Declaration of Independence as well as the Wright Brothers first flight at Kittyhawk

The only instance when they arrived at the intended date, however was when they possessed material which had actually existed at the specific location and time period they intended to arrive in. Obtaining materials from those locations was always problematic and usually illegal as this involved traveling to the sight that they wanted to visit in the present and somehow obtain an object that had existed during the time period they wished to visit.

Ron's next excursion to the 1919 World Series was successful solely because he was able to convince his father who was an avid collector of sports memorabilia and a White Sox fan, to loan him his original ticket to that World Series game, all in the interest of science.

Obtaining artifacts from a specific date in history was difficult as they were not always available, so Ron and Robert spent hours attempting to refine their calculations to make their arrival at the correct date in the past more precise.

"I simply do not understand," said Robert staring at the ceiling in their office, placing an emphasis on the word not. "Our calculations are exact, we energize and yet we arrive years away from our target date. I wanted to be in Philadelphia on July 4, 1776 when the Declaration of Independence was signed. Instead I arrived in Philadelphia on July 4, 1826; the day when both John Adams and Benjamin Franklin died."

"I repeated that experience in my attempt to see the Wright Brothers first flight in 1903," he added. "Aviation history being made and I arrived at an empty beach. At first I thought that the amount of energy supplied to the laser array might play a part in this, but I'm becoming more convinced now, that traveling backward in time becomes more unstable as you approach the horizon."

"But wasn't there a paper which suggested that that part of the time machine would be stable?" Robert asked slowly as he rose with purpose from his chair and walked over to face Ron. "The scientist in me is excited by what we've accomplished so far. At the same time I hate this hit and miss approach we apply to a scientific problem. We can't problem solve through luck and desperation. We must start at the beginning, focus and figure this out."

Robert and Ron agreed that their most favorable course of action would be to re-examine their approach to problem solving when Robert made a statement that neither of them had considered before while absentmindedly tapping his pen on a textbook.

"Wouldn't it be ironic if we continue working on time travel and discover that no one really wants to use this technology? What if we develop this and people only want to go from point A to point B faster and this becomes just another mode of transportation? It could be the beginning of an entirely new industry."

"It wouldn't be the first time that a scientific discovery became a practical consumer item, I suppose," Ron said thoughtfully. "Perhaps you should decide whether you should be focusing on your PhD or an MBA."

Whether they were discussing or working towards a solution, it still weighed heavily on their minds. The only time they weren't engaged in work on their time machine was during sleep and that ceased to be a refuge when they began dreaming about time travel.

Their individual priorities changed dramatically when Ron requested that they meet for coffee. He asked that they meet at the office instead of the Starbucks on South Lake Avenue and while Robert would have preferred to enjoy his coffee while sitting at a table outside and watching the world pass by, he relented when he recognised the serious tone in Ron's voice.

Ron appeared troubled and he sounded much worse when he spoke. "I spoke to my father last night," he said, his eyes wandering and focusing on nothing in particular. Raising his head and gazing at their office's white ceiling tiles, Ron sighed and continued, "My father has a very serious medical condition. I'm going home to Pittsburg to visit with him and his doctor. Here are the coordinates. I have a key fob and I'll return as soon as I can. I've notified Dean Fleming and Mrs. Spencer may stop by."

Robert energized the laser array and Ron entered with an anguished, downcast look on his face. Seconds later he was in Pennsylvania hoping to discover what his father's future might be.

It would be three days before Ron returned. If he had looked troubled before, he looked completely crestfallen now.

He stepped out of the time machine and sat in a chair next to Robert. He was tired but resolute. "It's called Creutzfeldt-Jacob disease," Ron began slowly. "It's a brain disease that is incurable and inevitably fatal. They have no idea how he could have contracted it and most people die within one year." He let the weight of his words be felt before continuing. "The doctor said there is research being conducted in London and Paris with limited progress to date. So there is hope for a cure but it will be too late to save my father." The manner with which Ron spoke suggested he wasn't finished and Robert waited for his friend to reveal his thoughts.

"But I've found a possible solution. You are going to send me to Paris in the future to the location where research is being conducted now. I want to see what progress they've made in fifty years. It is possible they will have a cure in the future which could save my father's life. I've already entered the coordinates for the research facility's current location, Hôpital Pitié-Salpêtrière, Boulevard de l'Hôpital in Paris. I can only hope that they remained in the same location."

Without hesitation, Ron stepped quickly into the laser array, the field energized, Robert's hand crossed the laser beam and the machine was suddenly vacant.

During the ensuing several days, Robert's mind was subjected to the eddies and swirls of his thoughts as he struggled to remain focused on the present, while trying to imagine what was occurring in France fifty years in the future. What were the challenges of arriving that far in the future without knowing what to expect? The ethics of Ron's plan also weighed heavily on his mind, as he thought about the conversation he felt he must have with him upon his return. He also remembered that he had not slept in quite some time and realised that he was losing his focus when drowsiness enveloped Robert like a fog and he leaned back in his chair and slept soundly.

Robert looked at his watch the moment he awoke and was not surprised to see that he had slept in his chair for eight hours. "Waiting for Ron's return is senseless," he thought. "I should return to Avery House, shower and change clothes." He stood up and glanced at their machine as an afterthought because his intention was to cross the room and leave the office. But there was an object lying inside the base of the machine.

All thoughts of leaving the office were now forgotten as he quickly stepped to the machine. On the base lay one of the objects that Ron and Robert had sent forward in time to act as triggers to return to the present. A piece of paper was attached.

Receiving notes from the future was something Robert had definitely not expected. Reaching into the laser array he picked up a note from the platform. As he quickly unfolded the note, he picked up the key fob and placed it into his pocket.

Rob,

Hope this works. I brought extra devices with me for this purpose. I am seeing an M.D. who specializes in my father's condition.

Back soon,

Ron

He imagined that the brevity of the note was necessary. As his mind struggled with what life may be like where Ron was in the future, he remembered that he had planned to visit his apartment at Avery House for that much needed shower.

Robert's apartment wasn't large, but it was comfortable and Avery House's on campus concept made it functional. Robert enjoyed cooking, but his apartment only offered a microwave and his work rarely allowed enough time to devote to something which involved preparing food, plus he really needed to cook for a group if he was to use the kitchen in the Avery House dining hall. The kitchen wasn't always available, unless the residents accepted the opportunity to have him cook for them, something they always did.

Relaxation and reflection were not options now, however. He needed to gather the items he required, if he was going to be present at the office when Ron returned. He warmed the remnants of an omelet with some bacon from the breakfast he had cooked for some of the residents in the dining hall yesterday.

Treating himself to a long shower left him feeling the most relaxed he had been in days. It may have been the time he had to himself or the bacon he brought with him for the walk back to the physics laboratory, but now he felt better able to reflect on the fact that while all his thoughts remained focused on time travel, they would soon involve significantly more than simply moving between time passages.

What had originally begun as theoretical research had now evolved into the need for them to consider to what extent their responsibility for the creation and use of the machine had become. The possibility that someone's life could be affected by their actions had not previously crossed his mind and now there was a near certainty that they could use their research to save someone's life. Was that responsible; was it even ethical? The fact that it now involved the parent of a colleague, who was also his friend made it that much more complicated. He was certain that there was a clear answer somewhere, but he wasn't grasping it just now. Robert finished his bacon just as he entered the physics building.

His pace was no quicker as he entered the physics laboratory and walked slowly down the hallway past Mrs. Spencer's office. Usually he would stop and say hello but today he was so deep in thought that his familiar routine went unobserved. While Robert's focus on the ethics question, it blinded him to the fact that Ron sat silently at his desk.

"You look well for someone who is 75 years old," joked Robert.

Ron smiled and nodded, "It's been a busy few days and I learned a lot. Paris became the epicenter of research on Creitzfeldt-Jakob disease about 40 years ago," Ronald paused and corrected himself. "I should say that in 10 years Paris will become the epicenter of Creitzfeldt-Jakob disease. Twenty years from now a cure will be discovered, which is why the doctor I consulted with thought it very strange that I would be asking questions about treatment for a disease that had been wiped out

30 years earlier. The drug that will save my father's life is available; it is just available 20 years from now."

Ron paused as he contemplated whether or not to confide in Robert the details concerning his next subject. He had been glancing anxiously at objects in the room while he described his visit to Paris. He gazed at the eucalyptus trees outside their office window, back to his White Sox cap and then to his desk top before raising his head, facing Robert squarely.

"I've discovered something we hadn't quite predicted when traveling forward in time. And that is the aging effect on our bodies. It is possible that some conditions may be influenced by forward movement in time. I experienced severe joint problems while I was in Paris. A doctor in Paris said that I may have arthritis."

Robert shifted uneasily in his chair. "And now?"

"Now I feel fine, I have no symptoms. What concerns me is this. If I take my father forward in time it could accelerate his disease. If he remains here, there is no cure and death is a certainty. I guess that I have no real choice but to proceed with my plan, which is to take him to Paris for treatment."

Having listened to all that Ron had said, Robert broached a subject he wanted to avoid; but knew that discussing it with Ron was unavoidable.

Robert walked to the window, leaned against the glass and glanced quickly at the campus below he said, "Had you considered allowing nature to simply take its course? I realize we are talking about your father, but what are the consequences of tampering with the future? Is it not wrong ethically to interfere in someone's circumstance, no matter how tragic? Because the reality is this really isn't why we created this machine. Is it wrong because we have no idea what consequences our actions might cause?"

Ron also rose quickly and approached Robert with deep furrows on his brow and his hands pressed upon the sides of his head. "Are you kidding me? We're talking about my father's life."

"I understand that."

"Do you?" he countered. "My mother passed away a few years ago. Now all I have left is my father. I cannot just watch him die when I have a chance to save him!"

"Have you considered what may happen if you somehow alter history? What if your father in the present, was meant to accidentally take the life of a stranger and that while your father resides in Paris twenty years in the future, that person deliberately kills people on a huge scale? Or even goes on to kill your father in Paris twenty years from now?"

"What if that random stranger's research discovers a cure for cancer or C-K disease? We can play this game forever." Ron's voice was gradually rising.

"You need to think about this objectively," pleaded Robert.

"I've thought all I need to about this," yelled Ronald as he turned toward the windows. "My father questioned whether or not he really wanted to live any longer when, after the death of my mother he suddenly found himself alone. Some people who lose someone close to them choose not to go on. My father said he wished to live. He believes we have a natural right to choose life over death without being concerned about why we die, and now I only care about how I can save him. I can tell you that my reality is centered about how I can save my father. We're not debating an exercise in ethical theory. We're talking about my father. If that means taking him to Paris, then that is exactly where I'm going," Ron said, turning his back to Robert as he stared out of the window with his hands resting on the window sill.

"I'm sorry Ron, but I can't be a party to this." Robert walked to the open doorway, glanced back at the window where

Ron stood motionless and entered the hallway. The hallway seemed emptier than ever and his footsteps louder than he had ever noticed them before. This late in the day all of the other office doors were closed as everyone else had left. Most light fixtures had been extinguished. When Robert stopped walking he noticed that the only sound came from some posters on the billboard being blown about by a large fan in the hallway.

He paused for a moment before turning toward their office door. When he stepped back into the office Ron was still gazing at the Caltech campus.

"How do we begin preparing for this? I'm all in," Robert said and waited uneasily for Ron's reply.

"You know, to be completely honest with you, I experienced the same thoughts as you," said Ron turning away from the window to face Robert. "However, listening to someone else say it was very difficult to accept. I misspoke when I said that they had cured C-K disease. It's more accurate to say that the disease is controlled by drug maintenance. He will need to remain in Paris in the future for as long as it takes. Unfortunately, there isn't any way to predict what exactly how long that time interval could be. Living there could be a permanent situation and he's prepared for that. Fortunately, medical treatment is not a problem in France."

"You're just going to move? Paris is an expensive city to live in now, but twenty years from now; how..." However, Ron had anticipated this question and was prepared with an answer.

Ron nodded in agreement. "I wondered about that also. After the conversation with my father's future doctor, I realized then that we would need to live there, perhaps permanently. Before returning to our time I researched the financial sector in depth. My father's assets are completely liquid. The investments that we make now will be worth enough in the future that we won't have any problems with money in Paris."

"What does your father think about all this?" questioned Robert. "To leave everything familiar behind to settle in a foreign country in the future is going to be pretty unsettling."

"He is actually quite positive about it now." Ron's anxiety was diminishing as he spoke more about it. "He hasn't had a lot to look forward to since my mother passed away and his health prospects are zero if we remain here. He is excited about the likelihood of surviving this disease now. He's much more relieved about having something to concentrate on other than his perceived death sentence from God."

Ron walked away from the window and stood before the desk. He picked up his pen and began tapping on a book.

"My father is making his investments today. When that part of our plan is completed, I'll return here with him and we'll be off to Paris. I had very little concept of exactly what the best plan was for this before, but now I feel that our best option is to move forward."

Ron was interrupted by the unmistakable sound of a cell phone vibrating and he began lifting papers and moving books aside, but the noise from the vibrations wasn't getting any louder. He was becoming progressively more agitated as each piece of paper he lifted from his desk, failed to uncover his cell phone. Robert lifted the sports section of the Los Angeles Times, picked up a cell phone and placed it on the desk in front of Ron. "Looking for this?"

He answered the phone quickly. "How are you? Very good. Is everything finished? Good. Go home and I'll see you in time for dinner. Make certain you have all your papers and then we'll leave. See you very soon."

Ron turned slowly and gazed at the corner of the room. "You have no idea what a relief it is, knowing that you support me. I need to travel to Pittsburgh and return with my dad. I need you to assist us in leaving for Paris and I want you to meet my father before I go." Glancing at his watch he continued, "It's nearly 2.00 PM now which makes it about 5.00 PM in Pittsburgh. I know the arrangements won't move as smoothly as we think they should, but let's plan on meeting here in 24 hours." Placing his phone into his right pocket, Ron strode across the room and stepped into the machine.

With the coordinates entered, Robert energized the laser array, returned Ron's wave and broke the laser beam with his hand. Ron disappeared and then sat at his desk. "It's funny how routine this is becoming," he thought as he rested his left elbow on the desk and rubbed his forehead. For a moment he considered remaining in his chair to wait until Ron returned with his father. "This is irrational," he thought. "I can't just sit here by myself. Stand up and start moving," Robert muttered to himself. Exiting the building with no real destination in mind, he felt the need to walk somewhere and at the moment, that was more important than his destination.

While he was acutely aware that he was very hungry, he was oblivious to the fact that he had strayed from the sidewalk while watching a pair of very tall palm trees sway in the breeze and was absentmindedly walking across someone's lawn. When the homeowner asked him to use the sidewalk, he attempted to explain that his uncle in Fremont had a pair of palm trees similar to his. The homeowner responded with a shrug and pointed toward the street.

He eventually reached his favorite Mexican restaurant on East Colorado Boulevard where he sat near the window and ate slowly, watching traffic and pedestrians pass by. Today, eating his meal was more like an exercise he had practiced over and over for years, something he was only stimulated to do by his hunger. Now, all his thoughts were centered on validating and balancing his actions versus their possible consequences. Could their work be something that would eventually be used to benefit people in general or possibly cause them harm? In a technological sense this was much more complicated than inventing the light bulb, but would Edison's contribution be considered a more profound benefit to society than what he and Ron and accomplished?

Robert glanced at his Titan watch. "It's nearly 5.00 PM" he thought, "tomorrow will be complicated in the extreme. I should try and get some rest." He returned to Avery house to refine some of his calculations. Laboring until nearly midnight, he laid down on his sofa for a moment to collect his thoughts before resuming his work but sleep soon overcame him.

When Robert awoke the following morning, he changed clothes, heated some huervos rancheros and returned to campus. His goal was to begin the day as normally as possible, knowing that the remainder would be anything but. He was much more aware of his surroundings now than he was last evening, greeting people whom he passed and avoided wandering aimlessly across someone's lawn. He was also aware of the presence of a car with government license plates nearly everywhere he went. It struck him as odd that a car like that had been parked outside the restaurant yesterday. "This is ridiculous", he thought. "I've seen cars with government plates before and there wasn't any reason for them to bother me then, it shouldn't now."

Accepting it as a symptom of exhaustion and apprehension about today's activities, he continued to walk at a brisk pace. It was much earlier in the day than the time that he and Ron had agreed to meet, but Robert thought it prudent to arrive at the lab early. Besides, there was something of great importance that he had to tell Ron before he and his father departed.

As he approached the physics laboratory, he looked up at their office window and was certain he saw someone moving in their office. Not knowing what to expect, he quickened his pace. As he entered the building, he concentrated more on the various sounds surrounding him; people speaking behind closed doors and sounds of solitary footsteps echoing down the corridor toward his office. Nearing his office door he heard a voice which was unfamiliar to him and as he turned door handle the voices stopped.

Cautious, he opened the door and stepped into the room. Ron looked up at Robert from his chair. "You look weird. Are you feeling all right? Maybe you just look this way when you sleep in your apartment." Before he could answer, Ron gestured to an older man who rose from his chair. "Robert, I'd like you to meet my father."

He turned to meet an older version of his colleague. "Dr. Dubé, I'm so glad we finally meet. Ronald has told me a lot about you. It's amazing how much you two have accomplished together."

"Thanks Mr. Maxwell," he began. "I'm not used to be referred to as Dr. anything just yet and I'd feel better if you called me Robert, anyway. It has been a great experience to work with Ron."

Ron and his father were very similar in appearance. Both were tall and thin and very dark, although his father possessed a bit more of an athletic frame than Ron, with broader shoulders and hands that belonged to someone who had spent their life doing manual labor. His eyes were very calm and intelligent looking and his hair had begun to turn grey around the temples but was still very full. With a firm and friendly handshake he smiled and said, "Robert, please call me Arnie."

Robert raised an arm and placed his left hand on Ron's fathers shoulder. "Well Arnie, are you prepared for this?" As Robert asked the question, he glanced casually in the direction of the laser switch used to energise the machine.

Ron interpreted Robert's glance. "Things were moving forward so rapidly that we decided to move now rather wait until this afternoon. I moved the switch next to the machine so we could operate it from there."

"Well, I'm glad I caught you before you left." Robert's tone became very serious as he sat next to the desk. He leaned forward, placed his forearms on his legs and interlaced his fingers. "I've accepted a position as a research assistant in the physics department at Syracuse University. Because you don't know how long you'll need to be in Paris, I'll take the machine with me until we can decide where to keep it permanently. That means you'll have no way to return to the present until I get it back on line. That shouldn't involve a lot of down time, but you need to be aware of that. I've been calculating a method to transport me and the machine together. I wanted to make that clear to you in case you wanted to delay your departure."

There was no hesitation either from Ron or his father. "We are committed to this; we're determined to go now," said Arnie decisively.

The three men shook hands and Ron and his father entered the machine. Father and son gave Robert a serious look and then smiled before both offered him a thumbs up. Robert energized the array, passed his hand through the laser beam and Ron and his father departed for France, 20 years into the future.

Over the next few days, Robert budgeted his time between teaching at the karate dojo, planning his move to Syracuse and solving the problem of transporting the time machine with him.

Using their time machine allowed him to make arrangements to relocate that much easier. He was able to meet with Syracuse University faculty members and rent an apartment close to campus that was large enough for him and the machine and still return to Caltech to complete packing his belongings in his office and his apartment at Avery House. Paramount in his mind was a method of testing the theory of transporting himself with the machine to Syracuse. Reducing the amount of time that the machine would remain off line would be critical, should Ron and his father need to return or communicate.

Late one evening, Robert was completing a task he considered to be singularly important, even if it only served to save time. He entered the coordinates for each location they had already used or were likely to use into the time machine's computer. Each location had a unique number and by entering that number the computer would automatically select the proper coordinates. It was one of the numerous chores he had given himself to complete before he could feel comfortable leaving Caltech

He appreciated that he really needed some rest when he awoke with his left hand supporting his head. "I really need to sleep a little," was a complete understatement, reasoning that he required a clearer mind if he was going to solve this problem. He also noticed that orange light was wrapping itself around the walls of his office, signaling the approaching sunset. "Should I sleep here or walk back to Avery House?" he thought.

That decision was made for him. The familiar sound of the machine energizing and powering down made him sit up and immediately turn to look at the corner of the room occupied by the machine. Half expecting to see Ron and his father returning from Paris, he was surprised and curious to see an envelope lying at its base.

The envelope was bright blue and made of a satiny material which opened very easily. A hastily written note was inside.

"Robert, we arrived OK but I really need your help. For some reason we arrived two months earlier than the date I entered. An envelope containing my father's financial documentation and medical records was accidentally left in my desk. We have rented a flat temporarily. The address is 97 Avenue Ledru Rollin, Paris; the coordinates are;

48 degrees 51minutes 7.7272 seconds North latitude
2 degrees 22 minutes 34.81 seconds East longitude.

We will be OK for a while, but will need my father's records by the time of his doctor's appointment, in about two months."

Sitting behind Ron's desk, he began opening drawer after drawer until he found an envelope with the address of an investment planner in Pittsburgh. Enclosed were records of the recent stock and fund transactions.

His first thought was that the envelope shouldn't be left in the office. This was much too important to risk losing or being misplaced. Robert left the office hoping that a walk to Avery House to sleep and to find a secure place for the envelope would solve those two problems.

In Robert's estimation, planning for his present and future events were either settled or nearly so. He was very eager to leave California and return to Syracuse. He had rented an apartment near campus and he would be working in his favorite field. The University had offered to move his belongings and his car. His only immediate concern was solving the problem of moving him and the machine together. He was confident that he had devised a solution.

He tossed his keys into the metal bowl he bought while on a trip he and some other students had taken to Ensenada and placed the envelope in the center of his bedroom chest of drawers beneath some of his clothes. He soon fell asleep thinking about buying the winter boots that he would soon need in New York.

That morning he was feeling much less anxious than he had recently and he devoted more time to preparing his breakfast than usual. He used olive oil instead of a spray, his omelet consisted of three eggs rather than two, he didn't include chopped raw onions on his omelet, instead he sautéed them until they were caramelized, made an extra cup of chai and of course, bacon. The notion of picking up a copy of the L.A. Times appealed to him, as would a trip to the local Starbucks. He intended to make this as relaxing a day as possible before settling into the work of transporting their time machine.

When his phone vibrated, a text message was waiting for him, something he was tempted to ignore but his curious nature won. What he read next both puzzled and alarmed him. He was reading a text message from Mrs. Spencer. "This is bizarre, "he muttered to himself. "I didn't think she even knew my number."

"Robert we need to talk NOW. Come to my house. Urgent. Linda Spencer."

His eyebrows drew close together. She had never once called Robert by his first name and he had always referred to her as Mrs. Spencer.

"Fine, see you in 10 minutes," he messaged back to her.

She replied immediately, "Good, cross through yard at 1572 Oakdale Street; passing under the bougainvillea will lead you to my back yard. Be looking for you."

Robert sat back in his chair, tapping his fingers on the arm of his sofa and looking at the text message as if it would somehow provide him with the answer he sought. In his mind he saw his relaxing day going up in flames, as he stared at the ceiling, searching for options that would allow him to remain comfortably stretched out on his sofa. Unable to think of any, he convinced himself that he needed to leave now and wrapped his omelet and bacon in a flour tortilla and quickly walked to South Holliston Avenue, toward the address Mrs. Spencer had given him while eating his impromptu breakfast.

He avoided even approaching his car. Walking meant using a circuitous route, but it seemed prudent considering her message. Soon he reached the house on Oakdale Street. He remembered that it belonged to a department head at USC.

Robert had only been invited to the Spencer's home once before. The Spencer's custom was to invite incoming physics students and professors to their house at the beginning of each semester and until today he had not received an offer to return. Now he was instructed to return to their home by crossing a neighbor's property and clandestinely entering through their back yard. Curiosity far outweighed his apprehension as he walked cautiously up the cement driveway of her neighbor's home, passing the garage on his left. At the end of the garage, he peered warily to this right. Seeing no one, he strode forward; moving to his left and continuing on, past the pool and beneath an archway of bougainvillea.

Once on the Spencer's property, Robert walked quickly on a gravel path, paying close attention to the rear of their house. The kitchen faced a very large flower garden filled with brilliant colors. From the sheer number of windows, he presumed that it must be very bright inside during the day. He noticed some movement as curtains were moved aside and then closed, followed by a door opening on his left as Mrs. Spencer appeared and motioned rapidly for him to enter.

This kitchen was spectacular. He paused in the doorway for a moment to examine it but Mrs. Spencer grabbed his arm, pulled him inside and closed the door. The cabinets were crafted from cherry as well as the floor and the center island. A brushed stainless steel refrigerator was recessed into the center of the far wall, surrounded by more cabinets and grey granite countertops. There were a variety of recessed and hanging lights which were unnecessary now as the kitchen was flooded by sunlight even this early in the day. The center island was built with a separate sink and had been designed so that a person preparing food would face directly into the back yard through a large bay window overlooking Mrs. Spencer's elaborate flower garden.

Her face bore a look of sincere urgency and her smile seemed a bit obligatory, but she greeted Robert with a hug, something else that was highly unusual.

He thought it very odd that she handed him a cup of coffee as Mrs. Spencer didn't even know if he liked coffee; but it seemed to put her at ease, so he accepted it without question. She took a deep breath and exhaled before speaking to him,

"Robert, men from the Federal Government are in the physics laboratory, speaking with Dean Fleming. I believe from their conversations that they are from the Department of Defense. They have sealed your office and have someone guarding the entrance to your office. They are asking everyone in our department to tell them where you are. One of them is also standing at the main entrance to the building and I believe that an agent has been sent to search for you at Avery House."

Mrs. Spencer paused as if to collect her thoughts and in a very serious and low tone said, "I heard a rumor that you and Ronald had actually constructed some sort of time machine. Is that even possible? I thought your research had been limited to data on your computer and those devices of yours that the cleaning crew complained about."

Robert hesitated for a moment to compose himself before answering. "There's no secret really. We have been doing research in that area and have had some success. We're not even close to reaching a point where we can make an announcement yet. There are no papers ready to be published or presentations to be made. All we have accomplished is mostly theoretical. There's nothing really sinister in any of this. We just haven't done much in a practical sense, aside from an experiment with a small dog."

Robert attempted to seem nonchalant about his last comment. He noticed that Mrs. Spencer's Yorkie had just rounded the corner of their island in the kitchen's center but backed away when she saw him. He wondered just how well developed a dog's memory actually was. As Sonya barked, he back tracked saying "Or it could have been a quinea pig or a very large gerbil."

"As a practical matter we've very performed little actual physical work. We've spent most of our time work on mathematical calculations." Robert noticed that Mrs. Spencer seemed to be focusing on his comment about a dog's involvement in his experiment.

Anxious to change the subject, Robert walked to where Sonya was now sitting, looking up at him and he picked her up, seeming to absent mindedly scratch her behind the ears.

"Mrs. Spencer," Robert began with a questioning tone, "does Sonya still have a thing about neckties?"

"If you're referring to what happened to Professor Stark's tie the evening of our party, yes she does; although I'd prefer to forget about it," her tone of voice sounding irritated. "Robert, why do you ask?"

Two years earlier as a guest in Mrs. Spencer's home, Robert and other unfortunate guests had endured the lengthy discourse by a particularly boorish, self-absorbed professor; who was doing his utmost to impress the other guests by enlightening them about his achievements in quantum mechanics. Mrs. Spencer's dog chose that moment to reveal a very special skill set. Sonya possessed an absolute hatred of neck ties and exhibited it completely, when she lept from Mrs. Spencer's arms onto the professor's chest.

Robert watched in amazement, as the professor lay terrified in his chair, paralyzed at first with his wide open mouth, unable to utter a sound; before beginning to scream and wave his arms wildly. Mrs. Spencer, a spectator to her dog's previously unknown talent, was stunned at first and stood like she was frozen in place. Overcoming her initial shock and realizing that Sonya's attack was not likely to conclude without some action on her part, she became determined to separate her pet's teeth from her guests tie. Unfortunately, her dog was equally determined to do her best to destroy the professor's tie and appeared to have the greatest success.

Robert laughed as though it was the funniest thing he had ever seen and hadn't been in the Spencer household again.

He placed his coffee cup on the counter. "Mrs. Spencer, I'm going to need your help. I need assistance gaining access to my office and I'll need Sonya when I do this. I would like you to take us to campus in your car and I'll explain as you drive," as he picked up a set of car keys from the counter.

"When you say "us", who exactly are you referring to Robert?" Mrs. Spencer asked slightly baffled.

"You and I and Sonya, of course," he clarified as he carried her Yorkie toward the kitchen door and continued to scratch behind her ears. "Is that your Mustang in the driveway?"

THE INTERVIEW

As Mrs. Spencer parked her car, Robert noticed something that was not entirely unexpected. A GSA car was parked in the lot closest to the physics laboratory. He turned to Mrs. Spencer and reached for Sonya. "Wait five minutes and then meet me outside of my office. I'll be in the hallway and you'll be stopping by to pick up Sonya from me. I have the extra set of your car keys. Don't move your car for two hours. After two hours have past, come to my office and retrieve your keys."

Mrs. Spencer nodded in agreement; committed to following his instructions, she felt a high level of excitement as she anticipated the unknown roles she and her Yorkie were about to play as these events unfolded.

Robert walked with Sonya across the campus in the direction of the physics laboratory. Sonya was very well trained, as she kept pace with Robert, remaining constantly on his left. When they approached the physics laboratory's main entrance, he noticed a person standing on the steps.

Usually people on campus were dressed casually and walked as if they had a destination in mind. This man wore a suit and stood, nearly rooted to the steps. "Certainly not academia," he thought and continued to walk past the entrance. As there was probably no possible way for him to enter unnoticed, Robert moved immediately to a service entrance on the opposite side of the building. Unless someone was standing inside, he hoped to enter unobserved.

Robert kept Sonya next to him and attempted to open the service entrance door. It opened easily and he slipped inside. Half expecting to be challenged by someone as he climbed up the staircase: he was very relieved to find it was unguarded. He knew that once he reached the second floor hallway, he would turn to his left, walk about 40 feet, turn right and his office would be the second door on the left. Robert picked up Sonya, who returned his glance and licked his face; "This will be interesting," Robert said to himself.

Rounding the corner, he saw another person who resembled the man standing at the main entrance, in front of his office door. Actually, he would have been very surprised if one present. The question in his mind was whether any of these DoD people knew Robert by sight. "We're going to meet anyway. This point is about to become moot," he told himself. Robert proceeded toward his office door, avoiding making eye contact with the person standing before it.

Other than a quick glance in Robert's direction, he paid scant attention to him and actually seemed more interested in Sonya.

Determining whether the door was locked or unlocked was most important now. As he walked closer to the door, he changed hands with the leash and placed Sonya on the floor to his right.

The DoD agent moved quickly in Robert's direction but it was too late. Robert reached for the door handle with his left hand. As soon as he turned the handle, the agent quickly reached and closed the door, but it didn't really matter. Now he knew that the door was unlocked.

Robert stood straight and looked with indignation at the person blocking his entrance. "What do you think you're doing?"

"Sorry sir. I am Agent Tyler with the Department of Defense. No unauthorized persons may enter this office."

Robert's voice rose immediately, "This is my office. If I'm not authorized to enter my office, who is?"

Agent Tyler impassively turned from Robert and opened the door and said, "Sir, Dr. Dubé has arrived."

A voice from inside the office called out, "Send him in." Agent Tyler opened the door wider for him to enter but Robert did not move.

Agent Tyler seemed stunned at first, then perplexed as to why he should be required to explain further. He looked again to Robert and said "You need to enter, sir. He is waiting."

Robert regarded the agent and said flatly," Me? I don't need to go anywhere. To begin; who is "He"? Second, this is my office. I do not get invited into my office. Third, I am meeting someone here, outside my office door. If "He" wishes to speak with me we can do that here, or I'm gone," and he turned to walk away.

Agent Tyler quickly spoke urgently to his superior, "Sir, he's leaving."

"Dr. Dubé, please wait. We need to talk." This voice from inside his office exhibited no urgency or condescension; in fact it was the voice most devoid of emotion he had ever heard. Robert stopped and turned back toward the office door.

As the door opened, a man in his fifties with graying hair, spectacles, a broad and wrinkled forehead and a serious expression entered the hallway.

Robert walked back to his office door, positioning himself with the door handle on his left, looking directly at the person who had just exited his office. When he closed the door, Tyler stood between them.

"I am Intelligence Specialist Franklin. I am with the Department of Defense. I am here to talk to you about your activities regarding your time machine".

Robert had anticipated this line of questioning. "I am not sure if our research qualifies as one of my "activities", Agent Franklin", Robert replied coolly.

"Research then", he said compromisingly. "The DoD is very interested in speaking to you and Dr. Maxwell, regarding the secret research in which you are involved."

Robert felt anxiety growing within him, as the tension between them increased.

Robert began, "First, Dr. Maxwell's father has been recently diagnosed with a terminal disease and he is more interested in spending some time with him. Second; there has never been any secret research or any intent to be secretive. Dr. Maxwell and I have been conducting research on theories surrounding time travel. Theories don't become scientific facts, Agent Franklin. We use theories to prove a fact. Presently, we have a lot of theories and a rudimentary model we are conducting research on. Dr. Maxwell and I are a long way from presenting our results or anything practical to the scientific community or anyone. There is really nothing here for you."

Any pretense of a cooperative nature from Agent Franklin ceased now as his impassive expression vanished. Replacing it was an authoritarian, condescending air which completely annoyed Robert.

"Dr. Dubé; the DoD is seizing your machine. Your office will be sealed until all information and materials relating to your time travel experiments have been removed. At this moment DoD personnel are examining your quarters at Avery House for anything related to your research."

To Robert, this intrusion exceeded the definition of bizarre. How could the federal government appropriate someone's intellectual property? He was also worried about what questions could arise if they located Ron's envelope full of financial documents.

Robert became aware of the sound of footsteps approaching behind him and from his observation of the glances of the agents; he did not feel the need to look for himself as he already knew who was drawing near.

"This is intellectual property. You can't just announce that you're taking it," he said defiantly.

As the sound of the footsteps became louder and the cadence slowed, Agent Franklin opened a file he held in his left hand and handed a document to Robert. "Do you recognize the signature at the bottom of this? " Franklin countered, sounding utterly bored and indifferent.

"Yes of course, that's my signature. I had to sign that when I interned for the DoD. That was five years ago. However, I never agreed to surrender property, intellectual or otherwise."

Franklin seemed to be losing patience with this discussion. "That is exactly what this means Dr. Dubé", he insisted. "This states that you agreed to allow the Federal Government to use any of your creations that it deems necessary to national security, at its discretion. The machine may have risen from your intellect, but it is now government property." Franklin's smugness enveloped him like a cloud.

Mrs. Spencer arrived just in time to hear the end of Franklin's declaration. She positioned herself between Robert and his antagonist and looked at Robert inquisitively.

Before she could ask, Robert raised his chin and explained." These men are Federal Agents from the DoD, Mrs. Spencer. They claim that the government has a legal right to confiscate the research which Dr. Maxwell and I have been working on."

Mrs. Spencer's eyes narrowed as her inquisitive expression turned hostile. As she engaged the DoD agents with shouts of indignation regarding they reprehensible action they had undertaken, Robert was about to proceed with an event he hoped would be reminiscent of the one he had already witnessed at Mrs. Spencer's gathering.

Sonya's day was usually spent no higher than the average person's knee and opportunities to repeat her assault on neckties were limited. Mr. Spencer always made certain that he had removed his tie before entering their home after observing Sonja's behavior, which earned her the title of "that treacherous beast".

If Robert had planned correctly, that could change very soon. While Mrs. Spencer and Franklin continued their debate about the federal government's intrusion into a private institution, Robert knelt down and lifted Sonya to face Tyler. She first made eye contact with her next victim, Tyler's dark mono colored tie. As Sonya struggled against his grip, Robert turned his head to his right so she could continue to look at the tie as if it was her next meal.

Robert turned to face Mrs. Spencer, "Mrs. Spencer, let me return your dog and your car keys". He held the dog with his left arm and searched clumsily in his pocket with his free hand. Feigning irritation, he pulled his hand from his pocket and he turned to Agent Tyler, "Would you mind holding Mrs. Spencer's dog for just a moment?"

Agent Tyler's arms rose almost involuntarily to accept Sonya, who launched herself from Robert's arms onto the agent's chest. In seconds, the dog had sunk her teeth through the confused agents tie. He protested, but it was much too late. Mrs. Spencer now understood what she needed to do and stepped in between Tyler and Franklin. Robert opened the office door with his left hand while blocking the guard's futile attempt to grab him with his right.

Robert slipped through the doorway, spinning to his left and in one motion, slammed the door shut and locked it. A grey metal file cabinet stood to the right of the door. He quickly pushed it against the door and positioned it so the top of the cabinet was just below the door handle. As the commotion in the hallway grew in intensity, he raced across the room to the time machine. Robert energized the array and selected co-ordinates from those stored in the computer. Pausing by the machine's threshold, he walked quickly to the windows facing the campus and threw some correspondence onto the shrubs below. He could hear Mrs. Spencer's protestations continuing to build and the noise of someone's efforts to open the office door.

Time was now at a premium and Robert wasted none of it. Rushing across the room past the desk, he opened the door to the adjoining office.

Franklin's efforts to regain control of the situation were becoming increasingly frustrating. Mrs. Spencer's dog had been separated from most of Tyler's tie, while some remained in her mouth as her personal trophy. He had unlocked the door with the keys that Dean Fleming gave to Agent Tyler, but Franklin was now stymied by the weight and position of the cabinet as the cabinet kept the handle from moving downward. In addition, being forced to endure Mrs. Spencer's diatribe while she cradled her dog in her arms; informing him of the possible consequences of destroying Caltech assets was truly the consummate distraction.

To complete his part of the plan, Robert continued to urgently rush through the office. After opening the adjoining office door, he returned to the machine, energized the array and set the time for two hours into the future, picked a key fob from the desk drawer and put it into his pocket. Stepping into the machine, he engaged the switch and instantly found himself seated at his desk with his back to the wall, looking toward the office windows and noticed clouds which weren't there a moment ago.

Glancing at his watch he confirmed that he had indeed moved forward by two hours in time. The file cabinet had been moved away from the door, but wasn't in its original position and the door was wide open. Inserting his hand into his left pocket he found the keys to Mrs. Spencer's car. Now he needed to activate the second part of his plan and could ill afford the luxury of reflecting upon what was occurring at this time or in Mrs. Spencer's time.

Cautiously exiting his office, he turned to his right, wondering if he should exit through the main entrance or his original route through the service entrance. It struck him as interesting that none of the DoD personnel were present. Franklin and Tyler were gone; he did not expect to see Mrs. Spencer as she had most likely taken her prized dog home for a reward and a nap. When he approached the staircase however, he became aware of the sound of someone advancing from the corridor to his left.

The option of running to the staircase occurred to him for a moment but he deemed it prudent to proceed as he was. When he reached the juncture of the corridor he nearly ran into a physics student. They exchanged startled glances and Robert took the staircase to the ground floor. Striding past the offices, he exited the building.

The campus was alive with the customary activities. Students and faculty were all en route to their various destinations. He wondered where all the people who had been with him in the hall earlier were now. He still didn't see any of the DoD agents.

'They wouldn't have just left the area," he thought. Crossing the parking lot, Robert theorized that it was possible that time periods possess their "real time". It was possible that he might not see any of his antagonists again until their time coincided with his. Arriving at Mrs. Spencer's red Mustang he glanced at his watch. He now had one hour and 55 minutes left and as usual, time was at a premium.

Franklin still struggled to gain access to the office. His only consolation was that Mrs. Spencer's rapid withdrawal also meant she had taken her accursed dog with her. Her barbed, malicious remarks, regarding intrusion into and seizure of private property, bothered him more than the task of seizing it in the first place.

Left to consider his options, Franklin became aware of noise from within the office. The unmistakable sound of the obstruction moving across the floor was immediately followed by the opening of the office door. Mrs. Spencer stood defiantly in the office, "I'd rather open it for you than have you smash it in".

Franklin's agenda did not include conversation. He rushed past her expecting a confrontation with Robert. Tyler followed closely and began surveying the room. As the only other occupant of the room was Mrs. Spencer's dog, Franklin's mood darkened.

'Where is he?" he yelled walking away from her.

Mrs. Spencer spoke very calmly," First don't raise your voice to me, Agent Franklin," she said with a penetrating gaze. "You have no idea who this institution is connected with. Unless you are prepared to defend your actions to your superiors, I would suggest you temper your tone. Second, I believe you can see that he isn't here."

Lowering his voice, Franklin glared at her. "You opened the door from the inside. I believe that you know where Dr. Dubé is."

Mrs. Spencer smiled shrewdly. "I never stated whether I was or was not informed of Dr. Dubé's whereabouts. When I entered the room it was empty. As I said earlier, I wanted to save you the trouble of destroying Caltech property."

Tyler called to Franklin from across the room, "Sir, there is an open window here. He could have exited the office through the window or the adjoining room."

"Check out the adjacent room and then examine the area beneath the windows and see how Davis is progressing at Avery House. I want him found now."

Robert drove Mrs. Spencer's Mustang out of the parking lot and turned onto Wilson Avenue. Within minutes he reached an electrical supply store on the corner of East Colorado Boulevard and North Meredith. He had already made all his plans in great detail and wasted no time in making his purchases and soon he was turning left onto South Hill Avenue toward the Caltech Parking lot. One stop for coffee and he'd be finished.

Upon returning to campus, Robert had about one hour to complete his task. His idea should work; in theory. This method as this was far more theoretical than he was comfortable with, but these recent developments had forced him to abandon his meticulous approach to research in favor of action.

"Sir, the adjacent room was empty," Tyler stated. "There are manzaneta bushes beneath the window where I found papers in the bushes and on the lawn with Dr. Dubé's name on them. If someone had jumped from the window they would have left foot prints or broken branches but there was no sign of that. Davis just arrived and reported that he was not in his apartment at Avery House, and a car registered in his name is still in the parking lot. I have checked on his cell phone and credit card usage and there has been no recent activity".

Agent Franklin seemed completely engrossed in the time machine's computer as he studied the display which showed the coordinates Robert had entered.

Robert parked Mrs. Spencer's Mustang just where she had left it. He hurried back to his office noticing that everything looked normal except for the absence of the DoD personnel. He expected them to be in the vicinity and that they would be meeting very soon. He moved as quickly up the staircase as he could while carrying with his backpack full of purchases from the electrical supply store and coffee from Starbuck's. The file cabinet was in its proper place, the door opened wide and the office vacant.

"Don't dwell on the DoD personnel," he told himself. "Get to work on the machine and prepare yourself. Robert left the coffee on the desk and immediately commenced work on changing the wiring of the machine. After he completed his modifications, he rechecked his efforts and pondered what success will look like if all worked as planned. All of the pieces of this puzzle will need to fit together perfectly for this plan to conclude properly.

Convinced that he could do no more than wait, Robert returned to his desk and placed his backpack beneath it. He sat with his back to the wall and faced the windows. His chair was old but very comfortable and its back was tall enough to rest his head when reclined. He checked the time once more and reached for his coffee with his right hand. "It won't be long now," he thought as he reached for the key fob.

"Tyler," shouted Franklin. "These numbers look like latitude and longitude coordinates. Find out where these are and we may find our missing doctor".

Tyler entered the coordinates into his phone. He raised his head quickly and stared at Franklin. "Sir, using GPS; these coordinates are," he paused as his voice trailed off, "this room". Franklin turned as Tyler continued. "Actually the location is this desk."

Franklin walked to the desk, pulled a chair to the front of the desk and sat facing the wall. He instructed both agents to stand on either side of the desk.

Suddenly, Robert and Franklin were staring at each other from across the desk. If Robert was surprised, he didn't reveal it. His expression was very calm. Franklin looked quite the opposite. His head had snapped back when Robert appeared and now looked like someone who was attempting to assimilate information he had difficulty comprehending. Tyler and Davis were clearly astonished and approached Robert from both sides.

Robert leaned back in his chair, smiling. "Do you still wish to talk to me?" Before Franklin could answer, Robert lifted an object he was holding in his lap and placed it on the desk. "Well, my other coffee mug. I haven't seen that one in a while."

He gestured to the corner of the desk where four containers of Starbucks coffee sat.

"Coffee, Agent Franklin? You seem like a tall drip guy to me."

"I want to know where you've been and what you were doing," Franklin said impassively

"I could answer your question; however I don't have to, so I don't believe I will, except to tell you that I did make airline reservations. I would use my invention to travel to my new position, but now that you're determined to steal it, I don't seem to have that option."

Franklin opened the file he was holding when he stood in the hallway earlier. "I understand that you've accepted a position at Syracuse University in their physics department."

Robert feigned surprise, "You certainly seem to know something about me," with ample sarcasm.

Franklin continued, "We know quite a lot about you actually. West Genesee school graduate, undergraduate degree in Physics and Masters in Theoretical Physics at Syracuse University and recently a PhD. from Caltech. You are about to become a research assistant at your alma mater in the area of black holes etc. etc. etc.," as he flipped through the pages of Robert's folder.

"That seems so unfair," Robert said looking straight at Franklin. Franklin's wrinkled forehead matched his worried brow. "I only know your role as a government bureaucrat who steals personal property," he said pointedly.

"We don't need to revisit this issue Dr. Dubé," ignoring his last statement. "This machine is now government property, which will be used in the country's best interests", Franklin said leaning forward in his chair and placing the folder on the desk.

Robert leaned back in his chair. He seemed to become calmer as Franklin's agitation increased. "And who decides what the country's best interests are Agent Franklin, and in whose best interests; mine, yours, some anonymous person in the Pentagon or at Langley"?

Franklin glanced at Tyler and Davis who in turn moved closer to Robert.

"Would they use this to stop Hitler, or the assassination Archduke Francis Ferdinand? Would stopping two World Wars be in our country's best interests? Perhaps Martin Luther King didn't serve our country's interests. Would you have stopped the 9/11 attacks; some think that the government was in league with Osama Bin Laden in that attack. Would you save all the people who drowned when Titanic sunk? Maybe saving the lives of civilians isn't in our countries best interests. Would you use it to discover whether Castro, the mafia or Lyndon Johnson was responsible for the assignation of JFK and save the life of an American President? You could stop the atomic bombings of Japan; but perhaps drop it on Moscow instead. Could you affect the supply of oil to the world or the availability of water to a region? That seems to be something that would suit your idea of our countries "best interests."

"Enough," Franklin roared as he slammed both hands on the desk, his eyes flashing at Robert. "This has gone far enough. Dr. Dubé, we are all leaving this building now and you will be placed where I can talk to you as needed."

"I have already asked if you want to talk," Robert said, resolute and obstinate. "Now you're arresting me? You won't take me anywhere voluntarily." Robert pointed at the machine. "You don't even know what you have here."

"I never said anything about being arrested," Franklin said coldly. "You will simply be detained and we have people who are capable of working with your device."

"Work with what? You people think you have a Bentley standing over there in the corner. This isn't even a Model T. This "device" as you call it is twenty feet of theories."

Franklin nodded to Tyler who stood on Robert's left. He placed his right hand on Robert's left arm. Robert looked at the floor, turned in his chair and appeared resigned to allow himself to be led away. As Tyler looked at Franklin, Robert rose from his chair and moved his left arm towards the wall exposing Tyler's torso. His side kick was delivered directly to Tyler's knee. Tyler screamed in pain as Robert felt the knee buckle. Following two rapid punches to Tyler's face, the agent began to lean forward. Robert grabbed Tyler's right arm with his left hand and with his right hand on Tyler's shoulder, forced him toward the floor. Robert's right knee smashed twice into Tyler's ribs. He whipped his left leg at the back of Tyler's leg. As Tyler knees touched the floor Robert delivered a front kick to Tyler's face. Blood spurted from his lips and he collapsed to the floor.

Robert had expected a reaction from Davis and almost immediately felt a hand gripping his right arm. Pivoting on his right leg forced Davis's arm to straighten and drove his left forearm into his exposed elbow. Davis's head snapped back from the pain in his elbow and tried to pull away from the chair, but he had lost his grip on Robert's arm and now found Robert using his right arm to pull him against the chair, leaving him off balance and his right side exposed. Sidekicks landed in his rib cage and as he fell forward a round house kick found the right side of his face, followed by Robert's straight arm soaring from his left side, which landed on the back of Davis's head, ending the ordeal.

Robert now resumed his discussion with Franklin. Turning to face him, he returned to his chair and pointed to his dossier. "With all the personal information you have, did someone miss the minor detail about my 4th degree black belt in Shorin Goju karate?"

Franklin bore the look of someone who was presented with a question he would prefer not answer as he surveyed his unmoving agents and reached for his coffee. "I would have to agree with you on that point."

Robert's response was interrupted as the office door opened and Mrs. Spencer entered the office. Observing the prone DoD agents, she walked to the desk and picked up her keys.

"I knew I'd left these somewhere." The agents were beginning to stir now and groaned as they attempted to stand. She looked at the agents and then smiled at Robert, "Dr. Dubé, if you can't play nice with the DoD boys they can't visit anymore," she said with more than a hint of mockery. "Have a wonderful day Agent Franklin," she said with complete satisfaction and headed for the door and closed it softly behind her.

Robert smiled as Mrs. Spencer left, but became very serious as his attention returned to Franklin and pushed the coffees toward him. "Here's the deal. I don't care who you say you have who can continue the work on this machine. You need to accept the fact that it was designed and constructed by Dr. Maxwell and me. If anyone else attempts to dismantle this they'll ruin it, guaranteed."

"You're forgetting your colleague, Ronald," Franklin said with a sense of enjoyment.

"No, I'm not forgetting Dr. Maxwell and I'll return to that matter," he said gazing intently at Franklin. "I will dismantle this and reassemble it wherever you want. You must, however; guarantee that it will remain energized. Now, regarding Dr. Maxwell's situation; as I told you before he can't be here because he is with his father, who is in Paris receiving treatment for a terminal disease. That may not be in the nation's best interests, but I trust Dr. Maxwell's decision making more than I would trust our government."

"What we discovered in our research is that a cure for his father's disease exists in the future. Dr. Maxwell used the time machine to take his father decades into the future to save his life. If we can't agree on my terms, you're action will prevent two U.S. citizens from returning home. Now, exactly where do you intend to transport my machine?"

Franklin listened attentively. "That is an interesting proposition Dr. Dubé. What do you expect in return?" as he disregarded his last query.

"I expect you to do your part to ensure the return of my colleague and his father. I expect you to allow me to finish this today. As you insist on taking our machine, I've booked a reservation to Syracuse from LAX tomorrow. I just wish to put this episode behind me."

Franklin rose from his chair. Considering all the events which occurred during the past 48 hours, this definitely seemed to be the most reasonable course to follow. He moved his gaze from Robert to his two officers, retrieved his phone from his jacket pocket and entered a number. "Yes, this is Intelligence Specialist Franklin from DoD. We are on site at Caltech and I need the vehicle and personnel you have waiting there for me. Also, I need a medical team. My two officers,"..... Franklin paused while he watched them sitting against the wall, "fell".

Returning his attention to Robert, Franklin looked announced sternly, "A vehicle will arrive soon to move the device to the U.S. Court of Appeals building on South Grand Avenue. The U.S. Marshalls Service will provide space and security within the building. Once the Marshall's have taken possession of the device, it will be secured in the building and my two officers and I will return to Washington."

Tyler held his nose and looked at the floor, "I think it's broken."

"It should be," offered Robert, barely looking in Tyler's direction. "That strike to the nose was perfect. In regards to the Court of Appeals building, I'm familiar with it. It was a very popular resort before World War II. People still go there today just to sit in the gardens."

Franklin answered Tyler's complaint with an air of indifference. "Walk it off. The medical team will be here soon. When we return to Washington, we'll address your lack of skills that got your nose broken in the first place."

Paying scant attention to the agents, Robert reached for his backpack and rose from his chair, stepping over Tyler, walked past Franklin and moved straight to his machine. He had planned on moving it at some point. He just hadn't foreseen relocating it under these circumstances.

The truck from the court house arrived in about fifteen minutes. Franklin wanted ensure the machine's protection and Robert was actually impressed with their level of preparation. He painstakingly dismantled the machine himself and was meticulous in his supervision as it was loaded into the government vehicle.

Anyone who had ever looked at the crest of the hill from the Colorado Street Bridge was struck by the way the building which housed the Court of Appeals dominated the view. Originally built as a resort hotel in the 1930's it had been used as an Army hospital during World War II. Now it was home to the U.S. Court of Appeals and the U.S. Marshall's Service. The building reflected the Spanish colonial style with its beige stucco walls and red terra cotta tile roof. Turning right onto South Grand Avenue, Robert could see the top of the six story tall bell tower and the rose covered pergola which covered the walk leading to the buildings entrance.

An oppressive nature now hung on him like a blanket, making it seem as if it had taken much longer than fifteen minutes to reach the court house. He remembered making previous trips by car or walking to this building to sit in the gardens to study and gaze down upon the Arroyo Seco.

The driver turned left into the driveway on the building's right side and proceeded to the rear delivery area. Robert glanced in the truck's side view mirror hoping that the GSA car would have mysteriously vanished, but it followed directly behind, carrying Franklin and two slightly damaged officers.

Having reached the end of the drive, the driver backed the truck toward the receiving area of the court house. Franklin had already left his vehicle and was speaking to a U.S. Marshall.

Franklin turned and walked purposefully with the Marshall to where Robert stood. "Dr. Dubé, this is Marshall Tate. He will show you to the area in the building where the device will be stored. They know that they are not to touch anything. You will be given all the time you require to reassemble it. If there is anything that you need, they will do their best to provide it for you. I have explained the importance of keeping the machine energized constantly. When you're satisfied that the device is properly reassembled and the Marshalls have the area secured, they will drive you back to campus. For my part, I'll return to D.C. with my officers, slightly impaired," he finished with a slight grin.

Acknowledging nothing, Robert turned and faced Marshall Tate. "Dr. Dubé, I'll show you where the item is to be stored", he said without emotion. They passed through the service entrance and walked to the end of a long corridor where he was shown the room where he would reassemble his machine. He estimated its walls to be twenty feet long, with a ceiling height of slightly higher than ten feet. Two computer workstations faced one wall. He counted five ceiling cameras; one mounted in each corner of the rooms eggshell white colored walls and one mounted in the ceiling inside a dark grey hemisphere. "I have most of what I need with me," he said pointing to his backpack. "I will require a step ladder. Some of the wiring needs to go through the ceiling."

Over the next several hours, Robert reassembled the time machine and finished the electrical work. Before leaving he pulled his cell phone from his back pack and took a picture of what he and Ron had spent so many hours creating. The Marshall had a puzzled look on his face. "I built this, Marshall. I want to remember what I built," and dejectedly returned his phone to his backpack and gathered his materials.

Securing the room, Marshall Tate closed the exterior door, entered a code in a key pad and escorted him from the building.

Neither the Marshall nor Robert seemed inclined to talk during their walk to the service entrance. The Marshall acted with an air of indifference to the entire matter and Robert was busy calculating what his next options would be. The Marshall began walking to one of the GSA vehicles Robert had been seeing so much of lately and seemed relieved when his offer of returning Robert to the Caltech campus was declined. Robert really needed time to think and the two mile walk would allow him time to plan. Intelligence Specialist Franklin may not have realized it, but this match was far from concluded and Robert was already thinking several moves ahead.

SYRACUSE

It was 75 degrees and sunny under a brilliant blue sky when a student from Avery House dropped Robert off at LAX. Hours later he landed at Syracuse Hancock Airport and he deeply inhaled the evening air. The brisk 45 degree air filled his lungs and reddened his cheeks. The cold air and a full moon partially obscured by clouds might have been disturbing to some. For Robert, this is what it felt like to return home.

During his initial confrontation with Franklin, he said that he had made one call to the airline to book his flight. He had made one other call but that was no one's business but his own.

Robert's call to his parents was to inform them of his planned return. What he saw surprised him initially, but seconds later he had collected his composure, stunned by the group of friends and family who were there to greet him.

After everyone had an opportunity to welcome Robert, the group moved to his parent's home for the inevitable dinner. Some were slightly perplexed what they perceived as indifference on his part. During the drive he appeared withdrawn and mostly gazed from the car into the darkness. He felt that he should be going to his apartment, so he could continue the process of reclaiming his machine. At the same time, he realized that he needed this time with family because hectic could not adequately describe how his life would be once he reached campus.

Upon reaching home, he found dinner waiting. It was very comforting to see Tandoori Chicken, tamarind rice, sambar and chole on the dining room table. The table was set as he had remembered it from the countless meals eaten there in the past. What made this meal special and noticeably altered his mood was what had been prepared just for him; eggs, bacon, Tuscan garlic bread and a large bottle of Frank's Red Hot sauce placed to the left of his plate. Robert couldn't recall a time when he felt more rested than he did while eating breakfast for dinner.

Robert was very excited about the prospect of spending the night at home and beginning the following day at his new apartment. The university had arranged for the shipment of his belongings but unpacking them was something he was actually looking forward to.

He had chosen a flat on Ostrom Avenue due to its proximity to the physics building, which along with several other buildings formed the border of the "quad". There was much that differed with his new flat compared to his apartment at Avery House. The constant contact with academia in his residence had been both convenient and confining. It had allowed him and Ron to work closely on their project, one which had by now absorbed their lives in a manner neither could have predicted. At the same time, the communal feeling was never really escapable and his new apartment would be a welcome change.

His new flat gave him what he needed and desired now, privacy and quiet. The building stood two stories tall and was painted grey with white trim. Walking toward the house from the street gave Robert an appreciation of its impressive large front porch. Two doors stood adjacent to each other on the left side of the porch, the one furthest to the left led to his upper flat. The entrance at the top of the staircase opened into his living room which was larger than his entire apartment at Avery House had been and one of its most outstanding features was the polished hardwood floors. There was a large window directly opposite to the entrance and to his right was what he favored most of all. That was an enclosed porch which was six feet wide and fifteen feet long.

From this height he could see cars passing by on the avenue below including students who had also found off campus housing along with homes where families lived. At times, staring down onto the street, the people looked like lost sheep. For one who was used to this area, it was a nearly perfect location.

The "Quad" was the epicenter of Syracuse University. Bordered by several buildings including the physics building, most students and faculty would probably cross through this area at some point during their daily routine. On sunny days, crowds of students would gather there for a meal on the lawn or to throw a Frisbee.

From his office window on the physics building's second floor, he could look out onto most of the Quad. His view lacked the expansiveness that some of the other offices possessed. However, he was quite satisfied with its northern exposure, as it included a view of the ivy covered red brick walls of Hendricks Chapel.

And while Robert's view may have been at least partially dominated by Hendricks Chapel, his thoughts were totally focused on his plans to reclaim his property from the Circuit Court of Appeals building in Pasadena. His strategies had begun to form as he drove from the Caltech campus in Mrs. Spencer's Mustang. Now it was time to implement them. A secure, barely noticeable, nearly invisible location was required. Once the machine was back in his hands, he was positive that Franklin would stop at nothing to steal it back and he wouldn't likely repeat his earlier mistakes.

Uneasiness with the local locations he was considering eventually led him to his parent's house for dinner. During a dinner of Tandoori chicken he revealed his dilemma to his parents. His father placed his fork down and raised his glass of Merlot. Glancing through their window at the hydrangeas in their backyard, he spoke like someone who was thinking aloud.
"The problem is your need to find a location which provides you with both anonymity and security. You need somewhere to store this where you can avoid giving your real name but in an area you can trust, which is an unlikely

combination. If the area seems more secure, they'll definitely require some form of identification. There's a word for this".

Robert had been waiting for this and leaned forward in his chair, "And what is it"?

"Conundrum", his father said positively.

"What?"

"Conundrum, it means puzzle."

"I know what it means. I don't need a definition. I need an answer to my conundrum."

His father grinned at both Robert and his mother, "The answer is The Nation."

"A nation", questioned Robert. "What sort of an answer is that"?

"Not a nation. The Nation; the Onondaga Nation", his father answered. "Out of the way, a sovereign nation within a sovereign nation and they don't appreciate outside interference. A fugitive from the federal government once hid on the Nation for months. Federal officers couldn't take him into custody because access could only be granted by the Nation. If you could convince someone in authority from the Nation to allow you to store your machine on their property, I think you would have a solution to your conundrum."

"But who would I speak to?" Robert's tone revealed a negativity that needed to be eliminated if this was going to work.

"I know someone in the Native American Studies Department at the University," said his mother. "Plus I believe he is an Onondaga. I could ask questions without going into too much detail about whom you could speak to."

The following day, as Robert sat before his computer studying data dealing with black holes, his computer alerted him to an incoming call. "Maithreyee Dubé, Syracuse University calling", announced a voice from his computer.

"Physics Department, office of Dr. Dubé," he answered cheerily. "How may I direct your call?"

His mother's tone was very businesslike, "I spoke to the person I know in Native American Studies. Go to "Firekeepers Restaurant" on the Nation. Ask to speak to Sarah about what you need. The person I spoke to said you should be prepared to look elsewhere, however. Oh, and wear a jacket."

Robert responded like he was entering into a covert situation, "Because they'll be looking for someone asking questions and wearing a jacket?"

His mother's voice was to the point, "No, it just looks like it might rain".

He left the building immediately, nearly colliding with some students on the staircase in the process. He raced back to his apartment on his bicycle and was soon driving his car south on Interstate 81 toward the Onondaga Nation.

The neighborhood where he first lived was in the vicinity of the Nation and he decided to drive through the Valley section of Syracuse on his way to Firekeepers Restaurant. Driving south on Route 80, he recalled the area with some vague familiarity. The red Cape style house where he lived until he was three was still there. Webster's Pond; where Ephraim Webster, the first white settler had erected a home was just at the end of his street. St. Paul's Methodist Church where he was baptized and the Valley Cemetery, where his grandparents were buried, followed as he continued driving south. Although they had moved from this neighborhood when he was three years old, he still remembered the rolling hills and endless trees.

The Nation is loosely bordered by Route 11 to the east and Route 80 on the west. To the north lay the town of Nedrow while its southern boundary terminates in the vicinity of the village of LaFayette. He stopped to consider the unnatural rectangular shape of the Nation, wondering who or what had determined these boundaries. The Onondagas had occupied this land for over 10,000 years. Today the nation encompasses 7,300 acres and had been much larger before the State of New York severely reduced its size. "They are appropriately called the "People of the Hills", Robert thought. He had always considered the view of fog hanging like clouds among the hills as one of the most striking scenes he had ever viewed.

Soon, he would enter a sovereign nation; a part of the Iroquois Confederacy, to ask for their help in hiding what he would always consider his and Ron's property. Would the People of the Hills make a decision that could possibly put themselves on a collision course with the federal government for the sake of a young physicist?

Entering Nedrow and continuing south on Rt. 11, he could see the restaurant only half a mile away as he traversed the boundary between Nedrow and the Onondaga Nation. Passing the cigarette shops, he turned off of Rt. 11 onto a side road and parked his car in front of Firekeepers restaurant. Walking past the "Area Closed "sign he entered a partially full dining room where several couples sat in booths. What he noticed immediately was an odd aroma which filled his nostrils and the darkness of the room. The booths were indistinguishable from one another, having been finished with identical laminated, mottled brown plastic and the aroma originated from the adjoining dining area where smoking was permitted. Passing the booths, he sat at the counter located near the far wall. A man who was seated at the counter wearing a cook's apron nodded to him as he sat, then stood and left after Robert ordered a cup of coffee and explained to the waitress that he was here to see Sarah.

The uninspired atmosphere of the restaurant was partly due to the small windows which looked out onto the parking lot and its inadequate lighting. What interior lighting existed was provided by the few hanging lamps. There was sufficient light however, to see that the ceiling tiles should have been replaced long ago. Logs extended across the ceiling from behind the counter to the windows but it was too dim to determine if they were actual timbers or just simulated wood. White tiles behind the counter covered the wall and eventually joined with a white tiled floor interrupted only by a narrow window where orders were shouted to the cooks and the waitresses picked them up.

"Nothing in this room matches" thought Robert.

As he considered what he would say when he met Sarah, a man about his age approached the counter and placed a steaming hot cup of coffee on the counter so deliberately that some splashed into the saucer, while the portion that managed to land on the counter disappeared against the unappealing brown counter. Robert turned in his stool as the person sat rigidly and glared at him with piercing black eyes, wearing his disdain for Robert like a mask. Raising his chin with a display of deep arrogance he growled, "What do you want?"

Robert returned to face his coffee, his shoulder pointed in the stranger's direction. "Well, I have my coffee now and unless your name is Sarah it doesn't matter what I want. I'm here to speak to Sarah", he said calmly, which only served to further irritate his inquisitor.

"My name is Nate and you can only see her if I say so and only if you tell me what you want," speaking with his self-appointed authority.

He began to sense that plan "B" was becoming more appealing when Nate began shouting at him. He looked around the restaurant as the patrons stared from their booths and began to feel extremely uncomfortable with the unwelcome attention this was attracting.

As his agitation increased, Nate became increasingly incoherent. Robert sighed, looked at the floor and rose quickly.

Reaching into his pocket he threw a five dollar bill on the counter, "Tell Sarah to keep the change."

As turned toward the exit, Nate rose from the counter, blocking his path and began screaming louder than before.

Robert knew that his agitated expression meant trouble. He felt someone grab his arms from behind, "Hold him Bob," Nate yelled. As the pressure of the grip on his arms increased, Nate approached Robert and drew back his fist. Robert struck first as he drove a front kick into his solar plexus and Nate dropped to the floor gasping for breath.

Raising his right leg, he sank his heel into Bob's foot. Bob had little time to react to the pain as Robert raised his left leg above Bob's knee and brought the sole of his shoe down, scraping along Bob's shin. He felt the grip on his arms loosen and leaning forward for a moment, he arched his back and threw his head backward. As his head connected with Bob's nose, the grip came free and Robert sank his elbow into his attacker's stomach. Taking one step forward he delivered two sidekicks; the first to his ribs and as he slumped forward the second struck his face. Robert recognized him as the cook who had been seated at the counter. Bob continued his fall to the floor and Robert heard the kitchen door behind him open as Nate struggled to rise.

He perceived some movement behind him, as a third person had left the kitchen and was moving toward him. Robert immediately spun around and dropped to his left knee. As the fist from this person sailed harmlessly over Robert's head, his right fist landed in this person's groin. His momentum carried him forward and Robert stood up with his shoulder lodged in this man's waist, he lifted him by his legs and dropped him face first onto the floor.

Expecting Nate to have recovered enough to attack him from behind, he turned to his right and saw Nate rushing towards him. As Nate's right arm drew back to deliver a punch, Robert moved left, blocked with his right arm and thrust his thumb into the right side of Nate's neck and his carotid artery. Nate's face already bore a pained expression as Robert's left leg swept and hit the back of Nate's knees and Robert's straight right arm hit him squarely in the face. Blood was now coming from Nate's nose and Robert gripped him by his collar, his head angled toward the floor; unable to continue, but possibly not ready to submit. With his left arm drawn back, about to finish the conflict for good, he heard a voice call out.

"Dr. Dubé, will you please leave my young men alone"?

He turned toward a woman standing at the end of the counter. "Sarah, I presume?" Robert looked at Nate and released his grip on the shirt, sending Nate to the floor.

Sarah looked at him with an emotionless expression, "I spoke to your mother. She said you'd be wearing a jacket."

"Was the jacket meant to be a method of identifying me?"

"No, because it looks like rain and she told you to wear one," she said simply.

"She didn't mention a karate demonstration, however," looking on as the three young men struggled to reach their feet.

"Dr. Dubé, your mother convinced me to listen to you and I'm willing to help you if I can." She motioned to one of the inexpensive looking booths and they sat opposite each other. Sarah was one of the Clan Mothers of the Onondaga's and was due an enormous amount of respect. Her directives were never questioned. She was an older woman with short white hair and now exhibited a pleasant smile. Her face was round with high cheek bones and she wore a loose brown dress with a beaded necklace.

Robert described what his needs involved and as Sarah listened, her young men slowly approached the table. Sarah diverted her attention from Robert and directed it to Bob and the other person from the kitchen. "You two will pick up all of this and then return to the kitchen and stay there. You have never seen this man and none of this ever happened. You are not to talk to anyone about this; although I can't imagine any of you would care to brag about being beaten by one man." Sarah looked at Robert, "Sorry, Dr. Dubé, I appologise for this reception. We're usually more hospitable."

Robert nodded appreciatively and smiled at Sarah.

As the debris was being cleared, Sarah's tone became very serious as she addressed his original antagonist. "Nathan you took it upon yourself to get involved in my business. That was a huge mistake. The person you were so rude to just now is Dr. Dubé. I agreed to meet with him because I'm convinced that he honestly needs our help and any assistance we can offer is the right thing to do. In addition, I share Dr. Dubé's skepticism when it comes to our government behaving responsibly. I am making you responsible for seeing to it that he receives whatever he needs from us. No one must know about any details of this. If there are any problems, I'll come to you for an explanation. Do you understand?"

Nathan was on the verge of protesting when he seemed to think better of it and responded the only way he could, "Yes Sarah."

"Fine. Dr. Dubé, you will go outside and wait in your car. Nathan, you will leave through the rear entrance and the Dr. will follow your truck. I have an outbuilding on my property. You're familiar with it?"

"Yes Sarah," said Nathan, painfully humbled.

"Do whatever you need to do to help him. Now go, both of you." She handed something to Nate before rising from the booth and disappearing through the double doors which led into the kitchen.

If Robert had felt any apprehension about waiting in his car for Nathan, he felt relieved when he began to follow him. Nathan slowed as he drove his Ford pickup truck past Robert.

Following the fight in the restaurant he expected a look of animosity from Nathan. He exhibited no smile; rather his look was one that someone wears when they have a job perform. He followed Nathan back to the road which had led to the restaurant, however rather than turn toward Rt.11 he proceeded in the opposite direction past the restaurant; onto a part of the road which was apparently used only by members of the Nation. The road descended, meandering until they reached the valley floor. Nathan's truck slowed and stopped at a crossroad. A right turn would lead across a narrow bridge to a highway in the distance. Nathan turned left and followed a still smaller road up a slowly rising hill and disappeared as the road curved around a tree line. He passed several homes of various sizes and designs on his right. To the left there were no buildings, only a steep hill covered with maples and birch trees.

Nathan had driven his truck down a driveway which led to a large home and continued past the garage before parking on the grass near a small two story house about one hundred yards from the road. This really was a brilliant location in which to store his machine. This structure stood in the corner of Sarah's expansive property, hidden by trees on two sides and from the sky by overhanging limbs. Located on a dead end road, off a seldom used road on Nation land couldn't be more secure.

Robert parked next to Nathan's truck and followed him to the front door of the small rectangular house with grey siding and maroon shutters. The front door was wooden with six panes of beveled glass which reflected sunlight and was located in the center of the house, while a large picture window was positioned on the right with two smaller windows on the left. Nathan reached for the door, stopped and looked at Robert. Handing him the key which Sarah had given him earlier he said, "This will be yours as long as you need it."

Robert nodded as he accepted the key, "I wish I could tell you more about this, but for now the less anyone knows the better."

"It doesn't matter. Sarah told me that you are my responsibility. That's all that matters," Nathan said without looking at him.

He inserted the key into the lock and thought he should ask Nate about an exit route but he had already walked away and was climbing into his truck.

Once inside, he was convinced that all the trouble leading up to this had been worth it. The ceiling was high enough and the room's length was adequate to accommodate the array. A sofa with matching end tables sat against the left wall. There was a roll top desk located by the right wall and a small but well equipped kitchen was situated at the far end of the room with a large window that afforded a view of trees and a stream that flowed across the property before disappearing into the woods.

The furniture was fashioned from blond oak which matched the color of the carpeting. A staircase next to the sofa led to a loft with an open ceiling; affording it a clear view of the living area. Sarah had several pieces of Native American art displayed prominently, including paintings, sculptures made from copper and silver and stone carvings.

Robert searched for his location's coordinates with his mobile devise and saved them to download into the time machine's computer. He made mental notes of what he would need to obtain before he returned to the house. Ideally, he would only need to travel here once more by car. In the future, he hoped to use his machine to arrive and depart.

Exiting the house he felt that there were a lot of challenges which he had overcome, but still many more remained. For one, he would need to stock provisions in the house which could last for a prolonged period of time. His major problem however, was avoiding detection by Agent Franklin. He was fairly certain that the amount of electricity used to energize the array was large enough to be measurable. If it could be measured, its usage could be traced and would lead Franklin to his location. This would be the next problem he needed to solve.

RESOLUTION

Robert reached the crossroad and stopped. Turning right would lead him to his original route and return to Firekeepers. Proceeding straight led to a highway in the distance where he could see vehicles moving past. He decided to drive straight on, passing a few houses on his left; nearly hidden by trees. On his right was a large field where some buildings stood just before this road terminated at the highway. A number of pickup trucks were parked at odd angles in front of the largest building. A sizeable wooden porch wrapped around it and several people stood beneath the roof or leaned against its posts. When Robert saw Nathan, Bob and the other combatant from the kitchen, they immediately straightened and glared at him, their arms crossed. Robert began to raise his arm to wave but didn't feel that his gesture would be welcomed or returned. Instead he turned his attention to the road before him. This was Route 11A which passed through the heart of the Onondaga Nation. Now he had at least two exit routes from Sarah's property. He just hoped he wouldn't need to use them.

He drove back to Nedrow and followed Route 81 to campus. In fifteen minutes he parked behind his flat and walked to the front porch where he found mail waiting for him. After climbing the stairs to his flat, he put the mail next to his chair on the balcony, walked to the kitchen and returned with a pint of Roasted Porter. Cars passed below heading to and from campus. A light breeze blew across the balcony and carried the sounds of children playing down the street while across the street two students casually passed a football to each other.

Robert was still concerned about Franklin's efforts to locate the machine once he had retrieved it and stored it on the Nation. The consequences would be different now. Regardless of Robert's interpretation of who actually owned it, DoD would view this as theft of government property. Any contact with Franklin in the future would make their initial visit seem cordial.

He returned to the question surrounding disguising the amount of electricity used when the machine was energized. The machine used a considerable amount of electricity and although it only lasted for a few seconds; he wondered if it was measurable and its usage could be traced to his location by someone who was searching for the machine. Would it be possible to construct a device that would dissipate or dampen the amount of electricity used, so that its usage would appear normal or be undetectable?

As a research assistant, he had certain resources available to him that would raise a minimum of questions. If these materials were needed for his research project, he might be able to procure them without much difficulty. Hopefully the necessary materials would be available on campus. In addition, from this point on he would avoid using his credit card for purchases. He was absolutely certain that Franklin would follow his credit card activity once Robert regained his property. Limiting the information the DoD officers could glean from following his transactions would be critical to his future success.

His efforts to deliver the package containing Ron's father's financial documents soon had become his priority. Hopefully, it would be as simple as sending pens, paperweights or Mrs. Spencer's terrier into the future.

Robert looked up at the rapidly darkening sky. Streetlights were coming to life and he could see rooms in some of the academic buildings lighting up as well. His life would be much more enjoyable if all these issues could be carried away like the breeze that blew dried leaves around the floor of his balcony. He thought it very odd that there was no escaping his involvement in all this. One foot followed the other down this steep path he found himself traveling. It had begun slowly, but his pace was definitely quickening now and he felt that as the situation progressed, it would be like running downhill with little or no control. It seemed appropriate that his research concerned black holes, for it seemed that once he passed this horizon, there would be no turning back.

THE PROPOSAL

"So Robert, let me see if I completely understand your proposal". Robert sat in the office of Dean Lenderman, head of the physics department who sat upright in his chair with folded hands and spoke in a soft quizzical tone. He had short brown hair, bright green eyes and a beard which could not mask his tremendous smile. But he wasn't smiling now as he strove to understand what Robert was proposing.

"We brought you here to work as a research assistant on a project studying black holes."

He paused and looked at Robert to let him know that he expected a response.

"Yes, Dean Lenderman."

"You've only just arrived and already wish to pursue something else? Not just something else; something we don't have funding for?"

Robert glanced at a photograph of Dean Lenderman and Dr. Kip Thorne shaking hands on the wall before him and the Dean's desk clock. It was fashioned out of a solid cube of mahogany and hinged in the center. A clock was recessed into the top of the highly polished wood and the bottom half held a magnetic compass.

"That's not entirely accurate Dean Lenderman," Robert said as he leaned forward and picked up the mahogany desk clock as his eyes narrowed.

"Relocating you to this university was not an inexpensive undertaking Dr. Dubé. It was part of a commitment on the part of this institution. I'm beginning to question your commitment to this program," he said in a voice that sounded like he was about to lose all patience as he stared uneasily at his precious clock.

Robert felt that he had the Dean's attention now as he moved his fingers across the sleek sides of the wood and studied the mechanism before returning it to its place on the desk. His back stiffened as looked directly at the Dean.

"To begin Dean Lenderman, I'm not suggesting that I have any intention of not performing my duties to this program," he said, conceding nothing. "I'm totally committed to the project. I don't think that it is entirely fair to call in to question my ability to commit. Anyone who completes a PhD. program at Caltech has to possess a strong sense of commitment. What I am attempting to explain to you is that in addition to work on my research project, I wish to continue work on my unfinished project from Caltech. This would not impinge on the amount of the time I spend researching black holes at Syracuse University. In fact, the two areas are so closely related that my work from Cal Tech will actually enhance my research here. My main purpose was to inform you in advance, so it wouldn't come as a surprise."

The Dean paused as he uneasily tapped his fingers on the desk. "That is quite a relief, Robert. Aside from the interest our department has in your success, I do not wish to interrupt the personal investment I have in your family. I play golf with your father and as for your mother," Dean Lederman paused for a moment and seemed to be searching for words on the office ceiling, "to be honest with you Robert, she frightens me and most department heads at the University. Ever since she so nonchalantly swore at Dr. Snowden, no one wants to oppose her, willingly that is."

Robert considered responding to the accuracy of this story and decided against it.

"Dean Lenderman, returning to my original subject, I wanted to speak to you about what is missing in front of the physics building." Robert continued as Dean Lenderman's expression betrayed his curiosity. "There are statues bordering the physics building that have absolutely nothing to do with physics."

"That's true," said the Dean thoughtfully. In all his many years at Syracuse University he passed these iconic statues on the quad without giving much thought to them. A statue of Ernie Davis, the football legend was situated on the western end of the physics building, while the Saltine Warrior was positioned to the east. Ernie Davis won the Heisman Trophy in 1961, the first African-American to do so. The life size bronze statue depicts him cradling a helmet with his left arm and holding a football in his right hand. The Saltine Warrior was created in tribute to an Onondaga chief who really never was. It occupies a prominent place in the south east corner of the Quad and shows an American Indian drawing his bow with an arrow pointed toward the sky. A member of the Onondaga Nation posed for the bronze.

"But what would be erected in front of this building?" questioned the Dean, his curiosity obviously piqued.

"Picture this," Robert said, uncrossing his legs and placing both feet on the floor. As he leaned forward in his chair, he gestured with his hands as his voice and expression became increasingly animated. "In the front of the physics building," pointing precisely in that direction, "a statue dedicated to the creation of the first device to make time travel a reality."

The Dean's eyes widened as they focused squarely on Robert.

"Consider what it would mean to the prestige of the University to be able to claim something like that. A full size likeness of the first functioning machine would be prominently positioned directly in front of the entrance to the physics building and the fact that you were Dean of the physics department." Before the Dean could formulate a response Robert smiled, "Because we've already built one."

Dean Lenderman looked a bit like someone who had just received an electric shock.

He revealed to the Dean, the details regarding the creation of the machine, including the point when it had been seized by the DoD.

"How does the government's possession of this machine prove that you and Dr. Maxwell created it?" asked a skeptical Dean, sounding decidedly guarded. "Why couldn't they claim that the government developed this?"

Robert stretched his legs, paused and looked more relaxed. "I'm in the process of reclaiming my property. The reality is that the government can't claim it was their development. If they did they would have to describe how they developed it and they couldn't because only Ron and I would be able to explain that. Additionally, I seriously doubt that it would be utilized for anything constructive. The DoD seized it because it was in the "government's best interests". The vagueness of that statement alone is scary. If they are using it, their purpose is most likely something the government would prefer that we aren't aware of. Once the conspiracy theorists learn about its existence, they'll attempt to blame the federal government for everything from Pearl Harbor to the JFK assassination. I'm prepared to retrieve the machine, use it for the purpose it was intended and give Syracuse University credit for its development. I only require that you understand my involvement in two projects simultaneously."

Dean Lenderman paused, absorbing all that he heard and looked back at Robert, "Dr. Dubé, I'm very interested in everything you've said. We had hoped that someday your name might be mentioned in the same breath as Drs.Chandrasekhar, Hawking, and Thorne, amongst others. I thought that might be overly ambitious. Please don't prove us wrong. If you need anything please let me know."

Robert rose from his chair and walked toward the door, but paused before exiting. The Dean had already turned his attention to closely inspecting his desk clock, expecting Robert to depart. When Robert stopped moving, he looked up from his desk. "Dean, in view of all that has transpired and may yet occur it may be best that we keep this conversation confidential."

Dean Lenderman smiled, "What conversation was that Dr. Dubé? Say hello to your parents for me."

Robert exited the physics building with much more confidence in the success of his plan than he had when he entered. His search for the necessary materials would be less encumbered now that his immediate supervisor was aware of his intentions.

Leaving campus on his bicycle and traveling down Euclid Avenue to his apartment, he continued the seemingly never ending mental exercise as to how he would put the remaining portions of his plans to reclaim his machine into action. Arriving at his apartment, he quickly pushed his bicycle up the inclined lawn and carried it on to the porch. He collected his mail without really looking at it and carried everything upstairs. Spending as little time as possible depositing his mail, backpack and bike, he continued into the kitchen and opened a door which led down a rear staircase into his backyard.

He remembered an alternate energy source he had seen at the University physical plant. Someone had proposed using an Uninterruptible Power Supply (UPS) as a method to provide immediate power for a short period of time in the event of a power outage. They would be connected between the power source and computers and would supply power until the primary power source was restored or a generator could be started. After comparing this method, it was abandoned in favor of solar powered batteries. Now, they sat as unused equipment in the physical plant building, but to Robert they represented several missing pieces of his puzzle.

A few weeks earlier, while visiting that building hunting for a book related to his research, he saw the UPS's sitting by the loading area. At that time, he suggested to an employee who was seated at the entrance that they looked out of place. In a disinterested tone, he explained about the aborted experiment and how he hoped they were only going to remain there long enough for someone to claim them. Now, he was driving down Comstock Avenue toward the Syracuse University physical plant hoping that everyone else shared the employee's lack of appreciation for them.

The person at the front desk didn't seem to have changed clothes since Robert's previous visit. His S.U. cap was still worn with the visor angled down obscuring his face, but it couldn't hide his full beard which hung over his tee shirt. He looked bored and sounded relieved that someone had arrived to remove this annoyance. There were six UPS's, each about the size of a PC arranged in a row against the wall. He wanted to take them all, but now he realized that his plan had only been to get here, not how to claim and remove them. However, he had reached a point of no return.

He turned toward the employee and placed both hands on the desktop. As the brim of the S.U. cap raised slightly in his direction, Robert began talking as if they were resuming a previous conversation. "It would be easier to take the UPS's from this loading dock and deliver them directly to the physics building on campus, don't you think?"

The man behind the desk paused for a moment and rubbed his hands across his face as if this action would somehow induce a decision. He rather quickly dropped his hands and placed them forcefully on his desk as if he had had an epiphany.

"You would need to have some paperwork for anything to be transferred from here. You can have the UPS's; but I need a work order," as he completed his statement with a satisfied expression on what little Robert could see of his face and emphasized his point by holding a copy of the required form above his worn cap.

"I've just left Dean Lenderman's office in the physics building," Robert countered. "However he's already left for a conference in San Francisco and he'll be absent for three weeks." Robert's confidence in concocting stories was growing by the minute. "You're perfectly welcome to keep these here for me for the next three weeks while I wait for the paperwork; or I can take them now and bring you the papers signed by the Dean when he returns."

"I'm not sure about you leaving them here for three weeks," said the clerk cautiously as he dithered about what course of action to take, remaining safely behind his desk.

"You want to keep them then?"

"I do?"

"You do?"

He removed his cap and ran his stubby fingers through his blond hair. "Yes I do; no; I mean, no I don't. Get them out of here now. Just bring me the paperwork when your Dean returns from San Antonio."

"San Francisco."

"Whatever. Just get them out of here," he said in a weary, broken voice, forcefully returning his cap to cover his hair.

Not waiting for an instant lest he change his mind, Robert walked calmly through the door, jumped from the platform to the ground and sprinted across the parking lot to his car. Weaving amongst the trucks in the lot, he maneuvered his car to the loading dock and 15 minutes later he was driving south to the Onondaga Nation and the house Sarah had loaned to him.

PREPARATION

Robert carried the UPS's into Sarah's house and placed them in a sequence against the wall on the left side of the living room. He knew that he had sufficient room for his time machine to fit in the living room in addition to with the additional power sources. The UPS's had the advantage of possessing the capacity to store enough energy to power the laser array for a brief period of time and not register a surge in energy usage. Their disadvantage was that recharging them could take hours, introducing the possibility that he could be stranded somewhere in time, waiting for the batteries to recharge before he could return. He decided that by dividing the six UPS's into three groups of two, that likelihood would be diminished if not entirely avoided.

Everything was ready now to reclaim his machine. He needed only to act and he would do that soon enough. There was one final addition he would make to his apparatus and that concerned the method of energizing his machine. From the beginning he had used a simple laser as a switch to send power to it. The situation was different now that his machine wasn't secure in his Caltech office. In addition to the possible intrusion from Agent Franklin, he felt that his concern about an intruder from the Nation, curious or otherwise was more than justified.

Sarah gave her blessing to storing his machine on Nation land and Nathan was charged by her with ensuring its security. He seemed steadfast in his intention to follow her instructions, but Robert still had some doubts about the level of his trustworthiness.

His adaptations included a device to recognise the image of a fingerprint before the laser array could be energized and a PIN pad. With these in place, Robert would be the only person who could operate the machine. These instruments were placed on the oak table next to where he would position the machine once he reacquired it. He entered his left index finger into the recognition device and stored it into its memory and selected his number to be used in his PIN pad.

He had selected enough freeze dried food to leave in the out building and still had enough remaining to take with him on his journey to France. While on his expedition, his goal was to visit the village where his ancestor, Mathurin Dubé was born and the port of La Rochelle where he had boarded a ship for New France. The year was 1660 when Mathurin left the village of La Chapelle-Themér. Like most émigrés he would never return to his homeland. Boarding vessels which would eventually relocate thousands of individuals thousands of miles from their homes was a concept which Robert found difficult to comprehend. A voyage across the Atlantic in a small wooden ship which would take weeks, made him wonder what drove a person to undertake something like that. He presumed that most were following their future, not escaping their past.

France was the most populous country in Europe at that time, but allowed fewer of its subjects to emigrate than Spain, Portugal or England. Of the few hundred thousand who were allowed to leave, only a few tens of thousands opted for New France. Most of them left for the warmer Antilles.

Also inescapable was that while it took weeks to arrive in New France after crossing the Atlantic aboard a wooden ship, Robert would travel the same distance instantly. His motivation was totally different from Mathurin's, however. He had no intention of living in France. Once he delivered Ron's documents, his objective was to return to the university and continue his research on black holes. He had been raised to always remain focused and his karate training had taught him to always be aware of his surroundings. This was fortunate. While he was in the process of completing the necessary connections to the machine prior to returning to campus, he became aware that he was about to be visited.

Turning quickly toward the door, Robert saw Nathan entering the house. His expression was unusually serious and this time; friendly. His defiant glare was missing, for the moment.

"I recognized your car. I thought I'd see how things were going and if you needed any help." Robert was struck by his sincerity, considering the circumstances surrounding their first meeting.

Nathan reclined on the sofa nearest to the door and leaned forward resting his forearms on his knees. "Looks like you've been busy. What do you use these for?" as he gestured towards the UPS's.

"Those are used to power electrical devises if the power fails," said Robert. The amount of goodwill he had felt toward Nathan was fading quickly.

"How about these things. What do they do?" Nathan rolled off the sofa and moved towards the table looking at the PIN pad and fingerprint recognition device.

Robert turned toward the table, "Those are just to keep my property secure. The more secure I can make this area, the sooner I can make it seem like I was never here."

Nathan's tone and demeanor became confrontational and caustic. "You sound like you don't trust us," he said with cold hostility.

"And now the level of trust I had is totally bankrupt," thought Robert. "I remember that Sarah entrusted you with keeping this area safe. I trust you to follow her instructions. You can't be everywhere however. This is just an added layer of protection. My primary level of security is you," Robert said as calmly as possible. Past experience had taught him that Nathan and his friend's emotions could become hostile without much provocation.

Nathan paused to absorb what Robert said, but glared at him with an intensity bordering on hatred, "I cannot believe that

I'm helping a white man conduct his business on Nation land. It seems wrong to me. After all your people have done to my people, we should be turning you out, not allowing you into our homes."

"I really don't have time for this," groaned Robert. Placing his hands on the table and staring back he said, "As far as "my people" are concerned, consider this; my mother is Indian. When England partitioned India in 1947, her country was split into pieces. Hundreds of thousands were killed during that period of relocation."

"If you imagine that you somehow are exclusively the only group that was a victim of prejudice or bias, then I think you should ask a Jewish person to tell you about the Holocaust. I'm not saying that what the U.S. government did to Native Americans was right, because it wasn't."

"My point is this: my parents weren't in this country during that period. I wasn't in North America when settlers and the government ran over your people. You weren't present in India during the partition, plotting to ambush trainloads of Muslims who were being relocated. The thought of deliberately committing acts such as these perpetrated on anyone would never enter my mind. Painting me with your broad brush, as you seem to conveniently apply to any non-indigenous people is totally ridiculous."

Robert could feel the tension rising and the thought of a reoccurrence of their first encounter at the restaurant seemed very likely.

He was anticipating what might happen next, when Nathan sniffed the air. "What's that smell'?

Robert suddenly remembered his skillet and its contents he had left cooking on the stove when Nathan entered the house. He walked hurriedly around Nathan and examined the contents of the skillet, which were by now bubbling and sizzling. Reaching for two plates, tongs and Tuscan Garlic bread he called over his shoulder to Nathan, "Do you like bacon"?

Nathan bore the look of someone whose curiosity had just been satisfied by such a needless question. "Are you kidding?" he replied enthusiastically, "Its bacon!"

"Have a seat in one of those chairs on the patio", Robert said pointing to the door with the tongs as he spread butter on several slices of toasted bread.

He carried two bacon sandwiches and two glasses to the patio and settled into the Adirondack chair next to Nathan. Robert thought this type of chair was nearly perfect to relax in. The seat slanted back at a slight angle and the arms were straight and broad enough to rest your arms and have room for a sandwich and a drink. With his arms stretched out on the arm of the chair, it reminded him of the statue of Abraham Lincoln in the Lincoln monument.

Neither spoke for a moment. Robert searched his mind for a way to break the silence and handed Nathan a glass of beer.

Looking at the southern hills, Robert glanced at the open sky. "I met someone from England once, who claimed that lacrosse was created there and they taught it to the Iroquois and it really is a girl's game."

Nathan nearly choked on his sandwich. "That's interesting. The game originated here in the 17th century and we called it "dehuntshigwa'es" (men hit a rounded object). Its purpose was to settle inter-tribal disputes and toughen warriors for combat. The English really don't know anything if they truly believe that."

Robert finished a bite from his sandwich. "Not only that, they call potato chips, crisps; and French fries, chips."

Nathan nodded as he drank from his glass and then studied it as he held it toward the sunlight. "That's crazy. What kind of beer is this?"

"Smoked Porter", said Robert as he raised his glass.

"Well, Cheers Robert."

"Cheers, Nate."

Robert continued to absorb all this. A tasty lunch with a previous antagonist, now a possible friend, sitting together was something he hadn't thought possible a short time ago. The din from traffic on Route 81 was barely perceptible and only a minor distraction as he sat comfortably in the Adirondack chair. This was relaxation at its best. "Enjoy this now," he thought. "Things are probably going to be anything but relaxing very soon."

RECLAIMING

Robert stood in the center of his living room, holding his mobile device in his right hand and one of the key fobs which would serve as the transmitter, in his left. Methodically, he practiced pressing the button on his mobile device and pausing a moment before nearly pressing the button on the key fob. The image displayed was the picture he took of his time machine in the basement of the Court of Appeals building the day he surrendered it to Agent Franklin. When he was satisfied with this procedure he activated his mobile device, uploaded the image, pressed the button on his key fob and vanished.

In an instant, Robert stood inside his time machine. Overcoming his initial impulse to step out of the machine, he looked quickly around the room. The changes since he was last here were dramatic. Though still dimly lit, he could see that there were still two desks against the left wall near the entrance, but a second pair of desks and one long table had been added near the opposite wall and a large screen was suspended from the ceiling. Each desk was now equipped with a computer and the table was awash with various texts and charts. On the screen, a series of calculations and formulas and diagrams were displayed. Robert shook his head as he studied their data. If this was the result of someone attempting to understand his and Ron's work, their progress had been extremely limited.

Robert began making changes in earnest in his connections to the machine in preparation for moving it to the Nation. The room was unnervingly quiet, but he recognized that all the equipment in the room was turned on. It was quite probable that someone would be returning at any moment. He noticed something at his feet as he was about to enter the coordinates to the house on the Nation. A hastily written note lay on the floor of his machine and there was a pile of similar appearing notes on the table amid the books and charts littering the table. Without hesitation he quickly stepped out of the machine, raced to the table and gathered the papers.

Not pausing to read them, he entered the coordinates for his next destination and stepped back into the machine. He energized the machine and instantly found himself and the machine in Sarah's house. The machine had positioned itself exactly as Robert had predicted. He repositioned the device he used to enter the coordinates so that it was placed outside of the machine and disconnected the original laser switch. After connecting the PIN device in sequence with the fingerprint recognition scanner, he joined the three pairs of UPS's which were already charged. Robert made the necessary connections and entered the coordinates for his apartment into the computer. When he was absolutely certain that everything was exactly as it should be, he entered his PIN, scanned his index finger, energized the machine and reappeared in his apartment.

His wing chair in the living room was his refuge, but the chair on the balcony was his retreat. Robert sat on his balcony, reading the papers he had collected in the basement of the Court of Appeals building. They were all from Ron, asking when he would receive the documents that Robert still had in his chest of drawers. He wondered if anyone on the government's scientific team had any idea that these messages had originated 20 years in the future.

One thing was certain; Ron's envelope would not leave his possession until he was able to deliver it personally. Franklin would undoubtedly respond when he discovered that the machine was missing and the envelope could not be allowed to fall into his hands.

Resting his feet on the balcony railing, he looked absent mindedly at the clouds hurrying past, driven by a brisk unseen wind; pondering what sort of changes he could expect in the future.

FRANKLIN'S REPLY

Intelligence Specialist Franklin sat in his office at the Department of Defense in Washington D.C. Since surrendering the time machine to be secured by the U.S. Marshalls in Pasadena, he had turned his attention to a cooperative effort with U.S. Cyber Command. From the moment he had driven away from the Court of Appeals building, he had tried to forget the entire matter regarding the time machine, as it had brought him no real sense of satisfaction. Quite the opposite, as it was closer to the truth to say that the young physicist's arguments were difficult to argue against. Simply telling yourself it was your duty wasn't a convincing argument.

He required some time to think about a long overdue vacation. This would be an interval when he needed to really leave his work behind and he could devote his time entirely to his family and none at all on anything related to the DoD. From the center drawer of his desk he withdrew a copy of "Yankee Magazine." Several pages of topics ranging from fishing and kayaking to photography had been folded over again and again. "Just imagine," Franklin thought, "no phone, no desk, no research results or meetings with anyone representing Cyber Security." He had merely desired time away before the Caltech assignment, but the entire Pasadena affair had nearly pushed him to his limit.

He could also do without his assistant, Intelligence Agent Tyler, who had somehow managed to stand next to him, unnoticed as he contemplated two weeks in Maine, away from him. He never really gave much thought as to why Tyler annoyed him so much. Just acknowledging the fact that he found him to be a colossal distraction was enough.

"Excuse me sir, I have something I thought you should see." Agent Tyler's serious look was difficult to ignore. Franklin sighed, re-folded the articles and returned "Yankee Magazine" to his desk for reflection at a later date. Leaning back in his chair he adjusted his glasses and rubbed his face with both hands. "What do you have?" avoiding looking in Tyler's direction.

"I was following up with some of the details regarding the assignment at Caltech," said Tyler gripping several sheets of paper. "To begin with I found records of a telephone call to book Dr. Dubé's flight to Syracuse and a credit card purchase from an electronics supply store about one mile from the Caltech campus".

Franklin's vision of a house on a lake in Maine, fishing from the shore while his children swam near the dock suddenly vanished. What remained was a sense of being lost and a wish that he had never heard of Caltech. He turned toward Tyler, "Why is this significant now and why didn't you see this before? You were supposedly checking on his cell phone and credit card usage when he went missing the first time." Franklin was clearly irritated.

"I did, I did;" Tyler insisted. "But look at the times listed on these reports. I made notes of the times when I began monitoring his phone and credit card activity. That was at 1.17 P.M., but the call to the airport was at 3.52 P.M. and the purchases occurred at 3.32 P.M. We had our contact with him at his desk 3.00. I can't explain it, but I think that the reason there was no record of any activity was that they were occurring in the future. Our real time was about an hour or two behind the period when Dr. Dubé was using his phone or making a purchase at the electronics store. And there is something else. I checked with the Caltech administration about monitoring electricity usage in the physics laboratory before we arrived in Pasadena. I wanted to monitor how much energy the time machine used within a certain time period. Pasadena Water and Power was able to monitor usage at that location and they found several instances of a significant amount of usage for a very brief period of time. They told me that their instruments showed a measurable but inexplicable brief spike in electricity usage from that location. Additionally, I just spoke to PW&P. I never told them that the investigation had concluded, so they never stopped monitoring the area surrounding the Caltech campus. There was a power surge exactly like the one in the physics laboratory; but this came from the Court of Appeals building where the machine is stored."

Franklin sat ramrod straight in his chair as if he had been shocked. Daydreams about Maine were over for now. "U.S. Marshall's Service, Circuit Court of Appeals, Pasadena California", he said to the computer. "Connecting United States Marshall's Office" appeared on his monitor. Moments later a person answered "United States Marshall's Office."

Franklin leaned toward the computer, sitting on the edge of his chair. "This is Intelligence Specialist Franklin calling from the DoD in Washington. I need to speak with Marshall Tate. It's urgent."

The voice said," Yes sir, I'm connecting you now."

Franklin waited a minute when a voice he recognized came from the computer, "Agent Franklin this is Marshall Tate. How can I help you?"

"I'm in my office in Washington, Marshall, and I have reason to believe that your security may have been compromised. I need you to check on that machine we left with you."

"Agent Franklin, I'm looking at the monitor right now. The room is actually the domain of the scientific team now but we still maintain security. The room is vacant at the moment, but I can see the machine clearly."

"Marshall, you need to go to the room and personally check this out. It is your surveillance system that I feel may have been tampered with."

"Very well," said Tate will a hint of annoyance, "this will take a minute for me check on."

Franklin glanced at his watch and turned in his seat to face Tyler. "Get us on a flight to Syracuse and arrange for transportation. I have a feeling that we will be meeting with Dr. Dubé soon if this proceeds as I think it will. Just get us..."

Franklin was interrupted by Marshall Tate. "Agent Franklin, I am standing in the room where your Dr. Dubé assembled that machine. Our security camera shows no activity outside the entrance since the scientific team left, but the machine is gone." Marshall Tate sounded completely perplexed.

"Marshall Tate," Franklin began slowly; "there was a grey metal object that was attached to the machine. It is approximately 6 inches square with a screen and a keyboard also. Do you see that?" Franklin waited impatiently to hear something positive from Marshall Tyler.

"No Agent Franklin," was the Marshall's reply. "Everything is gone."

Franklin took a deep breath and slowly exhaled. "Marshall Tate, Agent Tyler and I are leaving for Syracuse today to interview Dr. Dubé regarding the missing property. Please let me know what you discover when you check on the breach in your monitoring system. If you should find an electronic device that could be responsible, visit this electronics store on... wait a moment." Franklin stopped to read the paperwork handed him by Tyler, "on the corner of Colorado Boulevard and Meredith Avenue. I'll look forward to hearing from you Marshall."

"OK, what flights are available to Syracuse?" asked Franklin turning in his chair to face Tyler.

Reading from his mobile device Tyler said, "There are flights from Dulles later today. However we also could ride on a military flight from Andrews AFB to Syracuse, where the 174th Fighter Wing used to be. They pilot drones from there now, but they still have an airfield where a military cargo plane will be making a delivery today and we can requisition a government vehicle there for our use."

"Andrews it is then," said Franklin.

During the drive from the DoD to Andrews, Franklin thought about his upcoming confrontation in Syracuse. This time there would be no deals, no compromises. The only possible outcome would be regaining control of the machine and to have it secured, by him personally. They had just entered Andrews when his phone rang. "U.S. Marshall Tate" appeared on the screen. "Marshall Tate, hello. What do you have for me?" asked Franklin.

"Agent Franklin, when we began tracing wiring of the surveillance system, we found a device which had been connected to our surveillance system. We spoke to the owner of the electronics supply store on Colorado Boulevard who informed us that once installed, it has the capability to receive an image which would send that image to our monitors. It would appear that your Dr. Dubé had planned this well in advance."

"Well thank you Marshall. I have one question for you." Franklin's tone immediately rose from pleasant to aggressive. "How on earth did you allow this to occur? I left that machine under your supervision and now it has disappeared." Franklin sounded angry and annoyed.

"Well Agent Franklin," responded the Marshall dryly, "here's the thing. When you met me at the Court House, you told me that he was to be given "all assistance necessary" to install the machine and then you left. If you wanted to be more comfortable with the situation, you should have dropped your cavalier approach and supervised it yourself. Instead, you wheeled a Trojan horse into our building and ran back to D.C. The only person to blame for this fiasco is you." Then the screen read, "Connection lost".

Franklin paused for a moment before returning his phone to his jacket pocket. "I probably shouldn't plan on a Christmas card from Marshall Tate," he muttered.

After presenting his I.D. to the guard at Andrews, he and Agent Tyler were directed to the flight tower and from there to a waiting cargo plane. Meeting them at the door was Captain Carin.

The captain was dressed in his flight uniform, a tall, thick shouldered man with dark hair and an easy friendly smile and greeted them with a firm warm handshake. "Welcome aboard gentleman. We need to move now if I'm to remain on schedule." Entering the aircraft, the captain pointed to a pair of jump seats. "Buckle yourselves in gentlemen. The next stop will be Syracuse."

"Captain Carin, we certainly appreciate your help," Franklin said as the captain moved toward the cockpit.

"Our pleasure gentlemen. Our flight plan takes us to the 174th. After we deliver our load of materials for their flight systems, we have a delivery to make at the former bomber base at Plattsburgh. There is a joint American Canadian research facility there. If you need a return flight to Andrews, contact the 174th and they will arrange a connection."

"Thank you captain, we'll contact you if we need that." Franklin wanted to appear as cordial and appreciative as possible following his encounter with Marshall Tate.

Landing at the 174th Attack Wing was a culmination of a relatively uneventful flight. Franklin and Tyler departed from the cargo plane and looked out at a sky full of various clouds, all grey. Some areas of the sky were lighter than others, but the entire sky was as thickly overcast as any he'd ever seen. Captain Carin extended his hand and heartily shook hands with both agents. "Don't hesitate to call if you need help returning to D.C. This is Master Sergeant Shaw. He'll help you the rest of the way." Captain Carin returned to his duties of readying the aircraft for its flight to Plattsburgh.

"Specialist Franklin, Agent Tyler, I am Sergeant Shaw. Welcome to the 174th. I understand that you are to be here briefly. What do you require?" Sergeant Shaw was a man of average height with bright green eyes, thinning brown hair and sturdy looking hands.

"To begin with, Sergeant, we understood there would be a government vehicle waiting here for us." Franklin was making a statement, not a query.

"We had a mechanical problem with one of our vehicles Agent Franklin." Sergeant Shaw's pace didn't slacken as he strode in the direction of the control tower. "We don't have one to spare. However, we do have a solution," he said; opening the door. "Paige, come over here." He called to a young man seated before a computer who rose and hurried toward the Sergeant.

The sergeant introduced the three men. "This is Airman Paige. He will be your driver as long as you need him. We'll provide you with your own vehicle, as soon as one becomes available." The sergeant turned to Paige. "Paige, bring the vehicle here and take these men wherever they need to go."

Airman Paige disappeared but returned shortly and waited by the exit for the two agents to join him. Thanking the Sergeant, Franklin and Tyler walked with Paige across the tarmac to the waiting vehicle. Paige was tall with red hair, blue eyes, freckles and a very serious look.

Franklin leaned forward where he was seated behind Paige. "Airman, our destination is the physics building at Syracuse University".

"Oh, yes sir. I know exactly where it is. It's near the Carrier Dome. We'll reach it in about twenty minutes," as he exited the base and turned right onto Malloy Road. Airman Paige became more relaxed as they drove away from the airbase. Franklin asked him whether it was always so overcast. Paige thought for a moment, glancing at the clouds which extended to the horizon. "No sir, sometimes it rains too."

Reflecting on his comment and Franklin's rapidly darkening mood he continued, "It isn't as bad as a lot of people say. There are lots of golf courses and fishing is very popular too. Oneida Lake is near and the community hosts a Bass tournament annually where people come from everywhere to compete and anglers fish for salmon just north of here. The Fingerlakes Region and the Adirondack Mountains are very close and six Major League baseball clubs are five hours drive away. I hated here in the beginning, but I actually like it now."

"I once found a book written by Henri Nowen, who was a Trappist monk living in a monastery in Rochester; about an hour from here, titled the "The Genesee Diary," he continued. "The monks had a machine which ground up raisins for their cooking and occasionally a stone would get mixed in with the raisins and stop the machine. He felt that the stone was like the weather here. In some places people become so jaded by good weather that they fail to appreciate it. You really learn to appreciate sunny days more when the clouds, rain and snow are like those occasional stones".

Franklin thought about Paige's comments as Paige drove down the off ramp at the Syracuse University exit. "Airman Paige?"

"Yes sir?"

"If you were reassigned to San Diego would you be happy with that?"

"I think I could manage to pack in less than an hour," he answered good-humoredly. "I would however make one last stop at the Dinosaur Barbeque. They have the best pulled pork sandwiches on the planet."

By this time they had entered the campus and Paige stopped at one of the security stations. Paige looked up at the person in the station. "These men are from the Department of Defense. They have business here and I need to take them to the physics building and wait for them."

"You'll need a permit to park here," he replied in an uncooperative manner. "They're issued in the administrative building," and handed a map to Paige.

"Paige, pull forward would you?" said Franklin reaching for his wallet. Looking up at the guard Franklin presented his identification. The guard began to speak but Franklin wouldn't entertain it. "I'm Intelligence Specialist Franklin and this is Agent Tyler from the Department of Defense. We came here to conduct an interview. I'm not here to ask for your permission to park this vehicle." Franklin sat back in his seat, closed the window and tapped Paige on the shoulder. "Paige let's go. Park the car and wait for us to return."

"Yes sir," said Paige enthusiastically as a wide smile spread across his face.

When Franklin and Tyler exited the car they followed Airman Paige's directions, walking next to the vine covered walls of Hendricks Chapel and directly towards the "Quad". Once past the chapel, Paige said the physics building would be on their right. Franklin paused, looking at three buildings before them and quickly headed directly toward one in particular. When Agent Tyler asked how he knew which building was the correct one, Franklin continued forward and pointed to its second story. "It says physics building. We should begin there," he said unenthusiastically. Tyler caught up quickly as the two men walked across the brick covered plaza.

From his second story office, Robert watched with interest as two figures in suits walked directly toward the physics building, reached for his cell phone and selected a number from his contacts. "Hi Gina. Robert here. Hurry over would you? I need your help with that matter we were discussing."

Robert placed his phone back on the desk and returned to planning his trip to France. This trip had two purposes. Ron and his father needed the documents he had left behind and this would be an amazing opportunity for Robert to retrace the path his ancestor, Mathurin Dubé had taken before leaving France for the New World.

Mathurin was born in 1631 in the small farming village of La Chapelle-Themér in the Vendée department in Western France. Robert's plan would be to arrive in the port city of La Rochelle where his ancestor had sailed from, rent a car for the trip to La Chapelle-Themér and then travel to Paris to see Ron and deliver his package.

Studying a map of France on his computer screen, he considered a possible route to Paris by passing through Nantes, Le Mans and Versailles. He also learned that La Rochelle held the International Film Festival of La Rochelle from June 28th to July7th which aroused his interest. The quandary he faced was that the festival had begun a few weeks earlier than his actual departure time. He reasoned that he could conceivably go back in time to a few days prior to the beginning of the film festival. Following a visit to his ancestor's village and a leisurely drive to Paris, he could use one of Ron's key fobs as a transmitter, allowing him to go forward in time to Ron's location in Paris. With any luck Robert could see the film festival and celebrate Bastille Day with Ron.

The sounds of footsteps from the hallway were becoming louder and closer and he could sense that the anticipated interruption was imminent. He hastily closed the France website rather than provide the two people who were approaching his office any information regarding his plans and instructed the screen to open his files on quantum gravity and black holes research. Moments later there was a knock on his office door and the sound of someone entering his office. A familiar voice said, "Dr. Dubé we're here to talk to you regarding the theft of government property."

Robert turned slowly in his chair and stared directly at Franklin. "Well, Agent Franklin, what an unpleasant surprise. I'm sorry to disappoint you," Robert said, gesturing at the volumes of books on the shelves and fixtures in the office. "But if you're here to steal something today, all this is the property of the university; not that has been a problem for you before."

Agent Tyler stood just behind Franklin's right shoulder. Robert's last recollection of him was Mrs. Spencer's dog devouring his tie and then regaining consciousness on the floor of his Caltech office. Robert grinned at Tyler. "Nice tie, Agent Tyler."

Franklin stepped toward Robert and angrily gripped the armrests of his chair and leaned forward, his nose nearly contacting Robert's.

Robert's expression was calm and with a tone amounting to boredom looked back at Franklin. "Careful now Agent Franklin, you remember what happened the last time you boys got this close to me."

Franklin angrily pushed himself away from Robert's chair and stood as they suddenly became aware of the presence of a fourth person in the room.

"Gina, your sense of timing is remarkable," Robert said as he rose and walked past Franklin. "Gina Abramson, these are agents Franklin and Tyler from the Department of Defense

Gina walked to a chair near the window and moved it next to Robert's. "Gentlemen, please be seated," gesturing to the chairs facing Robert's desk. Gina was medium height, approximately 25 years old with a slender figure and thick black wavy hair and bright green eyes. She wore a dark blue suit and black glasses. Her demeanor was as businesslike as her clothing and she stared intently and directly at Franklin and Tyler.

"As Dr. Dubé has already mentioned my name is Gina Abramson. I am an attorney with the firm of Davis, Kaufman and Howe. We are the legal counsel for Syracuse University, representing the University's interests, assets and in this particular instance; its employees. If you all agree to it, we can begin a discussion in this office. Unless you are prepared to serve Dr. Dubé with an arrest warrant, I would suggest that you agree to either meet here, or in a conference room in our offices. I will remind you, that while you are visiting this campus, you are on private property.

Gina turned to Robert. "Dr. Dubé, have you been served with or asked to sign any documents?"

Robert merely shook his head no.

"Can we get on with this?" Franklin said, clearly irritated.

"You may ask anything you like," Gina said with authority turning to Robert before facing Tyler. "However, the doctor is not obligated to answer."

"Dr. Dubé, I believe you know exactly why we are here," Franklin hissed.

"Possibly," retorted Robert dropping his chin as he stared back at Franklin. "Are you here to steal my lunch money? You seem to have a propensity for taking things that don't belong to you. I have absolutely no idea what would bring you here and have less than no interest in why you are sitting in my office with my lawyer. My only real interest would be when you plan to depart."

"This concerns the theft of government property, as you know. We have evidence to support our suspicion that you removed government property from a Federal facility. I want you to tell me how you did it; unless you are willing to risk arrest." Franklin seemed very self-assured.

"I really can't answer your questions, Agent Franklin." Robert leaned back in his chair, looking up at quickly the ceiling tiles. "The only stolen property that I am aware of pertains to the personal property that you, as an agent of the federal government, stole from the Caltech physics laboratory. As for arresting me; I hope you have more to base that on than your false accusations. But please do it, because I'm sure that the news media would love this story: "Federal agents arrest research assistant on suspicion of stealing his time machine." That would be quite a story."

Franklin's patience was clearly reaching its limit. He moved forward in his chair; almost rising from it. "We're dealing in semantics now aren't we? Tell me now, yes or no, do you know the whereabouts of the machine you installed in the basement of the Court of Appeals building in Pasadena? I demand a straightforward answer to a straightforward question."

"Well now that depends, Agent Franklin," Robert said throwing another pencil at a ceiling tile.

Franklin looked at Robert waiting for his response.

"It really depends whether or not we're referring to what you stole from me", said Robert, smiling as he finally got a pencil to stick into a tile.

Tension was rising to a breaking point as the antagonists confronted each other. Franklin obviously had had enough.

Suddenly, he nearly lept from his seat and strode toward Robert. Gina seized the opportunity to move in between them. "Gentlemen, it would seem reasonable to presume that we have reached an impasse." She paused a moment, watching Robert and Franklin glare at each other from either side of her before continuing. "I propose that we meet in a neutral site to resolve your differences. The most logical locations would be a conference room either on campus or at our law office."

Franklin's seemed to regain his composure as he reached into his breast pocket and pulled out a silver business card holder. Handing his card to Gina he said, "Set this up as soon as possible and call me." Then he and Tyler walked out of the office.

Gina and Robert looked at the door and then each other. Gina was ecstatic and Robert seemed genuinely relieved. "You look very nice today," Robert observed as he stood looking from the window down to the pavement in front of the physics buildings entrance. Moments later, he saw Franklin and Tyler after they had exited the building and were walking toward Hendricks Chapel.

He turned and looked at Gina's beaming face. Returning her smile he said, "OK, you can start now."

"Oh my God, that was so much fun," squealed Gina as she hugged him. "They believed that I really was the legal counsel for the University."

"You certainly looked convincing enough," said Robert as Gina stepped back. "If law school doesn't work out, there's probably a future for you in acting. You were really brilliant. Where did the bit about the meeting at a neutral site come from?"

Gina shrugged her shoulders. "I may have seen it in a movie. I was just trying to defuse the situation. It looked like you two were on the verge of starting World War III."

"I just hope it doesn't return to haunt us somehow," Robert mused.

"Don't worry, nothing will come of this," assured Gina. "By the way you owe me for this one."

"Sure," Robert began, with obviously no idea of what to offer her. "Why don't we......

"And not just a couple of drinks on Marshall Street this time," Gina interjected with determination. "I think this is an occasion where you owe me dinner."

Robert thoughts were obviously nothing like Gina's, "Hmmm, OK, well we could......

Interrupting again she added, "And not that take out place on Westcott Street, a real restaurant this time."

"OK, let me think about this one. Shall I call you on your cell phone or leave a message at your law firm?" he said sarcastically.

Gina hugged him again and turned toward the door. "I leave you to figure that out Dr. Dubé. You're the PhD. not me."

Robert returned to his desk and continued to examine the map of France to plan his trip. He was studying the history of the Port of La Rochelle when his computer screen indicated an incoming call. "Communication from Chancellor O'Day's office." Perhaps the timing of the notification was designed to give no opportunity to ponder the message, because he had scarcely read the e-mail, when his phone rang.

The instant Robert answered his phone a voice said "Dr. Dubé, this is Mrs. Marshall in Chancellor O'Day's office. The Chancellor would like you in her office immediately. She asked me to stress the word importance of the meaning of "immediately" to you." Robert didn't question the reason for the call. He realized this was not a request.

The chancellor's office was located on the sixth floor of the Crouse-Hinds Building. Fortunately, it was a brief walk, but it also afforded him very little time to surmise what purpose would be served by meeting with the chancellor. However, the timing of the call suggested it probably had something to do with Gina's offer to arrange a meeting with Franklin at her non-existent law firm.

Robert was escorted to the doorway of the chancellor's office by Mrs. Marshall. Chancellor O'Day sat behind her desk talking to Franklin and Tyler on her left. Gina occupied a chair on her right and a vacant chair was directly in front of the chancellor's desk. "Well, this doesn't make me happy," thought Robert as he received the chancellor's stony stare. She gestured for him to be seated and her attention immediately turned to him.

"Dr. Dubé," she said; placing her hands together on her desk and looking at him intensely; "These gentlemen are federal agents from Washington. They say they are looking for stolen government property and they believe that you have knowledge concerning the whereabouts of this property. They want to search your apartment as well as buildings on campus without a warrant. What can you add to this discussion?"

Robert spoke as if the agents weren't present. "Chancellor, I don't know anything about stolen government property. I do however, have knowledge about property which the government stole from the Caltech physics laboratory and now they've managed to lose it. They of course are shifting the blame for their responsibility to me. It is simply not here."

The chancellor now faced the agents, "Well gentlemen, it would appear that Dr. Dubé isn't quite as confident as you that he is in possession of this property which you suspect he either has or is aware of. Regarding your request to search buildings on this campus, I will allow it this once without a search warrant. You must, however provide me with a list of the buildings you wish to search and I will provide you with someone to take you to those buildings. Regarding the search of a residence; I will not entertain even the suggestion that will allow you to enter the residence of anyone connected with this institution without a warrant. I will remind you again that this is a private institution and should you appear unannounced again, the University will not continue to be so cooperative and the issue will be directed to our legal counsel. I am telling you to contact me in advance if you return. Is that clear?"

Franklin looked calmly at the chancellor, "Yes Chancellor, crystal clear."

The chancellor continued, "While we're on the subject of legal counsel; Miss Abramson, if I am ever aware that you are engaged in an activity which could bring embarrassment to or legal action against this institution again, you will be finishing your law degree somewhere closer to home."

Franklin and Tyler both spun to their left and with stunned and angry looks scowled at Gina, who attempted to stifle a giggle as she returned their glares with a smile before directing her gaze to the floor.

The chancellor sat straight in her chair, placed her forearms on the desk and began to tap her Mont Blanc pen on the table until Gina looked at her. "Miss Abramson, return to your studies." Gina looked back as if not quite understanding what she heard. "That would be this moment, Miss Abramson", the chancellor sternly clarified.

Rising swiftly, Gina excused herself and withdrew through a large door which led to the chancellor's closet. Attempting to ignore the puzzled looks from everyone in the room, she walked confidently to the door which led to the outer office, opened it slowly and peered into the outer room, before closing it quietly behind her.

The chancellor resumed her conversation with the agents and Robert. She placed the pen on the desk and folded her hands. "Gentleman, I have no desire to revisit this issue. In the future we will keep our lines of communication open, yes?" as she nodded.

All were in agreement as the chancellor continued. "Excellent. Would you gentleman excuse us please? Our business is concluded for now and I wish to speak to Dr. Dubé in private. I trust there is nothing further to discuss?"

Both agents rose to their feet. "Apparently not. We will be in touch Chancellor. Thanks you for your time," said Franklin as he and Tyler exited the room quickly.

The door closed and the Chancellor directed her full attention to Robert as he felt the weight of the office walls closing in upon him.

"You know Robert; I've known you since you were in elementary school. I need to ask you something which requires an honest answer. Will you do that for me?"

"Yes, of course chancellor."

"This machine of yours; I would hope that it is not located on any property that is any way connected to Syracuse University."

A mischievous grin appeared across Robert's face. "No chancellor, I do not know of any government property which currently exists on any university property."

"That's good to know Robert," said the chancellor pointing toward the door. "I believe I've given all of you enough of a head start to avoid running into each other. Now go. Please say hello to your parents for me and keep yourself safe."

He rose and headed toward the door. "One more item to bear in mind," the Chancellor added. "If it is important enough to you to keep this property which the government claims you have, the location of which you aren't aware of; from these people, I will trust you to do what needs to be done."

He opened the door and turned to face the chancellor. "Yes," and just as she lowered her head to continue with her work, he added, "by the way, I only said it wasn't here." He smiled and slowly closed the door as the chancellor nodded.

For Robert this was a huge relief now that the issue with Franklin had at least been temporarily resolved. He felt that his machine was safe for now and was grateful that he had taken the steps to secure it on the Nation. Exiting the Crouse-Hinds Building, he began the return walk uphill to the physics building. Passing the Hall of Music he could hear the sounds of a piano being played through an open window.

Paige drove past the security gate while Franklin sat silently, looking in the direction of the chancellor's office windows on his left and at a person walking up the hill toward them. Robert and Franklin looked at each other for a moment as the car proceeded toward Waverly Ave. Robert appeared so preoccupied that Franklin wasn't sure if he recognized him. Tyler was studying a map of the university campus. "Sir, in which building should we begin our search?"

"Put it away," Franklin said in a relaxed tone. "He was right, you know. For us, there really is nothing here. From this point forward, I want him to think about nothing else than hiding it. Our best strategy now is to continue monitoring him. Continue to follow his credit card transactions, phone usage and talk to the local energy supplier so we can duplicate the same type of monitoring that was utilized in Pasadena. If he operates the machine here, perhaps we can use his electricity usage to locate the machine." Franklin leaned forward in and looked into the rear view mirror. "Paige, where are we headed now?"

Paige replied without looking back. "We're about to get on Route 81 North to return to the 174th sir."

"Isn't that Dinosaur Barbeque in the vicinity?" asked Franklin.

"It is about five minutes from here, sir."

"I'm in the mood for one of those pulled pork sandwiches and red beans and rice. How about you Tyler?" he asked speaking over his shoulder while Tyler attempted to convince himself that he wasn't imaging this conversation. "Paige, take us to the Dinosaur and get in touch with that captain we flew up with from Andrews. We will need a return flight with him. Then join us inside." Tyler thought that this was the most relaxed he had ever seen Franklin.

Paige replied with a very enthusiastic, "Yes sir".

Robert had noticed a car approaching from the direction of Hendricks Chapel. It could have been Franklin but he wasn't overly concerned with that now. He needed to finalize his itinerary for France. He suddenly became acutely aware of someone approaching him from his right side, when he felt an arm being slipped through his.

"Dr. Dubé, I do believe you still owe me dinner and this seems like the perfect time. I have no food at my place, no money and I'm certainly dressed for it."

Robert looked at Gina who confidently smiled back. This isn't exactly what he had been concentrating on, but she did have a point. Suddenly his eyes widened and his expression changed, "Do you like Thai food?"

"I do," replied a surprised stunned Gina. "But where.....?"

"There's a place on Erie Boulevard where my parents have taken me several times and they used to go there when they were dating. How would you like that? And after dinner I know of a place for drinks where we can sit and watch the sunset."

A few hours later, Agents Franklin and Tyler along with Airman Paige; had treated themselves to dinner at the Dinosaur Barbeque and the agents had boarded a return flight to Andrews AFB.

Robert and Gina sat facing west as the evening sky turned crimson. "Well Dr. Dubé, you certainly are full of surprises. A nice dinner followed by drinks with a view of the sunset. I didn't even know this place existed."

"It certainly helps to know people," he said handing Gina a glass of his favorite IPA. "It also helps to live on the second floor. Personally, I feel that an IPA tastes even better with your feet placed on the railing."

LA ROCHELLE

He savored each mouthful of his breakfast of scrambled eggs, bacon and Tuscan garlic bread because while he knew there would be eggs wherever he went, but the status of bacon would be less certain. It wasn't possible to predict how long it would be before he would return but he certainly hoped it would not take too long. After cleaning and storing the dishes, he resumed the task of rechecking everything, including the coordinates for La Rochelle and the date he wished to arrive. The PIN pad and fingerprint devise had both been installed next to the machine. Hopefully locating them next to the machine first rather than moving them as an afterthought would have a positive effect on its accuracy.

Robert entered his PIN and placed the index finger of his right hand to be scanned. He could see the first bank of UPS's coming to life, the array energized and Robert vanished.

"Nothing in this world can match the fresh smell which an ocean breeze brings," he thought. "No matter how tired a person may be, it is invigorating, intoxicating and something one can almost taste."

"To imagine that I'm looking out to sea from the same harbor that my ancestor Mathurin departed nearly 400 years ago is difficult to grasp," he reflected as he stood in the port of La Rochelle. Local residents were dressed in clothes from an ancient era and he suspected this had some connection to the film festival or perhaps there was another event being celebrated. Occasionally, someone passed by dressed like nobility, wearing breeches, a waistcoat and very colorful clothing, but the majority of the people he saw dressed like what he presumed peasants must have worn centuries ago: loose fitting, drab colored, heavy pieces of clothing.

He wanted to see more of the port before renting a car and driving to La Chapelle-Thémer. Walking closer to the harbor and looking away from the city, toward the open sea, he noticed that the city must have organized a flotilla of wooden boats and ships as the harbor was filled with them. "Shouldn't there be some pleasure craft anchored somewhere too?" he wondered. "Also that is Ile de Ré out there beyond the harbor. It's supposed to be connected to La Rochelle by a bridge, but I don't see one."

For a town in the middle of a film festival he expected people to be in a festive mood but most of them seemed very grim. Equally unsettling was the way people appeared to be staring him, especially the children. In fact, he was attracting so much attention that it was alarming. As he walked, they walked behind him. When he stopped, they stopped. When he turned to look at them, they scattered; only to reform their ranks when he resumed his progress along the street. He hoped to pass a shop window to examine his reflection and see if there was something wrong with the way he was dressed, but windows happened to be absent from these buildings near the port which were mostly one story affairs with walls fashioned from rock or stucco and tiled roofs. The cobblestone streets felt narrower as he continued to attract more attention. Now he simply wanted to rent a car and leave this place and these children behind.

"Monsieur? Pardon me, do you need help?" someone asked with interest. "You should get inside, now." A deep voice he heard behind him placed a heavy emphasis on the word "now".

Robert turned to see a man with a pleasant but urgent look on his face. He had deep set blue eyes, a little shorter than him and was plump and stocky. He was dressed very similarly to the other people in the street and wore and floppy broad brimmed hat.

"Come; join me for a glass of wine. It would be my privilege and honor to treat you as my guest and be away from these prying eyes." He led Robert by the arm and shouted at the army of children to go home. His entire manner seemed to be a mixture of concern and alarm. Robert was a bit suspicious of this man's intentions, but welcomed the prospect of getting away from the street and this fellow seemed the best choice at the moment.

The man held open a rough looking door and invited Robert to step inside. Its appearance was more like a tavern than a restaurant. Dark, with few windows and filled with men sitting at round wooden tables talking and laughing, it wasn't the most inviting place he had ever seen, but it was much more comfortable than walking around outside. A few of the men looked at them, glanced at Robert and nodded to the man with him, then quickly returned to their own conversations. After directing Robert to a corner table, he ordered wine for both of them and returned his attention to Robert.

"Forgive me for not introducing myself earlier my friend, but it seemed necessary to bring you away from the street first. My name is Bernard Badeau. Excuse me for saying this, my friend, but everything about you looks so very unusual."

"Yes, the reaction that some people have to my appearance does surprise me a bit," Robert agreed. "I am in La Rochelle to attend the film festival and some people act as if they've never seen a pair of sneakers or a backpack before. Until you brought me in here, I was convinced that now was the time to begin looking for a car rental agency so I can drive myself to a village located about 60 kilometers from here."

Bernard looked intently as if he was trying to absorb everything he had heard. Their wine arrived and Bernard continued. "Excuse me monsieur, but what exactly is a "film festival", or film for that matter? Also, I don't entirely understand your words, your unusual shoes and the sack you carry is unlike any I've ever seen. May I ask why you wish to be driven anywhere? We drive our cattle but people ride on a horse or in a carriage. May I also ask your name, my friend? Speaking with a new acquaintance is so much more pleasurable when we both know each other, don't you think?"

Robert didn't respond immediately. He just sighed as he tipped his glass from side to side and examined the way the wine ran down the inside of it. He emptied his glass and asked the waiter for another. Feeling that this had just become a colossal nightmare, visions of the Great Chicago Fire flashed through his mind. His new friend, Bernard Badeau was waiting for an answer and he responded by answering Bernard's query with one of his own. "Bernard," as his second glass arrived, "my friend, will you please tell me what year this is?"

Bernard's startled look was not unexpected. Dropping his chin, he looked at Robert with raised eyebrows and spoke quietly. "Yes my friend, the year is 1789." Bernard's quizzical stare centered on Robert as he searched his mind for a plausible response and contemplated a third glass of wine.

This was supposed to have been a relaxing visit to France but had now taken a turn of nightmarish proportions. Pausing for a moment to maintain his composure after learning he had arrived months before the French Revolution, he continued.

"Bernard, my name is Mathurin Dubé. I am from Riviere Ouelle, Quebec, Canada; although it was known as New France when my great grandfather arrived in 1660. I am here to visit La Chapelle-Themér, our ancestral home. After I visit the village, I intend to explore the Palace of Versailles and then I have business to conduct in Paris. When I have concluded my business, I will return home."

Bernard appeared little relieved but satisfied with Robert's explanation. Still, he remained rather concerned. "My friend, what you say is very interesting indeed. Your French is excellent, but your accent betrays you. This is not a good time to be an Englishman in France. You could be accused of being a spy for the British."

"I am no British spy," Robert declared softly, leaning forward, desiring that this conversation not be overheard by the other patrons. "My parents were born French subjects and remained so in their hearts. They were not happy when they discovered that we were lost to the British after the Seven Years War. The British offered passage to anyone who wished to return to France, but I never knew anyone who accepted their proposal."

"Of course, of course, my friend," Bernard said as he began to absorb what he was hearing. "You will draw far more attention from your appearance than your accent. That we can change easily. You will require new clothes and someone who can take you where you wish to go. If you would like to hire me as your guide, I can arrange all that."

In Robert's mind, this was an improvement, as well as his only option. Plus, a ride by carriage to see the village his ancestor came from, sounded like a relaxing journey. He had Ron's key fob and one of his own with him. He could visit the village and then use the key fob as the transmitter to send himself to Paris in Ron's time.

"My friend," Bernard said in a businesslike voice, "if that means you are hiring me as your guide that will require some money. Your clothes, a carriage worthy of you and my pay will make livres necessary. Plus," he added quickly, "someone needs to pay for this wine."

Robert raised his chin and nodded as he surveyed the dark ceiling and pondered this latest conundrum. While he was fairly certain that credit cards weren't very popular in 18th century France, he had not arrived entirely unprepared.

After he spoke to Gina regarding his plans to visit his ancestor's home, she convinced an acquaintance in the audio-visual department to scan French currency from different periods. Fortunately, she convinced her friend to produce an abundance of French livres after his previous experiences. If past experience had taught him anything, it was to be prepared for anything.

Bernard's eyes widened in amazement when Robert thrust his hand inside his backpack withdrew a handful of livres and placed them firmly into Bernard's waiting hand. "Will this do?" he asked.

Bernard nodded, dumbfounded and told Robert to wait, he would return shortly. Robert ordered a third glass of wine and began to question his decision to attempt to travel backward in time, even by a period of weeks given the problems they had already experienced. He recognized two relevant points; the scientist in him should not have engaged in something where they had repeatedly experienced a problem without having at least a probable chance of success. Secondly, rebuking himself now would serve no real purpose. He had arrived through his use of technology. Now he hoped that his lack of foresight which had caused him to arrive in the 18th century wouldn't stop him from returning to the 21st century. He still had his key fob and moving forward in time hadn't been a problem. For the present, his best strategy would be having wine with his new guide.

Finished chastising himself for his present position, he began to focus on a strategy to solve this new problem as Bernard returned with a satisfied look and good news.

"My friend, I have found for us, I mean for you, an excellent poste chaise. It will seat two persons and is very comfortable. You will have the look of one who is on the "Grand Tour". When Robert appeared a bit puzzled, Bernard attempted to explain. "My friend, the Grand Tour is exactly what the name implies. Young men from wealthy families tour the continent for months or even years to extend their horizons. It is a rite of passage for such young men. They are usually from nobility and they dress the part. However, my friend, this is not a favorable time to be connected with the English and in some eyes; nobility in general. The clothes I have selected for you are suitable for one who is of means, but not one who might look as if they have a sense of entitlement. It may be unwise to flaunt that position."

It seemed ironic to Robert that he understood the implications of Bernard's statement better than most. After centuries of worsening living conditions, the peasant's volatility was like a simmering pot. When their emotions boiled over, the nobility would be scalded first.

Bernard held the door as Robert stepped over the threshold and into the street. The post chaise was positioned directly before him and as he viewed it he felt his anxiety melt away. Not having any idea what to expect, he was immediately pleased with what he saw. It wasn't anything like the lumbering wagons he remembered from movies. The post chaise was smaller, sleeker and more nimble appearing. The front wheels were about half as large as the rear wheels and it was hitched to a pair of horses. A man rode postilion style on the left horse. At the rear of the carriage was a ledge where a coachman would stand and what looked like a box for luggage.

What appealed to him most were its windows. There were doors with a window on either side. It was designed for two passengers to sit abreast, facing forward through two large windows.

Bernard gestured to the man seated on the left horse. "This is my cousin Étienne. He will drive the horses as far as La Chapelle-Thémer. After that he will wait for a team that needs to be driven back to La Rochelle."

Étienne had a broad grin like Bernard's. He was much thinner, which is to say average width and had long brown hair over his shoulders. Wearing a riding coat with large silver buttons, he removed his hat, bowed slightly to Robert and replaced his hat. Bernard walked to the door of the poste chaise, opened it for Robert and held it until he climbed in.

Bernard closed the door, ran to the other side and with a little effort pulled his large frame in and sat next to Robert. Étienne seemed to acknowledge that as the signal to begin their journey and he turned the horses away from the ocean and headed inland.

Reaching under the seat, Bernard produced a baguette, some cheese and apples which he quickly sliced with a knife that seemed to appear from nowhere. He placed all this on a piece of cloth laid out on the cushion between them. "This is grand, is it not Mathurin? Samuel Johnson once said, "If I had no duties, and no reference to futurity, I would spend my life in driving briskly in a post chaise with a pretty woman." I have lived here nearly my entire life and I feel La Rochelle is the most beautiful city, besides being an important port. It could have been irreplaceable port city, if a river like the Seine, connected it to Paris."

"La Rochelle was once the home of the Knights Templar, my friend. According to legend, they left in the 12th century with their treasure laden ships and buried it in Nova Scotia. Perhaps you should search for it when you return to Canada, yes? Also, La Rochelle was a center of religious freedom for Protestants. Unfortunately my friend, that didn't last forever and religious freedom ended in the 1600's.The Catholic government wanted us to be Catholic again and thousands fled the country. Ours was also an important port for the slave trade from Africa, sugar from the West Indies and fur from the New World. Ever since France lost Canada to the British during the Seven Years War, our city has become far less important. It is a great pity, don't you think?"

It was becoming increasingly clear that Bernard was an incessant talker. He really hadn't put an abundance of effort into absorbing Bernard's dissertation about La Rochelle. Mostly, he observed the changes in scenery from the comfort of his poste chaise. He was also preoccupied contemplating what his next action would be following his arrival in La Chapelle-Thémer. Robert's reply was "That's very interesting, my friend," and Bernard would have to be satisfied with that.

As they progressed through the city it seemed to him that none of the streets near the port met at right angles. They all seemed to meander away from the port, eventually terminating on their own or joining another street, the way streams flow independently before joining to become a river. The streets were narrow cobblestoned affairs, lined on either side with two story buildings. What appeared to be elongated buildings which spanned the length of the main thoroughfare were actually a series of narrow independent structures, which shared common interior walls. A series of archways spanned the width of each section, creating a barrier between the street and the buildings and a walkway for pedestrians.

As the street further distanced itself from the port, archways appeared less frequently and when one was present, it usually led to a courtyard. The buildings that lined the street now seemed to be individual homes whose doors opened directly onto the streets with shuttered windows above.

Further on; the smell of the ocean air and cloudy skies gave way to fresh air and a cloudless blue sky. The narrow streets were replaced with wide boulevards lined with a variety of trees; individual trees at first, but these soon turned into heavily wooded areas on both sides of the road where small white houses with their red tiled roofs and several varieties of shrubs and hedges that filled the landscape.

Open farmland followed and he began to feel more comfortable in his cushioned seat and felt that he was now making progress having definitely made the right decision to hire this fellow as his guide. Bernard continued his dialogue about the region, his family and whatever seemed to creep into his mind. His ceaseless talking became part of the sights and smells and tapestry of the Vendée.

A sign eventually appeared on Robert's right, nearly hidden by a bush; "La Chapelle-Thémer". More structures rose from the fields of barley and wheat. He saw small white houses with terra cotta roofs, low shrubs and an occasional horse grazing in the meadows. The windows of the houses on the street leading into the village were all shuttered and faced a cemetery with its wall of stone and hedges. Upon their arrival in the village, Étienne unhitched the team and left them with a boy to be feed and watered. Bernard sliced more cheese and bread for Robert and poured him a glass of wine. "I will return quickly, my friend. I need to talk with someone and then I will take you to the village church." Robert enjoyed this meal and brief respite from Bernard's never-ending discourse as he looked at the ancient buildings, which all looked as though they were constructed from whatever materials the earth could be coaxed to part with.

Bernard returned soon and together they walked the short distance to the village's church.

The gravel in the narrow road crunched beneath Robert's feet as he approached the church which was small and ancient like the town. The side of the church facing the street had one small window. What he found interesting was the difference in construction between the tower and the chapel. The main body of the church had a red tile roof and exterior walls that resembled stucco or cement. The tower appeared as if it had been built of layer upon layer of stone and it rose nearly 20 feet higher than the church's roof. The side of the tower had a series of narrow slits for windows and the manner in which they were positioned suggested the possible outline of an interior staircase. A stone wall stood facing the street, spanning the gravel covered court yard was overseen by a solitary shrub.

"Mathurin my friend, Brother André is the village priest and he can assist you in contacting your relations in the village. I will leave you here, as I have already told him to expect you." Bernard turned and walked back in the direction of the stables.

He passed under an arch and surveyed the courtyard behind the church. Here was more gravel covered ground leading to plowed fields but no sign of clergy. Retreating to his right, he approached the church doors. They too, were ancient and weathered like everything else. His mind formed an image of this

Brother André, whom he soon expected to meet. He would be old, bent, thin and slow; someone who had been practicing the same duties for decades. He imagined that he would need to repeat his words several times to be understood. Robert sighed, grasped the iron handle on the heavy wooden door and pulled. He expected a loud creaking noise from a door which looked as though it didn't get much use. Instead it opened with ease, considering its considerable size and weight. Its interior was surprisingly bright considering the amount of light the two small windows would allow.

Stepping into the entrance he was amazed at the number of brightly burning candles. Someone had invested a considerable amount of time arranging the candles which provided so much light and were so pleasing to the eye.

"Still no sign of the wispy Brother André," thought Robert looking toward the simple altar.

Suddenly a loud voice boomed from the corner of the church. "Monsieur Dubé, I presume." This was hardly the voice Robert had expected. Hurrying from the location of the font, a rather large, young man emerged. His warm cherubic face bore a warm smile which was nearly as bright as the candles he tended.

He came straight to Robert and immediately embraced him. While he acted nothing like Robert's expectations, he was dressed very much like the image he had imagined. He wore a loose, brown tunic with a belt around the waist. Over the tunic was a scapula, a large rectangular cloth garment with an opening for the head and a hood which draped over his back.

"Ah, Monsieur Dubé it is such a pleasure to meet you. Bernard told me that you had an interest in meeting your relatives. There are actually quite a few Dubés in our village still and they live nearby. One of their children has already been sent home with a message that you had arrived and returned saying that his parents would be honored if you would have dinner at their home. Come my friend, I will take you there."

Brother André began walking with Robert toward the church's doorway. As they walked, Brother André spoke non-stop about the church, the village and shared what he knew about the Dubé family. "Yes my friend, the church does look different today because the original structure had been lost in a fire; only the tower had been saved. The village became smaller as more people left, just as your ancestor Mathurin did over one hundred years ago; to look for more land to farm or in search of a vocation other than farming."

The constant staccato manner of his speech was somehow familiar. After he had referred to Robert using the phrase "my friend" several times Robert cautiously asked, "Brother André, I'm curious. Just how do you know Bernard?"

The large priest paused and looked at him, wondering why he was being asked this obvious question when he felt that Robert must already know the answer, then began to laugh heartily, "Why my friend, Bernard is my brother."

"Well that explains a lot", he thought.

"Does that mean that you are Bernard's brother Brother André?"

"To my brother Bernard, yes my friend. Now then, allow me to accompany you to your relation's home before I leave you, as I plan to dine with Bernard and our cousin Étienne. I always enjoy seeing my brother but our conversations are a bit limited as I spend most of our time together simply listening to him. He can't seem to stop talking and it can be a little frustrating, as I don't have an opportunity to join in the conversation. Do you understand what I mean, my friend?"

"You have no idea, Brother André," Robert said flatly.

By now they had walked across the courtyard and Brother André motioned to an open door of a house about twenty feet distant.

"That is the home of your relatives. Before you enter I feel there is something you must know. You will undoubtedly get the sense that there is tension in their feelings toward you. They are afraid that you are here to claim your inheritance."

It was evident from Robert's blank expression that he didn't not understand the priests meaning at all.

Brother André continued, "When Mathurin quit France for the New World, he left behind his inheritance. As the first born son, he would have a birth right to inherit the family farm and all its property. As his closest living relative, you have a right to claim it as your own. They are concerned that after all this time; you have returned from Canada to evict them from what they see as their home. That is why they will seem apprehensive."

"In all honesty Brother André, La Chapelle-Thémer looks like a good place to be from," responded Robert seriously. "My intent was to visit this village, conclude my business in Paris and return home. I have no interest in claiming anything."

Robert's statement appeared to have relieved Brother André and surprisingly said nothing as he turned and continued to accompany him toward the house.

The Dubé home was somehow melded to a long rectangular one story structure with six small windows and one door where even an average sized person would have to bend over to enter. Together they looked as if they were constructed simultaneously by people whose intent was to construct two buildings with little nothing in common. His ancestor's home was very unlike other homes in the village because it stood two stories tall rather than one; but what made it really stand out was its roof. Rather than two gradually sloping sides, it consisted of six steep sides of different dimensions and angles, making it by far the tallest home in the village and only slightly shorter than the church's tower. Their windows were large, opening inward and had huge bright white shutters. Three stone steps led to the front door, where someone was already waiting to greet Robert.

The door opened and a man whose height and frame looked strikingly similar to Robert's, stepped across the threshold barely touching the stone steps and approached him nearly at a run. Brown hair, blue eyes and a broad grin; he reminded Robert of photographs he had seen of his grandfather. Now he really needed to use caution in what he said and remember that his name was, for now; Mathurin.

"Mon cousin, greetings to you. Welcome to our village and our home. How exciting it is to meet you. I am Simon, your cousin." Simon embraced him and kissed him on both cheeks. Brother André placed a large arm around each man and wished them well. "I will see you tomorrow. Enjoy yourselves tonight, my friends. I'm off to visit with my brother and cousin."

Simon and Robert paused and smiled at each other, searching for words and wondering what exactly they should do next. Simon extended his arm in the direction of the door. "Come and meet my family. My wife has prepared a special dinner for you." Simone's wife Charlotte stood just inside the doorway. She wore a simple cream colored cotton dress which closely matched her light brown hair. She had green eyes and a warm engaging smile. She immediately walked to Robert, held both his hands and leaned forward, kissing him on both cheeks.

"We are so happy to see you Mathurin. This is the most pleasant of surprises. Welcome to our", at this she paused and seemed to end the sentence with an awkward sounding, "our home."

Robert grasped the sense of what he had been told by Brother André. They were definitely tense about the issue of his inheritance. He held Charlotte's hand and returned her smile, "Thank you for inviting me into your home." The emphasis he expressed on the word "your" had a calming effect on Charlotte that was revealed in the way she looked back at him.

Their living room felt exceptionally comfortable. Its center was dominated by a large sofa with bright blue fabric and walnut end tables. Two wing chairs with matching fabric faced the sofa. The furniture was arranged upon a large rug, woven with designs of gold and blue. A fireplace had been built into the interior wall and on its mantle were two gold gilded candle holders with a large mirror hanging alone above it. The large window on the left opened onto the street.

Across the room a group of very anxious looking children stood silently. "Children, here is someone I want you to meet. This is your uncle Mathurin. His grandfather Mathurin and your great grandfather Jacques were brothers." This was followed by a chorus, "Bonjour, mon oncle Mathurin." "This is Marie, our eldest daughter", said Charlotte proudly. "And these are Joseph, Guillaume, Pierre, Louis and our youngest, Genevieve."

Robert looked at the well dressed, fair haired children. The boys all had blue eyes; the girl's eyes were green like their mothers. They all bore varying expressions ranging from mild excitement to moderate interest; except for that of Genevieve. Hers looked like one of complete captivation.

After Simon dismissed the children, he invited Robert to join him on the sofa, while Genevieve stood silently next to one of the end tables. Charlotte left the room for a brief period of time and returned with red wine and some cheese and sat on the chairs facing Robert. While the other children left the room as soon as they were dismissed, Genevieve remained behind and sat on the sofa next to Robert; trying her utmost to be invisible, hoping she would be allowed to stay.

Simon and Charlotte both apologized for their daughter's behavior and commanded her to leave her uncle and join the other children. "We don't often have visitors and certainly not a relative from such a distance as Canada. Still, that doesn't excuse our daughter's behavior," said Charlotte frowning at Genevieve. Genevieve looked up beseechingly at Robert, who was already looking down at her, "She's no bother at all, really. In fact I enjoy her company very much."

Genevieve took this opportunity to move closer to Robert, who saw that her appearance was unlike her siblings. Her hair was more blonde than brown, her eyes more hazel than green like her sisters, and a nose that was a bit rounder. Perhaps her most striking feature was her abundance of freckles. When she smiled which was constantly, they enhanced her already broad mouth.

Smiling back at her Robert said, "She makes me feel like a rock star." As the words escaped his lips he thought, "I really should not have said that." Interpreting the puzzled expressions on the faces of Simon and Charlotte's faces he said, "I only meant that she makes me feel important," hoping that they would be satisfied with that explanation and continued quickly, "I want to tell you why I'm here. Brother André alluded to something regarding an inheritance. This is the first I had heard anything about that. I have absolutely no interest in the land or the house or any property. As far as I'm concerned, all of this is yours as it really has been for over one hundred years. I have my own life in Québec, which I'll return to when my business in Paris has concluded. My only interest in La Chapelle-Thémer was to visit you, my family. If you need me to sign anything to prove that I quit any claim to your land, I'll be happy to do that. In any event I'll be off to Paris tomorrow. I could use another glass of wine, however."

Simon and Charlotte's relief at the news regarding their home and land was tempered by their sadness of losing Robert's company so quickly. While Charlotte filled their wine glasses, Simon stepped forward to take Robert's hand. "To begin with, thank you for putting our minds at ease. You of course, are welcome to stay as long as you wish, but if you must go; then God's speed. Our meal shall be ready soon, our cook is excellent and the meal will be a humble but tasty one.

While we wait, allow me to tell you something of our family. Our grandfather had other brothers: Simon, René, Jean and Jacques and some of their families live here still. Others left to find work as laborers. We decided to stay with the land. What family still resides here will come to visit soon."

As Simon spoke, Genevieve inched ever closer to Robert. During pauses in their conversation, she would ask him questions about his home and told him that she liked to draw. Her parents seemed very proud of her interest in art and told her that it would be permissible to share some her drawings with her uncle.

Genevieve lept from the sofa and disappeared through a doorway behind him. She returned nearly out of breath holding several drawings in her delicate arms. This time she sat immediately next to Robert, placed the drawings in his lap and described each one in detail. Except for the final drawing, all depicted rural life. Her work was alive with fields, trees and livestock as one might expect her subjects to be. What was unexpected however was her painstaking attention to detail. Fences had railings which weren't perfectly straight, horse's manes were uneven and their nostrils flared when exhaling in the cold winter air. This level of expertise would have been expected in an adult, but it was extraordinary for a child of four. When Robert finished looking at the second to last drawing, Genevieve quickly placed on his lap a drawing of a seascape. Again, it was not childlike in the least. Waves crashed upon the rocks at the foot of tall cliffs as waves beyond the surf awaited their turn to race to the sand. The rocks formed jagged borders between the beach and the breakers.

He was completely absorbed by Genevieve's drawing and the way she explained all of its aspects in great detail. He presumed that this was the result of an excursion to the ocean, La Rochelle perhaps. "That is the astonishing part," Charlotte explained. "Our daughter has never left our village. This is all from her imagination. Brother André described a visit he made to his brother Bernard near La Rochelle and what you see is the result."

"She possesses extraordinary talent," said Robert looking from the drawings, to her parents and back to her work. "Where did she ever learn to draw like this?"

"No one taught her," said Simon proudly. "She just presented a drawing to us one day. We try to obtain supplies for her but they are incredibly expensive especially for a family that makes its living by farming and La Rochelle is so far. What makes it even more amazing, is what she can do with the scant materials available here. Sometimes she makes drawings on wood or slate using charcoal from our fireplace."

At that moment, dinner was announced by their cook. Charlotte told Genevieve to inform the rest of the children to wash their hands and come to the dining room. He followed Simon through a wide doorway into the dining room. Another window to his left overlooked the street. An old man supported by two canes, moved slowly past the house in the direction of the church. Two more windows on the adjacent wall, offered a view of the yard and a line of trees about twenty feet away. The living room was square in contrast to the dining room's long rectangular shape. Their wooden floor was simple but polished and a long, sturdy wooden table dominated its center. The children began to arrive and quietly seated themselves. Charlotte and their cook carried the dishes through the kitchen door at the far end of the room.

Simon sat at the head of the table with Robert on his right. When all the dishes had been placed on the table, Charlotte took her place across from Robert. Marie, Louis and Guillaume sat to Charlotte's left. After a minor struggle, Genevieve managed to take a seat next to her uncle and Pierre and Joseph sat on her right. Simon led the prayers to give thanks for their bounty and Robert's presence and the plates made their way to Charlotte. Robert was served first which he did not fail to appreciate.

The bread was warm and soft with a buttery crust and the rising steam carried with it a garlic aroma. This was followed by leek soup in a creamy sauce. Genevieve said that her favorite was ratatouille, a dish made with peppers, onions and tomatoes. Understanding that was more of a suggestion than casual information, Robert gave her an ample serving.

The next offering caused Robert to inhale so deeply and with such a startled look that Simon and Charlotte asked if something was bothering him. "No, no this is fantastic. I love bacon. But how did you know?" Turning to Genevieve he said, "This is my favorite dish."

Without a word Genevieve carefully picked up the plate of bacon and stood on her chair to serve him. He thought that this was such a nice gesture and she was obviously repaying his kindness for serving her ratatouille. She carefully placed one piece on Robert's plate, four on her own and passed the plate to Pierre.

Looking at him with an impish smile she whispered, "It's my favorite too, mon oncle."

Robert's stunned look seemed to resonate with the rest of the family. Upon noticing Genevieve's energetic smile, her siblings began to laugh out loud. Her parents appeared to expect nothing less from their precocious daughter, but Charlotte soon retrieved the plate before Joseph removed its contents and made certain Robert received a share equal to Genevieve's. Simon grinned.

"We really have no knowledge of what happened to your grandfather Mathurin, after he quit France," said Simon. "When he left, all news regarding New France by any means was extremely limited. It was even worse after we lost control of it to the British. I was told that one or two letters were received, but little else to tell us what happened after he arrived in New France."

Robert was enjoying his last piece of some of the best bacon he had ever tasted. He swallowed and took a sip of the brilliant red wine they provided. Trying to recall everything he had heard about Mathurin he began: "As you know he was born here in 1631 and left for New France about 1660. He began farming on the Ile d'Orleans, north of where Québec City is today. There were not many settlers there and most were men. Very few women were willing to pay their own passage to relocate where the conditions were so harsh."

As he spoke, other family members filtered into the dining room who were also intent on introducing themselves, but were now silent as they listened to their distant relative's story.

"The Intendant of New France, Jean Talon, appealed to King Louis XIV to recruit women to relocate to New France to find husbands. They were called "The King's Daughter's" and between 1663 and 1673 approximately 800 young women were recruited."

Robert felt that dinner was officially over. His relatives were listening to him so intently that everyone was silent. In addition, while he was speaking, Genevieve had eaten his bacon. "This must be a family trait," he thought.

"The King's Daughter's came from various parts of the country and different backgrounds," he continued. "However, they all were held to scrupulous standards with special attention to their high moral character. About half came from Paris and 120 or so from Normandie, which is where Marie Catherine Campion; 16 years old, was from. Mathurin and Marie were married on September 3, 1670. They had eight children, the first six survived. Their names were; Mathurin, Marie-Madeline, Louis, Pierre, Charles, Laurent, Marie-Anne and Jean-Bernard. Mathurin and Marie were married for 25 years. He died at the age of 64 and he was buried at Rivere Ouelle on December 30, 1693. Marie died on January 28, 1697; at the age of 43.

Robert paused and exhaled, "I can't believe I remembered all that," he said leaning back in his chair as if exhausted. A few people chuckled. The room was full now and some of the children asked if their Oncle Mathurin from the Province of Québec could tell them more.

He thought for a moment longer and was about to admit that he could not, when he remembered something long forgotten. Leaping to his feet, he looked at the children who by now numbered about thirty. "Who would like to hear about Mathurin Dubé, a hero at the Battle of Rivere-Ouelle? I warn you; you will need to use your imagination." Thirty hands immediately were thrust up in the air.

"Very good," he said smiling. "Now let us all go outside," and he placed Genevieve on his shoulders and walked from the dining room, across the living room and through the front door.

There was a large field behind Simon and Charlotte's home, with woods forming one boundary and the stone wall which joined the church and faced the woods as the other. Robert told the children that they were all going to play the part of soldiers in the great battle.

"In 1690," he began as the children formed a semi -circle before him, "the people living in Riviere-Oeulle were very alarmed to learn that a British fleet commanded by Admiral William Phipps, had left the port of Boston and was advancing in their direction."

The children became more excited as Robert's description powered their imaginations. Pointing in the direction of the tree line he said, "From ships on the river, row boats filled with British soldiers headed directly toward our French settlers. They were told that the British were there to occupy our island. Should we let them?"

As Robert raised his arms, the children and some parents shouted "No!"

"Quickly, find something you can use like a rifle," as he picked up a long straight stick, held it against his shoulder and aimed it like a rifle. The children quickly found a stack of stakes used for planting in the garden and soon returned with their imaginary weapons.

Looking at his army, he instructed them to form a line and count by twos. When the children had finished, he separated them into two groups. "Good, now we need a British general", he said looking at them as a hand shot up in the evening air. "Pierre you are a British general who will lead your troops to assault the French settlers. "Your boats reach the shoreline here," as Robert drew a line across the grass. "Then you walk across the beach toward the village," pointing in the direction of the wall.

"You think that it will be very easy to take the village, but suddenly the settlers yell "fire" and shoot from their hiding places and you retreat to your boats. Are you ready?" Robert asked in a loud enthusiastic voice, expecting the children to join in his enthusiasm.

"But oncle Mathurin", said a voice from one of the older children. Robert saw it was Louis who had spoken. "I don't want to be British," he said frowning.

"Everyone will take turns being the heroes," Charlotte said from near the flower beds where the adults stood.

Now that the British question had been settled, Robert continued to direct his new recruits.

The "British soldiers" ran to the shoreline drawn by Robert, while he and his "settlers" hid behind the wall to lie in wait to ambush the "enemy". The children advanced across the imaginary beach, visualizing the blades of grass becoming the beach leading to Riviere-Ouelle. When their approach neared the wall, Genevieve and the rest of her band drew a breath and took aim with their "weapons". Robert yelled "fire", which was followed by an ear piercing scream from their hide behind the wall, resulting in more screams from their cousins on the lawn. Some of the children turned and fled back to their "boats" while some played the role of those unfortunate enough to be wounded. They saw flashes from the settler's weapons and the clouds of smoke they produced. With the results of the battle decided, the children gathered around Robert in the middle of the yard. Holding his stake high in the air, he finished his tale.

"The British were routed by the resolve and courage displayed by the settlers. Listed among the names of the snipers was Mathurin Dubé, originally from La Chapelle-Thémer and two of his sons; Mathurin and Louis."

The children took turns playing the roles of British soldiers and French settlers, re-enacting the Battle of Riviere-Ouelle until the sun was low and the sky began to turn red. Parents and children all thanked Robert for their history lesson and wished him well on his journey to Paris.

Upon returning to their home, the windows were all shuttered and the children said good night to Robert. Genevieve kissed him on the cheek.

"It is so good to have you here, and I can see that she adores you," Charlotte said as she carried his admirer off to bed.

Simon and Robert climbed the staircase from the living room to the second story. The hallway floor reflected the light from the lamps which were mounted on the walls. Simon opened a door on the left and showed Robert his room for the evening. A large, very inviting four poster bed was positioned against the opposite wall. There was a large window on either side of the bed with matching oak tables beneath them. A dressing table with a mirror above it and a wash basin with towels rested on its marble top. A desk sat at the wall facing the dresser.

Simon walked to the window. "Mathurin, here is a nightshirt for you. Place your clothes in the basket and put it in the hallway. They will be cleaned by the time you continue your journey. Also, if I am correct by looking at your bags, you could use more clothes. If you will accept some of mine to take with you, it will be my pleasure to make your journey easier. Have an excellent night's sleep. We will visit the graves of our ancestors tomorrow and would like you to accompany us. Good night."

Simon walked across the carpeted floor and silently closed the door behind him.

After changing into his nightshirt and leaving his clothes to be laundered, Robert stood at the window by the dressing table. From there he could see where earlier, British soldiers and brave French settlers had exchanged fire, before leaving for home and their beds. In the fading light, he could see fields separated by tree lines and a farmhouse in the distance. As he watched the remnants of the day gradually disappear into the night, he reflected how unexpected these events had been. He had intensely disliked this village when he arrived and now desired sleep to hasten morning's arrival to experience how the next day would unfold.

When he awoke in the morning, Robert found his new clothes in a basket in the hall where he had left his laundry in the evening. Dressing quickly, he retraced his steps and met the family in the dining room for breakfast. Simon and Charlotte told him that now he could easily be mistaken for a local resident.

Breakfast consisted of eggs, bread and tea and what little bacon Genevieve hadn't consumed. Everyone spoke in an animated fashion and wished that he would finish his breakfast soon, as the mornings focus concerned their walk to the cemetery.

Simon placed his cup of tea in its saucer and turned to Robert. "This morning we will walk to our village cemetery to place flowers on the graves of our grandfather Mathurin's parents, Jean and his wife, Reneé Suzanne. They were both born about 1610, no one knows for certain. We will take some of the irises and lilies that grow next to our house and by the time we return, Brother André and his brother Bernard should have returned and your journey can continue."

Walking past the church, the family trekked down the road Robert had used to enter the village. After walking a short distance, they reached the cemetery. A low stone wall formed the outer boundary, while a row of hedges with shiny green leaves and tiny white flowers lined the inner perimeter and rose about one foot above it. The dismal looking homes on the opposite side of the road looked on blankly as the Dubé family entered through one of the iron gates. All monuments bore a cross of stone and a few were large enough to be seen from the road. With Simon leading and Genevieve walking next to Robert, they soon stood before two graves. Both were simple stone monuments, worn by years of rain and sun but the names Jean Dubé and Reneé Dubé were still clearly visible. A crucifix had been chiseled into the center of each headstone and the year 1610 had been nearly worn away. These stones were like the village he thought. They were established, solid, aged and uncomplicated.

Charlotte handed the flowers cut from their garden to Robert and he placed them on the graves. Simon led them in a brief prayer and they silently turned to walk to their home. Soon, he saw the poste chaise in the church courtyard where Bernard, Brother André and Étienne stood together talking and now he could see their strong family resemblance. The team had been hitched to the carriage and Bernard waived as he saw them approaching from the cemetery. When Genevieve saw the post chaise, she realized that Robert was about to leave. She moved closer to him and squeezed his hand until they reached the church and he told her that he needed to speak to her priest alone.

Robert approached Brother André, the young priest smiling as when they first met. With his outstretched arms, he embraced Robert and kissed him on both cheeks. "My friend, I will miss you very much. You add so much to our little village."

"I will always remember my visit here, Brother André. I wondered if you could please help me with something," he said in a low tone to hide what he had to say from the others.

Brother André became serious for a moment and then beamed again. "Of course my friend. All you need to do is ask and it will be done."

"My niece Genevieve has a real talent for drawing. She needs proper supplies like drawing paper and pencils. I also want her to have brushes, paints and an easel. I would very much appreciate it if you would see to it that she gets what she needs."

Brother André was about to explain about the expensive nature of such things when Robert filled the priests large hands with lire notes. "I believe there is enough here for you to get her what she needs and have some left as an offering to your church."

The notes quickly disappeared into Brother André's robes. "You are a good man, Mathurin. Of course I will help you. Étienne routinely travels between here and La Rochelle. I will explain to him what needs to be done and you may consider the matter settled and the materials will soon be in her possession. Your niece will be well taken care of. Now, I have one favor to ask of you. Bernard told me of your plans to reach Paris. You will pass through communities where my fellow priests serve God. Would you please deliver these letters for me? There are only three."

Brother André produced three envelopes sealed in wax, from the same robes that the lire had vanished into. Impressed and willing to help, Robert couldn't say no. "Certainly, it would be my pleasure," Robert said taking the letters.

At this point, Bernard walked to where Robert stood and noticed the letters. "Ah, I see you have my brother's letters, my friend. Is there and invitation from the King to visit him at Versailles as well?" he said with a chuckle.

Robert rolled his eyes toward the sky, "I will be so glad to continue on my journey as I rest alone in the poste chaise and he drives the horses," he thought.

Simon, Charlotte and their children approached him as he stood next to the horses. Simon was first to hug Robert and then Charlotte who handed him a package and whispered in his ear "This is the remainder of the bacon. Genevieve adores you, but possibly not more than what is in this package. There is also a bottle of wine. Good luck," as she kissed him on both cheeks.

Robert shook hands with the boys and the girls giggled when he kissed them on their cheeks. Genevieve threw her arms around his neck and squeezed very hard. Robert looked intently at her extraordinarily brilliant, green eyes and freckles. "I will miss you too. Promise me you'll never stop drawing."

Genevieve smiled and nodded and Robert placed her back on the ground. "Promise me that you won't forget me," she pleaded

As Bernard mounted the horse, Robert stepped into the carriage. Leaving the village now seemed far less important than he had deemed it the day before and the task of delivering Ron's package was a much heavier burden now than ever. Yesterday, La Chapelle-Thémer had seemed like a village with no qualities. But becoming acquainted with his family had changed that and now the poste chaise seemed boring and cavernous. The only redeeming quality about departing now was that he wouldn't be bothered by Bernard's incessant babbling.

Acting impulsively, he reached into his backpack and leaped from the carriage. "Bernard wait! I need to do something." Raising his cell phone above his head he shouted, "I want to take your picture." Judging from their confused expressions, Robert was reminded why he needed to avoid acting impulsively.

Charlotte spoke first, "Mathurin, I gave you bacon, and now you wish to take our picture. What is a picture?"

He now faced the questioning looks of everyone except Genevieve, who scornfully looked at her mother for having giving away her favorite meal.

Robert's first thought was to return to the carriage and to simply tell Bernard to move on. Alternatively, he reasoned that because a device like his cell phone won't be available for over two hundred years, its secret would remain in their church's courtyard. Holding his cell phone in his hand he quickly and excitedly ran to a bewildered Simon and Charlotte.

"With this," he replied, "I can take your picture. Let me show you. This takes a likeness of you and you can see it on this surface as quick as you can blink and we call it a picture." Robert showed them some of his previous pictures. They understood, but scarcely believed what they saw. Robert took a family picture and astonished, they all wanted to touch the screen. Charlotte had such a perplexed look that he offered the only explanation he could, "Where I live, everyone has these," which really explained nothing.

Their amazement soon gave way to absolute delight, as everyone was allowed to take a picture and review it. Robert retrieved his device and turned toward his carriage, when he heard quick, light footsteps in the gravel courtyard. Turning without surprise, he saw Genevieve following him with the intention of having one picture of just her and her uncle. Pierre took the picture and Robert lifted Genevieve one last time. She smiled and he smiled in return saying, "Is there anything you want before I leave you?" Genevieve lowered her chin, turned her head toward the post chaise and stared resolutely at Robert. "You should know the answer," her eyes told him. "Oh come on," he shouted in vain, absolutely aware of what her answer would be. "All right you little bandit," he said reaching inside the coach and retrieving a package. He handed her the bacon that was his a few minutes ago, but now was the property of an extremely satisfied little girl. "Thank you oncle Mathurin," as she skipped happily back to Charlotte with her prize.

Robert looked at Charlotte who smiled at him and shrugged her shoulders. A strong breeze flowed past Robert that was warm and sweet, disturbing the dust in the courtyard as it gusted before them and continued past Simon and Charlotte's home. Robert looked at Bernard who guided the team to his right and onto the road as Robert waived good-by from his window. Under a clear, cloudless sky he left to continue his journey to help his friend Ron. He held the key fob Ron had sent to him. By just pressing the button, both he and the package would arrive instantly in Ron's Paris home. Bernard thought that Robert's next destination was Paris by coach, a journey which could easily last a week. He could not have known that the package and Robert would travel that distance and arrive in the 21st century in an instant.

CHOLET

As the road meandered away from the village, it followed a sizeable field on the left and extremely dense woods on the right which eventually gave way to farmland. Occasionally a solitary tree stood next to the roadside, but most of the heavily farmed areas on both sides of the road offered a nearly treeless landscape. Robert opened his backpack and glanced at Ron's envelope as he withdrew the key fob from a side pocket and put his right arm through one of the shoulder straps.

He glanced through the window at the complete inactivity of the fields. Whether or not he would prefer this to Paris in the mid 21th century was immaterial. He was prepared to say goodbye to 18th century France to help Ron and depressed the button of the key fob, expecting to instantly arrive 260 years into the future. A moment later he sat back in the seat of his poste-chaise, stunned as he looked at the same unplowed fields when he had expected to be standing in Ron's Paris apartment.

"This couldn't be any simpler," he thought as he continued to press the button. But the result was the same. The coach lurched when a wheel struck a hole in the road, shaking Robert a little. "There has to be an explanation for this," he said faintly. He fell to his knees and quickly opened the fob on the floor of the poste chaise; searching for anything that was obviously wrong, hoping he would find an apparent reason for the malfunction. Seeing none, he realized that his immediate options were extremely limited.

Cholet was far too distant to reach in one days travel. The horses would require to be exchanged at least once to continue their journey and they would need to find an inn before nightfall. His first experience with a country inn would add to the pain of his separation from La Chapelle-Thémer.

Sunlight was failing and the horses were tired. Bernard chose a poste house, which sat on the left side of the road. While the exterior appeared inviting enough, it only served to hide what would be unbelievably dismal once inside. Robert's room had bare walls and a fire place which was unusable because it smoked too much to bear. Supper was a perfect accompaniment to the décor. He was served, or rather endured a tough, miserable chicken, a cutlet, salad and a bottle of sorry wine. He went to bed hoping Genevieve was enjoying his bacon and wishing he hadn't left the wine Charlotte had given him in his coach.

Robert had no problem rising early in the morning. Quickly consuming a breakfast that looked amazingly like the previous night's dinner, he told Bernard to reach Cholet that day without failure.

Traveling through the countryside, he noticed features that remained remarkably unchanged. They stopped soon after reaching the Maine River, which Bernard announced meant that they had reached Cholet. After reaching the poste house, Bernard unhitched the team and led them to be watered and fed and Robert inquired of one of the stable boys where St. Pierre's Church was located. This was where the first of Brother Andre's letters was to be delivered. He was truly relieved to find that it was very close to the poste house.

The directions he was given consisted of a series of streets, more closely resembling narrow paved paths. The buildings on either side rose two and three stories above him which only added to its constricting nature. Looking forward, he was able to observe only an extremely limited view of what lay ahead, while the space above him offered a very limited view of a mixture of blue sky and thin tattered grey clouds. The street terminated at an intersection of several broad streets and the bread store he had been told to look for. He had not however, been instructed to look for a store front which had been smashed in. Broken glass and a missing door, plus various supplies strewn about the street, caused him to wonder if the entire city was on the verge of chaos.

Ten steps led to the arch work beneath the church's main tower. On either side of the steps, flowers beds were filled with plants of various brilliant colors. An old man sat on the steps next to the flowers and as Robert approached he looked up and met Robert's gaze through tired, vacant eyes.

"Look, look at what we have lowered ourselves to," as he waved his arm toward the street, littered with broken glass and pieces of wood while people on their knees scooped up random piles of wheat with their hands. Pointing at the cobblestone street he continued," The King knows that the want of bread is so great in every part of the kingdom that there is no extremity to which the people might not be driven. We are truly starving and this is the result." The old man, having said what he felt he needed to, returned to staring at the flowers.

Walking up the steps to the large wooden doors, Robert's thoughts turned to his first encounter with Brother André. He thought that this must be the new order of village priest. A young, enthusiastic and friendly cleric, who could be a member of his own flock and prevent his eccliastical duties from separating him from his parishioners.

Reaching the door, he pulled the ancient iron handle, but nothing happened. The door was unexpectedly locked and Robert was left with the option of knocking on the door or turning away. Several minutes elapsed since he had begun hitting the door with an ancient brass ring attached to a large metal Fleur-de-Lis; a victim of rust and apparent limited use. Receiving no response, he turned to walk away when he heard what sounded like the bolt in the door being slowly pulled back. As the listened to the sound of rusted metal scraping against more rusted metal, he could only speculate as to how much time had passed since it had last been moved. Holding the letter in his left hand, he expected a warm welcome and an expression of gratitude when he introduced himself as a personal friend of Brother André's.

The door was opened slowly by a small, mole-like priest who appeared as if he spent most of his time in the dark. From his vantage point, Robert thought the interior of the church looked rather dark and dismal. The priest appeared unfriendly and bore a mistrustful look, as he glared at him behind the safety of his partially open doors with a pair of dark, doleful eyes.

"Excuse me Father, my name is ....."

"Well, who are you and what do you want?" the mole like priest demanded in a morbidly irritated, high pitched voice.

"I am sorry to bother you Father, my name is Mathurin Dubé and I....."

"State your business before I close the door," repeated the wispy, squeaky voice.

Sensing that this was not going well, Robert tried to complete one sentence before tossing the envelope through the narrow opening provided by the distrustful priest, "I am carrying a letter for you from Brother André in La Chapelle-......."

"Brother André, why didn't you say so young man?" as a small withered hand shot from the narrow space between the door and its frame and snatched the letter. If this was the priest's opportunity to be cordial, he was not inclined to take advantage of it.

"Thank you was there anything else?" he said quickly, his eyes darting from side to side as if looking for other conspirators and giving the impression that this was now Robert's opportunity to leave.

"Why yes there is Father," Robert could almost feel the priest's despair as he realized he had to endure this intrusion longer than he wished to. "Brother André said that you may know somewhere my guide and I could spend the night." It was a lie, and the priest may have known it to be a lie, but how could this conversation be any worse? His initial hope was that they might be invited to stay in the church; but having experienced this form of hospitality, he wasn't very confident.

"What, there are more on you?" he said, horrified." "Well....no." and the heavy wooden doors were closed and bolted quicker than Robert could have expected.

Robert retraced his steps past where the old man had been seated, past people who continued to scoop up what few grains of wheat could be found and down the same narrow streets to see if Bernard was faring any better in securing accommodations.

"My friend, we are in luck," said a very happy Bernard. "There are two rooms available in the poste house owner's home. I have inspected them and it will be a welcome improvement over the disaster we slept in last night."

That evening's meal was much better as well. There was plenty of good wine with two courses and a dessert. There was also a large plate of some sort of fritter called chaudies, which Robert enjoyed immensely. During the meal, Robert told Bernard what he had witnessed in front of the church.

Bernard nodded, "Yes my friend, I heard the same from our host. On market day no person can buy more than two bushels of wheat to avoid monopolizing the supply. The situation was so bad, that they stationed dragoons to avoid violence. People began quarreling with the bakers because prices of bread are beyond the proportions of wheat. Scuffling began and then people began rioting. They took bread and wheat and ran away in every direction. When the dragoons left to chase those who had stolen the goods, the people turned on the store itself. Now the farmers and bakers won't supply goods until people pay for the stolen wheat. The people are starving now. All this will cause prices to rise further. The next time they will really need troops."

Bernard tapped his fork on the table for effect. "My friend, this can only worsen as we get closer to Paris. We will need to keep to the main roads." Smiling he cocked his head, "Perhaps your friend the King will invite us to spend the night at Versailles." Robert rolled his eyes at the ceiling and left to get ready for bed.

Their rooms were not decorated, but they were clean and warm, which was all he really wanted. In the morning a breakfast of fresh eggs, warm bread and hot tea were served. This was completely different from the miserable inn they had suffered in previously. Shortly they were continuing their journey to Angers, the second part of their journey.

ANGERS

As Cholet slowly disappeared behind him, Robert looked from his poste chaise at the same flat fields under an overcast sky. He appreciated the fact that France's roads were considered superior to British roads, but felt like he was proceeding at a snail's pace and clung to a slim hope of arriving at Angers before nightfall. He was still striving to solve the reason for the failure in transporting to Paris using Ron's devise. He labored on his calculations, which he already knew were correct, but hoped that the source of the problem might suddenly reveal itself as he renewed his efforts to determine a solution.

He noticed as he looked at the farms, that the elevation was gradually increasing and the fields seemed to follow a progression of sorts. The closest field lay fallow, one field filled with clover now would be ready for planting the following year. The next field looked like a plow had dug furrows for planting, but the ground was so saturated that planting was doubtful. Further on, he saw a much larger field with white stakes driven into the ground in a precise pattern, but nothing was growing. Two fields then came into view with bushes growing near the white stakes. The bushes in the first field were barely one foot tall, while the plants in the second field rose to about one yard. Robert guessed that this was a method of rotating planting fields during different seasons to save the soil from depleting its nutrients.

The trees in the fields were more abundant than they had been near La Chapelle-Thémer. The road narrowed as trees grew closer to the side of the road. Light was growing dimmer and Robert reasoned that any hope of reaching Angers this evening was lost. On both sides of the road, walls of rock sloped away from the road and hedges grew tall above them. In the distance on the left he could see three buildings; one large building with a smaller one on either side.

The smaller buildings were white with green shutters and the larger structure had a grey cement appearance with white shutters only on its second story. "This is our stop for the night?" thought Robert. "It couldn't possibly be worse than the previous inn."

He soon began to regret rushing to such a quick judgment. As he compared the two houses, he thought a more wretched place could not be imagined. After a dinner of stale eggs, bad bread and worse wine; they were shown to their room. Not only did they have to share a room, but there was only a mattress on the floor and no bed. After the door was closed behind them, Robert threw up his arms in disgust and exasperation, "Bernard, this room sucks."

"Excuse me Mathurin, but how does a room suck?" said Bernard inquisitively.

"No, no, I mean something else altogether. It's an expression we use at home. It means that something is awful or dreadful," he explained

"Well, I agree with you, my friend. This room definitely sucks," and he rolled into the middle of the mattress and immediately fell sound asleep.

In the morning the skies were overcast and threatening. The possibility of rain forcing Bernard from his horse and into the poste chaise, only served to further darken his mood. Following a miserable breakfast of warm tea and stale bread, Robert told Bernard to get the team ready and prepare to leave for Angers, while he went for a brief walk.

As he followed a path through a field of wheat, he was joined by a poor woman who said this was indeed a sad country. She and her husband had a small piece of land where they grew wheat and oats and raised their seven children.

"We have to pay heavy taxes," she said with anguished weariness. "The court system is unjust, the judges being ignorant pretenders, who are dependent on the landowners for their power. Besides the heavy taxes, the rental of the land usually consists of services we perform for the landowners. The industry of the people is nearly exterminated. There seems to be no escape for us," she finished with a heavy sigh. Robert looked at this woman who might have been taken for sixty of seventy years of age. Her figure bent, her vague vacant look, her face so furrowed by labor. When she told him that she was only twenty eight, he had no words. As she turned her back to him and headed toward a distant farm house, Robert heard Bernard calling to him that all was prepared to leave.

He told Bernard about his conversation with the woman. "My friend, even out here, there is disquiet. The owner of this miserable place said the idea is that people will, from hunger be driven to revolt and once they find any other means of sustenance than that produced by honest labor, all they will have left is fear. Their existence here absolutely sucks, my friend."

"We are leaving Bernard," Robert said opening the door and stepping into the poste chaise. He then made a mental note, "Never say anything could not possibly get any worse," even to himself, because it almost certainly will.

As they traveled further along the gravel road, Robert continued to devise a solution to the problem surrounding Ron's package. If using the key fob as a transmitter had failed, he theorized that arriving at the exact latitude and longitude of Ron's present location might require less energy and have an increased chance of success. How he could accomplish this in the absence of a mobile device connection to the non-existent GPS presented a problem. It did not mean it was an insurmountable problem, simply one that would require some innovation.

Soon, this train of thought was distracted by the absence of fields and the return of houses positioned close to the road. Gravel roads had become cobblestone streets. The homes here seemed statelier than those he had seen in Cholet. They were taller, with steeply sloped roofs covered with patterns of dark grey slate. The houses were beige or tan with white window sills and white shutters.

They were far from reaching Pont Verdun, which spanned the Maine River, but he could already see the twin spires of a cathedral extending above the roofs of the nearby buildings. The bridge was wide and made of stone with red flowers growing on its walls. Boats were docked at the embankment of the canal below, while the river moved slowly under a cloudy sky until it disappeared.

Robert wanted to simply cross the river to change horses, leaving Bernard to locate accommodations and a meal. While Bernard tended to these duties, Robert would deliver his second letter.

Bernard found the poste station among some trees adjacent to the river bank and while he instructed the stable boy to tend to the horses, Robert resumed his task of delivering Brother Bernard's letters.

This letter was addressed to a Father Julian of the Cathédral Saint-Maurice. When he asked about its location, he was told that he would not require directions if he simply walked in the direction of the nearest bridge. Robert walked back toward the Pont Verdun and crossed the street. There was a large plaza with a fountain located in its center and as he looked away from the river he understood why he needed no directions to find the cathedral. This promised to be completely the opposite of what he experienced when he searched for the church in Cholet. From the fountain, Robert looked uphill at a staircase which led directly to the twin spires he had seen before they crossed Pont Verdun.

The expansive steps reminded him of the way locks function on a river. After walking up a flight of steps, he continued on a level walkway until he reached the next set of steps. On either side on the steps, a wide level sidewalk was fashioned from grey cobblestone as well as lamps and small trees which led to the expansive courtyard in front of the cathedral. The front of the cathedral was not as ornate as the church in Cholet. The courtyard extended to its front and the doors which were recessed under a series of arches.

He held his breath as he paused to open the door, wondering what sort of a reception he might receive here. It swung open effortlessly and he stepped through the doorway. Once inside he was surprised how bright the interior was compared to the tiny church in La Chapelle-Thémer and the cavern like one in Cholet. Before him stood a statue of an angel holding a horn and above were huge vaulted ceilings and beautiful stained glass windows. On the other side of the church, artists had their positioned their easels on the tiled floors as they painted.

He spoke to an older priest who seemed very eager to assist Robert. When he said that he was here to see Father Julian however, the priest's mood turned very serious. He was asked in an abrupt, but very polite manner to please wait before turning and walking away.

While he waited, Robert used the time to examine the church's interior. Except for the tall spires, there wasn't much that he had seen from the outside that was very impressive. He was however, amazed by the intricacies of the stained glass windows high above the statues and woodwork. He became so preoccupied that he was a bit startled when he heard a strong, vibrant voice ask, "How may I help you, my son?"

Approaching him from across the church was a priest of about forty years old with greying hair, thick greying eyebrows and a concerned expression. Robert quickly extended his hand as a friendly gesture to put the priest at ease. He had been anxious earlier not knowing what sort of encounter this time he might have with Father Julian.

"Father, my name is Mathurin Dubé. I traveled to La Chapelle-Thémer to see my relatives and when their village priest learned that I was traveling to Angers, he asked me to deliver this letter to you." He began to pull his hand away to retrieve the letter from his shirt pocket when Father Julian held his hand fast and also lightly placed his left hand on Robert's shoulder.

"Yes my, of course I will hear your confession," he said with a smile and before he could protest, Robert was led to one of the confessional booths. He had never been inside one before and had only a vague understanding of what to say.

"My son, now you may please deliver the letter to me. There is a small opening in this wall separating us. Would you please pass the envelope you have through it?"

Robert located a small slot in the wall and managed to thrust it through.

"Fine, fine; you have performed a kind gesture by delivering this to me. I wish to thank you from the bottom of my heart. When you leave here, please take my advice and do not return."

The confessional booth suddenly began to feel very claustrophobic. The air somehow felt thicker than it had a few minutes ago. "Father, what is there about this letter that makes people uncomfortable? The priest in Cholet presented me with a very unpleasant response when I delivered his letter." Unpleasant was a charitable description of the manner which the mole like priest used to dismiss him, but he didn't want to burden Father Julian with the details. Yet there was no response from the other side of the confessional.

"Father Julian," he whispered, but was answered only with silence. Robert opened the door and stepped back onto the church floor. Uncertain if it was appropriate to do so and guessing it probably wasn't, he opened the door where the priest had sat moments earlier and found it unoccupied. Judging from the manner in which the parishioners glared at him, confirmed his suspicion that opening the priest's door was improper and he walked quickly toward the entrance and was soon standing alone again in the courtyard

He found his walk downhill from the church to be both a relief and very pleasant. Rather than dwell on the unusual reception these letters seemed to produce, he concentrated on the view from the crest of the hill. The steps led directly from the cathedral's courtyard, to the fountain in the center of the plaza. He had more time now to observe the houses which lined the walkway and the weeping willows which graced the front of them and their ubiquitous slate roofs as the Maine River bisected the landscape.

Near the fountain, some people sat on the lawn, a painter busied himself with his canvas overlooking the Maine River and an old man sat on a bench, leaning forward on his cane whose sole interest seemed to be centered on observing him. As he did not relent in his stare, Robert felt compelled to acknowledge his apparent interest in him.

He turned toward the old man and smiled, "Good day, sir. How are you today?"

The old man returned Robert's greeting with a smile. He wore a red coat over a white waistcoat with grey pants with black stockings. His smile accentuated the deepening folds of his forehead and lines in his cheeks and eyes. His snow white beard did little to hide his weathered face, but his mood was very bright.

He lightly tapped the space on the bench next to him with the palm of his hand, "Please sit young man. I don't get the opportunity to speak to many strangers."

As he sat on the bench, Robert was genuinely mystified by his last statement. "I'm sorry sir. How do you know that I am a stranger? This is a large city. I could be walking to my home, over there," Robert said gesturing to a house across the river.

The old man leaned against the bench, smiled and placed his hand on Robert's shoulder. "Yes, you might; but you aren't because you don't live in that house; I do. Besides, you look far too content to be one of our residents. People who live here are always in a hurry. It has become rare that one takes the time to merely sit and talk. My name is Jean-Pierre Roux and I own several slate quarries here, which is why you see so many of the roofs of Angers covered by it. Our city is sometimes referred to as the "Black City" because of our roofs."

Resting his hand on Robert's shoulder, he leaned closer as if he was trying to ensure that he would appreciate the meaning of every word he heard. "This is a very dark time around here and it is reflected by the faces of the people. You have something on your mind but you appear to be working on a solution. The people living here are generally centered on their problems. My fear is what will happen when they arrive at their solution. That plus," Jean-Pierre paused for a moment and looked toward the river while a mischievous grin swept across his face, "plus I saw you leave your poste chaise at the poste station and walk to the cathedral. I sit here every day and occasionally people talk to me. I knew you would return sometime."

Robert laughed at the joke that was played on him. "That was very clever, sir. Part of what you say is no joke however. You aren't the first person who has mentioned the unrest in your country." Robert told him what he had seen and heard since leaving La Chapelle-Thémer and his reason for visiting France.

"Yes, Mathurin, I did jest with you to some degree, however; what you have seen and heard unfortunately is all true. Throughout France there is a burning rage against the existing order. The entire structure of the ancient regime, under which the country operates, is in the weak hands of a corrupt and incompetent executive and is threatened by bankruptcy."

"There is neither fair taxation, nor political freedom and privilege pervades the state. The privileged clergy pay no taxes, the privileged nobles, mostly absent from their estates, collect their rents while performing no duties. The privileged lawgivers sell justice to those who can pay for it and impose burdensome taxes on those who cannot. Above all, the cultivation of the land is old and inefficient and the supply of food uncertain and haphazard. The people are hungry and bread riots are common. And here I sit or watch from my home at a city in turmoil, wondering if any of this can survive."

Robert was becoming skillful at judging time by looking at the sun's position in the summer sky since he had put away his watch and cell phone to deflect the attention they would draw. He was about to excuse himself from M. Roux to see how Bernard had fared with the arrangements for accommodations and dinner.

He turned to say good-by but Jean-Pierre spoke first. "Your guide Bernard has busied himself and secured rooms for you at the Hotel de Moulinet. However, your dinner reservations are at my home where you are to be my guests. Bernard is there now waiting for us. Shall we go?"

Standing, he motioned in the direction of his home. Robert noticed that the cane was really more of an accessory than an aid. Made of polished mahogany with a knob of silver, it slowly drifted with him; its aim being to enhance the appearance of the owner, not assist him as they made their way across the bridge to the embankment.

Jean-Pierre's home was very impressive. A large two story home, it was beige in color with white shutters and of course, a dark grey slate roof. The front entrance was located in the center with three large windows on either side. Second story windows were situated directly above those on the first floor with a dormer above each. The lawn was small but immaculate, surrounded by a black iron fence with gold accents and was reached through a gate which seemed to be adorned with a family crest. Above the entrance an expansive balcony looked out on the river.

Upon entering Jean-Pierre's home the doorman ushered Robert to a room where he could freshen up before dinner and left him after lighting a lamp and some candles. Beside the wash basin and towels the room had polished wooden floors and a table which sat upon a Persian rug. Several lesser tables had small vases and candle holders on them. There were large paintings of the countryside on the opposite ends of the room.

Entering the dining room, Robert found Bernard engaged in a conversation with Jean-Pierre and three other gentlemen. Jean-Pierre immediately introduced him to the other dinner guests: Paul Henri Micaly, a physician, Jacques Decretat, a manufacturer who owned cotton mills and Louis Volney a celebrated traveler from Nice, presumably wealthy.

Following a dinner which consisted of an excellent wine, roasted potatoes, a fat roast beef and plum pudding, Jean-Pierre suggested that they have cigars and after dinner drinks on the balcony which overlooked the front of his property and the river. Robert and Jean-Pierre chose Cointreau; the other men drank port, while they all enjoyed cigars and watched the river carry boats slowly past. They discussed a variety of topics, but the situation in France was truly an unavoidable subject. Jean-Pierre made certain that his guest's glasses were never empty.

"It is very sad that a country this size can't feed its own people, "said Jacques, leaning against the marble balustrade. "The most common form of peasant protest is the food riot. They are widespread and began last year when grain and bread prices reached their highest point. I employ as many men as I can in my mills and pay them well. Donations to the church help to reach out to the poorest, but it is never enough and when we see the opulence lavished upon projects for our King's comfort, it is very sad indeed, especially when one has to look into the faces of children."

Jean-Pierre placed his glass down and began pointing with his cigar to emphasize his opinion, "You know, sometimes when I stand here I feel that looking at the river flowing by is like observing the energy of France. I can never decide whether it is replenishing what has been lost or is leaving us without hope of returning before all is gone."

Before this day was finished, Robert wanted to retire to his room at the hotel. The enjoyment of the evening was one he would treasure like re-enacting the Battle of Riviere-Ouelle with Genevieve, but it was time to end the evening. His host was disappointed, but gracious enough to understand Robert's needs.

As they were preparing to depart, Louis spoke to Robert and Bernard in a very serious tone regarding that they would be wise to take care when sharing information with strangers. "I realize it may sound odd as we have only just met, my friends. However, what I've found in my travels is the closer you are to Versailles and Paris, suspicion and intrigue are at the forefront of everyone's mind. Some are simply interested, like spectators at the theatre. Others are nearly insane and will hide their motives until it may be too late. Watch out especially for those who only wish to absorb as much information about your intentions as possible. They have their own agendas to fulfill and will not care how they achieve them. Be as careful with what you say, as you are to whom you say it."

With that, Louis embraced them both, Jacques and Paul-Henri came to wish them both well on their journey and returned to their drinks.

Jean-Pierre ushered Robert and Bernard to his home's entrance. "I wish to thank you both for indulging an old man and allowing me to be your being your host this evening. If you wish, I can have my carriage take you to your hotel."

Looking at the river, he declined. It was a brief distance to the hotel and the lamps on the embankment looked inviting enough that he didn't want to forfeit the opportunity for a relaxing walk next to the river. "Actually Jean-Pierre, I would like to walk to the hotel. Thank you for your hospitality and your friendship."

Jean-Pierre held Robert's hand for a moment and kissed him on both cheeks. "My friend, my best wishes to you for a safe journey. Louis' intention was not to alarm you, but it is advisable to be cautious these days about who you disclose your plans to," he paused for a moment and lowered his voice, "or why one visits a church at mid-day?"

Robert tried his utmost to conceal how stunned he was by Jean-Pierre's statement. Did Jean-Pierre actually make reference to his visit to the visit to Father Julian? Could he possibly be aware of the letters from Brother André? The alternative was he knew nothing and his statement only referred to the fact that he saw him walk to the cathedral. Revealing nothing, he thanked his host for a wonderful evening and left through the gate.

He stood resting his hands on the rough, cool wall of the embankment, peering down into the river and listened to the waves lapping against the boats moored to their docks. His thoughts were interrupted by Bernard's remark, "Excellent diner, eh my friend," as he placed his arm on Roberts shoulder.

Thinking that what he really needed to concentrate on was the journey to Paris and delivery of Ron's package was all he could offer was, "Yes, it was fine," in a distracted tone.

The hotel was located on a street corner near the poste station. A large fountain was centered before its main entrance and was the most attractive part of any of his accommodations thus far. The ground floor of the building's exterior had a greystone appearance, while the next two floors looked like limestone. Once inside, Robert thought Bernard had redeemed himself for the disasters which were the inns they had stayed in recently.

The carpets in the lobby and staircase were red with flecks of gold. The handrail and baluster were painted in a deep gold color. Robert was extremely impressed with his room. It was spacious with a dressing table, large mirrors and a red chest of drawers with gold fittings. The windows were tall and wide with white curtains and they opened onto a balcony large enough for a small table and two chairs. "Too bad I won't have time to have breakfast out here," he thought. Most important, the mattress was soft. As the curtains stirred gently in the mild air he was tempted to close them and take sleep longer in the morning but opened them fully so his comfort wouldn't be allowed to compromise an early start in the morning.

LE MANS

Following a simple, but tasty breakfast of eggs, warm fresh rolls, tea and juice, Robert and Bernard rode toward the Verdun Bridge, turned left and proceeded upriver in the direction of Le Mans. Earlier, Bernard had again jokingly asked Robert if he'd heard any news from the King regarding an invitation to join him at Versailles. By this time, he ceased replying to what Bernard thought was humorous. His acknowledgement was limited to rolling his eyes, sighing and climbing into his poste chaise.

A mist lay over the town as they resumed their journey. The Maine River remained on their left for some time. The houses became fewer in number, more trees populated the roadside and he noticed the road gradually twisting toward the east. Soon the Maine was gone, replaced by an abundance of tall trees with and small, irregularly shaped fields whose borders were defined by tree lines and fences of stone.

Crossing the Loire River gave Robert a measure of hope that reaching Le Mans before nightfall was in the realm of possibility. Bernard soon dashed any hope by informing Robert they were much too far from Le Mans and would need to stay the night at an inn. He was not in a mood to hear this, but wanted to be reasonable and told Bernard to move as far as he could before darkness overtook them.

They eventually stopped before the oddest assortment of buildings anyone could imagine. Three or four buildings of different designs, materials, heights and lengths were somehow melded together in a manner that suggested someone had the misconception no one would notice what a disaster they had created. Chimneys sloped at opposing angles above roofs which looked as if they could collapse on a whim. Parts from a variety of carts were strewn about the property like the bones of cattle, dead in some forgotten desert. Roof tiles had separated and slid partially toward the eves, waiting for gravity to complete their descent. Vines rose randomly like fingers from the ground, waiting for the right moment to crush these structures and put them out of their misery.

Robert could not bear another night like those nightmares he had recently experienced and was prepared to sleep in his coach. The people at this inn changed his mind though, when he saw what lay beyond their dismal structures. After Bernard had left the team and coach with the stable boy, they walked around the property and found that the miserable looking buildings surrounded a well-kept, cozy courtyard where dinner was being served. They provided him with a dinner of delicious roasted chicken with garlic and basil, some fresh roasted vegetables, warm bread and surprisingly good wine.

He had noticed a large meadow beyond the circle of dilapidated buildings. In addition to the scattered pieces of carts, there were many men congregated in the field beneath trees, leaning against their bedrolls while eating their dinners. He had noticed men traveling like this since they left La Rochelle, but this was the first chance he had to meet them. Their appearance differed, but they did seem to have one thing in common: all carried the type of tools that a craftsman would require. He spoke to a boy of about fourteen years old with blond hair, round deep set eyes and lean sinewy hands, eating under a tree. Next to him lay what looked like carpentry tools. The boy introduced himself as Tristan Montagne, from Louplande; a village in the area.

Tristan was surprised that someone who was wealthy enough to travel in a poste chaise would be interested in speaking to a common laborer eating dinner under a tree, but he was quick to invite Robert to sit with him and passed his bottle of wine to him. "We are all journeymen and peddlers," Tristan explained. "Our movement is called the Tour de France. As our roads improved, so did commerce. As commerce increased, people had more money to spend and they could afford luxuries and to pay the craftsmen who construct them," as he gestured with his arms to the others seated around them. "And so here we are, we walk together because there is safety in numbers and we can't afford a carriage, so we share a cart. We travel from village to village, talking to peasants and working for the people who have money to spend."

"So Tristan, if you were to work on these buildings, where would you begin?" said Robert as he motioned across the meadow.

Tristan didn't speak. He grew thoughtful for a moment and gloomily studied the buildings, winced and raised his hands. Making a motion like someone striking a match, he made a sound like fire coming to life and then laughed at his joke. Robert nodded and thanked Tristan for the conversation. As he walked toward the buildings which Tristan had so casually joked about setting on fire, he doubted if he would ever think about the famous bicycle race the same way when he returned to the 21st century. His bedroom was sparse but clean and the bed was very comfortable. In the morning they left for Le Mans after Bernard asked once more whether Robert's invitation form the King had arrived. As usual, his question was met with a heavy sigh, accompanied by silence.

For the first time since leaving La Chapelle-Thémer, he noticed fir trees and fields of corn. Dairy cows, possibly Holsteins in great numbers, grazed in adjoining fields.

They crossed the Sarthe River via the Pont Yssoir and entered Le Mans. Directly before him stood the remains of walls built when Romans ruled. Above the wall on the crest of the hill, he could see the top of Le Mans Cathedral. It was not reminiscent of the majestic structure like the cathedral in Agners. However, its appeal was that he had one last letter to deliver and his promise to Brother André would be fulfilled and that was extremely attractive.

Just beyond the wall, was the poste station where the horses could be tended. Further on he found a narrow, meandering set of steps, confining and squeezed between homes with barely enough room for two people to pass. As he had now lost site of the cathedral he hoped this would eventually lead to a courtyard where he would find Father Francis and put an end to this tediousness.

When the steps ended he found himself across the street from the cathedral. He passed a small park on his left and stood before a landing as wide as the face of the church. While there were no tall spires like the previous churches, this cathedral, like Notre Dame had a series of flying buttresses on either side of the church. These had been added for support of the enormous weight of the walls.

These wooden doors easily opened and Robert walked from the narthex toward the central part of the church. He was immediately struck by the complexity of the ceiling. It looked like a series of domed or vaulted shapes, giving it the appearance of arcs which joined to form a circle. It was a very intricate design, supported by a series of arches which rested on very large columns. Although the interior's color was similar to an eggshell white, it appeared as pale pink or aqua depending on how the sunlight shone through the massive stained glass windows.

In the right corner Robert noticed an upright monument nearly 13 feet high. It appeared to be sandstone with a weathered surface like carved drapery. "It sure seems out of place here" thought Robert as he sensed someone approaching him.

"This is known as the Saint Julian's Stone," said a pleasant voice behind Robert. He turned to find a tall, thin priest with deep brown eyes and an inquisitive look. "It's a prehistoric monument called a menhir, and it is made of sandstone. Everyone who sees it comes away with a different opinion about its meaning. I am Father Francis, how may I be of service?"

Reflecting on the delivery of the previous letters to a priest who hid in the shadows and the other who simply disappeared, Robert was torn between being relieved and apprehensive now that he had met Father Francis, the final piece of his problematic obligation to Brother André.

"Father, I am very glad to meet you. I have a letter for you from Brother André," he said, hoping for the best. To his immense relief, Father Francis took Robert's right hand in his and held it warmly. "Please my son, let us sit. You have traveled a great distance."

The center of the church where the congregation sat consisted of a series of chairs rather than pews. On either side of the center aisle, 20 rows of 6 chairs each, led the faithful to the altar.

Father Francis barely seemed to notice the envelope when it was handed to him. He accepted it and with one quick motion deposited it in his robes without breaking eye contact. "You have done us all a great service, Mathurin, especially considering all the risks involved."

Robert's chin fell and his eyes narrowed, "Risks? What risks?"

Father Francis' smile faded and his tone became more concerned. "Are you telling me that no one told you what you were carrying?"

Parishioners were now beginning to enter the church and he knew this conversation needed to end quickly. "I only knew that I was performing a courtesy for Brother André. Father, you need to tell me what this is all about, "as he leaned closer to the priest.

Father Francis crossed his arms, leaned close to Robert and began to speak rapidly and quietly. "The letters Brother André entrusted to you, concerned options to ensure our safety, when and if the country turns against the Church. Many people have contempt for the priesthood and some of it to be honest, is justified. If conditions continue to deteriorate, the people may decide to punish the Church and will make no distinction between clergy who took advantage of their station and priests whose devotion was only to God and their congregation. These are plans for us to quit France for parishes in neighboring countries. To have been found with these in your possession could have been considered to be proof of treason, the penalty for which is death by hanging."

"But Father, France ceded New France to England after the Seven Years War. So you see I couldn't be guilty of treason as I'm actually a British citizen," he said sounding very positive.

Father Francis rubbed one of his hands on his cheek and exhaled, "Yes Mathurin, I see. That would be much different. In that case you would probably be arrested as a British spy; and then hung."

Robert put his head in his hands.

"Now, now," said Father Francis, placing his arm across Robert's back. "All the letters have been delivered. All is well. You should leave now and return by a different route. There is a door next to the Saint Julian's stone. Good luck my son." The priest rose and walked down the aisle toward the altar.

"This is really too much to consider and just sit here," Robert thought as he stood and walked quickly toward the exit. Next to the monument was a bright red door, he passed through it and turned to his left, the opposite direction of his original route.

Observing the far end of the church he saw buttresses which were much different from those at the church's entrance. Those were massive single arches which stood alone. The buttresses at this end of the cathedral were all interconnected. They were smaller, more slender, shaped like a "Y" and formed one long interconnected arch. It was spectacular and definitely invited his attention, but he had some pressing matters to attend to with his guide.

The circuitous route forced him to use some extra time in reaching the poste house but he eventually found Bernard sitting and smoking a pipe. Bernard looked happy to see him.

"My friend, I have found lodging for the night and not too far distant. But we should leave now if we are to arrive in time for the evening meal," as he proceeded toward the bridge they crossed earlier.

There was some urgency in Bernard's desire to leave, but Robert slowed his pace immediately with his first question. "Bernard, were you ever going to tell me about the purpose of those letters? Father Francis tells me I put myself in serious danger simply by carrying them."

Bernard searched his mind for an answer that wouldn't completely incriminate him and he stopped and slowly looked at Robert and placed his hands on his shoulders.

"Yes my friend, I admit we should have told you about the nature of the letters, but we were afraid that you would not agree to help us. No more than three letters are written by any one person so we limit the number of people who could be exposed. The priests you met know only that my brother, Brother André wrote those letters. The priests who receive letters from the priests you met will have no idea of Brother Andrés identity. Besides, you were in very little danger," scarcely conceding Robert's point.

Robert looked at Bernard in an accusing manner.

"Well perhaps it was moderately dangerous," Bernard conceded.

Robert continued starring as if to suggest that he was waiting for the correct answer.

"Oh very well, you were in extreme danger and could have been shot as a spy. But it is over now, eh my friend?" he admitted as he resumed his pace and tried to change the subject. "Our hotel is there," pointing to an unremarkable three story red brick building. An iron balcony spanning the length of the building's second and third floors was all that interrupted its monotonous facade.

Robert's interest was not in matching Bernard's pace. It was his cavalier attitude toward Robert's safety that he found disturbing. When they reached the entrance he allowed Bernard to stand waiting, holding the door open while he glared at him.

Everything about the hotel was non-descript. To begin with it had no name. The sign above the door only said HOTEL. It was neither well appointed, nor distressingly absent of taste. The staff wasn't friendly or rude. His room was adequate with a bed, chest of drawers and a wash bowl and the dining room consisted of one long table and a chandelier. If anyone had even bothered to expend the energy to name such an uninspired enterprise, their efforts and time would have amounted to a colossal waste of time.

However, the bed was very comfortable and clean and the evening meal's menu was a pleasant surprise. The fact that the building was mind numbingly boring, didn't seem to matter when Robert had a nice meal and a good sleep to look forward to.

Robert stopped Bernard as they walked to the dining room. "This is important," as he held Bernard's arm. "I have been advised to keep our plans confidential. If anyone asks, you are my guide and you are taking me to Brittany. You and your brother put us in this situation. I will reach Paris without further surprises or complications. Let's have a nice, relaxing dinner and an early departure in the morning."

Bernard turned sheepishly and proceeded toward the dining room. "Yes of course, my friend. I understand entirely," he said with a hint of remorse.

Passing through the archway and into the dining room, Robert saw three men seated at the only table in the room, which except for three glasses of wine, was completely bare. They seemed to be in the midst of a very serious discussion which ended abruptly when they realized they were no longer alone.

Robert wished to give them some privacy, but places had already been set for them next to these three strangers.

One of them rose and began the introductions. "Good evening, sirs. My name is Alfred Moreau. On my left is Antoine Durand and to his right is François DuBois. Please be seated. I believe dinner is about to be served."

Moreau was a gloomy looking man, with a nose too large for his face. Durand had a broad forehead with steel blue eyes and possessed a small physique that was apparent even as he sat. DuBois was a small narrow man; painfully thin who sat silent and absent minded while he looked at them with a dull expression.

These three men were similar to the hotel, not shabbily dressed nor elegantly attired. Robert and Bernard took their seats directly across from Durand and DuBois while Moreau sat at the head of the table.

Dinner arrived almost immediately and was a pleasant surprise. It consisted of roasted potatoes, fresh tomatoes and a cheese that reminded him of Gouda. Freshly baked bread and a well-seasoned chicken were offered, followed by a flavorful pudding. The wine was very good as well.

What concerned Robert about the conversation during dinner was that it centered on his reason for traveling to Le Mans. "Why is your business in Le Mans? What is your destination? How long did he plan to stay? What had he seen, whom had he met and most important; who was he meeting?"

He also thought it unusual that considering their interest in his business, they were all extremely evasive when Robert tried to discover anything at all about them. If he asked a question about them, Moreau and Durand managed to rephrase it to become a query about Robert and Bernard as Du Bois sat mute.

Moreau did the majority of the talking and the greater part of the interrogation.

Robert discussed his journey, beginning with visiting relatives and presently his guide was in the process of traveling to visit the coast before returning home. He also asked questions about the types of crops he saw planted during his tour and the discussion he had with the woman in the field beside the poste station.

When their meal was finished, Robert still couldn't recall the three men mentioning their occupations or whether they were residents of Le Mans or travelers themselves. The common thread they shared seemed to be the manner in which they glanced at each other whenever they gleaned additional information from Bernard or Robert.

Suddenly, Robert rose quickly from his chair and picked up one of the bottles of wine. The three men and Bernard all looked at him curiously as he drank generously from it and said, "We're really in no hurry to leave for Brest, Bernard. However, I am tired." Holding the bottle and pulling Bernard's sleeve, he bowed to the three bewildered men, "Gentlemen, it has been a pleasure, good evening to you."

Once in the hallway, he walked ahead of Bernard and motioned for him to follow. Speaking softly Robert asked, "Bernard, did you notice anything odd about those men back there?"

Bernard seemed to have enjoyed the wine a little too much. "Their poor clothing," he chuckled.

Robert sounded peeved, "No Bernard. They sounded much too curious about us. This is exactly the sort of thing Louis Volney had warned us to be certain to avoid. We need to be ready to leave in a hurry. It may be my imagination, but this entire evening just seemed wrong. This was far too choreographed for my liking. From the seating arrangements, to the way dinner just happened to be ready when we sat in the dining room and finally, the incessant questioning from those three. How did you decide that we should stay in this hotel anyway?"

Bernard realized the seriousness of Robert's question, "The people at poste station gave me directions and I followed them."

When they reached the doors to their rooms, Robert repeated his directions, "Be ready to leave when I tell you, Bernard."

"Yes, my friend," answered his guide as he was swallowed by the darkness in his room.

Lighting candles in his room using the one he brought from the dining room, Robert first emptied the wine into the wash basin. Re-entering the hallway, he poured some oil from each of the lamps into the empty bottle. Returning to his room, he hid his backpack and Ron's package in the mattress. Hoping that the need he felt to be cautious was really unnecessary, he lay down on the bed and soon fell asleep.

His sleep did not last long however, as it was rudely interrupted by a pounding noise that seemed to arise from a dream, gradually becoming louder and now joined by voices; like two powerful objects colliding. He was certain that he would need to be fully awake when he met these unknown forces and lept from the bed and dressed hurriedly. Then the door swung violently open and a group of hostile people burst into his room, flooding it with light from torches and incomprehensible noise from all who were yelling incoherently.

A man wearing a uniform that Robert had difficulty taking seriously, entered the room proceeded by two others and introduced himself as their commander. The rest of the mob brandished muskets, swords, sabers or pikes and shouted at him to follow their unintelligible orders as he attempted to make sense of their leader's attire.

His blue hat sat askew atop a mangled mess that was his hair. He wore a dark shirt buttoned unevenly as if he had dressed himself in the dark and his horizontal stripped vest was missing a few buttons, perhaps from the pressure exerted by his ample belly. Red pantaloons and shoes that didn't match completed his ensemble.

"Mathurin Dubé, produce your papers," the commander demanded. "We need proof that you are not a conspirator for the Queen."

Smiling in the darkened room, Robert doubted the commander would be satisfied with his U.S. passport. Trying to appear unconcerned as he stood before them with his arms crossed he answered, "I lost them at my relative's home in La Chapelle-Thémer."

The commander was plainly unsatisfied. "You create suspicions with your questions. This is a dangerous time with people like you who are allowed to move about the country with impunity."

"Is that what Moreau told you?" Robert shot back. "Are you his puppets to act as he directs you? The fact is that I am a British subject by an accident of birth. In truth, I am as French as you. I only happen to be born in a country which was once French and is now a British possession. Your questions bore me, commander and now if you don't mind, I want to resume my sleep. Why don't you go to your master Moreau and ask which of his commands you should perform next?"

His statement evidently failed to appease them. If anything it fanned the flames that burned their hatred of him. One bald man with a huge grey beard began brandishing his saber yelling, "If the English should attack France they will find a million men in arms to meet them."

The commander ordered the man to secure his weapon and be silent. Turning his attention to Robert he said icily, "We will leave a guard outside your door this evening and we shall see what disposition to take regarding you and your travels. Your guide will be free to go in the morning. We may decide to detain you here to question you further."

He ordered a heavy dark man holding the pike to step forward and instructed him to stand guard outside the door. The commander bowed to Robert, turned and with an odd gait caused by his mismatched shoes, exited his room followed by the mob.

Robert did not pause to decide what steps to take next. First, he slowly opened his door which led to the balcony. Looking down into the street he saw the commander and the remainder of the men in the midst of a serious consultation. He appeared to instruct two of them to remain at the entrance, left with the balance of his militia and gradually disappeared into the darkness.

Walking as silently as possible, Robert proceeded slowly along the balcony, his back scraping along the brick façade of the hotel until he reached the door which opened into Bernard's room. Thankfully it was ajar and he pushed it open quickly and silently to avoid any noise that might alert the guards below.

He walked to the edge of Bernard's bed, "Bernard," he whispered, prepared to cover his mouth if needed. The response he received was the loudest snore he ever heard.

"Bernard, wake up," he said a little louder. Bernard answered with additional snoring.

"This is just perfect," he whispered to himself. "A million guides in this country and I get one who can sleep sounder than the dead." Looking around the room he walked to the dressing table, filled the basin with water and unceremoniously poured it over Bernard's face.

Bernard's reaction catapulted him upright as he found Robert's hand gripped tightly across his mouth. Even in the subdued light he could see his bitter expression.

"Bernard," hissed Robert. "Those foul letters of your brother's resulted in a visit to my room by the local militia. They intend to detain us for questioning. We need to leave now."

He released his hand from Bernard's mouth "Why, what happened? I'm soaking wet," he said indignantly.

"I tried to wake you quietly, but you wouldn't stop snoring. Now get up, we need to leave immediately," he said impatiently.

Bernard paused as he got out of bed. "Odd that they didn't say anything to me about a guard or answering any of their questions," he said slyly.

Robert understood the implication of his remark. "Listen carefully to me Bernard," he replied ominously. "They may not be interested in you now. But I can guarantee that will change once they discover that it was your brother who gave me those cursed letters. A guard has been posted outside my room and there are two more at the hotel entrance. Use the balcony outside of your window to make your way to the end of the building. Move quietly to your right and when you reach the end of the balcony you will find a set of stairs leading to the street. Run and I mean run to the poste station and harness the team. When you reach the bridge, you will light one of the lamps. I'll be there directly, and if anyone asks where you are going remember that our destination is Brest. Do I need to repeat any of this?"

Bernard had risen and was putting on a dry shirt as Robert walked to the balcony.

"Bernard!"

"Yes?"

"Where are we leaving for?"

"Why we are bound for Brest, of course; my friend," he said with a hint of sarcasm.

"Thank you, Bernard. I'm relying on you. See you soon," and he cautiously returned to the balcony.

After returning to his room, Robert left money on the dressing table for payment his room and the damage that was about to occur this evening. Then, he removed the pillows from their cases and placed them and the blankets beneath the bed sheets. When they were covered in the dim light, it resembled a person sleeping. In bright light, it would fool no one. He took the pillow cases and tore them into strips. A few were inserted into the wine bottle so they would absorb the lamp oil. The remaining strips were tied together and left by the wash basin. In the event that he needed to bind the militiaman who stood guard outside his door, he would need to do it quickly.

As he stood by the balcony, looking for a signal from Bernard, he noticed figures approaching in the darkness. They came into the light and Robert realized that the commander and his militia had returned. He paused at the entrance to speak to the guards and then entered the hotel alone. A few minutes later he heard voices in the hallway.

The commander was busy speaking to the guard, but Robert was unable to understand what was being said. Then he heard a key being inserted into the lock. His heart was racing as he looked around the room and decided to hide next to the bed. If they approached that close, they would have discovered his ruse and he would have to act quickly.

From his position on the floor he saw something in the distance. A lamp was being waved from the bridge. Bernard was waiting! If Robert left now, they certainly would be caught. As much as it tortured him, he would have to wait until the guard left or he bound him with the cloth strips, so he remained crouched in the darkness.

The door opened quietly and the guard entered alone. He stopped when he reached the middle of the room and stood on the carpet, pike in hand. What was the guard's intention, he wondered? Did he intend to strike the figure in the bed? The guard nodded to himself and satisfied that all was well, then turned toward the door. There was some movement in the hallway as he backed out of the room and a moment later he heard the sound of a key turning in the lock and the sound of boots walking down the hallway. He hadn't been aware of it, but Robert now realised that he had held his breath while the guard was in the room. Exhaling, he wiped the perspiration from his forehead.

There were no more voices in the hallway. That was soon replaced by the voice of the commander speaking to his men in the street below. They were laughing now, as they had been offered several bottles of wine. As the bottles were opened, the mood of the men seemed to brighten and he could hear laughter. This created a new problem. As the men began to break their formation and walk away from the building they now had a clear view of the balcony and staircase. He needed a distraction because without one, they would definitely see him as he attempted to exit.

From his door overlooking the street, Robert saw a cart full of wooden crates with a horse hitched to it, to the left of the entrance. He pulled his knife and flint from his backpack and with painstaking silence he moved to his left. Every time his shoe dislodged a piece of debris on the balcony or a small piece of the brickwork from the building fell toward the street below, his heart froze.

Finally, he reached a position directly over the cart. Keeping his back to the street, he knelt on the balcony. Its uneven surface hadn't bothered him through his shoes, but now its weathered, uneven surface felt like knives were cutting into his knees. He desperately wanted to stand but he knew that moving too quickly would bring doom upon him and Bernard. Enduring the pain, he placed the bottle before him and struck the flint until the strips from the pillow case began to burn. As the wick burned, he turned away from the wall and positioned himself above the cart. One of the militiamen saw a light that seemed to fall from the sky, but before he could utter a word to his comrades, Robert's bottle landed directly into the center of the cart and shattered on the wooden crates, setting it ablaze. In an instant, the street was in complete chaos. The militia men dropped their wine bottles. Two men unhitched the horse, which bolted immediately and disappeared around a corner. The other men tried to extinguish the flames. Soon, other people arrived, including the carts owner, demanding an explanation from the commander. In the midst of the commotion no one saw a lone figure descend the stairs from the balcony and calmly walk down the street before running toward the lamp.

"Bernard, let's go," yelled Robert before he reached his carriage. "Head for Versailles and only stop to change horses. If we need to rest, it will have to be by the roadside. Hopefully, we can reach Versailles before they discover our true destination was never Brest."

Bernard headed the horses in the direction of the embankment and Robert sat back into the cushions. He hoped this was the end of the intrigue, but he sincerely doubted it.

THE DAUGHTER OF FRANCE

For the next two days, Robert and Bernard paused at poste stations only to change teams. When they did sleep, they were forced to find a secluded area away from the main road; taking turns sleeping so they could avoid being taken by surprise should anyone from Le Mans have decided to pursue them. There was an abundance of tall trees and shrubs lining the road, which provided adequate cover for them.

After passing through the village of Serge-les-le-Mans, the country side began to change. He saw pine trees and very tall shrubs and ancient farmhouses whose tiled roofs were covered with moss. These were followed by large stands of birch trees. One of the villages had some of the most interesting buildings he had seen since leaving Le Mans. A farm house was so diminutive that he was certain their horse's stables must be larger. Grey in color, it used red brick to frame the windows and corners of the house. In the center of the village stood the tiniest church he could imagine. It had a smooth beige exterior, a brown tiled roof and a charcoal colored steeple which is probably all that the congregation saw as there would only be room inside for their priest.

At the end of the second evening, Robert speculated about what had happened after the commander and his militia in Le Mans discovered that he and Bernard had escaped. Perhaps he had overreacted to the threat from the militia. The point was moot now as it appeared that they must be getting closer to Versailles. The day was drawing to a close now, and Bernard chose a spot to stop for the night. He wasn't certain how much further it would be before reaching the next poste station and decided it would be better to stop here, rather than risk moving about in the dark. They stopped near a bridge which spanned a small lake. A stand of trees shielded them from view from the road and there was water and grass for the horses and Bernard discovered an apple tree which provided a welcome treat for them. If anyone approached, Robert and Bernard would see them first.

In the morning Bernard awoke to a knocking sound. It was not loud or rapid. It was more like the cadence of a clock. With some effort, he began opening his eyes, having forgotten that he had slept beneath the apple tree. Lifting his head, he squinted as he looked directly into the rising sun. He remembered stopping next to the lake after having traveled for two days only stopping to exchange horses. He also recalled how weary he had felt and then fell asleep next to a large tree after unhitching the horses.

Shielding his eyes from the sun, he saw a thin blue mist floating above the lake as Robert walked away from him toward the coach. He was about to sit up when Robert spun around and with one motion, his arm and wrist whipped in his direction. This was followed by a black object which flew toward his head and imbedded itself in the tree. It was followed by two more objects and then Robert walked back to where Bernard now lay wide awake.

Rolling quickly away from the tree, he observed Robert dislodging several pointed metal objects from the bark of the tree. They were circular and had six sharpened blades that menacingly extended outward from the edge.

Bernard asked to hold one. "What are these?" he asked; carefully moving his fingers across the sharpened edges. "It looks like someone could be hurt with this."

"They're called Shuriken and I suppose you could hurt someone. They're intended use is to kill however," Robert replied emotionless, about to return them to his backpack.

"Kill someone!!" shouted Bernard. "You were throwing them at my head! Mathurin, what were you thinking?" He stood quickly, failing to notice a root from the tree sticking above the ground and quickly fell to the spot where he had recently been sleeping.

In rapid succession Bernard heard the same noise above his head, but now he knew what they meant.

"Actually Bernard, every time I throw one of these I think about just how much trouble you and your brother have caused me with those accursed letters of yours."

Bernard looked very concerned. "My friend, seriously, we had no intention of putting you at risk." Robert's silence and grave look made Bernard wonder if he would be sleeping here permanently.

Robert began to chuckle, walked over to Bernard and sat with him against the tree. "Relax Bernard. I'm really not angry. You were actually in the safest spot of all. If I miss the tree, it simply sails off in the grass and away from you. But I've been doing this too long to miss. Now get up and brush the bark from your hair."

He turned and faced the lake and the trees that surrounded it. "This is very peaceful here, don't you think Bernard? The lake and the trees make it seem as if we are far from any city; although it seems odd that I had the impression we were entering a large community earlier. The houses were larger and more numerous, but now I don't see signs of buildings anywhere. We should make plans to leave for Versailles now after we eat. I will begin preparing a meal now if you'll collect wood for a fire.

Bernard looked at the lake as he brushed pieces of the tree from his hair. "It is odd that you say that, my friend. I also noticed that the neighborhoods seemed to grow and then disappear. I have only been to Versailles once, however I feel that we are closer than it seems."

Bernard was about to see something that truly amazed him. Since leaving Le Mans, Robert had insisted on eating only a light breakfast and dinner in order to travel quicker. This also meant avoiding meals at any of the inns along the roadside, something that Robert didn't really miss, but was causing his hefty guide to grumble. While Bernard gathered firewood, Robert walked to the lake and filled a bucket with water. Bernard busied himself preparing to light a fire when he produced two pouches from his backpack. He separated the parts of the pouches and poured water into one of them, waited a minute and slipped one of the parts into the one containing water. In a few minutes he produced spaghetti and meatballs to a speechless Bernard.

"This is magic," breathed Bernard. "How is this possible? First you take the picture and now hot food from water?"

"It is an MRE, a meal ready to eat," explained Robert, as he handed Bernard a fork. "Just one more surprise I have for you." He handed Bernard his meal as they became aware of a noise approaching them.

The distant noise soon revealed itself as the unmistakable rumble of horses pulling a coach. Robert and Bernard walked to the edge of their shelter to obtain a better vantage point when Bernard pointed to a team of six horses. He drew a deep breath when he saw the carriage.

"Mathurin, what you see is a royal coach. A member of the royal family is traveling past us. They must be here to invite you to present yourself to the King," he said with his typically annoying chuckle.

This coach was different from any others Robert had seen. The rear wheels were much larger than those in the front. He was surprised by the number of springs supporting it and the large forward window. There was a door in the center and windows on either side of them. The windows had curtains but they were drawn. He was amazed, but not surprised by the ornateness of it. It was primarily white while the doors and roof were trimmed in gold.

A driver and a coachman sat forward to drive the coach, while a footman stood on a platform in the rear. Robert saw a woman through the open window who stared forward, seeming not to even acknowledge the existence of anything beyond the confines of her comforts.

While Robert turned his attention back to the lake and breakfast, Bernard continued to follow the path of the coach as it neared the bridge. "That's odd," Bernard said almost to himself. "Usually the royal coach would be accompanied by an armed guard."

"So?"

"So, my friend; there are none that I can see. Are you aware of any I may have missed?" as he suspiciously gazed at the coach.

Robert watched the coach for a moment, but lacked the appreciation of what the absence of guards implied and now wanted to finish their morning meal so they could continue their expedition to Versailles.

Bernard continued following the path of the coach as it slowed to cross the bridge. Just as the team reached the opposite side he saw a man jump from a hiding spot behind the wall. "He's trying to stop the coach," Bernard gasped at the same instant as the man fired a shot from his pistol.

Standing transfixed, Bernard could not believe what he was witnessing. As the first man held the team of horses in place by seizing their reins, others began to appear from beneath the bridge. The driver was pulled from his seat and disappeared from view. The other coachman climbed down from his seat and attempted to guard the door to the coach but was immediately struck down by a man with a large staff or a pike. The footman had disappeared also, but the man with the staff was repeatedly striking something on the bridge which appeared to be moving away from the coach.

A scream emanated from the coach's interior as one of the attackers tried to open the door. Reaching through the window, he grabbed someone and the terrible screaming intensified. Robert thought it sounded like a girl calling for help.

He looked at a skillet lying on the ground and grabbed his backpack. Bernard was startled as Robert ran swiftly past him in the direction of the bridge. Using the low shrubs as cover between him and coach, he could see five men on the bridge. The man who had fired the pistol was busy directing the others. Two were entering the coach, one climbed to the top of it and another continued to strike at what he presumed to be the footman.

Passing the cover of the hedges and running onto the bridge, he saw the footman, his face bloodied. His arm was held out to block the blows he was receiving. Obviously, he had no fight left; if he ever had any. His attacker stood over him with staff raised, ready to deliver another; possibly fatal blow when he heard an unfamiliar voice call to him, "Hey you." The startled attacker turned just as Robert's skillet landed squarely on his forehead, driving his head back. The momentum of his swing carried it over his left shoulder and he swept it back and hit him once again in the back of his head. He held the skillet above the man's head for a moment before the attacker slumped face first, to the cobblestone surface.

Now, a six foot long hardwood rod fell from the attackers hand and Robert was quick to arm himself with it.

To his left he saw one coachman lying motionless on his back but he was unable to determine if he was alive from that distance. He noticed some movement and then saw a tall man step over the coachman's body and advance with a pike pointed at Robert's chest.

Screaming as he charged furiously, Robert became aware that another man was attacking from his right with a sabre. Both approached with an air of confidence, for what defense could anyone muster against an attack such as this?

As the man with the pike ran toward him, Robert moved deftly to his left and with one motion, struck the top of the pike with his staff; driving it into the bridge surface where the spearhead snapped off. He delivered a blow to the to the right side of his head man's head, then struck his nose and repeated a strike to his head before hitting him in the back of his knees. His legs collapsed and before his knees touched the bridge surface the staff landed once again his forehead and he collapsed at Robert's feet.

The tall man now lay on the bridge surface between Robert and the man with the sabre. As his accomplice lay motionless on the bridge, the man with the sabre looked less self-assured. He paused for a moment, before charging with his sabre held high. Robert held his ground. By the time he had placed himself in a position to attack, Robert used his staff to deflect his blade, hit him squarely in the solar plexus and as the man dropped his sabre, thrust his staff straight ahead and striking him in the throat. Robert delivered a front kick on his chin and side kick in his ribcage. As he lost his balance, he held his staff with both hands and hit him squarely in the chest, forcing him over the wall and tossed his sword after him. A moment later a splash confirmed that he had landed in the lake.

In the interim, the tall man struggled to return to the fight. His determination was insufficient as he stumbled to his feet and attempted to swing his broken pike at Robert's head. Dropping on one knee, he easily avoided the path of this attack and placing both hands on his staff, raised himself with such force, that when it struck the tall man under his chin he was lifted off the ground. He fell backwards, and a few seconds later the lake received another outlaw.

Robert had lost track of the man who had been lurking on top of the carriage. During his preoccupation with the two men who now resided in the lake, he had descended from the carriage and approached him patiently. From his waistband he drew a short sword. Longer than a dagger and shorter than a sword, it seemed perfectly suited for close quarters fighting. He had the bearing of someone who had every confidence in himself and his weapon. He was shorter but powerfully built. His bald head, menacing eyes and great blank black eyes bothered Robert as much the weapon he held.

He did as expected, making thrusting motions straight forward. Neither person seemed able to gain an advantage. This man would move closer and Robert would block with his staff beyond the reach of the sword. Then the man would retreat to avoid a blow from Robert. This sparring continued for some time, each seeking an elusive deciding advantage. Then he noticed something interesting. The man had no shoes.

When he stepped forward again, Robert drove the end of his staff into the man's instep. As he stumbled in pain, Robert struck his staff against the man's left ear; followed quickly by a blow next to his right eye. He was rapidly becoming disoriented when Robert gripped the staff with both hands and swung his staff downward on the hand holding the short sword. His assailant screamed in pain as his wrist snapped and his weapon fell. He never saw Robert grip the end of his staff with both hands and pivot quickly. The staff delivered a crushing blow to the back of the man's head. The fight was clearly over for him.

Robert relaxed for a moment as the man lay motionless on the cobblestone surface and seemed to have capitulated. He had managed to support himself on his knees, bent at the waist and presumably in terrible pain; while Robert held the staff in one hand. Suddenly, the man produced a knife from his right sleeve and lunged forward. Now the man was too close for the staff to be of much use, and Robert let the staff fall. As the knife came forward, Robert stepped back to his right, grasping his wrist and began twisting his arm back. The knife fell to the ground, but the man refused to yield and began punching Robert in the ribcage. He continued to push his arm further until he felt it break. The man stood for a moment as his left arm hung uselessly and

Robert's side kick to his chest propelled him over the wall to join his accomplices in the lake.

A scream drew his attention back to the coach. He turned quickly to see the sole remaining attacker holding a girl with one arm, while he held a knife to her throat with his right hand. He had finally accounted for the remaining coachman who sat with his back against the wall of the bridge, his forehead bleeding and would be of no assistance.

His look was determined; nearly fanatical, as he continued to hold the blade while he searched for his next strategy. He had probably planned for every contingency except for interference from someone like this. Robert worried about what measures this one was willing to sacrifice to accomplish his goal. This situation was deteriorating quickly and Robert felt that he needed to act. Without breaking eye contact, he reached into his backpack and pulled out three shuriken as the terror in the little girl's eyes grew. Within three seconds the shukira were in flight. The first landed in the hand holding the dagger, causing it to fall from his grip. He screamed as the second hit just below his right cheekbone and he released the girl. He fell back in pain and shock. His stumbling ironically proved to be what saved him as the third would have landed in the right side of his neck, putting an end to the conflict and his life. Instead, it landed in the grass; he fell back across the bridge, ran through the field and disappeared into the distant woods.

Robert heard a distinct and familiar metallic noise, followed by a sound of something landing violently on the bridge's surface. He turned to see Bernard holding the skillet he had used to subdue the initial attacker, who had regained consciousness and decided to use his hidden dagger. Before he could deliver it to Robert's exposed back however, Bernard had acted. Now he held the skillet in his right hand, standing over his fallen foe. He smiled proudly and looked valiantly at Robert, "Sucks to be him, eh my friend?"

He smiled at Bernard's use of the phrase, "Yes Bernard, it definitely sucks to be him." He bent to pick up the dagger the man had dropped, put it inside his backpack and turned to the girl as she stood transfixed, a shocked expression on her face.

She wore a pale blue dress, which at the moment, was similar to paleness in her face. Just a moment ago a dagger was poised at her neck, her fate uncertain. Now someone's blood was splattered on her clothing and cheek. As he walked toward her, he heard the sounds of horses approaching. He was about to speak to her when he noticed the dagger which had been so close to taking her life, lying at her feet. He immediately recognized it as identical to the one he had just placed into his backpack. He turned it over in his hands for a moment before tossing it into the lake. The sound was becoming ever louder as he turned and saw six troops approaching, with an officer on the lead mount.

The girl slowly raised her eyes to meet Robert's as she began to recover from her experience, "You are my savior, brave man. You have done me a great service. Should you not be bowing before me?"

"Well, you're welcome," Robert returned sarcastically. "Wasn't there a woman in the coach with you? I haven't seen her since your coach passed us."

The girls eyes widened and a look of panic swept across her face. "Yes, yes. Our governess is inside. Please tend to her." Robert had already climbed into the coach as the girl completed her sentence.

The governess was about 40 years old with dark brunette hair and very white skin and he thought; astonishingly beautiful. She was just beginning to stir, having apparently fainted when the girl had been dragged from their coach. When she opened her eyes, she revealed deep violet eyes which regarded him with deep distrust. She suddenly sat forward with an anguished face and shouted at him. "Where is the King's daughter?" she said nearly in a state of panic.

"King's daughter?" thought Robert. "Is that what Bernard alluded to earlier?" With perfect timing the previously unknown girl stood by the coach door, glaring at the woman who had yelled so venomously at Robert. "Duchess, control yourself. This man is my savior. He defeated the men who attacked us. He only entered our coach when I ordered him to see to your condition. If he hadn't intervened we might all be dead."

Robert was quickly growing weary of his involvement in the relationship between child and governess and now that he was certain they were unharmed, he felt there was more important matters to tend to outside the coach. Quickly bowing he said differentially, "Mathurin Dubé, pleased to meet you and to be of service," and started to turn back to where Bernard stood over the only remaining highwayman.

The governess extended her hand to Robert. He guessed that she wanted to be assisted from the coach. He held her hand as she stepped onto the bridge and then she continued to hold his hand. "I am Gabrielle de Polastron, Duchess of Polignac and Governess of the children of King Louis XVI. You have just saved the life of Marie-Therese, the daughter of France," she said confidentially.

Robert quickly released her hand and continued in Bernard's direction, "You'll pardon me duchess, but I have a prisoner to tend to and I believe your guard has arrived. This matter may not be finished."

By now the soldiers had dismounted and were securing the area. Robert looked at this girl differently now, then when he saved her from her attacker. "I have never met anyone who could say they were royalty," looking sincerely at Marie-Thérese. "I'm not certain how to address you."

"You may address me as Marie-Thérese," she replied with a poise that surprised him. "I know your name is Mathurin, but I will refer to you as savior, and I will never forget you or what you did today."

Robert touched her shoulder, recalling how a young girl like Genevieve had also affected his life recently by promising to always think of him.

He expected that by now the attackers would be in custody and the injured coachmen would be treated for their injuries. However, as he walked past the coach with Marie-Thérese, what he saw perplexed him. Bernard was being held by a soldier while others had drawn their swords, brandishing them at him and the man who had attacked the coach. Robert and Bernard exchanged glances.

Bernard's terrified expression was directed to an officer on horseback, which caused Robert to look in that direction. This situation seemed to be deteriorating rapidly without explanation. The officer pulled a pistol from his belt and without speaking, took aim at him. A noise like a cannon erupted, and the officer disappeared behind a cloud of smoke, while Robert knew that the shot was intended for him and a ball of lead was headed in his direction.

THE KING'S INVITATION

The report from the pistol startled Robert and he instantly felt the resulting impact of the ball as it smashed into the corner of the Royal coach next to his right shoulder. His natural reaction to the noise was to shut his eyes and this probably saved his sight. With his lids narrowed, the injury to his eyes from the shattered wood was significantly diminished. Still, he was forced to close his right eye from the pain of splinters which had become lodged between his eyeball and his lids. Through a watery image, he could discern the officer dismounting and advancing toward him, sword drawn.

He knew that running would only result in being caught from behind, but standing to fight with no weapon and poor vision was certainly no option. He was about to turn toward the wall of the bridge and dive into the lake when he felt someone brush past him. With his left eye partially open he could see Marie-Thérese positioning herself between Robert and the officer.

"Captain Petit," she yelled. "You will cease this madness immediately. While you were missing, we were attacked and this man saved both my life and the governess'. You and your men will take the prisoners away, now." She demanded.

The captain protested, "But Princess, I need to discover what these men were doing so close to your coach." He had stopped but stood menacingly, pointing his sword at Robert's chest.

"I believe, Captain; that the larger question is why you were missing when you were needed to perform your duty. It is a question that I am quite certain my father the King will demand to be answered." Robert could feel the chill in the air from the icy tone of the daughter of the King as she spoke directly to the captain, ceasing his authoritarian tone.

The footman Robert had saved from being beaten had regained his feet and slowly walked to where Robert stood. He knelt on the bridge and took Robert's hand. "This man saved my life. He defeated five armed men armed with only a staff and a pan. And that man," stretching his arm to point at Bernard, "came from nowhere to stop my attacker from stabbing him in the back."

The other coachman, who had lain motionless on the bridge earlier, now came to his aid. "It is true. I have never seen anything like it. One of them was about to kill me when this man came to save us. He defeated two men at the same time by using that staff. He deserves a reward from the King, not to be treated as a criminal by you, Captain."

Robert shielded his right eye from the bright sun, enabling him to open his left eye a little more. He could now feel some of the loose splinters being washed away by his tears. When he wiped the tears from his cheek he winced in pain as he discovered more splinters imbedded in his cheek. He looked scornfully at the captain. "This man," pointing at the outlaw whom he had struck first, "is your prisoner. Three of his accomplices went into the lake and the one who held a knife to the throat of Marie-Thérèse is on foot in those woods. He has wounds on his right hand and right cheek. Release Bernard. He is no concern of yours."

The captain never responded to Robert's statement, but relented and released Bernard under the incriminating gaze of Marie-Thérèse.

"I have this for you," said a voice behind Robert. Looking back toward the coach, the second coachman who had been sitting against the wall of the bridge came forward. He covered his wounded head with one hand while holding something in the other. He opened his hand revealing the shuriken which had missed the assailant's neck. "I retrieved it for you while the captain was releasing your friend."

The duchess now turned and faced Robert. She took his hand from his face and began tenderly removing the splinters form his cheek. "My child," she said to Marie-Thérèse, "we need to see that your physician tends to our hero."

Turning to Captain Petit who seemed to be tending to the matters of the outlaw in his custody and the search for the remaining outlaws with a very cavalier attitude, the Duchess took charge of the situation. She summoned him to stand before her and spoke in a loud voice, "Captain Petit, we need to return immediately to Versailles. Send two of your men to the palace to inform His Majesty of the attack on our coach and order one of your men to drive their poste chaise to the Palace and send the remainder of your troops to search for the other attackers.

Petit reluctantly complied with the instructions from Gabrielle; as he had always considered her to be a meddling civilian whose main power was drawn from her close relationship to the Queen.

. Bernard ran to the poste chaise and drove it to the bridge. One of the cavalrymen hitched his horse to the coach and drove it behind the Royal coach while Bernard rode inside with the injured coachmen. Inside the royal coach, the governess insisted that Robert call her Gabrielle and focused her attention on removing the fragments from his cheek while his right eye continued to water.

"Mathurin, my savior; what plans do you have now?" asked a concerned Marie-Thérèse.

"I am traveling to Paris to work with a colleague," he explained. "Once that is concluded, I will return home. Locating him is proving to be a bigger challenge than I had anticipated and that will determine how long my stay is. My only real plan was to continue my journey, although I seem to have encountered a delay."

Marie-Therese sat across from Robert, "I hope you will remain with us," she pleaded. It was interesting to him that the daughter of the king of France was imploring him to be their guest at the iconic Palace of Versailles, as he might have asked a friend to do the same when he was a boy growing up at his home in Camillus. Robert could not recollect ever being invited to spend the night at a palace of a king whose garden alone encompassed over 2,000 acres of landscaping.

"Certainly he will child," confirmed Gabrielle. "The King himself will insist that Mathurin remain with us," she said smiling. "Heroism such as his will not go unrecognized or unrewarded. His majesty will take great pleasure in being generous beyond measure to the person who saved his daughters life."

Contemplating the duchesses' last statement, Robert was positive that what she said regarding the measure of gratitude the King would be willing to bestow was accurate. What he desperately needed to do however was continue to his original destination: Paris. He thought also about his immediate needs as he hadn't slept or eaten well since fleeing Le Mans.

Robert was now able to blink and open his right eye and his vision was returning reasonably well. He could still feel some irritation, but felt extremely fortunate that the ball had struck the coach and not him. He smiled at the King's daughter as Gabrielle gently wiped the tears flowing from his right eye.

"It's ironic that you feel I rescued you, when I consider how much worse my condition would be if you hadn't interceded. That captain would surely have tried to kill me if you hadn't been there when I needed help. For now, I would welcome more than anything a hot bath, a warm bed and something to eat. I'm sure that I speak for Bernard too. The past few days have been beyond difficult. Oh, and some bacon would be nice too."

Gabrielle and her young charge both looked at Robert and were stunned into silence after listening to his incredibly simple request. Marie-Thérèse giggled, "My father can grant you anything you wish."

He had other concerns on his mind at the moment, but if the King would grant wishes as his daughter said; it might be more advantageous to formulate them after he had slept.

Bernard was absolutely correct about Versailles being in close proximity to the lake. Shortly after crossing the bridge he saw a tall iron fence on his left, eventually leading to a gate and much larger buildings in the distance. A manmade rectangular lake lined with trees appeared on his left and a very long tall stone wall to the right. As the wall became closer to the road, he could tell from the noise of the horses hooves that they had left the gravel covered dirt road and were now on a cobblestone street. They passed through the main gate with its emerald green fence and gold medallions, beneath the coat of arms of the Bourbon Dynasty. This was the real center of power for France. Marie-Thérèse's great–grandfather, Louis XIV, had built this palace to be the most magnificent in Europe, if not the world.

As the coach slowed to a stop, its doors were immediately opened by servants dressed like the coachmen. Robert was the last one to exit the coach and what he saw took his breath away. The courtyard was enormous, the buildings massive and so ornate that they seemed unreal.

The activity present in the Royal Courtyard was like stepping into that of a cyclone. People were rushing in all directions, but there appeared to be no confusion. Each person knew what his role was, and it was choreographed to the minutest detail. The soldiers had ridden ahead to report on the assault upon the royal coach and now a host of servants and soldiers descended upon the area.

Bernard and Robert were left to stand and watch as servants swirled about the courtyard, all with a duty to perform. The injured coachmen were taken to the infirmary, the Royal coach and his poste chaise were taken away to feed and rest the teams. Robert and Bernard were both staring at the buildings in amazement when their eyes met. Robert's eyes widened, he lifted pressed his hands to his face and said, "Holy Cow, Bernard!!"

Bernard looked puzzled. "My friend, I see no cows. And if I did I don't believe I would consider them to be holy. Is this another one of your odd expressions?"

Robert was about to explain when two servants approached them. "His Majesty will see you now, please follow us," and they turned and walked across the immense courtyard. A door was held open and they entered a large lavishly decorated room where the focal point was a gaming table that resembled a billiard table.

"The King's games room," said one of the servants in a monotone voice.

They passed through an archway into the adjoining room. The servant stopped and faced them. "This is the State Apartment. To your right is the Drawing Room of Plenty. On your left is the Venus Drawing Room, this will lead to the Hall of Mirrors." He turned, expecting Robert and Bernard to follow him. The next six rooms were all connected through a series of doorways located on the right side of the room, so that one could literally see to the end of the State Apartment by standing in a doorway of any of the rooms.

Robert seriously wondered if any of these servants ever smiled. Bernard walked next to him and whispered, "Do you realize what this means? We can ask for anything and it will be granted. We could leave Versailles as nobility." Bernard smiled broadly at that prospect and he behaved as if he already possessed his chateau and the royal pension he expected to receive.

He immediately placed a firm grip and his guide's arm. "Bernard," he uttered in a very low tone, "listen carefully to me. The very last thing you should leave Versailles as is a member of the noble class. Accept anything you like, but being a member of the ruling class could be a death sentence. Have you forgotten what you said to me the day we met in La Rochelle? Haven't you remembered anything you have heard during the past few days? Consider all that before you wish to be a part of that class." Then he withdrew his hand from Bernard's arm as they continued following the servant while he described the names of the rooms in the State Apartment.

The Diana Drawing Room was next, followed by the Mars, Mercury, Apollo and War Drawing Rooms. Each was different, each as impressive as the last and although each was a feast for his eyes, walking through the Drawing Rooms, he was never overcome by the profusion of gold, marble, bronze and mirrors, for throughout the palace the sense of luxury was heightened with its artistry.

Upon entering the War Drawing Room, the servant turned left. Robert sensed an abundance of natural light flowing from the area outside the doorway. They passed through another doorway and into the Hall of Mirrors.

King Louis XVI was seated on his throne immediately inside the entrance to the Hall of Mirrors. Robert later learned this throne was regularly inserted and relocated depending upon the occasion. If the situation warranted it, or depending which country he was from, a representative might find it necessary to walk the entire length of the Hall of Mirrors while the King waited at the end in an orchestrated display of authority.

The King had a very round full face and a large nose. He wore a white powdered wig and a long flowing grey coat with a blue sash worn over one shoulder. A very large; star shaped gold medal was fastened to his coat, directly over his heart.

Marie-Thérèse stood on her father's left. On his right Queen Marie-Antoinette sat very straight and looked at Robert with her deep blue eyes as if attempting to determine exactly what function he should serve at Versailles. Her hair was a light brown color; she had arched thin eyebrows and a dainty nose. Robert thought her dress was enormous. It was light blue and expanded outward from her waist with large blue bows connected to more and more cloth which matched her hat. There was also a dark blue train with gold fleur de lis embroidered into it.

Marie-Therese smiled at him with adoration. "My savior," she shouted as she rushed toward Robert and embraced him. The King smiled but the Queen frowned at their daughter's momentary lack of deportment. Bernard seemed nearly overcome by the introduction to the royal family. Robert briefly placed an arm around his small admirer and quickly released her.

The duchess was positioned just behind the children and continued smiling at him. When she smiled he thought she had the absolutely the whitest teeth he had ever seen. One boy remained standing where Marie-Thérese had been. This was her brother, Louis-Charles, four years old.

Robert knelt before Marie-Thérese as he spoke to her. "How are you feeling? I didn't have a chance to speak to you about those men at the bridge."

She spoke quietly and confidently. "I was terrified in the beginning; but then I saw you turn and face him and I knew that I would be saved," and she threw her arms around his neck.

Bernard began clearing his throat, giving Robert the sense that this meeting was completely about being presented to the King and not a reunion with Marie-Thérese. Robert stood and tried to look apologetically at the royal family while their impish daughter returned to their side.

Sunlight entering the Hall of Mirrors created a sensation so intense that Robert was disoriented for a moment. The throne was positioned in such a way that the illumination seemed to emanate from it.

Bernard looked straight ahead, "Holy Cow," he whispered.

"Bernard?" Robert questioned. "Shouldn't we be bowing or kneeling or something?"

"I am guessing that a very deep bow would be appropriate," he murmured; staring down as if the answer was on the floor.

"Should we say something to the King?" whispered Robert.

"I just guessed about bowing. It is your turn to guess how to address him," Bernard whispered back.

Bowing sincerely in unison, Robert managed to say, "Your Majesties," slowly enough to give Bernard time to repeat the address. They cautiously looked up from the floor to see the King walking toward them.

"Arise, arise my brave young men," the king said in a voice that made the Hall of Mirrors ring. "My daughter and the duchess have both told us about your valiant defense of them. As a grateful father and the sovereign of France, I am forever in your debt."

Placing his hands on Robert shoulders, the King kissed him on both cheeks and repeated this gesture with Bernard. "Eventually, I want you to tell me everything that happened on the bridge today. But first I understand that you are tired and need rest. These servants will show you to your rooms. When you are rested, we will talk."

The King gestured to servants who without a word led them through the Hall of Mirrors. Bernard was shown to his room first; Robert's was located further down the corridor. They opened the doors for him and escorted him into a room that was beyond description of any chamber he had ever seen or imagined. The floor was an amazing hardwood parquet design with a large painting hung before him which looked like a gathering of several royal families. A door was positioned at either end of the room and a painting hung over each. Several large windows about twelve feet high afforded a magnificent view of the grounds, which the servants were now closing. Against one end of the room was a beautiful fireplace. It was made of pink marble with a gilded mirror above it that rose to the ceiling. The bed was positioned next to the fireplace and a large partition had been placed nearby. Behind the partition, the servants showed Robert an inviting tub of hot water with steam rising from it. A clothes rack with new garments hanging from it stood ready for him when his bath and rest were completed. After he slipped into the tub the servants bowed and left him to his thoughts.

These recent events in his life, since he left the borrowed house on the Nation and arrived in La Rochelle, began to filter through his mind. How all these incidents could have culminated as the guest of Louis XVI at Versailles could not have possibly been imagined. Now he was immersed in both his thoughts and bathtub in his private salon. Soon he changed into a sleeping robe and settled into the most comfortable bed he could have conceived. He laid in it, placed his backpack next to him and Ron's envelope under his pillow as he studied the intricacies of the two chandeliers hanging from the white, gold trimmed ceiling and was soon fast asleep.

When he awoke, he couldn't recall a time when he felt more refreshed. As he dressed before one of the mirrors, he admired his appearance in clothes made of silk and linen and felt these might be the most splendid clothes ever made. He had an aqua colored coat with gold trim with a matching vest and pants and white breeches and black shoes with gold square buckles.

He opened some of the windows and felt the warmth of sunlight on his face. Pleasing as his room was and now fully rested; he felt a desire to get out of these surroundings and explore the Palace gardens.

One of the servants had remained outside in the hallway. As he opened the door, the servant bowed, "Sir, I am to take you to the Hall of Mirrors. The Duchess and the Daughter of France have requested that I take you to them," he said dispassionately. He led Robert to join Bernard who was preoccupied with alternately looking through the windows to first admire the view of the gardens and then to admire the reflection of his new clothes in one of the many mirrors.

"The Hall was originally built to link the north and south apartments," the servant explained. Robert counted seventeen immense arched windows, offering an amazing view of the gardens and beyond that stretched as far as the horizon. The vaulted ceilings were decorated with paintings that celebrated the reign of Louis XIV.

"Magnificent as it is, its purpose mostly serves as a passageway from the King's apartment to the Queen's, men and women live separately. The Hall contains 357 mirrors. When the Palace was being constructed, the secret of making mirrors was owned by the Venetians. That secret was stolen, allowing the mirrors to be made locally, which saved money and time." The servant smiled for the first time that Robert was aware of; when he mentioned the fact that the secret had been stolen without mentioning by whom.

"My friend," said Bernard, still mesmerized by the view of the pools and gardens and his own reflection, "I realise that I joked about your plans to visit the Palace of Versailles. Now that we are guests of the King, I will never doubt you again."

"You are a wise man, Bernard," he answered with his arms folded, looking at the view of the magnificent gardens.

He felt an arm reaching through his, while another partially encircled his waist. To his right stood Gabrielle and on his left he saw Marie-Thérese smiling up at him and holding her brother's hand, she asked Robert to kneel in front of her. "The King is speaking with the Russian Ambassador. We decided," nodding to Gabrielle; "that we would all walk through the gardens until we are called to dinner."

Gabrielle gently squeezed his hand, "It would give us great pleasure and would be an honor to show you our favorite parts of the gardens. Later, the King will show you how he can demonstrate the level of appreciation he has for the acts of heroism you and Bernard performed."

Marie-Thérese and Louis-Charles chased each other, as the party walked from the chateau toward an exit which led to the gardens. They were followed at a respectful distance by a different pair of servants who rushed forward to open doors and then retreated until their services were required.

Their tour began by walking across the open courtyard between two large rectangular pools with the Palace behind them. Reaching the end of the pools, Gabriele turned left and continued down a path lined with tall manicured hedges like one would find in a maze. Gabrielle strode through an opening in the hedges into a circular area with a multi-tiered waterfall at the opposite end of the circle.

The area surrounding either side of the waterfall resembled an amphitheater consisting of eight grass covered tiers. This incredible waterfall needed to be observed from both a distance and very close to be fully appreciated. Separated by several very low narrow cement walls, water cascaded until reaching a pool. Next to each pool stood a base large enough to support a stand, upon which rested a large gilded vase, about 5 feet tall. The sections of the waterfall alternated between seven and eight tiers in height. As Robert drew nearer to the waterfall, he noticed how unusual the surface appeared. It was not smooth as it had appeared from distance; in fact it was very uneven; constructed of shells which enhanced the rippling effect as water spilled them.

Robert turned to question Gabrielle about the waterfall when she walked over and held his hand. She spoke quietly as she pulled his hand into the falling water and ran his fingers across the shells. "Mathurin, those shells were fetched from

Madagascar solely for this waterfall. The colors they provide are why Louis XIV wanted them."

She led him away from the others and held both his hands. "You are our hero, but the attention and gratitude you will be shone is much deeper than that. The King loves his children dearly. His son, Louis-Joseph recently passed away and to come so close to losing his daughter, who was saved by you gives him hope. That is why you will always be welcome here by their family and in my home as my brother."

He paused to absorb what Gabrielle said. While most of Louis XVI's subjects were aware of the misfortunes that had already befallen the Royal family, none but Robert was aware that of the Royal family members, only Marie-Thérèse would survive the French Revolution.

Gabrielle continued to talk, but Robert's thoughts centered on the impact of what was about to occur. Everything was so peaceful here. He knew that he could remain in Versailles and be nearly invisible. He also was conscious that Versailles was as surreal as the talk he had with the aged looking woman behind the miserable excuse for an inn. Living in Versailles is like living in a dream world; but they were sitting on a powder keg without realizing it.

Gabrielle slipped her arm through Robert's and they exited the Rockwork Grove. They walked past fountains, statues and down paths lined with trees and shrubbery. He noticed that Bernard was falling behind and seemed to be losing interest in their walk. He waited for Bernard to rejoin them and asked if he really wished to continue.

"My friends, I would like permission to take my leave of you now. I feel a need to sleep in the bed I slept in last night at least once more. It's doubtful that I will ever be that comfortable again."

Robert grinned and looked away, knowing that it was really Gabrielle's permission he needed. The Duchess merely nodded and turned to a servant. "Guide monsieur back to his apartment and wait outside while he sleeps. He will join us for our evening meal with the royal family in the dining room."

Bernard and the servant both bowed to her and he was led back to the Palace which dominated the skyline.

Gabrielle next took Robert to The Colonnade. Within a perfect circle of about one hundred feet in diameter, rose an inner ring of 32 columns of pink and blue variegated marble; which in turn were connected by 32 arches to an outer ring of 32 marble rectangular piers for support. Each of the arches was decorated with a marble cornice, placed in the center of the arch. Beneath each arch, level with the ground; was a fountain on a base about two feet tall.

The children ran among the columns playing some pre-arranged game. Robert couldn't resist staring at the workmanship involved in creating this. It was like standing inside a work of art.

"It is beautiful, is it not?" said Gabrielle.

"Beautiful can't begin to describe this," he agreed, gazing at the intricacies of the marble. He wandered around the columns and across the open center of The Colonnade, looking at it from every conceivable angle. When he was satisfied, he returned to the bench where Gabrielle waited. She seemed to be concentrating intently about something, which made him a little anxious.

"Mathurin, my dearest brother," Gabrielle said pulling herself closer. "Have you given any thought to your future?"

Continuing to look skyward he thought, "Well Gabrielle, very soon; I hope to be 240 years into the future," but for the moment decided to keep that comment to himself.

"With the great service you have done for His Majesty...."

"Here it comes."

"I am positive His Majesty will bestow upon you a title and land and arrange a suitable match for you. Your future couldn't be better than in France." She spoke so seductively that for a moment, Robert actually gave her proposal serious consideration.

"I am certain that His Majesty would be very generous," he replied. "However I'm not interested in profiting from my actions. My plan is to conclude my business in Paris and to return home. Although, I definitely intend to ask His Majesty for his assistance in one particular area. The remainder is very complicated."

"Is there someone who will be waiting for you to return?" she asked softly.

Robert thought for a moment. The closest he had been to any sort of a relationship lately had really been sharing drinks and pizza with Gina Abramson. "No, no there is no one waiting for at home, Gabrielle."

"Well then perhaps there is someone here is waiting for you," she said prophetically.

He wondered how or even if he could respond to Gabrielle's suggestion, when he was distracted a truly amazing fountain. "This is the Fountains of the Animals," as she swept her arm before them.

It was comprised of two fountains, surrounded on three sides by groves of trees. The water from these fell into two smaller fountains. There were three statues that stood like sentinels, guarding each of the pools.

Further on was something he could not have expected. Gabrielle called it the Hamlet. It was a village that had been created on the banks of the Great Trianon Lake. He counted twelve houses around a pond whose water was so still that it looked like a mirror. The Queen had a cottage built there just for her, although referring to it as a cottage was not very accurate.

Very large and surrounded by trees, it stood two stories tall with dormers above each window and a balcony which ran the length of the cottage. It even had a gazebo, which didn't look as it had been used to any degree.

As they continued their walk, Robert realized that The Hamlet was more than a collection of simple homes; it was actually a working village. A family waved to them from the front yard of a simple house, amid roaming fowl and livestock.

"Here the gardens are cultivated, the fields plowed, the trees pruned and the fruit gathered. From the gallery of her cottage, the Queen and I can watch Serge using his donkey to carry corn to be ground at the mill," explained Gabrielle, nodding in the direction of a man dressed in peasant's clothes.

As the path turned away from the Queen's cottage, a woman busily washed clothes on the banks of the pond next to Gabrielle's cottage, a gift from the Queen. It was a much smaller cottage, but he felt that it was actually more attractive than the Queen's dwelling. "Its odd how people sometimes feel that possessing something solely because it is the largest, is somehow equal to it being the best," he thought.

Gabrielle's cottage was surrounded by a low, very dense hedge with a small wooden gate. It was positioned across the pond from the Queen's cottage and while it was distinctive in its own right, it was clear from its appearance that it was never meant to overshadow her benefactor's.

What he especially liked about this cottage was how it would never be confused with any other. While the roof line appeared to have been designed with no planning, the gardens in front of it were completely organized. The upper story had doors that opened outward where no balcony existed, while a graceful staircase wound its way around the cottage, connecting the gardens in front with the pond in back. There were potted flowers everywhere there was space for them. It was like Gabrielle controlled the parts of her cottage that she could, leaving the remainder to the King's builders.

He was totally captivated by both the tranquility and irony of The Hamlet. This was one of the most relaxing, peaceful places he had ever seen. At the same time, he pondered why someone who lived in one of the most magnificent palaces on earth; would build a simple village in its shadow. Is this what the King thinks that life is like for his subjects? He doubted that the King was aware or even cared about the true condition of those who lived and starved or participated in food riots simply to survive when they lived beyond the walls of The Hamlet.

He was about to broach the subject with Gabrielle when a servant approached them from the direction of the Palace. "Pardon me Duchess; the King has requested your attendance for the evening meal."

Returning to the Palace, the Duchess, as someone who had already walked over every inch of the gardens, explained why she loved it so. "In the gardens, the patterns with their embroidery of colorful flowers, the pastures and the paths lined with marble statues and carved fountains; everything echoes the splendor of the palace, through on a much larger scale. It extends into infinity, beyond the views of the Royal Avenue and sparkling waters of the Grand Canal."

Robert had had the idea that because Versailles was the King's residence, he would only see people who lived and worked there. But it was just the opposite. He was surprised to find visitors ranging from the very wealthy to the commonest laborer walking about the gardens and in the palace itself. People of less than noble birth seemed to have access to areas of Versailles that he felt was intrusive.

When he mentioned this to Gabrielle she quoted Pierre de Nolhac, "Ever since the days of Louis XIV, foreign tourists and ordinary Frenchmen had been permitted to wander about in the gardens and inside the palace from apartment to apartment to watch the King and his relations leading their lives in public in an animated waxworks show."

She admitted that she had questioned the Queen, who was not an advocate of the nearly unlimited access to the royal family. She was always worried about security, but there was never an incident. The King wished to above all, uphold the tradition of unfettered access to Versailles. He could only hope that they would have dinner without being a sideshow for some of the tourists whom they passed in the Gardens.

The dining room had a full length mirror at either end and two slightly smaller mirrors on the opposite walls. A large table of very dark wood, with three drawers trimmed in gold, was positioned beneath one of the mirrors. The room itself was an eggshell white with a gold colored border. There were large paintings above each of the doors with smaller paintings at various places on the walls. A substantial intricately designed chandelier hung near each of the floor length mirrors. The dining table itself wasn't as large as Robert had expected. There was just enough seating for the Royal family and a few guests. The chairs were covered in a bright blue fabric, while the wood and table matched the dark wood of the gleaming floor.

Two chairs at the head of the table were unoccupied for now, but the royal crest embroidered into them left no doubt who they were reserved for. Robert was directed to a chair on the left side of the table closest to where the King and Queen would sit. A servant had been sent to fetch Bernard and he placed him on Robert's right and next to Bernard was seated a very distinguished looking gentleman. He wore red and silver robes with an emblem that Robert didn't recognize. Slightly bald with grey hair and a long thin nose, he stared ahead as if waiting to be introduced before conversing.

He was searching for some way to begin a conversation with him, when a servant stepped into the doorway and announced, "Their majesties, the King and Queen." All stood and seats. The King was seated closest to Robert while the Queen sat on the Kings left. Another man stood in the entrance to the dining room, waiting to be introduced.

"His Majesty Joseph II, the Holy Roman Emperor," announced a servant.

As a servant pulled a chair away for him to be seated, Robert thought he looked remarkably like the Queen. He smiled and nodded but didn't speak to Robert or Bernard. They smiled back and Robert looked across the table at Gabrielle. Next to her sat the children, Marie-Thérèse, and Louis-Charles. Marie-Thérèse looked adoringly at Robert, while her brother fidgeted in his chair.

Gabrielle looked intently at Robert and then to the as yet to be introduced gentlemen. "Monsieurs, you may be acquainted with the exploits of these two men. They defended the life of Marie-Thérèse against five armed men. They are the King's guests of honor this evening. Allow me to introduce to you, Mathurin Dubé and Bernard Badeau."

As the older man now turned to Robert, Gabrielle continued; "Robert and Bernard, I would like you to meet Joseph II, the Holy Roman Emperor; brother of the Queen and Ivan Simolin; the Russian Ambassador to France." Ivan rose and bowed deeply to Robert and Bernard, while Joseph II nodded, with a pompous attitude in their general direction; they also rose waited for the royal couple to be seated before returning to their and bowed in return; still uncertain if it was proper or not.

The King wore completely different clothes than he had earlier, of course. They were however, no less resplendent. He spoke alternately to Robert and Bernard and his other guests while the Queen and Gabriele became absorbed in a private conversation with Marie-Thérèse. The Russian ambassador and the Emperor were both very curious about learning every detail surrounding the attack, especially the facts connected to their victory over five armed men. The King was silent, but seemed to listen with unmatched interest.

His willingness to describe the details of the attack had nearly reached his limit, when the ambassador suggested that Robert re-enact the entire episode. Gabrielle sensed his weariness to continue and Bernard seemed perfectly content to remain mute and focus on his wine. Gabrielle was about to intervene on Robert's behalf when a servant announced that the meal would now be served.

Robert's curiosity about the King's menu was about to be answered. He was certain of one thing; whatever had been prepared; there would be abundance, as the King looked like he was no stranger to food. While the dishes were served, he thought this was much more than simply serving, it was a major presentation.

The courses consisted of four different types of soups, stuffed pheasant, roasted duck and mutton with gravy. This was followed by salad and then pastries, fruits and jams.

One of the chefs spoke to Robert directly. Bowing, he addressed Robert, "Monsieur Dubé, we understand that you have a certain love of bacon. While we don't serve that particular dish at Versailles, we do make Lardons, which are cubes of pork and we use them as part of a salad. We hope you will enjoy them." He bowed again and stepped away.

Before he could respond properly, another chef approached and bowed. He was tall, blond and had deep blue eyes. "My name is Jan van Ryn. I am one of the chefs of the royal kitchen and my home is in the south of the Netherlands. We have prepared a very special dish we call Spek, or in English; bacon. It has been marinated in spiced oil and seasoned with salt, pepper and herbs and slowly cooked."

A servant placed a large plate before Robert, consisting of separate pieces of bacon wrapped around scallops. Gabrielle's advice about accepting the possibility that the King would propose he remain at Versailles, was becoming increasingly attractive. "We hope you will approve," said Jan, bowing and exiting the room.

He was stunned. By the time he recovered from this surprise, Jan had left and Gabrielle softly suggested, "Mathurin, the Spek looks very appealing; you may want to eat some of it as well."

This was quite possibly the most flavorful bacon Robert had ever tasted. As he consumed his third piece, he considered the possibility of returning to the 21st century with one of the King's chefs. After all, Gabrielle had informed him that nearly 500 servants were involved in serving the King his meal. Surely they wouldn't miss one chef. So many people were involved in the ceremony of seeing to the wishes of the King, that pouring a glass of wine seemed to take forever. "I don't want to even think about how long it would take to pour me a pint of a Smokin' Indian," he thought.

The meal was nearly finished when a servant entered the room, whispered to the King and stood waiting for instructions. Barely acknowledging the servant, the King raised his right hand and spoke in a nearly imperceptible tone while he communicated his instructions and then motioned for him to leave.

While the servant backed away from the King in the direction of the doorway, the King smiled and looked first to the Queen and then at Gabrielle and his children, before turning to Robert and Bernard.

"There is something of tremendous importance that awaits us outside; courtesy of Marie-Thérese."

Robert caught the gaze of his young admirer whose widening grin was obviously hiding a very large secret. Now the servants began to follow their instructions and almost immediately the dining room became a center of the prearranged activity he was becoming accustomed to. Doors were opened, chairs were moved from the table and all were assisted as they rose and walked to the doorway. The King was the epicenter, acting totally oblivious to it all. The servants gave the royal couple the illusion of weightlessness, as the entourage swept them away like the rushing waters of some great flood.

He stood, observing these proceedings and noticed that the servants were now waiting for him to react.

Fortunately, Gabrielle knew what was about to happen next and she slipped her arm through his, while Marie-Thérese walked beside them. They followed in the wake of the King and Queen's departure.

Gabrielle noticed Robert's intense curiosity regarding the orchestration required to move the King from the dining room.

"Mathurin, you too would become accustomed to this, if you remained here. The King's every action and gestures are the pretext for a ceremony, his rising and retiring, his meal or his walk in the Gardens. A dazzling audience is present when the King attends Mass, or grants an audience to a foreign ambassador. The court fills the palace with a life, a vitality that will last forever."

Robert considered what she just said, especially the implication of the last sentence. He winced when she ended with the word "forever". The King's grandfather, Louis XIV was referred to as the "Sun King", Louis XVI was now referred to as the "Restorer of French Liberty". Soon he would be tragically remembered as "Louis the Last". He did have to admit however, that the spectacle surrounding the King was truly amazing, while at the same time very sad. He wondered if Louis XVI spent any time whatsoever contemplating the reality that his subject's colossal suffering made this illusory existence possible, when he could engage his immense power to help lift them out of their misery. He thought the answer would be a defining no.

Soon, they were seated outside the palace, on a dais built purposefully for this evening's event. With the Hall of Mirrors as a backdrop, Robert looked at the twin pools and the distant trees surrounding the gardens.

In the faltering daylight, streaks of red adorned the sky before retreating as evening approached. Robert sat between Marie-Thérese and Gabrielle. Bernard busied himself with wine and entertaining the Russian ambassador and the Emperor with his account of his role in the rescue of the King's daughter.

Commoners were still wandering through the Gardens. Several guessed that Robert was the King's guest and while most were content to glance and smile at him, a few were forward enough to hesitate and approach him; after bowing before the King and Queen. Some merely wished to touch his hand and one very emotional woman kissed him on the cheek.

A servant arrived with a silver tray with several small glasses containing a dark liquid, first presenting them to the King and Queen before being offered to their guests.

"This is Cointreau," explained Gabrielle as she raised two glasses from the tray, handing one to him and Bernard. "It is the King's favorite liqueur to enjoy after dinner, which comes from a village next to Angers. I believe you visited that area on your travel to Versailles."

They sipped Cointreau and as Robert enjoyed its warmth, Marie-Thérese tugged on his sleeve. She was looking up at him as he turned to face her. "This is in your honor my savior, and Bernard as well." He welcomed her smile as always and his puzzlement about her last statement did not last long. A deep popping noise arose behind him followed by a thunderous explosion. A brilliant red starburst appeared overhead. The greater part of the evening was spent by royalty and commoner alike, witnessing a dazzling fireworks display that he would not have thought possible in the 18th century. He guessed they were launched from the roof above of the Hall of Mirrors. While the evening sky was rocked with explosions from the fireworks, the Gardens were quiet and peaceful as everyone sat still, enthralled by a girls expression of appreciation for her rescuers.

When the fireworks had concluded, the whirlwind that accompanied the King and Queen, swept them away again as they retired to their apartments. Before he left, the King told Robert and Bernard to stand before him and the Queen. Following their bows before the King, he spoke, "Tomorrow morning you will be served breakfast in your apartments. Following that we will meet in the Hercules Room to discuss your futures. Bonne niut."

Returning to their apartments, Bernard exuded gratification. With a contented grin he passed painting after painting as if he was convinced that he belonged here. "Our futures," he repeated dramatically. "The King wants to talk to us regarding our futures. Would anyone imagine that I could depart La Rochelle a common laborer and return a member of nobility, with land and wealth and a title. Who could wish for anything grander?"

Robert stopped Bernard, grabbed his arm and spun him so quickly it startled him. He lowered his chin to give Bernard the full effect of his glare.

"Bernard, be very careful what you wish for. We have had this conversation before. Making the wrong choice here could be fatal. Don't get blinded by all this wealth and influence around you. We will return to the real world soon and you need a clear mind to make the right decision."

Bernard glared angrily and forcefully pulled his arm loose from Robert's grip. "You don't want me to become as significant as you are. That is it; you would always have me as your servant. Well, not after tomorrow; not after tomorrow." He turned and stormed down the hall.

"Bernard, what I want for you, is to live to see your next birthday. Make a good decision tomorrow." There was no reaction to his remark and he returned to his apartment and hoped seclusion would help his guide to choose the proper path. A bath had been drawn for him and a fresh night shirt hung next to the tub. After his bath he had time to more closely examine the fine paintings, dazzling sculptures and woodwork in this magnificent room. Then he climbed into his bed and focused on the chandelier, wondering how tomorrows events with the King would influence his plans to move closer to Paris.

THE DECISION

The following morning, he was awakened by a soft steady knocking at his door. It was opened slowly by a servant whom he recognized from dinner with the King. A silver cart was wheeled into his room pushed by Chef Jan, who seemed very pleased to find Robert awake. Two more servants entered the room and placed a small table next to an open window which faced the Gardens. A single chair was positioned so he could look out onto the Gardens while he enjoyed breakfast.

Jan positioned the cart next to the table and enthusiastically revealed what lay beneath the silver lid. There were teas and fruits with a variety of jams and breads on the tray. Jan paused for dramatic effect before lifting the smaller lid to reveal a plateful of spek.

"The serving of meals is usually left to the lesser servants, however I wanted this to be special so I delivered it myself," Jan said as he pulled the chair back to properly seat Robert.

"Is this what they meant by the royal treatment?" thought Robert.

"Jan, I want you to know this is beyond anything I would have expected. Why don't you join me? A meal like this should be shared."

"Oh no, M. Dubé, that would absolutely be improper for someone in my station to sit in the company of a guest of his Majesty." Jan paused somewhat awkwardly before continuing. "I do have one request to ask of you monsieur, however."

Robert turned in his chair and looked inquisitively at Jan. "Yes of course, Jan. What is it?"

Jan fidgeted uncomfortably. "It has been rumored that his Majesty will bestow a title upon you for you action in saving his daughter. Your chateau will need a kitchen staff and a chef to operate it properly. If you would please consider me when you select your staff, I would be eternally grateful. My family remains in Gorinchem because they're not allowed to live here with me. If I find a position away from Versailles, they could possibly join me; if you would allow it."

Robert stood and placed a hand on Jan's shoulder, "Of course, I'd consider you Jan. Are you telling me that you are capable of doing everything it takes to run the kitchen; staff and order the food?"

"Yes sir, these are just a part of my present duties."

"That's interesting Jan. What does one do when they are in charge of a kitchen and its staff?" Describe to me what you would do in a in a typical day as the chef of my kitchen."

Jan proceeded to explain in detail, the intricacies of being in charge of a kitchen. It was clear to him that Jan could perform the details involved with operating a kitchen, whether it was his own or if he performed these duties in the Palace.

They shook hands before Jan left him to savor his breakfast and an excellent view of the Gardens. He wanted to appreciate the food and the view because he couldn't tell how long each would last after his visit with the King.

When breakfast was finished, the servant removed the cart from the room while another entered and stood next to the doorway. "The Governess of the Children of France," he announced and a moment later Gabrielle entered the apartment.

To say that Gabrielle simply walked into a room was the epitome of understatement. She was so graceful in her movement and exuded such confidence that she seemed to drift across the threshold and fill the room with her energy. Robert thought that of all the memories that he would carry from this adventure, hers would be one of the most enduring.

Today she wore a long yellow dress with a matching hat and lace surrounding her neckline. She walked to Robert holding her outstretched hands, taking his and kissed him on both cheeks. "Mathurin, my brother, today is such an exciting moment for you. The King will bestow whatever honor you desire upon you. You must be excited beyond measure." Turning to stand beside him, she put her arm inside his and with a beaming smile said, "Come let us see what his Majesty has in store for you. But before we do, there is something very special I wish to show you."

As they exited this room for what would be the last time, Robert reflected that she never asked if he wanted her to walk with him. Was it presumptuous on her part that one would not want to be in her company or was she merely a gracious host on behalf of the King, or a good friend making him feel comfortable? In the end he decided it was best not to over analyze this, because as a practical matter, it really didn't matter. He would, of course; be totally lost at Versailles without her; she was simply a joy to be with. He also imagined that she could be a valuable friend and judging from the amount of deference, sometimes bordering on fear shown her by the staff, she could doubtless be an extremely powerful enemy. Plus it was always nice to be in the company of a beautiful woman, it made him look especially charming.

They passed through the State Apartment, which he remembered led to the Hall of Mirrors. Then they entered two unfamiliar rooms on his right, one which overlooked the Marble Courtyard and the Royal Courtyard. What struck him about this room was an abundance of pink in a variety of shades. A very handsome carpet lay in the center of the room with a predominantly pink influence. The floor was an intricate wood pattern with a reddish color, and the floor length curtains matched the carpet. White walls were framed in gold borders with gold ornamental work between. However, the room seemed to be built around a desk which Gabrielle stood next to.

"This is the King's Private Cabinet," she said, resting one hand on it. "I saw how much you appreciated the Colonnade and thought you would also appreciate his Majesty's desk. The King wanted a desk where he could hide his papers and this is was created for that purpose. It took nearly ten years to create."

Gabrielle was right. This was an incredible creation. A small clock was surrounded by a metal ornament which was centered on the desk's top. It was handmade artwork crafted from inlaid tableau and bronze. Just viewing it from various angles was indeed a reason to pause and remember that this was the effort of one man. When he thought he had absorbed everything about the desk, Gabrielle had another surprise. From her dress, she produced a key and placed it in the desk's solitary keyhole, which was surrounded by a metal Fleur-de-Lis. It turned effortlessly one quarter of a turn and the top as well as the drawers all were unlocked.

He spoke to her, while still looking at the desk, "You were absolutely accurate about this, Gabrielle. This desk is the definition of unique. There can't be any equal to this on earth." He paused to collect his thoughts before changing the subject to a more serious matter. "Gabrielle, I hope what I am about to tell you doesn't shock you, but I'm not sure if I can accept a gift of lands and wealth from the King. I feel more inclined to serve him in some capacity, than to be a part of all this," as he swept his hand across the room.

Gabrielle locked the desk with another turn of her key and merely smiled at Robert. "Now it would be the first time anyone has ever witnessed anything like that. A gift from the King is not something that is easily cast aside, so I trust you to speak from your heart, Mathurin. More than anything, I believe that his Majesty trusts you and values your happiness. Tell him exactly what you desire and he will grant it."

"We should leave now to meet with the King so he can discuss your future. I believe that if you are honest with him, he will grant you whatever you wish. He will see us in the Hercules Salon. It is a truly amazing room." She led him through the King's library at the end of the State Apartments and into the Hercules Salon.

Some people had preceded them, including Bernard; having also been summoned by the King. The first that he noticed were two men in military uniforms. Their backs to Gabrielle, they stood next to each other, facing the courtyard outside without speaking. When the servants saw Robert and Gabrielle enter the salon, they both bowed and one immediately left the room; presumably to possibly notify the King. Both officers then turned and bowed to Gabrielle and nodded courteously in Robert's direction. The officer on his right immediately smiled and approaching her, took her hand and kissed it and she in turn kissed him on both cheeks. He was tall and handsome with dark brown hair, blue eyes and a moustache. He was unfamiliar to Robert, but he immediately recognized the second officer as the one who had shot at him on the bridge.

Gabrielle enthusiastically introduced Robert to the first officer. "This is our captain of the Royal Guard, Joseph Hyacinthe François de Paul Rigaud, the Compte de Vaundreiul. Captain, I wish to introduce you to our gallant heroes, Mathurin Dubé and Bernard Badeau."

"Mathurin, I believe you are acquainted with Captain Petit." Petit nodded expressionless as Robert involuntarily brushed his cheek where the splinters had become embedded in his skin and returned his nod with an icy stare.

With that, the captain's face beamed as he embraced Robert warmly. "Pardon me sir, but this is an honor to meet you. Your action on the bridge is already a legend. Disarming ten men in defense of the King's daughter and the Duchess is the epitome of bravery. You must tell me sometime how you accomplished that."

Robert could feel himself blush. In addition, the praise the captain accorded to him, made the officer who shot at him, look worse than when Marie-Thérèse had admonished him on the bridge and it was completely apparent from the tortured expression face.

Trying to defuse the situation Robert said, "Well captain, there were actually only five men, and we had a frying pan." Although, when he heard his words leave his lips, he thought he may have just made matters worse.

Captain de Riguad laughed out loud. "A frying pan, a frying pan, well perhaps we should start arming our troops with pans, eh Petit?"

That barb was clearly intended for Petit and it hit its mark. Robert gathered that François didn't care at all for Petit and was using this affair to insult and embarrass him. François refocused his attention on Robert and Bernard's defense of Marie-Thérèse.

"Seriously Mathurin, can you show me how you managed to disarm those assailants? As a military man, I am very interested. What weapons did they carry?"

He briefly described the short sword and daggers and the pike which seemed to interest François immensely. He once again, used this information to sow more seeds of disquiet with Petit who stood uncomfortably by the window.

François spoke loud enough for all to hear, "So Mathurin, do you think that Captain Petit and the troops under his command could have stopped these highway men from attacking a royal coach by using frying pans? I guess we will never know because they arrived just in time to arrest you and your friend Bernard, leaving us to wonder where are those who escaped? That is just too hilarious for words, don't you agree?"

Robert glanced quickly at Petit who was seething and tried to change the subject by questioning Gabrielle. "One difference I seem to notice about the Hercules Salon, Gabrielle, is there are only two paintings here, while so many of the other rooms have numerous artworks. Here I see only the smaller one above the fireplace and the grand painting against that wall." He hoped that her explanation would deflect this baiting of Petit by Françoise, although judging by her enthusiastic smile she appeared to enjoy the discomfort being inflicted on him.

"You are very observant Mathurin," she replied. "This room gets its name from the ceiling painting, "Apotheosis of Hercules". The wall paintings were by the same artist, Veronese. The large one is, "The Feast in the House of Simon". It was a diplomatic gift from the Republic of Venice in 1664."

The mere size of the artwork itself was impressive. Robert estimated it to be about fifteen feet high and thirty feet long. It seemed that he had al last found a subject that didn't lend itself to the incessant verbal onslaught waged by Françoise.

His respite didn't last long, as Françoise found yet another way to embarrass Petit. "Yes Mathurin, what a magnificent work of art. How fortunate for you that one officer was derelict in his duties, forcing you to intervene on the bridge. If he had been at his post, you would not the guest of the King today."

Robert wished that the floor would open and swallow one of them. He was occupied with his thoughts, considering whether he would like to be swallowed first, when he heard two loud, distinct noises, Gabrielle's scream and Petit's shriek. Gabrielle had turned just in time to see Petit racing toward Robert's back, his dagger drawn. Robert moved by instinct and spun to his right, placing himself in front of Gabrielle. He saw a figure approaching over his right shoulder and as the knife intended for his back, passed against his clothes and heard it slicing through the air. Having failed in his initial strike only added to Petit's rage. His face was red and full of hate. Robert distanced himself from Gabrielle by moving left as an amused François looked on and Bernard waited for an opportunity to assist as needed.

Petit held his dagger with the blade facing down, meaning the next attempt would again begin from above his head and sweep downward. Petit rushed forward as Gabrielle screamed "Mathurin!" When he was close enough, Robert stepped forward, grabbed Petit's wrist with one hand and used his other to strike his elbow and then deliver a knife hand blow to his neck. Petit's momentum carried him forward and Robert wrapped his arm around his neck and threw him over his hip. Petit was aware that he had lost control of his weapon and when his back hit the floor he found to his horror, his blade pressed against his throat. "What does this remind you of?" hissed Robert.

Petit looked bewildered and stunned. A moment ago he was the aggressor. Now he wasn't certain how much longer he had to live. He panted furiously but would not beg for life. He reasoned that if Robert had wished to take his life, he would have done so by now. What worried him was an absence of malice in his expression. Robert's eyes were devoid of emotion, as if thrusting the dagger into Petit's throat would require no more thought than breathing. He was beginning to panic now. Was his life to end quickly on this floor, witnessed by Hercules? Sweat formed on his forehead and his breathing became more rapid, when a voice announced, "His Majesty the King."

Continuing to hold the blade against Petit's neck, Robert looked up to see Louis XVI already standing in the salon. Usually the King was announced prior to entering, which meant that he had observed at least a portion of the altercation. He stood some fifteen feet past the doorway, surrounded by his family and his entourage, staring coldly at his prone officer.

A pause seemed to linger forever in the silent room until the King's reaction broke the silence. "Explain this!" he shouted. Petit turned his head toward his monarch, with a dumbfounded expression that offered no explanation.

The last person in the room to acknowledge the King was Robert. Quickly he stood and bowed to his monarch. "Your majesty, Captain de Rigaud asked for a demonstration on disarming an opponent and Captain Petit was good enough to participate. Thank you Captain." Robert offered his hand to Petit, but continued to hold his dagger.

Petit's face bore a stunned expression and chose to rise on his own; then bowed to the King.

"Captain, I believe I have something of yours," said Robert handing the dagger back to Petit. "Odd that it looks identical to the one I saw at the throat of the Daughter of France."

As Petit returned his dagger to its sheath; he could only respond with, "These daggers are very common. I'm sure that it looked very similar."

Robert looked at François who appeared to be digesting Petit's last statement.

The King reminded everyone the purpose they were serving by attending in this room as he waved his hand to a servant who stood before him. He began by addressing Robert, Bernard and the two captains. "His Majesty commands your presence, now."

All four presented themselves before Louis XVI who was very solemn. He either was exceedingly serious or tremendously angry, perhaps both.

"I summoned you here as I have an honor to confer upon each of you," he began, looking at all four subjects seriously.

Gabrielle was whispering to the Queen while smiling at Robert. He could only guess that the Queen was now aware of the actual events which placed a knife in Robert's hand aimed at Petit's neck.

"Captain Petit," began the King, "until a moment ago I had decided that your best position might be lying in a cell at the Bastille. All that saved you was Mathurin's explanation for your part in this episode I have just witnessed. You will leave Versailles immediately where you will report for duty at the Bastille. Your duty will be to control security of the entrances to the Bastille. You will report directly to the officer who stands next to you. Captain de Rigaud, you are henceforth promoted to the rank of Major with official title of Lieutenant de roi (Lieutenant of the king). You will be responsible for general security and will be second in command to Captain Bernard-René de Launay, governor of the Bastille. That will be all." With a wave of his hand they were dismissed and in a moment, it was as if they never existed.

"As for you Bernard Badeau, for your part in the rescue of my daughter; you will be granted the title of Baron, with lands in Brittany; near the town of Saint Martin des Champs and a yearly pension of fifty thousand livres."

Bernard could scarcely believe what he just heard. Until recently he rode horses as a guide and whatever small jobs he could find in La Rochelle. Now, he would walk away a nobleman, with defined rights and responsibilities. Chance had provided him with an opportunity to meet a young traveler in need of a guide and locating a skillet just when he needed it. Now, he would join one of the smallest noble classes in Europe. He would have the right to hunt and to be exempt from paying certain types of taxes. He would also have defined responsibilities. Nobles were required to honor, serve and counsel the King, often by military service. Bernard wasn't too sure how he felt about military service, but he was too elated with his new status to care. He was also told that he could lose his title if he engaged in manual labor; he would certainly have no problem with that.

Bernard's situation concluded, the King's full attention now focused entirely on Robert. The sun had risen slightly and now bathed the Salon more brightly than before. With Bernard at his side, a beam of light fell upon him. In a room constructed of so much dark wood, he became the focal point of the room.

"Mathurin Dubé," the King began solemnly, "for your courageous service to the Daughter of France, I bestow upon you the following title and request your service. Henceforth, you will be the Duc of Anjou. You will receive an annual pension of 100,000 livres and your first responsibility will be to teach your fighting skill set to my troops.

While he didn't fully comprehend the scope of what the King had just bestowed upon him, he gathered from Bernard's quiet whistle that it was substantial. This title was the highest that a non-royal person could be granted. To be granted this amount of land and money was an enormous gift for one person to receive.

Standing in this surreal setting, having been just given enough wealth to last a lifetime; the entire royal family and Gabrielle nodded in approval and smiled at the newest members of nobility. Marie-Thérese broke the silence, "My savior is now a Duc."

What Robert did next, few could have imagined. After the King had bestowed on him, title, respect, wealth and responsibilities; he voluntarily returned it. He did not feel that he had done enough to have earned a title to begin with, plus in a very short period of time noblemen would be hunted by the people they had previously governed; usually very poorly. He didn't feel that respect could be granted or purchased, but must be earned. He wanted to accumulate his own wealth and responsibilities were something he was ready to accept. After he bowed and took a very deep breath, he faced the sovereign and his family.

"Thank you, your Majesty for this great gift and honor you have given me. In good conscience however, I admit that I feel uncomfortable accepting payment because I simply did what I felt what right. So I would ask of you to allow me to serve you in some other fashion. If I am to accumulate wealth, prestige and respect, I prefer to gain it by my own good works. I only sought to aid a girl in trouble, not because she was the daughter of Louis XVI."

"Holy cow," said Bernard.

Considering the shocked expressions of nearly everyone in the room, the surprise was complete. The King however, was rather stoic considering a commoner had just refused his gift. Marie-Thérèse looked like she was about to cry, while Gabrielle turned her head aside and stared at the floor.

Robert's voice remained strong and confident. "Your Majesty, my request is to be given responsibilities. I will gladly instruct your soldiers in the martial arts. There are two additional areas where I would like to serve you. You have some of the finest balloonists in the world in France. I wish to create a more accurate method of mapping the earth. I can combine these tools to be useful to your Majesty's army. I would like to serve you as an officer in the French Army."

The royal family and Bernard listened intently, although Bernard stared in disbelief; his mouth open and Gabrielle merely nodded. The King was now resting in a large chair brought into the Salon by servants, while his chin rested on his fist.

Robert continued, "One remaining task is to locate the person who held a knife to the neck of your daughter. He needs to be held accountable for his action. I want to see that he is brought to justice. Whatever I receive after that will be due to my having earned it, not because it was granted to me."

Robert felt that this was the proper time to crease talking. Anything else could probably only serve to make matters worse. Gabrielle began smiling proudly, while the King seemed to be pondering this strange twist in events.

Louis XVI walked across the Salon and embraced Robert, kissing him on both cheeks. "Mathurin Dubé titled or not, you are the noblest man in France. My country would be a better place if half its citizens were as selfless as you. Very well then, I suppose you have earned the right to demote yourself. An officer you shall be. I will make you an officer with the rank of..." the King paused. "Perhaps you should tell me what rank you prefer so I don't have to demote you twice in one day," he said laughing.

"And I will make you a citizen of France. I can't have a British subject serving in my army."

Marie-Thérese was smiling again as Robert responded. "Your majesty, I believe the rank of major would be perfect....."

Before he could complete his sentence the King stopped him. "Your friend, the governess of my children, had suggested what your wishes might be. A uniform is waiting for you now in my bedchamber. Others will be sent from the Satory military camp."

He motioned to one of the servants. "When Major Dubé's uniforms arrive, they are to be packed immediately for him and placed in his coach. Take him to my bedchamber now, so that he may change into his new uniform and then return him to me." The servant and Robert both bowed and exited through the dining room door and led him to the King's bedchamber.

The servant walked to an oak closet and opened the large doors. Inside were several officers uniforms, but each carried an insignia of a different rank. The servant selected one with four stripes on the sleeve signifying that he carried the rank of major with an unfamiliar symbol on collar and hung it next to a changing curtain. He turned and faced Robert, "Congratulations on your promotion to his Majesty's cavalry, Major. I will wait outside to escort you to the King."

"Cavalry, did you say cavalry?" he said, stunned as the door closed behind the servant who offered no reply. "I hadn't even imagined horses as a possibility," as he examined his uniform.

His uniform consisted of black knee length boots, white breeches and a waist coat with silver buttons. The coat was blue with a red collar and cuffs with more sliver buttons and white trim. His hat was black with gold trim. A cutlass hung on his left hip and dagger on his right.

The servant nodded approvingly at Robert as he stepped from behind the dressing curtain. "You look excellent, sir. His Majesty will see you now."

They retraced their steps to the Hercules Salon and Robert was surprised to find it empty. The servant did not seem concerned however, which put him at ease. Without hesitation, he continued toward a doorway and turned slowly to wait.

"This is the Royal Chapel vestibule," he said in a hushed tone. "The royal family always attends Mass at this time. The King and his family sit in the Royal Gallery. You will sit in the side gallery."

He was escorted quickly to a seat next to Gabrielle who smiled and nodded upon seeing him in his uniform. She gently squeezed his hand before returning her attention to the Mass being celebrated in the nave below. Bernard sat on the opposite side of Gabrielle and looked as though he was very impressed by Robert's appearance. The gallery was formed on the upper portion of the chapel. At one end stood an incredible organ with the royal gallery located prominently at the opposite end. Marie-Thérese greeted Robert with a smile, until the Queen, with a disapproving movement of her head, instructed her to pay attention to mass.

The public sat in the nave where people divided their time between the priest celebrating mass and turning in their seats to view the King. Gabrielle whispered, "Very few people listen to the Mass, most are too busy looking at the King."

The arches, walls and columns were almost exclusively white with gold accents which made the multicolored marble floor even more brilliant. When the priest stood with his back to the altar, he looked directly at the royal gallery. The altar was made of white marble and adorned with a variety of gold statues. The marble floor contained variations of pink, grey and orange. Six columns in the upper ambulatory were far enough from the wall to create enough space for people to sit in the upper gallery above and room to walk around the nave below. Like most of the other chapels he had seen, the vaulted ceiling was adorned with religious paintings.

Following Mass, servants escorted Robert, Bernard and Gabrielle to the Royal Gallery where the King and his family waited. Marie-Thérese immediately left her mother's side and ran to Robert as he and Bernard bowed to the King and Queen. She hugged him around his waist and looked up at him admiringly, "My savior is a Major in our army." Robert knelt in front of her, "I will do my best to serve you; Marie-Thérese." She smiled broader and as he saluted her, she laughed and returned his salute before she dashed back to the Queen, who offered only her disapproving stare.

The Royal Gallery wasn't very large, but it afforded a wonderful view of the chapel. It occupied the upper end of the chapel and looked directly at the altar and organ. It was also very private as there was only one entrance and was on the same level as the King's Apartments.

The King approached Bernard and standing before him, placed his hands on Bernard's shoulders. Thanking him for his assistance, he kissed him on both cheeks. He then stood before Robert, "Major Mathurin Dubé, I thank you again for your deed which saved my daughter and the Daughter of France. Know that you will always be welcome at Versailles and if you ever have need of anything, you only need ask me and it will be done." He stepped back next to the Queen.

"I know that you feel a need to leave and pursue your own path. Your carriage will be made ready for you in the Chapel Courtyard in the morning. You will have fresh horses and clothing and provisions. A livery servant will drive your carriage to Paris. A horse worthy of one of my finest cavalry officers goes with you, Major. Your new post will be the École Militaire."

The King seemed to be speaking introspectively when he said, "This has been a most interesting day. I don't believe any king has ever had two subjects renounce their titles on the same day. It's a new world I suppose."

Robert gasped and turned to Bernard who was already looking at him with his familiar grin. "Well someone has to be your guide to Paris, my friend."

"And now my two noblest men, I will leave you now as there are matters to discuss with the Russian ambassador which require my attention. Good luck to you both." The King strode forward as two servants opened the gilded doors and he exited along with the Royal family, followed by his ever present entourage.

Robert and Bernard spent the remainder of that day in pursuit of their favorite experiences from Versailles. It was doubtful that either of them would be returning to the palace and they wanted to remember their fondest memories of their brief moments there. For Bernard, that meant returning to sleep in his comfortable bed, while Robert enjoyed a tour of the remainder of the gardens of the Palace of Versailles led by Gabrielle and the King's children.

In the morning, Robert and Bernard enjoyed one last breakfast with Gabrielle, Marie-Thérèse and Louis-Charles. Although they were saddened that their friends were leaving them, the children promised Gabrielle that they would be appreciative for the extra day they had with them in the Palace. Jan served them a special breakfast with a very large portion of spek in Robert's honor. He was reluctant to finish his breakfast, knowing it meant he was closer to leaving Versailles, but knew that it was unavoidable and his visit ended with his cup of tea. Gabrielle and the children walked with them to the Hercules Salon.

"Let this not mean that we can never see you again, Mathurin. Just because there are other tasks you need to undertake, doesn't mean that you can forget us." She kissed him on both cheeks, the children hugged them both and they returned toward the King's apartments.

One servant remained to escort them to the Chapel Courtyard. Flanked by the Royal Chapel and the Royal Court with the Hercules Salon behind them, they looked out as the Royal Courtyard lay before them. The servant gestured to the poste chaise, bowed, wished them good luck; smiled for the only time either of them could remember and returned to the Palace. Next to the poste chaise, a man dressed stood at attention when he saw them approaching and bowed. "My name is Pierre. I am to drive your coach to École Militaire. Your coach has been packed and your horse is hitched to it.

They stood in the shadow of the Royal Chapel as the sun hadn't yet risen high enough to illuminate the entire courtyard. He moved closer to look at his horse and noticed a man standing with his back to him, stroking the horses flank. He turned to face Robert and he realized Jan would indeed be traveling with them.

"His Majesty wanted to be certain that you ate well, Major," he said with a great smile. "Besides, only you appreciated my spek. I believe they will be just fine without me."

Jan turned toward the horse. "The King has really given you a magnificent animal, Major," he said reverently. "You will be the envy of anyone who knows anything about horses. My family has raised horses for years on our land next to the Loevestein Castle. Our land lay between the banks of the Mass and Waal rivers near Gorinchem. We had some very nice animals but never anything like this one. You have an Arabian stallion, Major. The Bedouins bred them for centuries for war. Among horses they are the elite of the elite. They are renowned for their intelligence, endurance and loyalty."

He walked past Jan and began to stroke the horse's muzzle. He was drawn by his large lustrous brown eyes and the long white stripe that began by his ears and passed between his eyes, stopping just before his nose. His dark brown coat was incredibly smooth and his mane, tail and legs were all jet black. Three of long muscular legs had white socks and he looked at Robert in a way that conveyed an understanding that he was now his horse. He spoke to his horse loudly enough for all to hear, "Time to return to the real world. Jan, there isn't a lot of room in the coach, would you like to ride my Arabian?"

Jan was pleased to no end and could barely breathe. "Yes, yes of course. Major, I can't tell you how much it would mean to me."

PARIS

Robert and Bernard climbed into the poste-chaise, Jan mounted the Arabian and minutes later they were leaving by the same gate they had entered to conclude their brief stay. It seemed to both as if their stay had been much longer.

"So Bernard," Robert began in a questioning tone, "I'm curious to know why...?"

"Why I gave up my title and privileges?" interrupted Bernard. "I wondered how long it take before you asked, my friend. When you left to change into your uniform, I started feeling selfish, which is usually not a problem for me. After listening to what you said and seeing the reactions of those close to you, I felt it necessary to ask the King to make me an untitled subject once again. Besides, I'm really still employed as your guide and I feel responsible for getting you safely to Paris. Also, you have yet to pay me."

The road they traveled on would eventually cross a wide river their right. "That is the Seine, my friend." Bernard said.

Robert looked at the walled embankment on the opposite side where buildings became more numerous and much taller. It was evident that he was entering a great city. There were also numerous vessels docked there and the river was busy with commerce conducted by boat.

"If you don't mind the occasional smell from the water, it is the most beautiful river in Europe. It brings everything to the people of Paris. It divides the city and brings it together as well. The Seine meanders slowly and gracefully through the City of Lights. When we leave the Bastille for the École Militaire, we will cross the Seine on Pont Neuf. It is the oldest bridge in Paris, which crosses this jewel of a river."

Robert could see Pont Neuf from his seat. It crossed the Seine in two places actually. A shorter span crossed from the left bank to an island in the middle of the river and the larger section continued onto the right. He noticed the carriage slowing as it approached the river and suddenly stopped.

The driver of their horses dismounted and approached the poste chaise. "Major, monsieur; my instructions are to report to the Bastille and return to Versailles by carriage from there. I am told Major, that your quarters are waiting for you at the Military School which is not far from here. If we go directly to the Bastille now I can return by carriage to Versailles, but then you would need to drive your coach to the Military School yourselves. I can take you to your quarters now or proceed directly to the Bastille if you wish. It is your decision."

"My guide knows the way; we will go directly to the Bastille," he said as Bernard nodded. Now he got to examine Pont Neuf more closely, which was what he wanted to do anyway. There were five arches in the first span, which connected the embankment to an island in the middle of the Seine and seven arches in the second. In the center of each arch was a battlement, giving it a fortress like appearance. The surface was made from stone, but much smoother than the cobblestones used in the streets.

Soon after crossing the Seine they turned right and soon he saw an enormous structure, which meant their next destination had been reached as well.

"Ah, there is the Bastille; my friend," said an excited Bernard. "It has been used as a fortress but it is mostly just a prison now. There are some who say the inmates are well cared for, but some criticize it. Who can tell what the truth is? It separates the Le Marais, the wealthy section, from Porte Saint-Antoine; where the poor, working class live. The Bastille used to guard the entrance to Paris to keep people out, but Paris grew too large and the walls were eventually torn down. It's a shame that they kept the prison too. These walls were built with the intent to separate people. Now it is wealth that keeps them apart."

Only Robert knew that the Bastille would be the flash point of the French Revolution, but if the sentiment of Parisians toward it was anything like resentment he experienced from the people who rioted in villages he had visited; its role in the Revolution would surprise no one. He could see a stone wall surrounding the Bastille about forty feet high. The prison itself stood about seventy feet tall with a tower in each corner and one in the center of each wall.

"There are actually names for the towers," said Bernard pointing toward them as the carriage slowly moved across the cobblestone, amongst the throngs of people in the crowded street. Even the livery servant's yelling could not persuade them to quicken their pace. "Let me see if I can remember them," as the coach came to a halt. "They are, La Chapelle, Trésor, Compté, Baziniere, Bertaudiere, Liberté, Puits and Coin. A few were named after persons, possibly prisoners; one for the chapel; the others I'm unsure of."

The Bastille seemed smaller than Robert had expected. Perhaps being the icon of the Revolution had created a larger image in his mind. It seemed that it was slightly more than two hundred twenty feet long, about ninety feet wide and eighty feet tall.

As they approached the south entrance, he wondered if he would see either of the fort's newest officers.

Bernard was busy concentrating on an area adjacent to the prison. "This area is open to the public," he said whimsically. "I understand that the governor rents out the shops for 10,000 livres a year. You have to wonder whose pocket that money goes in, eh, my friend? Many of the prisoners are here as a result of the whim of someone in authority, including the King himself. Prisoners can be detained using a "letter de cachet (letter under a Royal seal)."

"After the King decided to have someone imprisoned, they would be tapped on the shoulder with a white baton and formally detained in the name of the King. My personal favorite is when a person can be imprisoned through an action by members of their own family. It is usually by parents who have their children held here for rejecting parental authority, disgracing the family reputation and others. Sometimes it involved a spouse taking action against their husband or wife. How convenient eh, my friend?"

He was about to answer when the coach turned to enter through the Bastille's south gate. The hive like atmosphere of the pedestrians outside was now replaced by soldiers following orders shouted by officers. Men, horses and carriages were in a constant state of organized movement. The sun was high in the sky, heating the courtyard and eliminating any shadows. The fact that the Bastille was rather small prevented any relief from a breeze to dissipate the heat; something the soldiers hoped for but rarely happened.

The poste-chaise stopped near the center of the courtyard and the livery servant jumped to the ground and walked calmly to Robert's door and began to speak immediately.

"Major Dubé, I stopped here where no one can hear us talking. You would do well to be very careful now that you are in Paris. The servants at Versailles hear......things. Someone has too much wine, a casual conversation between an officer and a female servant; I'm sure you understand. The rumor is that Captain Petit has vowed revenge against you. He blames you for his transfer to the Bastille. He will never forget what happened and won't rest until he feels he has received satisfaction. Be very careful how you choose your friends."

No sooner had he finished when their conversation was interrupted by a bellowing voice, which was coming nearer. There was no doubt that someone objected to their carriage's location.

"You there. Move that coach immediately. You are in the way," someone shouted in a furious voice.

The livery servant walked toward the horses and began stroking their heads as Robert stepped down from the coach as they both searched for the source of this yelling. Soon he could see who was creating the distraction.

A very agitated, stern faced officer glared at the servant as he quickly approached. The moment he stepped in front of the horses, the officer saw Robert. His stern look vanished and was replaced by a huge grin. He stood face to face with Major Françoise de Paul Rigaud, who immediately shook his hand and embraced him.

"Mathurin, what a surprise it is to see you. You have arrived just in time for our afternoon meal. You must join me and you also, Bernard."

"You," he said to the servant, "take your team to the stables to get them water and then you and your chef go to the enlisted men's kitchen and tell them I sent you to be fed, although Jan may choose to cook his own meal."

He then led Robert and Bernard through an entryway in one of the towers where they climbed a series of stone steps until they reached the upper story. The coolness provided by the stone walls was in sharp contrast to the oppressive feeling of being baked in the courtyard. The upper story housed the senior Bastille staff and their dining quarters. Robert and Bernard followed François into a room with a stone floor and several wooden tables. Robert walked to the closest window and looked at the congested mass of people in the streets below. "This Le Marais," said François. "It is the aristocratic section of Paris. The Bastille separates it from the working class district, Porte Saint-Antoine."

Officers who sat for their afternoon meal took notice of the two strangers. As Robert and François were senior officers, they were saluted by anyone who approached them. Bernard was the curiosity however, as the officers dining room was customarily restricted to French officers. However, once they were aware that these were the men who had saved the Daughter of France and Robert requested to serve in the cavalry as his reward, while Bernard rejected a noble rank as well to serve as a guide for Robert, all were extremely happy to make them welcome.

All except for the officer who entered just as their meal was being served. The kitchen staff then brought them a bottle of red wine with slices of beef and fried artichokes in a marinade, fresh grapes and they were told that coffee would follow soon.

Captain Petit saw this and became visibly agitated when the same staff member served him bread, some watery soup and a salad.

When Françoise noticed Petit seated across the room, his verbal onslaught from Versailles resumed. Speaking loud enough so that all in the room could hear, he began, "Well Major, we are certainly honored to have you with us today. The king offered you the title of Duc for saving his daughter but you asked to be rewarded by serving with us."

Petit had been staring at Robert's back, now realized who their guest was and believed this was the reason his rations were so meager in comparison.

The kitchen staff returned to ask Robert if there was anything else he would like. "I'd really like this to go", he thought. He had experienced this interaction between Petit and François before and it was an experience he was in no hurry to revisit. "Not, this is perfect," he said eating as quickly as possible.

Not in any hurry to allow his prey to escape, François pressed on. "I understand that your duties will be to train our army in hand to hand combat skills. Perhaps you could train officers to follow orders as well, so they will be present when the person they are assigned to protect is attacked."

Everyone in the room heard the sound of a chair sliding across the stone floor, followed by its impact when it smashed against a wall. Robert heard the sound of boots quickly advancing in his direction. Not wishing to expose himself to being assaulted from behind like in the Hercules Salon, he turned quickly to face Petit.

François swiftly rose and stood before Robert while other officers rushed to stop Petit's advance. He looked at Petit's reddening face. "Captain, isn't it customary to salute a superior officer?" he taunted while staring at him.

"There is nothing superior about you!" screamed Petit. His arms were outstretched as if he could somehow reach François' neck from where he stood.

Robert noticed that Petit had quickly withdrawn his hands. "His hands, where are his hands?" he yelled.

Several of the officers looked in his direction but didn't appear to understand his question or its significance.

"Look at his hands," he repeated. "What is he doing with his hands?" The sense of urgency in his voice finally resonated with the officers; they looked down when suddenly arose the deafening report from Petit's pistol, followed by a cloud of smoke. Fragments from a hole in the ceiling fell like rain onto the dining room floor and tables. A dejected Petit glared at Robert as he was quickly escorted from the room by his fellow officers.

François returned to his chair with a very satisfied look, while Robert was left with a sense of relief and bewilderment. Bernard had covered his plate, managing to save his food from being showered with debris and had resumed eating in earnest.

An exceedingly infuriated officer marched to where François sat and slammed the discharged pistol on the table. "You are an idiot! One of these adventures of yours will get someone killed someday. Don't involve others in your drama. Why don't you two fight a duel, so one of you gets eliminated?"

François grinned slyly. "Petit is well connected and incompetent, but he's no fool. He does nothing to cause me to challenge him and he won't enter a fight he knows he can't win."

Robert and Bernard had finished their meal and neither saw a reason to remain further. Robert wanted desperately to be settled in his quarters at École Militaire before it became too late in the day. As he thanked François for his hospitality, François moved closer and lowered his voice. "Mathurin, remember what I say. Petit, really hates you and blames you for his current situation. He cannot accept the blame for the attack on Marie-Thérese and so he holds you responsible. He is from a privileged family and has never been held accountable for anything until now. His family felt that serving as an officer would make a man of him, but you have witnessed his obvious lack of progress. He feels as though his honor has been tarnished and he will search for a way to strike out at you."

"In addition, while the King has commanded you to instruct soldiers in hand to hand fighting, there are virtually no officers who will support you in this. They will tell you that the only civilized combat comes at the end of a sword. You will do better to concentrate your efforts on other tasks. Those programs which won't interfere with the army's agendas will have a greater chance of success. You will find that the King doesn't deal well with those who fail him. Until we meet again, Mathurin. Good luck." He shook hands with Robert and Bernard and departed through the doorway where Petit had been dragged.

Walking across the courtyard, he noticed how the Bastille seemed more dismal now than before entering it and he was going to be eager to be rid of it. They found Jan standing next to the Arabian, stroking his muzzle.

Jan had seen them approaching and looked as if he had something urgent to discuss.

"Major, the livery servant made certain that your horse and the team were fed and watered. It will take some time to arrive at the Military School. I wondered if I could continue to ride your Arabian until we reach your quarters."

Jan and the horse looked at each other as if they were waiting for an answer.

"It sounds perfect to me," said Robert as he climbed into his carriage. "I will ride in the coach, you ride the Arabian and Bernard drives the team." Also Robert would get some much needed solitude.

Aside from the calming effect of riding in quiet, he felt more hopeful following the advice of François. Previously, Robert thought he was the only in France person who had no interest in teaching karate to French soldiers. His goal would continue to concentrate on locating Ron's coordinates and finally sending the documents to him.

Crossing Pont Neuf, he looked at the Seine and felt he was closer to his goal now and could afford to be less concerned about the encumbrance of teaching those who didn't wish to be taught. Now he needed to propose his plan to the Military School's commander in such a way as to ensure its failure. Dealing with a superior officer who will undoubtedly be opposed, openly or otherwise should make his task simpler.

Bernard turned the coach away from the tree lined banks of the Seine onto a straight avenue in the direction of a long multi storied building with a large gold dome rising behind it. This was the Hotel des Invalides, a hospital which was built for wounded soldiers during the reign of Louis XIV.

Bernard followed a straight narrow tree lined avenue to the right, which soon entered a much wider street made of stone. The sounds resonating from the horse's hooves and the wheels of the carriage against the avenues surface dissipated now that the buildings stood further from the street.

Ahead was the École Militaire. It was two stories tall, constructed of tan colored stone and a dark grey roof. It appeared to be at least two blocks long, with a grand center entrance and two smaller entrances, one on either side. The first entrance was a large grey door with the word "Cavalarie" above it. Just beyond a gate led to a narrow passage between two buildings. The main entrance was noteworthy for its six great columns, three stories tall and three very tall dark grey doors. Robert could just see another entrance with the word "Artillerie" above it. Bernard turned from the street through a second gate where they were stopped by a sentry. As he stepped from the carriage, the guard snapped to attention and saluted. Robert returned the salute and asked to be directed to the commanding officer and to the stables where his horses could be fed and watered.

The guard directed Bernard and Jan to the stables at the far end of the parade grounds and told Robert that he could find the commanding officer, Colonel DuPont talking to a group of officers on the parade grounds.

He walked toward the group of men that the guard had indicated. By the time he reached them they were being dismissed by the colonel. Robert hoped this encounter would conclude quickly. He had practiced what he would say to the colonel several times in his coach. Carrying his orders in his left hand, he strode to an officer he was certain could make his life unbearable.

The colonel appeared about fifty years old, tall with grey hair, dull brown eyes and a weathered face. Robert was expecting a more scholarly look from the commander of a military academy. He seemed more likely to have earned his commission on the battlefield than in the classroom. A wave of doom washed over him.

Robert presented his most precise salute, "Major Mathurin Dubé, reporting for duty sir." Robert continued to stand as erect as one of the flag poles he had passed in front of the school. He tried not to make eye contact with the colonel and stiffly presented his orders to the commander.

To his complete surprise, the colonel immediately returned his salute and accepted this orders without looking at them.

"At ease Major. I received a set of your orders earlier today and I have eagerly anticipated your arrival. How exciting this will be. My parade grounds will be full of our soldiers being taught hand to hand combat when they should be instructed in the art of fighting with the sword."

He felt the colonel's comments had been laced with a heavy dose of sarcasm. "I appreciate your enthusiasm, sir."

"You understand Major," the colonel continued, "that while I have open space, I don't have an abundance of resources at my disposal....."

Disliking the idea of interrupting, but not wishing to endure the Colonel's unwanted opinion any longer, Robert did exactly that. "Colonel, I understand and completely agree with you. My needs are small. I need quarters for myself and space in your stable for my horse. I am unfamiliar with Paris and if you can arrange for someone to provide me with accurate directions; that would be very helpful. As soon as my duties have been completed, I will be able to excuse myself from your hospitality, your time and your resources. I'm certain that His Majesty will appreciate your assistance." Robert was absolutely positive that the colonel could detect the sarcasm in this message.

DuPont pondered both this information and insubordination by this young officer. He could make an issue of it or ignore it. If choosing the latter would result in his earlier departure, then at least for now; that was the course he would follow.

Robert wondered why the colonel was staring at him. His desire was to situate himself in his quarters and resolve his problem quickly. Now it looked as if he may have created an additional problem.

DuPont looked quickly from Robert to someone on the parade ground. "Garnier," he shouted, "get over here."

Robert turned to see an officer slightly younger than himself, running like he was fleeing from the devil. Stopping immediately before where the colonel impatiently stood, he saluted while panting. Returning the salute, DuPont's voice lowered but only slightly.

"Lieutenant Emile Garnier this is Major Dubé. You will serve as his aide while he is quartered in the Military School. You will follow his orders and see to his needs. Locate the supply officer, get the Major proper quarters and see that his horse is stabled. When his duties have been fulfilled, you will be reassigned. You will want to disassociate yourself from this project as soon as possible, Lieutenant."

Garnier looked quizzically at the colonel as he finished with his prophetic advice. "No one who hopes to be promoted someday desires an assignment on their record which ended in an epic failure, Lieutenant. Dismissed."

Colonel DuPont strode off as soon as Robert and Garnier had saluted, searching for other officers to afflict with his unpleasantness.

Garnier pivoted to face Robert and presented him a very stiff and proper salute. He was certain that his salute would be considered lackluster by the lieutenant, but he had larger issues to consider.

"Lieutenant, let's begin with me and my quarters. Once you have located them, report to me here." Turning to Bernard he said, "Once Garnier returns, we'll carry my belongings to my quarters," ignoring Bernard's puzzled expression.

Robert decided that he and Jan would walk the stallion to the stables alone. They crossed the parade grounds to the stable located near the far gate. Robert introduced himself to the sergeant in charge; a short stout fellow of medium height, lucent blue eyes and a pair of the largest, strongest looking hands he had ever seen. Jan removed the horse's saddle, obtained a stiff brush and began brushing him.

"Sergeant, I am Major Dubé and I will be quartered here for some time. Would you please see that my mount is well taken care of?"

The sergeant seemed mesmerized by Robert's horse as he stared at him with instant admiration. "He is magnificent," as he gracefully and reverently rubbed the horses flank.

"What do you call him?" asked the sergeant, never diverting his gaze from the stallion.

"I'm not sure, to be honest sergeant. The King just presented him to me today. No one mentioned his name."

"It is you, the one who saved the Daughter of France," gasped the sergeant. "We heard what you accomplished. This is truly an amazing day, meeting both of you," although Robert sincerely wondered who the sergeant was happiest to meet.

"A gift from the King should have a worthy name," said the sergeant, gazing intently at the Arabian. "Arabians are extremely loyal animals, Major. They can become your best friend also."

Robert raised his head as he did when be believed that he had arrived at a solution, "I believe that Sadeek is an Arabic word meaning, "true friend". I think that would be a fitting name for a horse like him."

The sergeant looked at the stallion and stroked his muzzle, "Sadeek, is it true, my friend? Will you be a true friend to the Major?"

Sadeek seemed to respond as if Robert had made a wise choice by shaking his head up and down.

"Sadeek it is then," exclaimed Robert. "Sergeant, I will also need space to store a carriage. Can you help me with that as well?"

"Oh Major, I'm not sure. A poste-chaise like yours is rather large. It may be difficult to safely store it here." The sergeant was searching for something and Robert was certain it wasn't bacon.

Stepping closer to the sergeant Robert placed his arm around his shoulder and spoke softly, "Sergeant, in the first place my carriage will be considerably smaller than the poste-chaise and I will see to it that you are compensated for your assistance." Handing him a few notes he added," Do you still feel that taking care of my carriage will pose a problem for you?"

The lire disappeared quickly into the sergeant's pocket, "No sir, that will be no problem at all. In fact, it will be an honor sir," he answered enthusiastically.

Robert thanked the sergeant and walked with Jan to his poste-chaise, where Bernard and Garnier were standing. Slowly, he talked to Jan about what his future plans might be and his family in the Netherlands. Jan spoke in a guarded manner about his desire to be near to his family and his dream of cooking in his own restaurant.

Garnier snapped to attention and saluted as Robert reached his carriage. "Sir, I have your quarters ready and rooms have been requisitioned for your chef. Your quarters are in the officer's wing and Jan will be located where the enlisted men live. I can take you to your quarters now if you like."

He returned Garnier's salute, clearly tiring of this formality. "Lieutenant, do you really need to salute me every time we meet?"

"Yes sir, I do. It would be awkward for me to be seen not saluting a superior officer."

Robert sighed, "Very well, lieutenant. We will salute on the school grounds. However, there will be no need for it in my quarters. Would you and Bernard take my belongings to my quarters, please? I will wait here with Jan."

As he watched his belongings being carried through the large wooden door leading to the officer's quarters, Robert told Jan to join him in his poste-chaise.

Jan looked puzzled at this request. He wanted to see his quarters and the kitchen. How could he plan meals for the Major, if he couldn't familiarize himself with his surroundings?

Sitting in his poste-chaise for perhaps the last time, he placed his backpack on the floor between his feet. Unfastening the top, he pulled out a cloth bag. "I can guess what you are thinking Jan. You wonder why you aren't in the process of being shown to your new quarters. Did you wonder why I asked you what you really wanted to do? I know that you would prefer to be with your family. I'm going to admit something to you. While I was very happy to learn that the King would allow you to accompany me, I really had misgivings about keeping you separated from your family. Additionally, I can't imagine that your life's ambition would be to cook for a French officer."

Before Jan could protest, Robert told him to listen to what he needed to say. As Jan sat patiently, Robert placed lire notes from his backpack into the drawstring bag. Drawing the bag shut, he turned to face Jan and handed the bag to him.

"There is enough money in this bag for you to return home and open your own restaurant. Very soon, this city; this country will be a very difficult and dangerous place to live. The sooner you can establish yourself somewhere else, the better. There are events which are about to take place here, which a family should not be exposed to. You don't understand it now, but believe me; Versailles will be far from a safe place as well, especially for one who serves the King."

"When Bernard returns from my quarters you will accompany him to a poste station to exchange the horses. From there you should be able to arrange for passage to Gorinchem. I foresee you owning your own restaurant, overlooking one of the canals and serving the most savory spek that one can imagine."

Jan was astonished beyond words, attempting to believe all he heard. He stared straight ahead, squeezed the bag and nodded, "I'm going home". He turned to Robert as if explaining to him and repeated the words that he often wondered when he would be free to utter them, "I'm going home."

"Yes, you are Jan. I would never feel right knowing that I had the ability to return you to Holland but prevented it so you could remain here to meet my needs. Look, Bernard and Garnier are returning. Tell no one what we just discussed. Say only that I am sending you to visit your family, but not that you are leaving permanently." Exiting the poste-chaise, Robert motioned for Bernard to join him.

"Bernard, pay attention," Robert said evenly. "I need you to take the poste-chaise and the team and sell it all. I think someone who knows people the way you do, will be able to obtain the best price. I also need you to find a smaller carriage for me, one that is more suited to a large city. Take Jan with you and leave him where he can get passage to the Netherlands. When you return, meet me in my quarters. This will likely take you awhile, so you will need to leave now."

Bernard and Jan could both tell from Robert's tone that the discussion was finished. Bernard mounted the horse on the left as Jan climbed inside the coach and looked back toward the stables hoping for a last glimpse of Sadeek. As he watched with Garnier, his poste-chaise traveled slowly between buildings until it reached the street and turned right. Parting with his carriage seemed to add new vitality to the real purpose of his effort which was returning Ron's documents to him.

Robert slapped Garnier on the back, "Let's go Lieutenant, we have work to do," and nearly sprinted to the building that housed the officer's quarters. He would have continued his pace had Garnier not offered to show him where the officers were quartered. "Lead on, Lieutenant;" said Robert cheerily.

His quarters were located on the second floor, overlooking the courtyard. It was not nearly as well appointed as the hotel in Angers, but not as miserable as some of the inns he had experienced. A very large room, it was separated into individual areas. To his left he found a wooden desk and chair, and a small fireplace near the windows which overlooked the parade grounds. A small sofa and chairs and a coffee table faced it. On his right were his bathtub and dressing area with a large standing mirror. His bed and another fireplace were located next to the other window. This would be perfect for his needs, he thought.

"Lieutenant, I need you to do several things for me. First, when Bernard returns with my new carriage, use it to transport him to wherever he needs to go. His business with me will have concluded and he will need to hire a carriage to get home."

"Second, part of the reason I am here is to fulfill the King's request to instruct soldiers on hand to hand combat. I will begin by requesting a list from our general officers; I need recommendations of officers to select for training. You will write those letters."

Garnier's puzzled look told Robert that his second order was vague enough that his project was doomed. "Epic failure," he thought. "Perfect."

"Third, there are two people I wish to meet." He directed Garnier to the desk and positioned a piece of paper and handed him a pencil before continuing.

Robert was searching his memory for the names of two prominent balloonists from that period. "I need the addresses for Jean-Francis Pilatre de Rozier and Jacques Charles."

"Fourth, I need something large enough to draw on; a large easel with paper or a blackboard and some chalk or pencils."

"Fifth, I will need to visit the Royal Academy of Science. You will help me find its location. That should be all for now."

Garnier finished his writing and started to review his list. "Yes sir, Major. All of this is possible with the exception of the scientist de Rozier."

Robert lifted his head, looking at Garnier with an icy stare. "And why would he present a problem, lieutenant?"

"Well sir, it seems that he died a few years ago in Pas-de-Calais," Garnier replied flatly. "He was attempting to fly across the English Channel when his balloon fell from the sky. He and his companion were both killed. That poses a relatively minor problem, sir."

Now Robert remembered de Rozier. He and his companion, Pierre Romain had the dubious distinction of being the first aircraft fatalities. "Oh. Then could you help me locate Jacques Charles, provided, he is alive?"

"Yes I can sir," Garnier said rising from his chair while attempting to suppress a grin. "I believe there is a large drawing table which could be "borrowed" from a classroom in the adjacent building. "I'll find someone to help me carry it here."

He removed his coat, threw it on the sofa and headed for the door. "You've found him, lieutenant. Let's go and "borrow" the drawing board. I have work to do," and he walked into the hallway. Garnier followed, shocked that a superior officer would do manual labor which Garnier would have relegated to enlisted men.

In the adjacent building, they found a very large easel with large sheets of paper, perfectly suited for drawing and a supply of pencils. Fortunately, it was mounted on a wheeled platform which made it easy to move past a few shocked enlisted men and soon it was positioned near the window adjacent to the sofa and fireplace. This was the most organized he felt since leaving the Nation. As he drew, his plans began to coalesce on his drawing board. While Garnier was following his latest order to locate a bottle of wine, he began to write. When Garnier returned with dinner and wine he saw the initial pieces of Robert's plan to deliver the documents to Ron.

1- Letters- Lt. Garnier will write
2- Jacques Charles- Lt. Garnier will locate
3- Latitude and Longitude- sextant and quadrant
4- Hydrogen v. Helium equations

Garnier placed the bottle of wine and glasses on the table near the sofa and stood waiting for orders.

"Pour us some wine, would you; Lieutenant?" asked Robert as he studied the list from his chair in front of the easel. Garnier passed a glass to him, waiting for Robert to drink first.

"This is our project list, Lieutenant. The items on this list comprise the tasks which I need to accomplish while at the Military School. When I have nothing left to add to this, it will be a signal that it is time for me to leave.

"A question, Major, "asked Garnier; pouring wine for them. He stood before the list, "what does this have to do with your instructions to teach martial arts to army officers?"

Robert relaxed in his chair and replied nonchalantly. "Not much at all actually," he replied. "I am uncertain how much success we will have in a project that no one wants. The remainder involves a project utilizing an observation balloon and a special instrument to coordinate troop movements. One problem is that the instrument doesn't exist, yet."

His real purpose was to use a balloon for an aerial view of Paris which would lead him to Ron's coordinates, something he was extremely reluctant to reveal to Garnier.

A knock at the door interrupted their conversation and they faced the door in time to see Bernard entering his quarters. Smiling broadly, he handed Robert a cloth bag which was tightly drawn.

"This is the remainder from the sale of your poste-chaise and the purchase of your new carriage, my friend." Robert gestured to a spot on the sofa next to him. "Bernard, sit and have a glass of wine with me. We have some business to attend to."

While Bernard filled his glass, Robert emptied the contents of the bag onto the table and instructed Garnier to bring three meals from the officer's dining room for them.

"Bernard, have you already deducted what I owe you, from the remainder of the money you used toward the purchase the new carriage?"

Bernard paused for a moment before answering. "No my friend, it is all there," as he studied the pile of money.

"Good, that will make this much simpler," Robert said as he formed the notes into two equal stacks.

Bernard's curiosity steadily increased as the stacks grew higher. When he had finished counting and separating the notes, Robert pushed one pile toward Bernard and pulled the other toward him.

"Bernard, I couldn't have made this journey without your assistance. Half of the money left from the sale of the carriage is yours."

Bernard looked stunned and speechless, which was something Robert hadn't experienced before. "My friend, I don't know what to say. Your generosity is beyond my expectations."

"It was worth all of this Bernard. By the way, I like your new boots and topcoat very much. They're new aren't they?"

Bernard shifted uneasily on the sofa while attempting to appear unfazed by what Robert's observation had implied.

"Relax, Bernard. You really needed and deserved the boots and coat. Besides, I remember that it was your skill with a frying pan that saved me from a knife in the back. This is really the least that I could do for you. Now, it is getting late and our business is concluded. If you like we can have one last meal together. You can spend the night here and have a fresh start in the morning, or you could take your leave now. Either way, Lieutenant Garnier will take you wherever you need to go in Paris."

"My friend, I appreciate your offer. One final meal together and I will excuse myself. It is a sad but perfect way for us to part company."

So these two fantastic companions, who had experienced so much in a short period of time; shared one last meal together. They both ate heartily, although it was most significant for the silence on Bernard's part. Robert thought that his traveling companion seemed rather sad and he would regret seeing his guide leave him.

As the last bit of roasted chicken was consumed and the remainder of wine had been drunk, Robert pulled his backpack from where it sat next to the sofa and placed it on the table. He divided all the lire into stacks as he had with the money from the sale of his coach and added it to the sum he had already offered to Bernard. An empty draw string pouch lying on the floor next to Robert was soon full of lire and he handed it to a speechless Bernard.

"My friend, I don't know what to say," said Bernard as he tightly gripped the pouch in his lap.

"Don't say anything at all Bernard. Your silence is enough for me."

Following their meal, they walked to the parade ground where Bernard presented Robert with his new carriage.

"This will be perfect for you, my friend. This is a phaeton, a small nimble carriage; perfect for a large city." Bernard had selected a sturdy grey horse to pull it. "And this fellow is well suited for the city also. He won't generate attention the way Sadeek does, but he is good natured, quick and will happily take you wherever in Paris you need to go."

There really wasn't much left to say between them. Robert and Bernard both knew they had experienced so much in their brief time together, but now it was time to move forward. After a brief handshake, Bernard placed his large hands on Robert's shoulders and embraced him. They shook hands firmly and Bernard climbed into the phaeton beside Garnier. Garnier commanded the small grey horse to move and they trotted across the parade grounds to the gate and left the Military School. Robert thought it was peculiar that he forgot to ask Bernard what his plans were. After all they had experienced together, it felt odd that he had absolutely no idea what they were planning to do separately.

But he had other matters to attend to now and he quickly returned to his quarters. He brought paper to the sofa and started composing a letter to an unspecified officer about his participation in a training that he would not be supportive of and Robert had no intention performing. He would leave it to Garnier to supply the name of the officers.

"Lt. Garnier, write this letter to the general officer who can command others to participate in the task given to me by our King," he wrote across the top of the paper.

Major Mathurin Dubé

École Militaire, Paris

Most esteemed sir,

It is the command of his Majesty that I develop a system to instruct his young officers in the skill of martial arts. I humbly request a list of twenty officers whom you feel would be well suited to this endeavor. The purpose of this training would be to return these officers to instruct their own troops. Training will take place at École Militaire.

I look forward to your reply.

Your servant,

Major Mathurin Dubé.

He had originally considered requesting that one dozen officers to be committed to this training, but hoped that the general officer who read this letter would feel that twenty officers would be an impossible number to agree to. He felt that this had been a full day for him when he found that he was having difficulty keeping his eyes open. He changed into his nightshirt as the faltering sun sent scattered beams of orange and red light across the wall of his room. He was asleep before his room became dark.

The morning sun shone down upon the parade grounds of École Militaire and through the curtain less windows of the officer's quarters. The sun's rays were quicker to warm Robert's room than they were to awaken him. In his state of being half awake and half in a dream world, he nearly expected Ron to enter the room with his customary cups of Starbuck's coffee. Soon, he remembered that he was in Paris and a very long way from Ron's morning delivery. Deciding that the best path to follow was washing his face; dress in his uniform and work toward formulating a solution.

He was verifying his calculations in an effort to discover how the key fob that Ron sent had initially failed him, when he became aware of footsteps approaching in the hallway and a moment later Garnier entered with a tray containing tea and rolls. "I thought we'd get started early," he said placing the tray on table.

"I suppose that for now this will be my best substitute for a tall drip," he thought.

"Here is the letter I want you to send," said Robert handing the paper to Garnier. "You will need to supply the general officer's name."

As Garnier read the letter, furrows appeared in his forehead and one eyebrow arched.

"Is something wrong, Lieutenant?" Robert questioned him as he peered at his aide over his teacup.

"It seems to me that this letter could be more strongly worded, sir. I could suggest some changes and present them to you for your approval; if you like."

"All I really require is the name of the proper officer to send it to, Garnier. I feel it is perfect just as I wrote it. Let's do that and focus on the rest of the items on my list."

"Yes sir," said Garnier holding the letter at his side. "General Claude Libley would be the best officer to receive the letter. He has many years of service and has commanded both armies and small units of men. He would probably best understand what you are attempting to accomplish."

"Also, I know where Jacques Charles lives. It isn't actually his home, but he spends so much time in his workshop, that it may as well be his residence. His workshop is located at the

Place des Victories. It is a small building, surrounded by much taller structures. It should be easy to identify."

Garnier pointed to another item on the list. "The Royal French Academy of Sciences meets in rooms on the second floor of the Louvre. This is very close to the workshop of Jacques Charles. We can visit them in whatever order you prefer."

Robert considered this for a moment and determined that locating Ron's coordinates were unquestionably his first priority. "We'll visit the Louvre first. Then we'll call on Jacques Charles. By the way, where did you take Bernard?"

"Actually, I didn't take him anywhere definite, sir. We rode a short distance beyond the front gate. Just after turning onto Place Joffre we witnessed a large gathering on the Champs de Mars. They were demonstrating against the price of grain, as usual. He jumped from the carriage and before I could stop him, he disappeared into the crowd. I shouted to him that it could be dangerous. The King has informers everywhere and one could easily find himself in prison for simply attending an event like that."

Robert stood quickly and threw on his hat. "Bernard's a big boy and he can take care of himself. Plus, if he does get into trouble, he can always talk his way out of it. For the present, I want to concentrate on locating the Academy and Jacques Charles. Let's get the carriage ready and be on our way, Lieutenant."

With one motion, Garnier placed the letter on the table and put on his hat. "Yes, sir," he nearly ran to the door and paused before entering the hall. "Sir, wouldn't you prefer to ride Sadeek? He is such a magnificent animal that it seems a pity to not ride him. I could have him saddled also," he said enthusiastically.

"I am not familiar with Paris yet Lieutenant, so until then I will need you to help me with directions. I will meet you at the stables." What he failed to mention to Garnier was that he didn't know how to ride a horse.

Walking across the parade ground Robert saw that his phaeton was ready. The sergeant was busy brushing and talking to Sadeek. He immediately came to attention when he saw Robert approaching and was a little disappointed when he was told not to saddle his stallion. Robert drew the sergeant close to him as Garnier inspected the phaeton.

"Sergeant I have something very important to share with you and no one else. Can I trust you?" nearly whispering to him.

"Yes, sir," the sergeant affirmed. "Of course, your secret is safe with me."

"I don't know how to ride a horse," he admitted. "I've never even been on one, much less owned one like Sadeek. But I would like you to help me change that. Every morning at 7.00 I will be here and I would like you to show me how to saddle my horse and how to ride. Will you do that for me?"

The sergeant was moved by the sincerity of this officer asking him for assistance, not demanding it. He could barely contain his elation. Sadeek's ears stood up as if he understood the conversation while Robert climbed into his carriage rode off with Garnier to move another step closer to his goal.

ACAMÉMIE ROYAL DES SCIENCES

As Garnier guided the carriage to the right, Robert immediately saw the embankment of the Seine on his left and recognized this as the route Bernard had taken when they first entered Paris. As they crossed a bridge he looked up river and in the distance he could see Pont Neuf, which meant that he was one step closer to his first objective. .

"This is Pont Royale," announced Garnier, "and that is the Louvre," as he pointed to a large three storied structure before them, which was the corner of an enormous building that seemed as long as the Seine itself. It was extremely ornate with dark grey rooftops

After crossing Pont Royale, the lieutenant turned the carriage to his right again. They had travelled about one hundred yards when they passed to their left beneath one of three archways and into an expansive plaza, whose size reminded him of the Royal Courtyard at Versailles and with good reason.

"This was the residence of the royal family until Louis XIV decided to build the Château de Versailles," Garnier explained as he halted the horse, hitching it to a post near the Louvre. "You would have difficulty recognising it now, but this was originally a fortress. If what I understand is correct, the entry before us leads to the meeting rooms of the Academy of Sciences.

Robert picked up his backpack and walked across the gravel covered courtyard, following Garnier through the entrance and up a flight of stairs to the second floor. As they marched down a long hallway, they could hear the sounds of a loud discourse emanating from one of the rooms.

The noise from their riding boots must have been recognized by the group of men in the rooms since the moment Robert and Garnier stood in the doorway, all talk ceased. Robert and Garnier looked at six men who stared back at them. Two of them looked especially angry while the remainder seemed curious; as if waiting to learn something about these two officers before reaching a conclusion. None smiled.

Acting first, Robert dismissed Garnier and instructed him wait at the carriage. Smiling, he ignored the hostile expressions and entered the room.

"Gentlemen, please pardon my interruption. My name is Mathurin Dubé. I have come to the academy to ask for your assistance in providing a solution to a scientific problem. I can wait or return if you wish." Robert looked earnestly from one person to another, waiting for a response of some sort. "This group is as unpleasant as the priest in Cholet," he thought.

The man nearest to him broke the silence.

"I am Jean-Charles de Borda," as he approached and shook Robert's hand. "First, allow me to introduce you to our members. This is Jean Delambre, then Pierre Méchain, Jérome Lalande, Joseph Lagrange and finally....".de Borda's introduction abruptly ended when the last man angrily burst forward.

He was one of the men who bore a hateful look from the moment Robert stood in the doorway. His pace quickened as he approached Robert while raising his finger at him.

He was about to say something when Robert completely disarmed him by saying, "And you of course are Pierre Simon Laplace," and shook the hand which had been taking aim at him a moment earlier. Laplace was sometimes referred to as the Isaac Newton of France.

The mood in the room brightened slightly at Robert's attempt to defuse the situation. Laplace had white hair, great reproachful blue eyes and was probably capable of a brilliant smile, but Robert had no idea whether he or anyone would see it today.

Laplace resumed his animosity by sneering at Robert's mere presence. "And what does his Majesty require now? What would someone from the military possibly want from the Science Academy?"

He was rapidly losing patience with Laplace if not the entire group. "Latitude and longitude," he said flatly; waiting for a reaction from anyone in the group. "I need an instrument capable of accurately measuring a pair of co-ordinates. If an instrument like this doesn't exist, I need someone's assistance in fabricating one. I reasoned that if anyone could understand what I need, it would be the members of the Academy."

This seemed to agitate Laplace further, for a reason that seemed to be known only to him.

"We have been conducting researching on this subject for some time ourselves. Who are you to arrive, unannounced; expecting us to stop and assist you?" His face had become nearly as red as his suit.

"Oh, I am perfectly capable of working with you on a solution if you're having difficulty understanding it," Robert said as if speaking to an undergrad. He thought, "Wait for it, wait for it. Here it comes."

Laplace's rage exploded. He "refused to stand for anymore of this nonsense" and stormed from the room, taking the members with him.

"Actually the priest was friendlier," muttered Robert.

All of his attention had been focused on Laplace, but now; glancing slowly about the room he observed that nearly half of their meeting room resembled a classroom. The wall where the academy members congregated had a large blackboard mounted on it. A long wooden table, full of loose papers was surrounded by a dozen chairs, all on a tiled floor. The remainder of the room was like a very comfortable, expansive living room; with sofas, stuffed wing chairs and a number of coffee tables. The furniture was upholstered in subdued shades of browns and greys and where the tiled floor ended, the meeting area was heavily carpeted. He surmised this area must be where the members sat near the fireplace to discuss the topics they had encountered in their academic portion of the room. Tall windows afforded a wide view of the plaza where he could see Garnier waiting by the carriage.

Now he looked back at the blackboard. It seemed they had indeed been discussing longitude and latitude from the equations written on it.

$$\Delta^1_{\text{LONG}} = \frac{\pi}{180} a \cos \phi$$

He recognized this as the formula for the length of a degree of longitude of a sphere. However, he knew that because the earth spins on its axis; it is really an ellipsoid and the formula is different. He picked up a piece of chalk and wrote:

$$\Delta^1_{\text{LONG}} = \frac{\pi a \cos \phi}{180(1 - e^2 \sin^2 \phi)^{1/2}}$$

$$e^2 = \frac{a^2 - b^2}{a^2}$$

Laplace's screaming seemed to have subsided, but Robert was uncertain if that meant he had ceased his rant or had just moved to a part of the Louvre. He still had the room to himself, so he included the formula for measuring the length of a degree of latitude.

$$\tan \beta = (1 - f)\tan \phi,$$

$$P = \frac{\beta_1 + \beta_2}{2} \qquad Q = \frac{\beta_2 - \beta_1}{2}$$

$$X = (\sigma - \sin \sigma)\frac{\sin^2 P \cos^2 Q}{\cos^2 \frac{\sigma}{2}} \qquad Y = (\sigma + \sin \sigma)\frac{\cos^2 P \sin^2 Q}{\sin^2 \frac{\sigma}{2}}$$

$$\text{distance} = a\left(\sigma - \tfrac{f}{2}(X + Y)\right)$$

Robert stepped back and sat on the table. Satisfied, he pushed himself from the table, turned toward the door and noticed several members standing behind him, studying his notations. Crossing the room, he walked to where de Borda stood, took his hand and placed the piece of chalk in it. "If Laplace has difficulty understanding what I've written, I'll be happy to explain it to him. My quarters are at the Military Academy." He bowed slightly, walked down the same hallway and met Garnier in the courtyard.

Garnier climbed into the carriage and grabbed the reins. "Were the members as cordial as they were in the beginning?"

"Charming," he replied sarcastically. "Did we ever discuss the location of Jacques Charles and his workshop?"

"I was still unable to locate his residence. However, the workshop at Place des Victoires is probably still the best place to find him as he spends most of his time there. He works with the Robert brothers; hopefully they will be present also. As I understand, he stopped ballooning some time earlier and now only the Robert brothers take to the air.

The workshop was located not far from the Louvre. After traveling down one narrow street after another, they saw a large opening ahead. The merger of six streets created a circular plaza with a statue in its center. A statue of Louis XIV, standing high on a pedestal; sword in hand was surrounded three and four story buildings with grey slate roofs, with the exception of a small one story building tucked away between them and nearly forgotten, in a corner of the plaza.

The expansive width of the entry way reminded him of a barn, very well suited for someone who moved large objects either in or out of his workshop. He found Jacques Charles studying a drawing of a basket with oars attached to it, which was suspended from a large balloon.

Speaking before he knew who was standing behind him, Jacques began," Brilliant is it not? Who would have realized that you could steer and propel a balloon with oars?" Pausing as if waiting for an answer, he continued; "No one, that's who. Once it became airborne, we found them to be completely useless. They use them on boats for a reason; they're useful on the water."

Turning slowly, he saw it was two French officers who had been listening to him.

"Pardon our interruption sir," Robert began. "I would like to discuss with you, a very important matter of the King's business."

Jacques began to grin at the mention of the King. Jacques was about forty five years of age with very wavy long brown hair and a long straight nose. His increasingly friendly grin accentuated his high cheekbones.

"The King, what would his Majesty want or need from me?" he asked defensively.

"His Majesty has instructed me to develop a method of using latitude and longitudinal measurements to identify specific points on a map and a balloon would be an integral part of achieving my goal," Robert explained. "You are the best known balloonist in France and I am here to enlist your help."

Jacques returned to his drawing and stood next to it. He looked up to the rafters of his workshop as if searching for the answer. "We've been attempting to develop such an instrument for some time now," he said, not sounding very hopeful. "What we have is very good for locating an area like an island at sea, but not a rock on the island. I gather you want to locate the rock," as he glanced back to Robert and Garnier.

"Yes, exactly," said Robert, taking a few steps closer. "It will fulfil some military, as well as scientific objectives. Plus, once it is accomplished, I will have completed my duty to the King and can return home. The King didn't send me to you. I chose to come here because I know that you pioneered the use of hydrogen gas in balloon flight."

"Well yes, that is true," said Jacques as he waived his hand toward the drawing of a balloon with oars. "We sent the balloon aloft which was filled with a gas. It was a huge success, until it landed and peasants attacked it with pitchforks. I will help you with the balloon ride Major, but I'm not sure if I can help you very much with your instrument. You should try visiting the Louvre for that."

When Robert hesitated to speak, Jacques guessed that Robert had already been there.

"Ah, so you have already visited the Academy, have you? I would guess that your visit was not fruitful? "

"Actually," he began, "I think I know how your balloon felt when it met those peasants."

"Well, I guess that means you had the pleasure of meeting Pierre Laplace," he said confidently. "He will help you in his own time. He needs to protest when he feels that he has been disturbed, give him time to consider the circumstances and he'll nearly beg to help you. But, we are wasting time standing here. The Robert brothers are preparing a balloon at Champ de Mars and you definitely should meet them."

Robert and Garnier followed Jacques' carriage for the short ride to Champ de Mars which was located directly across the street from the Military School.

In the center of Champ de Mars, he was introduced to the Robert brothers; Anne-Jean and Nicholas-Louis. They were surrounded by a growing throng, captivated as they watched a balloon slowly inflate. Lead pipes connected the balloon to its source of gas which was being pumped into it by Anne-Jean.

The Robert brothers had erected a rope barrier to keep the curious at bay. "We have about one quarter of a ton of sulphuric acid reacting with half a ton of iron in that vessel," Nicholas-Louis said. "We need the barrier because these people keep trying to show their children the big experiment. That would be just what we need; to have a half-witted parent drop their child into this soup."

Anne-Jean spoke between drawing heavy breaths as he continued pumping gas into the balloon. "This is quicker than when they used to fill a balloon with hot air from a fire, but it is still a laborious process," as he operated a large device that reminded Robert of a bellows.

Robert intently followed the pipe which carried the gas to the balloon from the vessel several times.

"Cold water," he said to himself while he studied the pipes. Jacques Charles and the Robert brothers looked at him waiting for an explanation.

"A gas expands when it is hot and contracts when it cools," he began. "If you run the pipes through cold water before pumping it into the balloon, you will be able to fill it with more gas in less time."

The brothers and Jacques looked at each other, then nodded at Robert and then at the pipes. "Of course, that makes perfect sense. Why hadn't we thought of this before?" said

Jacques. "Mathurin, whenever you wish to go aloft, you only need to ask."

Robert's eyebrows immediately rose. "May I ride in your balloon when it is full?"

"It will be ready soon, Major, and it will be our pleasure," said Nicholas-Louis.

Robert excused himself so that he and Garnier could return his carriage to the Military School's stable. After he changed to his riding boots, he returned to the stable where the sergeant instructed him how to saddle and mount Sadeek. Sadeek seemed to sense his apprehension and maintained a slow gait, as one would to assist a child learning their first steps. Wind blew through his hair and brushed against his face as Sadeek moved effortlessly back and forth across the parade ground. When he returned to the stable, the sergeant then instructed him how to properly care for his horse after he had been ridden. He removed the saddle, brushed his slowly and gave him water and oats.

Robert never walked more briskly than today, crossing Place Joffre as he returned to the Champ de Mars. Jacques and the Robert brothers were in the final stages of preparing the balloon. He could see it above the trees now, as the balloon strained against the mooring lines.

From the balloon hung a large basket, which measured about six feet square. Nicholas-Louis told him to climb into the basket first and after checking the tension in the lines and the ballast, he joined Robert.

He signalled to the people on the ground that it was time to release the lines and within seconds the ropes grew slack and had fallen away as their balloon was ascending rapidly. "This is as much wind as we dare make an ascent in," yelled Nicholas-Louis. "Any windier than this could be very dangerous," as Robert listened to the creaking of the suddenly very fragile looking basket, while it swayed in the wind.

As they quickly rose to nearly one thousand feet, he could appreciate what an advantage the balloon could be in locating a specific area on the ground, once he determined their coordinates.

It was interesting as he viewed how the Seine meandered through Paris. The thousands of streets which seemed to be so illogically arranged when he was on the ground, actually intersected and converged like spokes on a wheel in a very logical pattern. He knew that one of them must be the Place des Victoires where Jacques' workshop was located, but from this height, he couldn't tell which it was. It seemed to him as if they were drifting out of Paris and toward the suburbs.

"This wind is blowing in the same direction as it was when we last ballooned from the Champs de Mars," said Nicholas-Louis as he held the ropes and peered over the edge of the basket. "We landed in a farmer's field like our first flight, but we weren't attacked by peasants. At first they were excited when a balloon landed on their property. Now we have to pay them a landing fee. Hopefully, this time we can return to Paris before it costs us anything."

After a while, Nicholas-Louis pointed to a village that looked like a promising place to land.

"This is Gonesse. It is small and surrounded by fields. It is a perfect spot to land."

As the distance to the village narrowed, Robert noticed that the same was true of the distance to the ground. He began pointing in the direction of a church and tapping his flight partner on the shoulder.

"Ah yes, that is Notre Dame de la Paix, the village church." Then he saw the alarmed look on Robert's face as they were now on a collision course with the church's steeple.

"Oh, this is not good," which was as much of an understatement as Robert had heard in some time.

Nicholas-Louis moved quickly to the side of the basket opposite Robert and told him to release a sandbag when he gave the signal and soon two sandbags were rapidly falling to the village below. The jettisoning of the ballast had the intended effect of gaining enough altitude to just avoid the steeple. However, while the first bag narrowly missed a cart drawn by a small dark horse, the second scored a direct hit in the center; sending its contents and the driver into the street. The driver got to his feet, grabbed the horse's reins with one hand and shook his fist at the occupants of the basket with the other.

Pedestrians were now aware that something unexpected was taking place and gathered near the cart to see what might happen next. As they made the connection between the disappearing balloon and the irate cart driver, they began to follow the direction of its flight on foot. The balloon had by this time passed the church, the cart and driver vanished from view and the two men in the basket were hoping that their recovery crew would arrive at their landing site before any angry villages.

Nicholas-Louis released some gas from the balloon's envelope as they drew nearer to the fields while Robert attempted to quickly plan to what degree the crops below would cushion their landing. Rows of plants on stakes rising from the field beneath them became more threatening as they were now seconds from impact and he felt very concerned that they could become impaled on the stakes

More gas was released and they gently landed in a field of grape vines. He couldn't tell exactly how many stakes were broken, but the destruction was considerable. From the point where they snapped their first stake to their final stop measured nearly sixty feet long and about ten feet in width. Unfortunately, they were also a considerable distance from the road, which would present a problem for the retrieval crew.

As he attempted to guess how this would be accepted by the local farmer, two riders arrived on horseback. Their job was to follow the balloon and then direct the wagon to the site so the balloon could be transported back to Paris. He could only guess who would arrive first.

His answer came sooner than he would have liked as a man with a pitchfork arrived, leading a small group of people. Judging from their direction, Robert presumed that he came from the farmhouse in the distance. As he began to hurl insults and threats against him and Nicholas-Louis, an equally calamitous looking person arrived in his cart from the village.

The cart had been carrying a load of grapes bound for market when the second sandbag landed and Robert had seen the mess lying in the street from the balloon. Now it looked like the driver was wearing a large portion of his crop. His clothing was a mass of juice and pieces of grape stuck in his matted wet hair. Between the destroyed crops and the disagreeable looks on the faces of all parties concerned, Robert concluded that the cost of appeasement would be high.

Nicholas-Louis quickly came to an arrangement with the farmer, who nodded when he had money in his fist and turned with his family, plodding between the ruined crops in the direction of the distant farmhouse.

The disquiet caused by the farmer and his family had subsided now as Nicholas-Louis walked back to the basket. "That was expensive," was all he could utter before the cart driver ran to him, shouting and waving his shovel. When he turned his pockets inside out, the cart driver exhibited emotions that would not easily be subdued. Advancing toward Nicholas-Louis, he shoved him against the basket and seemed determined to raise this confrontation to whatever level he felt necessary.

As Robert approached from his left, the cart driver swung the shovel back to strike Nicholas-Louis, who could do no better than to raise his hands in a feeble attempt to ward off the blow.

Stepping forward, Robert whipped his leg into the back of the drivers knee and he fell into the field as the shovel sailed harmlessly past Nicholas-Louis' head. Robert's hand quickly produced several lire notes from his pocket and extended them to the fallen man. He sheepishly accepted the payment and Robert's assistance from the dirt, before returning to his cart.

By now the wagon arrived and the crew loaded the balloon onto it and began their return to Paris. During the excursion to their workshop, Nicholas-Louis told Jacques and his brother how Robert had defused a potentially dangerous situation. "There is no doubt in my mind that there would have been terrible consequences in your absence, Major. I will be forever in your debt."

Upon reaching Place des Victoires, a throng of spirited people were waiting for them, who applauded as they greeted the carriage. They lined the path to the workshops, very excited, cheering and applauding as the wagon crossed the Place des Victoires and entered Jacques' workshop. Jacques and the Robert brothers were beside themselves with joy. "We accomplished so much today," they said as they hugged and danced across the workshop floor.

"Great, and what exactly did we accomplish today?" thought Robert. "We rose in a balloon, bombed a grape farmer's cart, crashed into a farmer's field and paid a lot of money for crops we destroyed."

The celebration was short lived as most of the revellers returned home almost as quickly as they had arrived.

He was certainly assured a balloon ride at any time in the future, but now he questioned the value it held in determining Ron's location.

After all had been dismantled and stowed away in Jacques' vast workshop, Jacques and the Robert brothers decided that the excursion had been a great success, although

Robert still hadn't discovered what their triumph was measured by. Jacques opened a bottle of wine and they all toasted to the day's events and to their new friend. By now the sun was setting and Robert decided to walk to his quarters rather than accept a ride in his new friend's carriage. He had a lot to consider and preferred use the time alone as an opportunity to put as much effort as possible into planning.

Later, as he lingered on Pont Royal watching as the Seine flowed steadily past; he decided that tomorrow he would return to the Science Academy. This time, he would not allow Laplace to hinder his progress.

In the morning Garnier brought a breakfast of rolls with butter, fruit and tea, but found that Robert already had risen and dressed. The board was now filled with new information. A new set of numbers was written in the center which meant nothing to him.

48 degrees 51 minutes 7.272 seconds North

2 degrees 22 minutes 35.0754 seconds East

Garnier stood as he attempted to decipher the information. "Major, may I ask what this all means?"

Realizing that divulging all the details could create more questions than answers; Robert placed his tea on the table. "The numbers on the upper portion are coordinates to a specific location in Paris. The problem I need to solve is how to identify that location. It could be anywhere in Paris. It might be just outside our gates or it may exist across the Seine. They are more than just numbers, however."

He drew a large circle on the board.

"This is our planet and it can be separated by lines called latitude and longitude. Where these lines intersect identifies a specific place. The solution involves the current and future meetings with the Academy of Science and Jacques Charles."

Robert put the pencil down and retraced his steps to the table and took a sip from his tea before sitting down.

"The project which I proposed to his Majesty involved the development of a system using an observer in a balloon, who could coordinate troop movements with those units on the ground, using matching charts."

Garnier continued to gaze at the board and asked a question as if he already knew the answer.

"Does this mean that you give the idea of training troops in martial arts a low priority?"

"Lieutenant," began Robert slowly, "teaching martial arts or anything to those who don't wish to be taught is a colossal waste of time when the alternative is completing a project that is far more important and useful," as he pointed at the board. "Now you may relax and enjoy your tea. I am going to the stables."

Robert felt exhilarated as he crossed the parade grounds and felt its hard surface crunching against the soles of his riding boots. The sergeant saw him and fetched Sadeek from his stable to be saddled. Sadeek was excited also, as he saw who approached him. Robert gave his mount some sugar and stroked his muzzle. He spoke to Sadeek like a companion as he saddled him and very shortly they were riding together.

As he approached the entrance on Avenue de Lowendal he noticed a coach which had been stopped at the gate by a sentry. The sentry appeared to be speaking to someone in the coach and then turned and pointed in Robert's direction. He wanted to break Sandeek into a gallop but wouldn't use his spurs on his stallion. Instead he crouched forward and pressed his knees against Sadeek's flank. Robert wasn't sure if his horse understood until he suddenly felt like he was flying toward the coach.

They were now racing across the parade ground as officers and students sprinted to get out of the way. Robert's hat flew off adding to the excitement. He could hear Sadeek's heavy breathing as his nostrils flared and they dashed past the startled coachman. Sadeek moved effortlessly in the open space to show everyone, "This is why God created Arabians!".

As they approached the gate, he remembered the reason they were headed in this direction and reluctantly eased back on the reins and the pressure with his knees. Sadeek slowed to a trot and made a wide turn to where the coach had halted. Passing the stable, the sergeant saluted, with an enormous smile and tears in his eyes. Most of those who had stopped to watch Sadeek's fluid movements resumed their duties when they realized that he wasn't going to resume his exhibition of speed.

Approaching the coach, Robert stopped and dismounted as a man emerged. Old and bent with white hair, pale green eyes and large sideburns, his movements were as slow as Sadeek's were swift. Regarding him with complete indifference the old man inquired, "Are you Major Mathurin Dubé, sir?"

Robert nodded and he reached for an envelope and lifted it to Robert as if it were made of lead.

"My name is Aubrey, sir" He spoke as if every word was going to be his last. "I am secretary to The Royal Academy of Science. I am to wait for your reply and return with it to the Louvre."

"Monsieur Aubrey, would you please wait in your coach and I will give you my answer in a moment?" Robert unsealed the envelope as Aubrey returned to the carriage with his odd shuffling walk.

Royal Academy of Science

My Dear Major Dubé,

Please honour us with your presence at our meeting this morning at precisely 11.00. I believe we have much to discuss. A meal will be served. Aubrey will await your decision. I pray it will be a positive one.

At your service,

Laplace

"First he screams at me and now this," murmured Robert as he walked to the carriage. Aubrey's pale, round face stood out against the coach window like a painting of the moon. "Monsieur Aubrey, you may tell the members that I am very excited to accept this invitation."

His enthusiasm was tempered by Aubrey's lack of interest as he settled back in his seat, obviously void of feeling and expression. "Very good, sir," was all he offered. Raising his cane, he banged once behind the driver's seat. "To the Louvre," he shouted, and the carriage made a slow turn to exit the Military School.

Robert watched as the coach slowly retreated through the gates before recovering his hat from the gravel covered ground and the sergeant strode out to meet him, taking Sadeek's reins with his hand.

"He is magnificent," as he stroked the stallion's head. "The way he moves is more like gliding than galloping. Major, this is the most marvelous horse that has ever existed." Without really looking in Robert's direction, he led Sadeek to an area where the saddle could be removed and his coat brushed.

The sergeant watched as Robert groomed Sadeek. "You are becoming an excellent horseman, Major. Both of you move so well together. You move together as one, not merely a horse and a rider. That is why people stop to watch you."

Robert continued to brush Sadeek. "It's him making me a better rider, sergeant. When he galloped just now, it was like he knew what to do before I did. Do you think I'm ready to ride away from the confines of the Military School? I have a meeting before noon at the Louvre. Also, would he be safe? I wouldn't want to lose him to a thief."

"If you are not ready Major, he certainly is," the sergeant replied as he leaned against a column. "Concerning his safety, Sadeek is too recognizable to steal. If he was stolen, he couldn't be hidden forever and once seen, wouldn't remain a secret for long. Also, he is wearing a military saddle. Although he is a gift to you from his Majesty, that symbol on the saddle makes him property of the King. To steal your horse, would invite a death sentence. When you arrive at the Louvre I'm sure that you will find people who will consider it an honor to watch him for you."

After he had finished grooming Sadeek, he thanked the sergeant for his valuable assistance and returned to his quarters; walking across the parade ground while he brushed the dust from his hat. Selecting a new uniform for his meeting, he laid at the foot of his bed; head propped up on his intertwined hands, staring at the coordinates on the drawing board. He wished there was some way to assure Ron that his package was going to arrive soon. However, all he could do was to remain focused on working rapidly and use his time efficiently. He knew instinctively that his inability to transport Ron's package was tied to the key fob, but all he could do now was use his abilities as a scientist to explain it and find a solution.

The knock at his door broke his train of thought. When he told the person to enter, Garnier opened the door and entered with letters in his hand. "Correspondence for you, sir;" he announced with a straightforward tone.

Robert continued studying the board, completely disinterested in the mail. He sounded like someone, who was lost in his thoughts. "Just tell me who wrote them please, Lieutenant."

"Yes sir, the first eight are likely to be responses from your letter regarding combat training, judging from the names on the envelopes. The last one......, Garnier's voice trailed off as he studied the envelope. Normally he would be peeved with this lack of information, but Robert simply did not care. "I would rather have all the junk mail in the world, than reactions to martial arts training," he thought.

"This final one is from the Duchess Gabrielle de la Polignac. Major this is from the Governess of the Children of......," the lieutenant's excited tone was cut short as Robert lept from his bed and tore the letter from Garnier's hand. He walked to the sofa and carefully opened it. "Just read those letters and tell me what their responses are."

While Garnier opened letter after letter, Robert relaxed and read Gabrielle's correspondence. She mentioned how Marie-Thérese had pestered her to write to see how his life in Paris was progressing and how much she missed him. Gabrielle went on to say how life at Versailles has not been the same since he left. Everyone was still talking about the manner in which he dismissed the arrogant Lieutenant Petit in the Hercules Salon.

He was about to read her letter for the third time when Garnier interrupted. "These are responses from the commanding officers who received letters from General Libley. They all question the reason for this training. Few agree about the need for it and they all agree that they only responded because it was a directive of the King. They request more information before they will release any officers for this type of training. How would you like to respond to them?"

"First, thank them for their response. Then ask then for their suggestion on how to implement this plan."

Garnier sounded confused and annoyed. "Sir, let me make certain that I understand your meaning. You are ordering me to respond to these officers who don't want to participate in this program and ask them how they can accept a larger share of its planning?"

Robert was already putting on his coat and had just picked up his hat from the bed. "Yes Lieutenant, that's exactly what I want. I am leaving now for the Academy of Sciences. You may embellish those letters however you like." He glanced at the fireplace and for a brief moment considered tossing Gabrielle's letters into it, instead he chose to carefully fold it and place it inside his coat.

He anticipated a magnificent ride on Sadeek to the Louvre considering that it perhaps would be a greater experience than the uncertainty of the meeting he was about to attend there. He knew what to expect with Sadeek, but he accepted that his reception at the Louvre could be far less predictable.

Sadeek began prancing and whinnying when he saw Robert approaching with his saddle. As they rode onto Rue Joffre, Sadeek seemed to be in high spirits and all the people they passed stopped to admire him. When they entered the courtyard of the Louvre, Robert dismounted and a small group approached to look more closely at his stallion. Among them were two young boys aged about 13 years; one taller than the other but both painfully thin who approached and asked if they could touch Sadeek's coat. When they were offered a ride around the courtyard, they could barely contain themselves. He could tell from the manner in which the boys and Sadeek responded to each other that they would probably be interested in the chance to tend to him while he visited the Academy of Science meeting.

The smaller boy saw an opportunity present itself and drew himself as straight and tall as possible. "How much will you pay us to watch your horse, Major?"

Having foreseen this possibility, Robert drew a lire note from his pocket. This was already more money than they had probably seen at one time and they both gasped as he held it in front of them.

"He will need to be walked occasionally and you need to devote all of your attention to his needs. His name is Sadeek. It means "true friend". Can you boys be a true friend to him?"

Both boys nodded, as their attention was divided between the horse's reins and the money, both of which now resided in Robert's hands.

"I want you to think about this," he said pointing to a window on the second floor of the Louvre. "I will be in a room up there and will be able to see you both easily. So be certain to properly care for him. Do you see my saddle?"

Again they nodded.

"That symbol means that this horse is the property of the King. If anything happens to him you could be sent to the Bastille forever. Do you want to go to the Bastille?"

Both boys shook their heads and said softly, "No, sir."

"What are your names?" he said with a serious look on his face.

"I am Henri and this is my friend Gerard," said the taller boy.

"Very good," Robert replied. He held the note and tore it in half. He handed half of one note to Gerard. "Take good care of Sadeek and you'll receive the other half when I return." The boy quickly snatched the note from Robert and stiffed it in his shirt with one hand, while snatching the reins with his other.

Robert turned and walked quickly toward the entrance to the Louvre. He began to steel himself for his second encounter with Laplace and the other society members. He didn't wish to presume that this meeting would be any more cordial than his initial visit. Walking through the doorway of the meeting room placed him directly in front of Laplace who apparently had been waiting for him. Discussion amongst the members ceased as when he had arrived with Garnier in his initial visit. However, this encounter was completely different. Laplace smiled and with an outstretched arm, shook Robert's hand vigorously and appeared to be genuinely glad to see him again.

"Major Dubé, thank you for accepting our invitation. Please accept my apologies for my reaction to your presence yesterday. The Royal Academy of Sciences was created by Louis XIV to be apolitical; however we are not always treated in that manner. Lately, it seems that when people from Versailles arrive unannounced, they always require something which is not science related and only offer us their ignorance in return. When we saw the formulae you left, I realised what a colossal mistake I made. Here, let us sit and talk."

From the part of the room where all the chairs were arranged in a circle, the members had risen and all stepped forward to greet him. Everyone thanked him for returning and they were very grateful that he accepted their invitation. They were extremely interested in learning more about their guest and when they were told that their guest was a scientist also, they were very impressed; but had to admit that the California Institute of Technology was unfamiliar to them.

Old Aubrey stood by the doorway, mute and expressionless. As their discussions ranged through a variety of scientific topics, he could see how invaluable Aubrey really was. He orchestrated all that occurred in that room which supported the Society. When everyone was settled in their chairs, he directed the staff to serve the meal. As plates were emptied, they were whisked away. Drinks were supplied and cigars were lit. Curtains were opened and windows raised or lowered depending on the height of the midday sun. If any of the members were asked to identify any of the staff, they would have been unable to. Aubrey made them invisible. His management of the meeting made everything flow seamlessly, like water flowing downhill and allowed them to be completely unaware of whatever occurred around them, enabling them to concentrate solely on their conversation.

Now that their wine glasses were filled, Laplace turned in his chair and faced Robert.

"We were all intrigued by the equations you left us with, Major. Our calculations function well in general when measuring the length of a degree of longitude. It fails when measuring some parts of the globe, but we didn't understand why. Can you explain it to us?"

Robert paused for a moment, wondering how best to begin. He walked to a large globe which was positioned next to one of the many windows. Depositing his hat and coat onto a vacant chair, he glanced out onto the courtyard and saw the boys walking Sadeek as the ever present throng of onlookers followed.

Turning the globe slowly on its axis he looked at the members. "We can all agree on the basic measurements of the earth. The earlier equations work fine on a sphere at rest. However, the earth is not at rest. It rotates like this globe at about 1070 miles per hour and in doing so its shape becomes elliptical. It is this difference in shape that renders your equation incapable of accurate measurements in latitude and longitude."

He stopped the globe for effect, walked to the blackboard and began to write.

"And this gentlemen, is why I came to you. The reason I am in Paris is to determine the location of these coordinates;
48 degrees   51 minutes   7.272 seconds   North

2 degrees   22 minutes   34.0754seconds   East.

I need an instrument capable of accurately measuring these coordinates."

Jean Charles de Borda was the first to speak. "I can appreciate your interest in this, Mathurin. An accurate measurement for one's location has been sought for centuries. When I commanded French ships during the American Revolutionary War, I tested several methods of determining our location. Measurements taken when a ship is at sea will result in giving you the location of an area, but not as specific which is what you would desire on land. It has never been attempted before and perhaps that is the best reason to attempt it now."

"The primary scientific topic that we planned to discuss here today is, coincidentally; the same matter which you brought to us," he continued. "That is, whether a practical method exists to accurately measure longitude on land using the marine chronometer. This is a very expensive instrument and we are very fortunate to have one loaned to us by the Navy." De Borda finished speaking and gestured in the direction of a chair closest to Aubrey, who looked on sullenly.

A young naval officer walked to the large table near the blackboard where a wooden box had been placed in the center. It had brass fittings and a handle on its side for carrying and when he pressed a button, it unlocked the front. Inside the box, sat a clock resting on hinges. "This is Lieutenant Maingon, our liaison with the Navy," began de Borda. "He developed a new method of determining the distance between the sun or a star at noon to determine longitude at sea. We feel that his findings may help us better understand how to apply his methods to locating those measurements on land."

Picking up a piece of chalk, the lieutenant bowed and turned to the blackboard. He drew a circle with a line across the center and another connecting the two poles. "The problem with a marine chronometer is that it is most effective at sea level," he began. "We need to determine the effect altitude may play when using it to measure latitude on land. We know that the equator is 0 degrees latitude. For our experiment we have decided to permanently use Greenwich, England as 0 degrees longitude. We will take our measurements at noon: Greenwich Time, which it will be shortly. Let's move quickly to the courtyard and begin our experiment."

As they exited the Louvre, de Borda walked straight to a specific spot in the courtyard. Robert was about to question him regarding its relevance when de Borda motioned to a medallion which had been embedded in the ground.

"This is our latitude, as accurately as we could measure it anyway," de Borda explained. "It seemed to make sense to establish a reference point nearby. Now let's see what if we can measure longitude."

Robert knelt and read the medallion's notations.

N 48° 51', which to Robert seemed incomplete.

"Excuse me Jean-Charles, but I don't see your measurements measured to the seconds position. The accuracy which I require is to the hundredths of a second."

"I noticed that as well from the coordinates you wrote on the board, Mathurin," replied Jean-Charles. "We are capable of measuring the degree of accuracy which would be adequate on the deck of a ship. What we are seeking is much more accuracy than that, however. I suspect that the location you are looking for is in our vicinity. My best guess is somewhere in Porte Saint-Antione, possibly near the Bastille. I can't tell how great a variation exists between those we measured here and your coordinates until we visit that area. My suggestion is this, we visit the probable area today and return tomorrow morning at 11.30 Greenwich Time. Then we can measure latitude and longitude and compare those measurements with yours.

As he spoke with the members of the society in the courtyard, Sadeek and the boys watched him intently. Sadeek was visibly tired of the admiration from these two boys and seemed aware that the entire affair would mercifully end soon. Robert excused himself from de Borda and joined the boys, handing them the missing half of their lire note. They quickly ran across the courtyard, in the direction of their neighborhood which lay beyond the walls of the Louvre. Robert mounted Sadeek and left for the congested streets of Porte Sainte-Antoine.

Amidst the crowds and tall, desperate buildings, they stopped before an open area. It was the size of a small park, lacking any desirable attributes. The surface had been denuded of any sort of grasses. This should be an arena where children play, or adults gather to discuss the events of the day. Instead, it was a depressing caricature of the poor section of Paris where children played on an uneven plot of land with rocks and sticks for toys.

De Berg struggled to describe the depressing nature of this part of the city. "In this section of Paris, people are more likely to eat adulterated food, consume and bathe in water with high levels of pollution and suffer with the resultant malaria. It was said that in the 17th century, people here died from hunger, in the 18th century they just suffer from it. Rousseau once referred to Paris as a place "dominated simultaneously by the most sumptuous opulence and the most deplorable misery. Some well-intentioned people have attempted to bridge the gap between rich and poor. They formed the Société Philanthropies in 1780 where all members were equal and private people come together to speak publicly, but they can only do so much"

Robert acknowledged de Berg's description and walked with Sadeek while he tried to ignore the surroundings and entertained the notion that conditions here could improve without the intervention of someone who possessed a very strong will.

De Borda talked about an area in which he felt might have some promise. "I know a person who is an expert in constructing precision instruments and is very interested in becoming involved in this project. His name is Étienne Lenoir and he lives on Rue Vendome, which is not far from here. I have invited him to meet our members and you here tomorrow. Until then, Mathurin."

As de Borda returned to his coach, Robert held Sadeek's reins and walked in the general direction of the Bastille. He was inclined to continue walking, as it helped him to think. However,

Sadeek was attracting a new crowd of devotees and to escape the crush of pedestrians, he mounted his horse and joined the flow of carts and wagons until he reached the Seine.

His optimism was growing however, now that events seemed to be proceeding in the proper direction. It was tempered however, by the fact that he was still proceeding much slower than he wished, accompanied by an irritating degree of uncertainty. He continued to follow the Seine as far as Pont Neuf. He could hear voices from the river below, as people worked to secure their boats to the embankment for the evening. It reminded him that he had a long day before him also, and needed to quit this circuitous route and return his quarters.

After brushing Sadeek and giving him water and an apple, he returned to his room intending to send Garnier to bring him dinner. He was surprised to find him sitting on his sofa, engaged with something in his hands.

Garnier stood up so quickly that it mildly startled Robert and he examined the expression on his aide's face that was a mixture of guilt and surprise. Robert quickly looked back to the table as his heart froze. Garnier was holding his cell phone!

Garnier began speaking so rapidly that Robert could barely comprehend what he was saying. "I'm so sorry Major. I was cleaning for you and found this on the table. When I picked it up to move it, it...." Garnier found it difficult to describe something he had no words for. The lieutenant stammered as he searched for words to explain.

He remembered now, when he was searching through his backpack earlier, he must have removed his cell phone and had neglected to return it.

Garnier looked upset and worried. Unauthorised use of a superior officer's property was a serious offence. Many young officers' careers had been ruined for far less.

"Show me what you found, Lieutenant," said Robert patiently, trying to put him at ease. "I'm not angry. I'm only interested in what you found."

"It's Paris, sir. It's like magic. This is like viewing the city as a bird might see it. I saw the Seine, the Bastille, and Pont Neuf. And when I touch this surface like this it moves."

Garnier's fright had disappeared now as he became more animated and handed the devise back to Robert.

"I had an app for this?" he thought.

His index finger slid across the screen until he recognized the area near the Bastille and located the open area he had visited earlier. As the cell phone focused on that area, numbers appeared across the lower portion of the screen. They were coordinates!! He continued to focus and slowly move his finger across the screen until he found a point that matched Ron's coordinates exactly. "Garnier, you just found my ticket home. Thank you." Powering down his device, he returned it to his backpack, next to the envelope containing Ron's documents. When his device had been upgraded to be of service in Europe, his provider had included this feature and never mentioned it to him.

Garnier looked relieved and completely puzzled. He had been caught in possession of someone else's property and was being thanked for it.

"Lieutenant, my favorite meal would be a roasted fowl with roasted potatoes, warm bread and the best bottle of wine you can locate. You are, of course, welcome to join me," he said enthusiastically

Garnier could not believe what was happening and thought it best to exit quickly before anything changed. Robert could not believe his good fortune including the irony of it all. With his all his planning and effort, the solution had been uncovered by a junior officer who still had no idea what he had done. The visits to the Royal Academy of Sciences, talking to some of the greatest scientific minds of the eighteenth century, were outdone by Lieutenant Garnier while playing with his superior officer's cell phone.

Robert took time to have a bath drawn and when Garnier returned with the meal, he was really ready to relax. He instructed Garnier to put the meal on the table and pour wine for them both. Garnier was surprised and elated when Robert looked at the solitary glass of wine and reminded him to pour a glass for himself. The notion that a superior officer would ask his aide to join him for dinner was very unusual. Quickly pouring a glass for himself, was followed by toasting to the success of their careers, which seemed to complete this part of the evening. Robert was buoyed by the weight that had been lifted from him due to Garnier's recent accidental discovery.

Tomorrow, he could deliver Ron's package personally, certain that the key to his return to Syracuse would be realized. When the wine and dinner were finished, both officers felt very satisfied. Robert hoped his excitement would allow him some much needed sleep because tomorrow would certainly be a day of days.

He arose at first light as it was his practice now to keep his recently hung curtains open and be awakened by the morning sun. On this sunny day, he exercised in his quarters, practicing his katas until Garnier arrived with tea and a simple breakfast of eggs, cheese and bread. Robert could not disguise his uplifted mood and had difficulty finishing his morning meal. He would sit and drink some tea, eat some bread and cheese; and walk to the window. Then he would pace and return for more tea and a bite of his egg but before he could finish, he felt compelled to return to pace and discuss one topic after another. Actually, discussion was not an accurate description as Garnier never contributed to the conversation.

The walk to the stables was brisker that morning. The sun felt warmer and his pace was more energetic. The sergeant noticed that Robert's mood was more robust than usual and at the end of his ride with Sadeek; he spent extra time brushing his mane and coat and stroking his muzzle.

"I will return in a few hours sergeant. Sadeek and I will be observing a very important scientific experiment in Porte Saint-Antoine. Plus, it is a perfect day for a ride."

The sergeant smiled, wondering which event was most important to the Major.

Robert decided to attempt a new route to the meeting place where he would find his fellow scientists. He was becoming more familiar with Paris now and felt that as his time here was limited, he and Sadeek should see as much of Paris as possible.

Exiting through the gate closest to the stables, Robert directed Sadeek to turn left and traveled down a cobblestone street. They passed a park which reminded him of the gardens at Versailles with its meticulous symmetry of lawns and tree lines. A small chapel with tall columns and a gold dome dominated the center. Behind the chapel, a long beige colored two story building with grey slate roofs, formed a perimeter around the gardens. Shortly, he could tell from the sounds of boats and glimpses of bridges on his left that he was approaching the Seine. Pont de Sully crossed the seine at this point and Notre Dame could be seen in the distance on his left.

He arrived before the miserable park just as several coaches approached and stopped. Laplace and de Borda stepped down and walked to him first, looking very excited. While the ever dour Aubrey oversaw the erection of tables and instruments for the experiments, de Borda approached accompanied by the naval lieutenant and a man he was unfamiliar with.

"Mathurin, I would like you to meet Étienne Lenoir, expert maker of high quality instruments and you have already met Lieutenant Maingon."

Robert shook hands with both men, while de Berg explained further.

"The lieutenant will measure longitude with the marine chronometer, while I use the sextant to measure latitude. Étienne will then give us his opinion on increasing the accuracy of our existing instruments or the need to create something new."

Lenoir was short and thin with coarse lips and apparently uncontrollable grey hair and an impish grin. He had the longest, most delicate fingers Robert had ever seen.

Lagrange, Lalande, Méchain and Delambre gathered around the table where Aubrey was making preparations and all were in especially good spirits. As Robert walked to join them, a crowd of the curious began to form around the perimeter of the dirt covered plot. He glanced in Sadeek's direction and noticed that a crowd gathered near his stallion and quite a few of them were backing away as well. He diverted his path from walking toward the Society members and proceeded directly to his horse, as he suspected the cause of the disturbance.

Lieutenant Maingon and de Borda stood and watched as he approached the crowd, reached into his pocket pulled out a lire note, tearing it in half before wading through the onlookers. He managed to move through the throng where he heard shouts emanating from the center of the commotion. When he finally reached the center of the crowd, he confirmed its cause. Henri and Gerard had seen Sadeek and now had taken up posts as self-appointed guardians, keeping all at bay. They snapped to attention when Robert pushed way into the center, and saluted him.

"We have been keeping all this riff-raff away from Sadeek, Major. But some won't listen," said Gerard as he kicked the shin of someone whom he felt had come dangerously close to the horse they felt deeply responsible for.

Robert handed one half of the note to Henri. "Listen boys, it's perfectly fine if people want to look at Sadeek, but they need to form a line. Being surrounded like this would make anyone nervous," as he made eye contact with Sadeek and stroked his muzzle.

Robert announced to the throng that everyone would need to wait their turn in line if they wanted to see his horse, or he'd see to it that none would. This time people allowed him a large path to exit as he appeared like someone who had no time to debate the issue and departed to rejoin the Academy members, Étienne and the lieutenant.

Noon was fast approaching as de Berg and Maingon each raised their respective instruments. Lagrange stood over the chronometer with Lieutenant Maingon, as de Borda lifted the sextant from the table. Lagrange yelled "mark" as the chronometer measured 12.00 Post Meridian, Greenwich Time. Quickly Maingon located 2 degrees 22'minutes East longitude, while de Borda measured and calculated 48 degrees 51' minutes North latitude. All of the measurements were recorded by Lalande and Méchain.

Determined as they were in their attempt to refine their measurements, even using the accurate formulae supplied by their newest acquaintance, nothing remotely close to Ron's coordinates could be obtained. Even Étienne, who was the finest maker of instruments, admitted to Robert that he could not make an instrument capable of measuring the coordinates to the degree of accuracy he required which he had presented him with.

This would pose a huge problem, as a difference of one degree was equal to a difference of one mile in either direction. This would clearly be an unsatisfactory situation if he had any hope that he and the package could arrive in Ron's living room.

With this sort of accuracy, he might arrive where he intended; but could just as easily land in the Seine.

Aubrey now began the laborious process of returning all the equipment to their coaches for transport back to the Louvre. Robert stood and talked with the Academy members, who were all very excited with the results of their experiment. This was their proof that dividing the earth into grids defined by latitude and longitude, was feasible and validated the use of the meter as a unit of measure and accuracy by using the correct formula.

As for his plans, Robert desperately needed the members to remove themselves from here, so he could move on with his personal task. Aubrey had managed to effortlessly move all the equipment back to their coaches and they were soon ready to return to the Louvre. Laplace suggested to him that he should begin attending their meetings on a regular basis. "There will always be room for an intellect like yours in our Society, Mathurin. Please consider that I speak for all the members." He extended his hand and vigorously shook Robert's. Laplace turned and walked to a carriage where the ever present Aubrey held a door open for him. Laplace entered without really acknowledging Aubrey, who in turn, faced Robert and bowed respectfully. Without waiting for any gesture in return, he followed Laplace into the coach and ordered the driver to proceed.

Now that the entourage was departing, he returned his attention to Sadeek and the boys who were left tending to him. A line had indeed formed just as he had ordered and he could see more clearly now that the crowd had melted away as the carriages departed. The boys were keeping everything very orderly as charged, but they had included something Robert had not anticipated. They were demanding a fee just to touch Sadeek, who had clearly had enough of this sort of attention.

"That's enough boys," he said handing one of them the remaining half of the lire note, and regaining possession of the reins.

"But we've collected money from all of these people already," they protested in unison.

"Not my problem boys," said Robert sternly. "I paid you to tend to my horse. You didn't rent him from me," looking at their pockets, bulging with money. "In all fairness, you two crooks should be paying me. Now refund their money," and he walked away with a very relieved Sadeek.

One segment of the problem was that while his app did identify the coordinates he sought, the image of Paris he was using as a reference now was taken in the mid-21st century, not the year 1789. Standing in the street, he viewed an open lot. On the screen of his mobile devise, he viewed the store front of a pharmacy with six floors of apartments rising above it.

Robert found a spot in the street in front of the lot that corresponded to: 48 degrees 51' 7.727 seconds North,

2 degrees 22' 35.0754 seconds East.

Calculating the difference in the distance from that spot in the street, to Ron's coordinates, he walked with Sadeek; due east until he reached the location in the lot that he was positive was the same as Ron's.

Opening the pouch he carried, he removed the envelope along with the key fob Ron had sent. With a push of the button he could accompany the package too, but he looked at Sadeek and reflected about how circumstances had placed him here for a reason and believed he could delay his departure for just awhile longer. He placed the envelope in the dirt with the key fob on top. If ever a theory of his needed to be validated, this was it. He stared at the envelope, took one deep breath, knelt down and pushed the button.

LISETTE

Robert stood and backed away from the spot in the dirt where he had placed the envelope. The envelope had vanished, Ron should have his package now and his theory ought to have been validated. He drew an enormous sigh of relief and then became acutely aware of the sound of voices behind him.

This attention was something he was becoming increasingly accustomed to. The fact that onlookers constantly wanted to get closer to this incredible horse was becoming very predictable.

He was astonished when he turned to face the most openly hostile looking group he had ever imagined. All were directing their most hateful, vile gazes at him. A woman stood at the apex of the crowd and seemed to reflect the sentiment of all those who stared at him cold and scrutinizing manner.

He thought that despite her hateful stare, she was the most beautiful woman he had ever seen. Her long ashen blond hair lay gently across her shoulders. She had deep blue eyes and skin like alabaster. Judging from the extent of the animosity she directed at him, he thought she was a person who would be unwavering in whatever task she undertook. He was also positive that if looks could kill, he would be dead by now.

But Robert stood straight and returned their hateful stares with the look of complete tranquility. He could have mounted Sadeek and reached the street before anyone could stop him. However, he was Major Mathurin Dubé of his Majesty's cavalry and feeling that he undoubtedly presented a very impressive appearance in his officer's uniform, should make a proper impression and receive an appropriate amount of respect from this incredibly gorgeous but overtly antagonistic creature.

He stood straight, looked her in the eye and said; absolutely nothing. Stunned, as he attempted to comprehend what happened as his mouth remained open but he couldn't speak. His forehead began to perspire and the dryness in his mouth increased while he rubbed his forehead in confusion and saw the hatred in the eyes of the mob softening. He decided to try again. His mind seemed to lose its focus as he looked at her again.

"Your name what is?" Something inexplicable occurred between the moments when his thought arose in his brain and his words sprang from his mouth. A moment ago the crowd seemed bent on attacking him. Now they seemed ready to take pity on this obviously brain damaged young man in an officer's uniform.

The outward animosity so apparent earlier, was diminishing while some in the crowd began discussing who could volunteer to take charge of this poor man.

The woman who was the reason for his difficulties was not so easily convinced and was waiting for an answer that satisfied her. He was certain that the amount of time he had to make anything positive of this was quickly waning. He thought for a moment and then surprised himself and everyone else when the word "playground", forced itself from his mouth. Now that the crowd heard him speak, they returned to listen for more.

Robert attempted to collect his thoughts and continued. "Yes, that's right. A playground, right here," he shouted, pointing to the barren ground. "The King wants build a playground somewhere in Paris for the children. He sent me to search for a suitable sight and this is it!" Using his index finger for emphasis, he moved his hand in a circular motion until he uttered the word "it" and pointed at his foot before continuing.

"I see a slide, monkey bars, a teeter totter, a........" It was apparent by their blank expressions that he had lost their attention beginning with the mention of monkey bars; as they returned to their initial reason to question his sanity.

"Why would the King send a single officer into Porte Saint-Antoine to do anything for the children?' she demanded. "His majesty has never shown that he values his subjects as anything but grist for his mill. I believe that there is something very sinister in your visit today," as the people in the crowd now began nodding in agreement with the woman who seemed bent on discrediting whatever Robert said.

It was clear that this woman could incite this group to agitation very quickly.

"They're not buying any of this," thought Robert.

"No, no that's not the case at all," he pleaded. "We really intend to build something special for the children, to avoid playing with these," as he bent down where the envelope had been, picking up stones and dirt and then dropping them for effect.

A part of him wondered why he was carrying on so, when the real purpose for being in Paris ended the instant Ron's package disappeared. It would be easy to mount Sadeek and disappear from here forever. But children in this poorest portion of Paris were in such a plight that he became convinced that he was in a position to do something truly special for them before returning to his time.

"This then is my plan," he shouted. "It is to convert this nothing piece of your neighborhood, into a place where children can have fun while they are still young, before time robs them of their childhood in the present and replaces it with futility in the future. How is this something that anyone could possibly have any objection to?" He spoke to the crowd, but he looked directly at this woman who seemed to be at the center of all the hostility brewing here; and she knew it. When he heard nothing in reply he continued. "I will be here quite often and I would like your help. My name is Mathurin Dubé. Please come to me with any questions or offers to help."

As the uninspired crowd slowly melted away in the direction of the street, Robert led Sadeek toward the street and was very surprised to see the woman who had just been his accuser, look at him and smile. Feeling a bit emboldened by this melting of her original icy charm, he stopped Sadeek.

"What's your name, mademoiselle?"

She paused for a moment with a look of uncertainty, as if revealing her name was beyond her comfort level.

"Lisette."

"Lisette. Lisette what? How do I find you?"

She looked at him for a moment, as it was now someone was waiting for her to answer their question. Her response was to turn and become part of the crowd. In a moment, he lost sight of her. Hurrying to the street, he met the two boys who, until recently had been earning a good living from Sadeek. Their pockets were still full of coins.

"Boys, I need some information from you"

"Yes, Major?" was their first reply.

"What will you pay us for this?" was their second.

Robert stepped closer to them and knelt on one knee. The boys were a little startled when he quickly closed the distance between them. "Let me tell you little thieves something. You have earned a great deal of money from me and Sadeek. Telling me where she works is the least you can do for me. Otherwise," he said as he withdrew his dagger, "I will slit your," they retreated with a terrified look on their faces; "pockets and you can fight to reclaim your coins from everyone in the streets."

He was certain that this was his most unpleasant look as the boys continued to back away from him. They began to babble the way he had when confronted by the angry crowd earlier, but soon regained their composures and then faced him. "Major,"

Henri said in a very sincere voice. "Is that really the cruelest you can look?"

Robert realized he wasn't fooling anyone. "Gerard, Henri; I really need your help with locating the woman who led that crowd," he continued. "You can keep your money. I only need to find this woman who calls herself Lisette. Will you ride Sadeek with me and show me where she works?" he asked.

That seemed like their best option and soon all three were riding as two very excited boys pointed out directions and waived to anyone they knew.

"What is Lisette's' last name?" Robert asked.

"They just call her the "Bread Lady", offered Henri, shouting over Robert's shoulder. "We didn't even know her first name until you spoke it just now. She owns a bread shop on Passage de la Bonne Graine. She bakes bread and gives it to the children of Porte Saint- Antoine.

Henri and Gerard directed him from the lot on Avenue Ledru Rollin and after a short distance, instructed him to turn Sadeek sharply to his right. This reminded him of the narrow streets he encountered in Cholet as he searched for the church inhabited by the mole like priest. The street bent until it became scarcely wide enough for a coach. In the middle of this sad excuse for a street, the boys pointed to a store front with a hitching post in front of it. The sign over the door read simply "BOULANGERIE" in large gold letters. Robert dismounted and helped Henri and Gerard to the ground. "Mind Sadeek, would you please boys? This probably won't last long," as he handed them the reins.

The front of the store was painted dark green, with a door in the center and breads of different sizes and varities visible through the large windows located on either side of it.

He walked purposely to the door and entered without hesitation. When he reached the counter he stopped. Lisette's back was to him as she checked on something in her ovens. Wooden beams ran across the exposed ceiling and the floor was made of stone. Walls of brick extended to the ovens in the rear of her shop and bins filled with loaves of bread and baguettes were everywhere.

Everyone in the shop now stood aside and looked at Robert. The person talking to Lisette stopped in mid- sentence and peered over her shoulder at the stranger waiting at the counter. Lisette slowly turned and faced Robert.

Her expression was similar to what he had seen earlier. Her shocked appearance was quickly replaced by her scornful glare, magnified by the placement of her hands upon her hips.

"What do you want, Lieutenant?" she asked sharply.

"To begin with mademoiselle., my rank is Major, but I would rather you to call me Mathurin. Second, if you weren't already aware, it is very rude to turn your back on someone when they are speaking to you. I asked you your name and you gave me your back. I would like to know why you greet me with such hostility when you don't even know me. All I've done is perform a scientific experiment here and offer to build something for the children. Explain to me why it is bad for me to offer help the children by building a playground, but good for you to give them bread?"

"I give bread to starving children because I live here, and it is the right thing to do," she countered. "Not because our King tells me to do so. I am not motivated by the whims of this monarchy. The monarchy and its representatives have brought nothing but misery here. I sincerely doubt the sincerity of someone who, like you; must have achieved his rank due to his family connections."

By now, Robert and Lisette were completely oblivious to the bystanders in the shop. He felt that the force of her venomous attack wasn't going to lessen as it seemed too deeply rooted. He paused and looked away for a moment before turning to face Lisette.

"What you claim to know about me isn't true at all. I wasn't given my rank because of who my family is, but because of a service I performed. The King had offered me the rank of Marquis of Anjou, but I requested to serve France, not take from it."

"You refused a gift like that from His Majesty? What could someone like you possibly have done to be granted anything approaching that?" she scoffed at Robert, leaning further across the counter as her harshness grew.

"It was to repay a debt His Majesty felt he owed to me." His voice was growing louder, but there was no anger in his voice. He placed his hands on the counter also, leaned forward and now their noses were nearly touching.

Lisette raised her voice again and said mockingly, "What would the King possibly be indebted to you for?"

He paused a moment and reluctantly answered. "He felt indebted to me for defending his daughter, Marie-Thérese from attackers."

Now it was Lisette who paused and stood up straight as her eyes widened and her mouth opened. "That was you? You're the one? Why didn't you tell me?" she said meekly.

Murmuring began to replace the previous silence in the shop. "He defeated 15 men single handedly. And they were all heavily armed," said one. "No, no," corrected another. "There were twenty men on horseback," as more comments swirled about behind them.

Robert continued to lean forward and stared at Lisette. "Why would I explain anything to you, when you wouldn't simply tell me who you are? Which, by the way was my original question and I'm still waiting for an answer."

The comments in the room were impossible to ignore now, making Lisette aware that they had never been alone and just how close she now stood to this young officer. She stood up and nervously brushed her hair for no apparent reason.

"You want to know my name? Why would you ever want to know my name?"

"Because," Robert said as he stood on his side of the counter, "if I am going to ask you to share lunch with me, I would like to call you by something other than, "The Bread Lady".

"Lunch? Who said anything about lunch with a stranger who simply walks into my shop with the expectation that I would go anywhere with him." She sounded as if her antagonistic side had returned, stronger than before.

"To begin, I just now introduced myself and it appears that you knew who I was before I entered your shop; so how can you refer to me as a stranger? I want to bring a drawing with my plan for the playground to show you while we have some wine with a little meat and cheese. Perhaps you know where we can find some nice bread?"

Lisette's harshness evaporated as she smiled, "Yes, I believe I do know where I can find some very nice bread. We can have this lunch of yours tomorrow."

Robert wasn't sure if kissing her hand was the proper thing to do, but he did it anyway. Turning to leave, he noticed all the women in the store smiling at him. One of them said something to her in a voice so low that he couldn't understand what was being said.

"It is Lisette," she answered pleasantly. "My name is Lisette Lebrun. I suppose that I would like you to call me something other than "The Bread Lady" also".

"Until tomorrow, Lisette Lebrun," he said, this time with perfect composure.

Smiling and walking past the grinning women, he found Sadeek, still in good company with his adoring boys, who eagerly accepted a ride with Robert. They would go no further than the courtyard of the Louvre, however. His offer of a ride to their home was declined as they both agreed they would prefer to walk.

His ride to the Military School didn't seem as long as it had previously. His spirited dismount took the sergeant completely by surprise. After spending extra time grooming Sadeek and treating him to carrots, he questioned the sergeant about where he would suggest to take a girl for a picnic.

"That depends, Major Dubé. What is it, this picnic?" When he explained further, the sergeant's puzzled look changed to a knowing smile and a nod. He suggested a spot where he took his wife, long ago as a private. "It may work for you as well, Major," he said with a sparkle in his eye.

Before returning to his quarters, Robert visited the officer's mess, where he instructed the cook what he would need to prepare for him to take in the morning.

Walking across the parade ground toward his quarters, he heard the unmistakable shriek of Colonel DuPont's rant being leveled on yet another hapless soldier. Robert hoped his good luck would continue and he would be able to slip unnoticed through the doors leading to the officer's quarters, but it appeared his luck had ended when he heard the unmistakable roaring of Colonel DuPont calling his name.

"Well, well, Major Dubé, I see you are still our guest." DuPont stood gloating at Robert shouting as he rocked on his heels with his hands held behind his back, positive that he could inflict some fatal wound with his foul insults. "I'm sure the King must be as impressed with your progress as I am. How much longer will we have the pleasure of sheltering you and your horse?"

Even the colonel's condescending tone could not dampen Robert's mood. He saluted the commanding officer and smiled.

"His Majesty and I certainly appreciate your support, sir. Most of my progress is actually taking place outside of the school grounds. When I see the King, I will be certain to bring to his attention how your attitude and leadership qualities are inspirational to us all."

DuPont's sarcastic smile quickly vanished in the face of Robert's retort and he showed his clenched hands. "Carry on," he grunted and stomped away in search of easier prey.

He found Garnier waiting for him in his quarters. After he sent his aide to obtain dinner from the officer's mess, Robert had a bath drawn for him and cleared his drawing board. By the time Garnier returned, he was busy diagraming his plans for the playground. He wasn't positive how to refer to it, so he titled his diagram "Exercise Yard." Garnier had opted to eat with Robert and immediately began questioning him about this latest project.

"This is an exercise yard, Lieutenant," he began, running his hand across the sheets of paper. His illustration displayed the playground bordered by buildings on three sides and Avenue Ledru Rollin on the fourth. "The idea is to provide an area for troops to work on their strength and endurance conditioning. This will begin with men who volunteer to join our unit, and hopefully will teach the skills they learn here to other troops." Garnier gave the impression that he actually believed what he was hearing.

"This is designed to work in such a way that you can begin anywhere, but you have a circuit to complete. Each piece of equipment presents the user with a different challenge and works a specific muscle group. At the completion, a person will have worked on their arms, abdomen and legs. We will have a minimum of eight pieces."

He continued drawing outlines of the equipment but avoided referring to them as, monkey bars or jungle gym. Instead he described them as; gravity slides, leg conditioner and traversing bars. Following his dissertation to Garnier, he added dimensions and a list of materials that would be required. Robert stood near his bed to view it from a distance and he felt that his impromptu attempt to build a playground was nearly perfect.

His decided that riding in his carriage made more sense than to expect Lisette to ride Sadeek. After his customary breakfast with Garnier, he spent more time than usual riding Sadeek. They rode around the Military School for some time, but soon became bored with the monotony of passing the same buildings and left to ride somewhere unfamiliar. Sadeek seemed to come alive as he and Robert explored the surrounding streets.

When they returned, he instructed the sergeant to hitch his grey horse to the phaeton. Convinced that Sadeek understood and would be displeased when he was left behind, he spent additional time with his Arabian stallion before walking to the officer's mess to retrieve the items he ordered. The few officers present, paid scant attention to his presence and the cook appeared to be glad to see this special request leave his kitchen before other officers began making similar demands.

Robert eagerly walked to his quarters with cuts of veal, cheese, fruits and a good bottle of wine.

He had nearly forgotten what the horse Bernard had purchased for the phaeton looked like. Arriving at the stables, he found that the sergeant had already hitched his horse to the carriage and was leading him to the parade grounds by the reins. It was smaller, grey and very sturdy looking. The sergeant told him it was well suited for pulling a carriage like this and while it made sense to leave Sadeek here, he was already looking forward to his next opportunity to ride again.

The ride to Porte Saint-Antoine took longer and was not as enjoyable as riding his stallion, but for once he attracted no attention in his ubiquitous carriage and was soon hitching his grey horse to a post near Lisette's bread shop.

Entering the boulangerie, he couldn't help but notice the number of women present who weren't shopping and wondered if they were there for the sole purpose of watching Lisette and him leave together. Two women stood behind the counter and assured her that she should enjoy her time away from work and not return too quickly because everything would be well taken care of.

Her pace was quick and light as she left the counter carrying a brightly colored cloth bag. "Did you bring me some food?" as she smiled and put her arm through his.

"What is it with women and food?" he wondered.

"Yes, I did. Did you manage to find some bread?"

She acknowledged his query with a slight nod and a broad smile. "Yes, Major, I did manage to find someone who makes excellent bread. Also, I noticed that you are more attractive when you aren't acting so hostile," as she stood facing Robert, holding her bag in front of her.

"Um, thank you; I think," he replied as he helped her into the carriage. The carriage passed the window of her shop and as it did, he noticed that the eyes of every woman in the shop were peering through the windows at them.

"They seem to be very interested in watching over you," as they turned from her narrow street onto a broad tree lined boulevard.

"We look out for our own here Major, especially when a single woman is leaving with someone who is unknown to them. The only reason they are not upset with us leaving together is that we heard about you before you arrived in Paris. Your defense of Marie-Thérese was well known already. Our neighborhoods are our responsibility and whenever we see soldiers present, it is usually when they come to arrest beggars. That is why you attracted such a crowd. We presumed that you were here to make trouble for our poor. Ironically, it is the government who creates our beggars."

"Here, being poor means dressing in rags and eating only in good times. It means an entire family living in a single room with inadequate heating. It means that rent and food prices rise faster than wages do. I'm sorry if listening to this makes you uncomfortable, but it's far worse when you have to witness the effects that hunger has on these children. That is why I bake bread for as many of them as I can, but I never feel that what I give is sufficient."

Turning to Robert, she rested her hand on his arm. "Forgive me for burdening you with the problems of Porte Saint-Antoine. They are not yours and the afternoon belongs to us. Let's enjoy our good company and the best bread that Paris has to offer. Plus, I am very interested to see how well you draw. You never did tell me where you are taking me. Is it far?"

"I believe we are very close, if we're crossing Pont Austerlitz," he said confidently. To his right he could see Notre Dame. Now that they had escaped the narrow streets, the advantages of riding in an open area without tall buildings on either side presented themselves. The sky was blue and the sun was warm on their faces and if he was correct; their destination lay immediately on the other side of the river. The sergeant had told him to look for a large two story grey building with a dark roof and a domed addition on either end. At the end of a long mall filled with flowers and flanked by trees he was sure he had found it. "I believe this is our destination," he said hopefully as they crossed the bridge.

"Oh, Jardin des Plantes," exclaimed Lisette excitedly. "It's odd that I live so close, but almost never take the time to visit here. I used to come here with my parents." She abruptly stopped talking and looked away.

Robert hitched the horse to a post near a large tree, helped Lisette from the carriage and picked up the bag containing their lunch.

They joined the throngs of people strolling through the gardens in picturesque groups and found a spot next to the paths, beneath a tree with branches full of pink and white petals. As people casually strolled past, Robert gathered his drawings of the playground. Lisette pulled a blanket from her bag and spread it on the ground. She sliced the bread and cheese as he opened the wine bottle and poured them each a glass.

"I want to show you something," as he spread his drawing on the lawn. Lisette became very excited as he described the activities children could become involved in. "I could use some help from people in the neighborhood with this. Do you think anyone would be interested in building this?"

Lisette was now kneeling on the blanket, drawing her index finger across the paper; tracing the circuit and imagining what this could become for the poor children she saw so often. "Yes, I'm certain Mathurin. You will soon come to realize that my shop is the focal point of life in our neighborhood, for the women anyway. When we return, we can talk to them about the playground, they in turn will talk to their husbands and the husbands will come to our meeting."

Robert nodded. While looking at the gardens, he was mindful of the timelessness of this scene. The manicured lawns, sculpted shrubs and amazing array of flowers would look the same in this century or any other. He hoped very soon to be looking at this garden in the 21st century with Ron and his father. There were gardens like this in America and he had seen them in England and the Netherlands too. If it weren't for his uniform and the fact that he was driving a horse and carriage and not Mrs. Spencer's mustang, he could be having lunch with this beautiful woman in any time period.

He refilled Lisette's wine glass. "This is very nice." Taking a bite of bread and cheese he asked, "Tell me how you became known as the "bread lady"?

She laughed and covered her mouth as a smile came to her deep blue eyes. "Oh, I see you have been talking to those two little spies of yours, Henri and Gerard. I used to operate the shop with my parents until they passed away. I suddenly found myself alone and my family in Nantes told me to return home. "Paris is no place for a single woman. Come home and we will look after you," they said. "But Paris is my home now and I didn't want anyone to look after me. I decided that I would remain here and operate our boulangerie alone. Although in this neighborhood, I never truly feel alone until the last customer has left and I lock the door for the evening. My parents always told me to be sure and give back to our neighborhood. We don't live in the most glamorous section of Paris; so there is a lot of giving to be done."

"Every year, people die from the cold and children are abandoned by families who can't afford to feed them. Thousands of them are malnourished and sickly. It's like that in other cities too, but it is worse here because the people live where the city is so congested. Maybe you haven't noticed because you live on the other side of the Seine, but I see these people every day and I feel that I need to give them something to eat and perhaps a little hope."

It was true that Robert didn't witness poverty in the area surrounding the Military School on the level that Lisette spoke of. But that didn't prevent him from noticing the children who suffered with all sorts of maladies. There were many who were deaf, lame or in some way deformed; almost useless to that society.

He sat closer to her. "I think building this would be a great start. Who can predict what effect on other neighborhoods it might have. Your parents would be very proud of you."

Lisette nodded and looked at a long row of brilliant red poppies before renewing eye contact with Robert.

"Thank you, Mathurin. My parents thought they had planned on everything. My mother was from the city of Bath. They met when my father was in England on business and after they married they returned to Nantes where our family owned farmland. It was our home until the government revoked our religious freedom. After that it became an uncomfortable place for a Catholic man to live with his Protestant wife. That's when we moved here and opened our bread shop. Things went well until a sickness passed through our neighborhood. Now I own the business and the building."

She filled their glasses with the remainder of the wine." If we leave soon, we will arrive at the time when laborers are returning home from work. It will be the best opportunity to gather people together. Before we finish this excellent wine of yours however, I would like you to tell me about yourself. I know almost nothing about you, except that you tend to babble when you're nervous."

Without supplying her with too much information, he briefly told her about his parents, his education; his reason for being in Paris and his plan to return home, which was more than he had divulged to anyone.

"That is interesting, Mathurin. You are a scientist in a foreign country, serving a foreign King, after rescuing his daughter and are planning to build a children's playground. Do you plan to do anything that you're trained to do while you're here?"

He smiled and nodded. "Well, I have been trained to defend myself, but not for a living. I will say that it was difficult to refuse the title of Duc of Anjou but I was never trained for that either. Perhaps we'll find an opportunity for me to show you an experiment soon." They both finished their wine and he said, "I believe it is time to return to your shop."

The sky was turning grey and the wind blowing from the Seine reached Pont Austerlitz felt much cooler now as the sun sat lower in the sky. When they reached Lisette's shop, Robert wasn't sure if anyone had left since they went to lunch, although there were definitely children present now. As he stood exchanging smiles with some of the women, their children came to him with questions about his uniform and his grey horse and carriage.

While he sat on the floor answering their questions, he could see that Lisette was busy in conversations with many of the women, whom were soon exiting through the entrance or the back door. Soon she joined him to share some news.

"I have just spoken to several women who are going home now to speak to their husbands. We can meet upstairs in my apartments. Come; let me show you my shop."

The children reluctantly released their new friend, after he promised them all rides in his carriage and especially on Sadeek. They soon discovered other interests.

Although the floors creaked a little and the counter was worn, he couldn't help noticing that her shop was entirely spotless. The floors and shelves which held supplies of flour and herbs almost sparkled due to their cleanliness. Lisette did something with her breads that other bakers chose to ignore. She used different types of flours, oils, all mixed with varities of spices and herbs to create something special.

"My father always taught me to add value to whatever I do. I use what I can, when I can get it. Sometimes it's tomatoes, sometime peppercorn or citantro. The various flavors make the children happy, and my customers come from all the neighborhoods of Paris. The money of customers from the wealthiest neighborhoods enables me to make bread for children from the poorest."

"It is surprising how similar the ingredients that you use, I find in my parent's house. Although it's so far in the, the....." He stopped himself before revealing anything about which century his parent's pantry existed in, but not before Lisette gave him a quizzical look similar to the one he received the day before.

"What were you about to say, Mathurin?" as she walked to him.

"Oh, um, ah in North America. Yes. They live very far away. That is just what I meant to say."

She placed her index finger on his lips. "I don't understand why someone as educated as you speaks that way, Major. I would expect you to be more articulate," she said with a wink.

Robert turned his attention to the sounds of people climbing the stairs above the bakery. He could tell from the difference in the sounds their shoes made on the steps and their pace that people of all ages and vocations were arriving. Lisette led the way from the shop to her apartments above. The staircase was old and worn, like the counter and very dark, as it's only light source came from the floors above and below and a small window at the top of the staircase.

There were several couples in attendance, some with their children; who were engaged in conversation and stopped immediately when Robert and Lisette entered her apartment. This was her living room, with imposing oak furniture that must have been in the family for generations and had a comfortable feel, without being pretentious. A fireplace was located in the center of the right wall. There were two dark cloth covered sofas facing each other and six simple wooden chairs scattered around the sofas. A dining table and chairs were located at the far wall of this room, next to a large window. A substantial wooden dresser stood against the wall by the dining table with three sets of drawers and a pair of glass doors above.

Robert was introduced to M. and Mme. Moreau, Bucher, Champney, Montaque and Vasser. They all seemed mildly interested, or at least curious about the purpose for this meeting: and wasted no time in introducing themselves to Robert.

He immediately removed his coat, hat, saber, dagger and pistol. Looking for somewhere to hang the plans and seeing none, he spread them across the narrowest portion of the floor, and invited everyone to move closer. He explained what the pictures represented, how they worked and where they would go.

Emile Montague, a short and very thin man; was the first to speak. "Why do we need this?"

"You don't need this, the children do," Robert responded.

Guy Vasser sounded even more skeptical. "The King didn't care about us before. Why would he do this now? What does His Majesty hope to gain by this?"

"I can't speak for the King. I can tell you that I was instructed by His Majesty to find something beneficial for the children. In my opinion, they look like they could profit from some time playing in a safer environment than in the streets. He is a parent too. Perhaps you should think about it in terms of one parent doing something nice for some other children, whoever they are."

Charles Champaney spoke with angry disapproval as he stroked his full greying beard. "Why doesn't he just give us the money that it would cost and be done with it?" he said in a loud contemptuous voice.

The others quickly began nodding in agreement and added their voices to Champney's sentiment.

"This isn't going well," thought Robert. This reminded him of his confrontation with Ron. He hoped it would be resolved by a discussion, but his hopes were fading quickly. He looked toward the doorway to the staircase for his exit and as he started to rise, he felt a hand on his shoulder. Lisette stood next to him as she looked sternly at the people in the room.

"Tell us what you need, Mathurin," she said calmly.

He looked at her gratefully. "First of all, I need nothing." He paused a moment for their attention. "I only wanted to talk to you about this idea. If any of you are able to help, I would appreciate it. If not, it will simply take longer to finish. Before anything can be put into the ground, the area needs to be leveled. It will make installing everything easier. All the stones must be gathered together in a pile. We can use them to make cement. We will need a kiln to heat limestone too, before mixing it with the gravel to make the supports strong. We will also need metal to place over the wood to make a slide for the children. Then we need people to construct the pieces."

Joseph stood furthest from Robert and had seemed the least interested. "I run a kiln making bricks. If I could get some limestone, I can heat it but I don't know exactly how to handle it."

"If we can obtain some, I'll show you what to do; Joseph," Robert said confidently.

Jean-Paul Bucher spoke next. "The King is always building something, whether or not it benefits his subjects. Limestone is used for road construction. I know where they are building a road and constructing a building. I can get your limestone. Plus, the King's buildings use metal sheeting for their roofing, which can be used for your slide. I'm sure that the King would agree to "donate" these materials for your project."

"This is very good," said Robert. "We make the slide from our donated material."

Charles shouted, "That depends how much will the King pay. If this comes from the King, I should be paid plenty!"

It was apparent that Charles already had enough to drink and his additional comments were immediately shortened when his wife Claudia's elbow found his ribcage. "What I meant to ask is how much wood will we need for this slide? If the King is about to be good enough to donate materials, then we should make it. What do you think would be a fair price, Major?"

Robert decided that the real test would be for Charles to answer that question. "Charles, I believe you would know better about the cost of wood than I. Figure out the cost of materials and add your time to it. Tell me before you leave."

Joseph wanted to know more about the limestone. "How do I prepare the limestone for this cement we are going to make?"

"You're going to heat it for hours until it crumbles after you remove it from the kiln. But we need to add some water and use it soon or the carbon dioxide in the air will seep back into it and turn it back into stone. We'll need to dig holes in the earth for the supports before we'll be ready to make the cement.

As Robert heard nothing further, he decided it was time to leave and rolled up his plans as Lisette's apartment emptied. Everyone paused briefly in front of her shop before leaving, but Robert remained to talk with Charles and his wife. Lisette watched from her counter while they spoke next to his phaeton for a few minutes before Robert reached into a pocket and handed Charles several lire notes. They shook hands and Charles walked away with his wife.

Robert was about to climb into his carriage, when he heard the bell above the shop door ring.

"This isn't the King's project, is it Major?" Lisette's stance resembled the infamous pose she had made the first time he saw her at the head of her mob. This time however, she was smiling. He raised his head and closed his eyes as if caught committing some awful crime.

Now she walked closer to him and he knew he needed to think of something quickly.

"Well, ah, you see, um," and Lisette came closer; put her finger on his lips and kissed his cheek. "Are all scientists such terrible liars, Mathurin?" She took his hand and looked him in the eye, "I do believe that this scientist is a very good person, however terrible a storyteller he may be. Now, return to your quarters, Major. You have work to do," and she returned to her shop. Robert waited to hear the bell ring once more and the sound of the lock turning, before heading his grey horse back across the Seine toward the Military School.

Robert didn't need to be convinced to spend time with his stallion when he reached the stables. After he tended to his grey horse and carriage, he fed Sadeek carrots and assured him without fail that tomorrow they would ride together again.

Walking toward his quarters, he began organizing these recent events together in a way that he felt would eliminate uncertainly as he moved forward. Knowing now that his theory was able to solve his time travel problem and he could leave at any moment was a tremendously liberating feeling. Now, he had the luxury of deciding between remaining in the 18th century or returning to the 21st if he chose to and for now, he chose to remain.

The playground project was becoming increasingly important to him. He honestly felt that it was entirely possible to accomplish his goal of transporting Ron's envelope and now doing something positive for the children. When he returned to his quarters, he had an orderly draw a bath and while Garnier left for the officer's mess, he spread the drawing out on his easel.

Garnier seemed very interested in the planning details and sat upon the sofa as Robert painstakingly measured where the holes would need to be dug for the supports and the placement of the pieces of playground equipment.

In the morning when Garnier brought breakfast to Robert's quarters, he found an unoccupied room. From the windows on the second floor of the officer's quarters, he looked on to the parade ground below and saw Robert already riding Sadeek, devoting absolutely no attention to any influences but those of his horse. Garnier walked slowly to the stables and stood next to the sergeant, who was busy in his tack room repairing a saddle.

"It was the most unusual display of affection I think I've ever seen," said the sergeant; laying down his tools. "The Major arrived an hour earlier than usual and Sadeek seemed to be waiting for him, as if he was expected. I'm not sure how long they've been riding like this today, but they look like they've been riding together forever."

There were some tasks which he wanted to undertake today, but as it was much too early to expect that people would be ready to see him, he seized the opportunity to ride Sadeek to the Hotel des Invalides and back several times. He estimated that about two hours had elapsed since leaving the stables and when he returned, the sergeant commented on Robert's increasing abilities in handling Sadeek and felt that he was becoming an excellent horseman. Robert could feel it too. The communication between horse and rider was becoming nearly as much mental as physical. Sadeek seemed to anticipate what Robert wanted, before any command needed to be given.

His breakfast was cold, of course by the time he sat on his sofa. Garnier had delivered his tray on the table at the time when Robert usually ate. The cold meal couldn't dampen his spirit, however. The tea was cold and his eggs were room temperature, but he had just finished riding Sadeek for hours. He considered it to be a good trade.

His first stop this day was to the Military School's carpentry shop, located on the opposite side of the parade ground. Robert spread his drawings on the workbench before the sergeant in charge. He looked and acted gruff at first, but after Robert explained the project to him; the sergeant smiled and used his weathered, brown hands to smooth the paper. His carelessly parted hair was either the same color as the wood he worked with or simply full of saw dust.

"I don't expect you to make all of this Sergeant Boré. The orders will be split between you and others." He went on to describe what each would look like and how they would be used when finished.

"Well, if you ask me; this is a colossal waste of my time and the King's materials, Major," was Boré's unexpectedly disinterested response.

Robert leaned against the workbench and folded his arms. "To begin with, Sergeant Boré, I don't recall asking you about anything. I am a little surprised at your reaction, after you seemed interested at first. I came to you because this project was commanded by the King. When I came into your shop, you were sitting drinking tea. It seems as though you are quite adept at wasting time without anyone's assistance. I was told that you were a person who could accomplish this properly. If I've been misinformed, I'm sure the carpenter at the Bastille can handle this. Perhaps it wouldn't be asking too much to have you assist him."

Robert began to slowly and methodically fold the plans when the sergeant slapped both hands with fingers spread out, across the paper as a cloud of sawdust rose from the table.

"The Bastille? You would entrust the King's project to that idiot Pelletier?" he shouted with irrepressible indignation. "My wife is a seamstress and she knows more about carpentry than he does. I will finish these three which you need and transport them also."

Robert grinned.

The sergeant drew a line with his finger beneath the parallel bars and the monkey bars on Robert's drawing. He thanked Sergeant Boré for his commitment and left him to drone on about his contemporary at the Bastille.

It was now close to noon as he saddled Sadeek and left the Military School for his next stop, the Bastille's carpentry shop. Once there, he found Sergeant Pelletiere at work in the back of his cavernous carpentry shop. Pelletiere was a person in deep contrast to Boré. He was tall and slim with great dark eyes, and wore a towel over his head to protect his black hair from sawdust. Robert had to follow him as he raced from one project to another, explaining his need for Pelletière to give this his attention while speaking mostly to his back. What surprised him the most was his ability to move wood around like they were match sticks.

"I would like to help you, Major. But they have so many projects for me to do here that I have difficulty keeping up with it all. And now you expect me to stop everything to help an officer from, where did you say you were from, anyway?"

"I am currently stationed at the Military School, Sergeant Pelletiere."

"The Military School!!" he shouted with a voice like thunder. "There is a carpenter there, why are you here with this?"

"For one thing, sergeant; never take that tone with me again and look at an officer when he speaks to you," Robert began, speaking with authority. The sergeant reluctantly turned to face him. "Secondly, this is not my project. It comes directly from the King. Also, I heard that you were the man for the job. But perhaps Sergeant Boré was right and I should let him do this."

Robert didn't think Pelletiere was capable of speaking louder, but now he hollered, "Boré!!" That idiot, that pig, that parasite! His wife is a seamstress and is a far better carpenter than he could ever hope to be. Tell me what you need, Major, and consider it done."

Robert left his drawings for the spinning platform with the compliant sergeant and left for his next objective; the Louvre.

When he arrived at the Academy, the members were deep in discussion about the experiment they performed in Porte Saint-Antoine. De Borda looked up, saw Robert and almost instructed Aubrey to set another place for lunch. Aubrey, who was, after all; Aubrey, had already seen to that task. As usual, he said nothing. He merely raised his eyes toward the ceiling and instructed one of his ancillary workers to perform the task.

De Borda invited Robert to be seated near the center of their meeting area. The room was very large and in contrast to the functional stationary blackboard and table, it was very fluid as they constantly moved chairs to different areas of the room dictated by the tenor of their discussions.

De Borda began to elaborate on his initial statement. As he talked about the experiment in Porte Saint-Antione, the other members didn't seem interested in an opportunity to offer their opinion. They appeared to be waiting for Robert to provide an answer.

"We were discussing the results of our measurements for that day, Major. It does raise another question which we were hoping you could answer for us," De Borda began.

Looking at the circle of academy members, he had a fairly good idea what question lay on this horizon.

De Borda spoke first. "I believe our question is, Major Dubé; who are you really?"

Robert appeared to be puzzled. "I'm a bit confused Professor de Borda. If you know who I am; why would you ask that question?"

"We are aware of who you claim to be, Major," de Borda responded calmly. "The actual question is who you really are. Lieutenant Maingon and I sat in my coach discussing navigation, when we witnessed you use what appeared to be a small black devise to locate the coordinates on your own, that we unable to with our best methods. We also saw you place a package in the dirt and press something in your hand and the package simply disappeared. We agree that you seem too knowledgeable to simply walk into our meetings without any of us having heard of you before."

Robert rested his head in his hand for a moment and slowly rubbed his forehead. This was another instance where it would be easier to maintain his silence and leave, than to remain and answer questions. However, he felt that the members had raised a valid question and they had each earned a highly valued level of respect and trust.

He sat back in his chair and kept both feet on the floor, looking at each member before answering, "Gentlemen, I must have your word that you will treat what I am about to tell you with complete confidence." He waited for a moment until they all gave him their word.

"Everything that I have told you about me is absolutely true. What I didn't mention was that I earned my PhD. in theoretical physics from Caltech and I am a research assistant at Syracuse University; studying black holes." The members acted a bit confused, but were listening intently. "You may also be interested to know that neither of these institutions exist in your time and I will be born 213 years from now. The device I used to locate those coordinates is based on the experiments we performed in Porte Saint-Antoine. However, the information in my device is accurate enough to locate those coordinates anywhere on earth to within a meter. That information was gathered from manmade satellites which orbit the earth in my time, and that information is stored in here," he said pointing to his cell phone. "My original destination had always been Paris; however it was supposed to be in the middle of the 21st century. It would appear that traveling back in time requires more accuracy to be as precise as we need it to be," he finished realizing he had just uttered an enormous understatement.

If the benign expressions of the members were any indication of their thoughts regarding Robert's disclosure, he wondered what their responses would be.

"Mathurin, if our present events are already history to you, can you tell us what we can expect in our future?" asked Laplace.

His question contained certain vagueness, making the question both easy and difficult to answer.

"I can answer that in two ways," he started. "First, this country will soon fall into a great turmoil. Everything involved with the Monarchy will be discarded, including the Royal Science Academy. Your society will be abolished by the new government, but will be reinstated as the Institute of Sciences and Arts. All of you will be invited to become members of the renamed society. One of you won't accept."

Now the members began to debate amongst themselves, which of their areas of expertise would be most relevant two and a half centuries from now. The conversations became so protracted that Robert watched and listened as the ever attentive Aubrey delivered lunch to him and made sure that everyone was able to concentrate on the debate. While all the details in the room were in Aubrey's capable hands, Robert walked slowly to the windows to see how Sadeek and his guardians were spending their time.

The members looked on as he froze for a moment before bolting madly from the room. As he ran down the hallway, the members could hear the sound from his boots diminishing as he reached the stairs. He ran onto the courtyard just as the members reached the windows to see what had caused his sudden reaction.

Sadeek was not at his hitching post and a mild sense of panic had begun to grip Robert as he looked across the courtyard until he heard the sound of breathing behind him that only his stallion could make. He turned to see Sadeek pulling Henri along who was struggling to maintain both his grip on Sadeek's reins and his footing. His stallion seemed content to place his muzzle on Robert's shoulder and breathe heavily. "He said he wanted to go for a walk, Major," Gerard said sheepishly.

By the time he returned to the meeting room, the discussions were in such a pitch that one would not have known that the entire membership had earlier raced across the room to watch Robert search for his horse and then hurried back to their seats to continue their discourse. Aubrey and already freshened their drinks and rolled his eyes at the ceiling when Robert returned.

After answering the member's specific questions regarding their individual fields in science, everyone wanted to know why someone who could create a machine capable of time travel wouldn't make it accurate enough to place himself in the correct century.

"This inaccuracy is something we are refining," replied Robert. "At the moment, traveling back in time is similar to my balloon ride courtesy of Jacques Charles and the Robert brothers. We knew we were going up, we just weren't so sure where we would land." The members nodded, acknowledging his analogy as he continued. "My colleague and I attempted this as an experiment. Circumstances forced us to do things we hadn't planned for and now he is in Paris about thirty years ahead of the time I last saw him. His address is that spot of dirt I stood on while you watched me send his package forward in time."

He explained also, the problems the DoD's intrusion had presented in their research, when the Comte de Cassini spoke.

"So, you have the same problems with your government as we do with ours?"

Laplace and Méchain asked if they could accompany him forward to the time he left Syracuse.

Robert shook his head slowly. "No, that can't happen now. First, we've only travelled in time with another person once. I am certain that we need more research in that area, before we attempt it again. What would concern me most, would be returning you to your time. Going back in time past the date where the machine is located...... well look at my situation. We could target your time period and you could find yourself discussing science with people who worship rocks and trees. For the present, it would be best to concentrate on protecting your works. One of the results of the change in your government will be a distrust of science and scientists."

"We wish you could remain with us, Mathurin. Your membership would be a welcome addition," said Comte de Cassini. Everyone nodded, except of course Aubrey. His contribution was focused solely on his operation of these meetings.

"Don't think for a moment that I haven't been tempted to stay," admitted Robert. "Working with so many learned scientists would be an incredible opportunity, but I have many things to do before allowing myself a luxury like that."

"May I tell you why I came here today?" Robert asked, piquing their interest. "I need a device which will enable two objects to spin on top of one other. At home we would call them ball bearings." Walking to the blackboard he proceeded to draw a diagram of two pieces of metal with bearings between separating them. "It needs to be strong enough to support the weight of the equipment, but small enough to fit inside the center column."

"Mechanical engineering isn't really a problem we concern ourselves with, but this looks very interesting," de Borda said as he stepped closer to the blackboard. "Give us a day to work on this," while he stared intently at the drawing.

Robert excused himself from the members, returned to the courtyard and found Sadeek being tended affectionately by Henri and Gerard just where he left them. The boys seemed to be enjoying themselves more than Sadeek, who exhibited a very bored look in his eyes. The instant they saw Robert, each boy grabbed the reins, attempting to be the one to deliver the Major's horse. Sadeek looked like he simply wanted this ordeal to conclude.

"Thank you boys," as he reached out and took the reins with both hands. "I don't believe there are two better horse minders in all of France." Clearly they were more interested in pay than accolades and smiled the most when he paid them their fees.

"For tomorrow, I could use someone to keep Sadeek in good company," he began. "I will first go to the area where we are building the exercise park and then to the boulangerie on Passage de la Bonne Graine."

The boys looked puzzled at first, and then Henri blurted out, "You mean the bread lady."

"Yes, that's right, the bread lady's shop," agreed Robert. "You can ride Sadeek with me to her shop, if you like."

"Oh yes sir," the boys shouted; full of excitement. "We will meet you there tomorrow," as they saluted and then ran across the courtyard.

It was too late in the day to visit Lisette, plus he couldn't think of an excuse to visit her boulangerie. He thought his time could be better utilised by visiting the carpenter's shop at the Military school.

He found Sergeant Boré working on a table top. He was much less inviting than their first meeting. While he wasn't openly hostile toward Robert, he seemed reluctant to answer questions about the parallel bars and monkey bars. Robert looked in the center of shop and saw them standing alone, finished.

"Sergeant, thank you, well done, "said a very satisfied Robert. "When can you deliver these to the exercise yard in Porte Saint-Antione?"

"Th-that may be a problem, sir." The sergeant seemed very evasive and began to stutter. As Robert attempted to understand this change in his attitude and the sergeant's persistent stuttering, he realized what the explanation for Boré's uneasiness was. Someone was obstructing his plan and he had an excellent idea of who it was.

A stern voice shouted from behind him. "Major Dubé, returning to the scene of your crime, I see."

The sergeant barely looked in Robert's direction and continued to sand the table top.

"Don't worry sergeant," Robert said loudly. "I believe I have found the source of the problem." The sergeant half-heartedly nodded and sanded even harder, staring straight at the wood before him.

"Excuse me, Colonel DuPont," as he crossed his arms and turned to face possibly the most negative man he'd ever encountered. "I was just discussing with the sergeant when I can expect the delivery of this equipment. He claims that a problem now exists."

The colonel seemed angered at Robert's lack of intimidation. Red faced and exasperated, DuPont began his diatribe by screaming. Robert perceived this as a bad omen.

"Major, this is my installation. I am the commanding officer here and I decide what I will allow to be made and what will not. Nothing, nothing happens here without my approval; nothing! And yet you ordered this man to make objects for you without receiving permission from me," he shrieked and glared at Robert with utter contempt.

DuPont's face was now scarlet and he began to spit out his words as he worked himself into a frenzy.

"I'm sorry, Colonel," Robert said softly. "Did you say nothing happens here without your approval? I shouldn't have to remind you that I am here at the command of the King. Unless I am mistaken, we both serve at the pleasure of our sovereign; do we not?" Not waiting for an answer, Robert plunged ahead. "I was assigned here by his Majesty and I am bound by my duty and honor to carry out my orders. So please colonel, tell me why anyone in France, would order me not to follow a single command of the King? I could travel to Versailles tomorrow and ask him personally, why you would deny me the right to complete his Majesty's orders. That is as they say; a bad career move. Colonel, would you please allow the sergeant to transport this exercise equipment, so I can move forward with the King's wishes? The sooner I finish this, the sooner I will be reassigned. The alternative will be for me to travel to Versailles for breakfast with the King, because unlike you Colonel; I really do have that sort of relationship with our King."

Robert paused and calmly looked at the colonel whose breathing was becoming increasingly rapid.

"Do what you wish and don't remain one second longer than you need to," screamed the colonel as he turned on his heel and stormed out of the carpentry shop.

"You'll sand a hole in that table if you're not careful, sergeant," said Robert in a jovial mood. "I will give you directions where you can deliver this within the next two days and all this will become a bad memory."

The sergeant straightened himself as sawdust fell from his hair. "Actually major, this will be a memory I'll keep forever. Just tell me where they need to be and they will be delivered wherever you like."

The sound from his boots created a hearty resonance as he walked across the wooden floor and onto the parade ground. Darkness was casting its shadow onto the parade grounds reminding Robert that he needed to rise early but he wasn't particularly hungry. When he encountered Garnier, he asked that he bring him something light to eat. His plans were drawn again on his easel and after changing for bed, he confirmed in his mind, how this would affect the lives of the neighbourhood children when it was completed.

In the morning, Garnier sat by the window as Robert practised his katas. Garnier was curious about how close was Robert's project.to completion.

"If Colonel DuPont will simply remain in his office, it would be an enormous help," Robert offered.

He saddled Sadeek after breakfast and rode in different patterns around the Military School. His confidence was growing now and he actually looked forward to riding in an open area where he could let Sadeek gallop. In the congested Paris streets, there weren't many opportunities for that. However, he was becoming increasingly adept at moving a horse through areas choked by pedestrians and carts.

They left to travel to the playground and when he arrived, Robert stopped and stood up in his stirrups in shock as he witnessed the efforts to clear the playground. As he surveyed the area, he was astonished. The entire area had been levelled. Gravel lay in piles in the far corners of the playground.

"How could this happen?" wondered Robert. "This area looked like a washboard two days ago and now it is as level as a table."

"It is a wonder what a few tools and many hands can do, Major," exclaimed a voice behind him.

Robert swung in his saddle to see Charles Montagne standing with his hands on his hips and a broad smile on his weathered face.

"We only had a few of these," he said; holding a shovel. "But we had many of these," holding up his hands. "Nearly one hundred adults and children worked together on this. When people heard what you had proposed, so many volunteered that we worked in shifts."

"This is amazing," Robert said as he dismounted. "Some of the equipment is ready. We can begin preparing holes for the supports and I need to talk to Joseph about getting the cement ready."

Charles nodded. "Jean-Paul got limestone for Joseph to heat in his kiln. The King was also nice enough to "donate" metal sheets for the slide. We are working on that and it should be completed tomorrow." Robert held Sadeek's reins as he and Charles walked to the edge of the playground. He pulled his diagram from his bag and Charles produced a surveyor's wheel to measure the correct distances from a spot next to the pile of gravel, while Robert spread the diagram on the ground. Visualising where he should begin, he paced off the distance to where the slide would be located.

"This is perfect," he said to Charles. "He tossed his coat and hat on top of Sadeek's saddle. "That shovel is good, but do you have something for smaller holes? We'll need to dig holes to pour cement in for the supports"

Charles had anticipated Robert's question. "Like the kind one uses to dig fence posts, yes? I believe the King "donated one of those and the surveyor's wheel just the other day," he said smiling.

Over the next several hours, Robert dug holes in the softened earth with a "donated" tool and carefully marked the locations for the other holes to be dug with the other. A continuous gathering of onlookers watched the proceedings of the emerging playground with interest. A few volunteered to help, most of them children. Robert wondered if they gathered to watch him dig holes or saw it as an opportunity to come closer to his horse.

The sound of retreating hoofs made him realise that no one was too interested in him. Sadeek had seen Henri and Gerard and was now lowering his head to offer his handlers the opportunity to rub his muzzle and talk to him. When the boys approached him hoping to receive a lire note, Robert handed them a bunch of carrots.

"This is an opportunity for you to give back something today, boys. I will give you carrots for Sadeek, but I'm working on something for children like you. Would you please offer to help me with my horse?"

"Will you let us ride him to the bread lady's shop?" countered Henri.

"Yes you can, on one condition," he answered. The boys wondered what the cost of this condition could be. "You must stop calling her the bread lady. She has a name just as you do. You will call her Mademoiselle Lebrun from now on. Do we have an agreement?" asked Robert as he sat in the dirt.

Both boys readily agreed and immediately asked when they could ride Sadeek to Mlle. Lebrun's shop.

Jean-Paul, Charles and Joseph arrived with some wine and bread. With nowhere to sit, they walked from one side of the area to another and as Robert began to describe his plan in detail, a picture of the finished playground arose in each of their minds. The incline and the slide were already finished and the cement could be mixed anytime.

"Let's begin tomorrow," said Robert, handing the bottle back to Charles. "I will have the equipment from the Bastille and the Military School delivered tomorrow morning." And with that, he walked to Henri and Gerard whom he lifted onto Sadeek for the brief ride to Lisette's shop. The boys acted as though they would never tire of the thrill that came from sitting on a horse like this.

When they arrived at Lisette's shop, Robert placed the remaining carrots in to their eager hands and spent a moment appreciating what a magnificent animal he owned. If he was fortunate enough to own a horse when he returned to Syracuse, he doubted that there would be another like him.

He found Lisette kneading dough on a board. She was surrounded by salt and flour and some of her extraordinary spices. She looked at him and blew a strand of her hair away from her face. Examining him, she stated, "You are a mess, Major, What would the King say if he saw you now?"

"I would tell him that I have been digging holes in the dirt for a new playground. I feel that it's about time I got dirty. Besides, I happen to have clean clothes with me," as he held out his backpack.

"Well don't be dirty in my bakery," she demanded. "Take yourself upstairs and change. Leave your uniform there and I will wash it myself. Then come back here as I have a question for you."

"Yes ma'am," said Robert as he saluted.

Lisette placed her hands on his face and kissed his cheek. "And don't forget to wash your face. It's covered with flour."

When he returned, she pointed to some bread and a bottle of wine. "I thought that we could visit the Jardin des Plantes again, if you have the time. There is so much of it that we didn't see the other day."

Robert removed cheese and fruit from his backpack and placed them next to the bread. "I think that is an excellent idea." He thought for a moment. "How did you know I would be here today?"

"I knew that you couldn't stay away," she said with a smile as she turned the dough over. "Besides, your boys told me earlier that you would be working on the playground."

Lisette excused herself to get ready for their visit to the Jardin des Plants. Robert was carefully placing the items into his backpack while he talked to Claudette Montagne and Charice Vasser about their continuing project when the bell above the door rand and a young officer entered.

He wore the uniform of the King's cavalry and seemed oblivious to everyone in the shop but Robert. "Lieutenant Richard reporting, Major Dubé," as he saluted and when Robert returned his salute, he produced an envelope from his courier pouch. "With His Majesty's compliments, sir." He handed the envelope to Robert, sealed in wax with the royal stamp upon it. "You are summoned to Versailles, Major; immediately."

"Yes, thank you Lieutenant," said Robert as he opened the envelope, with most of his attention focused on its contents. "Very good."

The lieutenant turned to leave, but stopped when Robert laid the letter on the counter. "Lieutenant, I am going to leave immediately. Before you return to Versailles, you will proceed directly to École Militaire and tell Sergeant Boré, in the carpenters shop to make his delivery tomorrow. I will give him the location, but he needs to prepare today."

"Yes, sir; but I'm not stationed at Versailles. I'm stationed at the Bastille."

Robert stopped for a moment before returning his gaze at this young officer. "Lieutenant?"

"Yes, sir?"

"Did I ask you where you were stationed when I gave you an order to proceed directly to the Military School?"

"No sir. You did not"

"Then what difference does it make where you are stationed?"

"None sir."

"One other thing I want you to remember Lieutenant. Remove your hat when you enter someone's home or place of business. It's just plain polite. You are dismissed Lieutenant."

The bell above the door rang again, signaling the lieutenant's departure but Robert was only aware of the sound of Lisette descending from her apartment. She stood in the middle of her bakery as he emptied the contents from his backpack and placed them next to her dough.

"What is it, Mathurin?" she asked as she attempted to understand his disappointed look.

When he saw Lisette, Robert's heart sank. She had pinned up her hair, and had changed into a bright yellow dress and a matching bow in her auburn hair. Clearly, the idea of visiting the gardens was very important to her.

"The King has summoned me to Versailles," he said dejectedly. "I need to leave immediately. But I promise to return here first, if that's all right with you."

Lisette winked. "I think the wine will be fine until you return. However If you take too long Major; I may have to come to Versailles myself."

"No need for that," he said as he walked to the counter. "Just don't open the bottle until I return."

BLOOD IN THE FIELD

Approaching the gate to Versailles, Sadeek slowed to a trot before Robert brought him to a halt just as a member of the palace guard was walking in the Royal Courtyard.

"Corporal," Robert said as he was immediately saluted. "I am here to see the King. Take my mount to the stables and see that he is tended to. After I see His Majesty, I need to return to Paris."

"Yes, sir," said the corporal as he took Sadeek's reins. "I believe you'll find the King by the reflecting pools before the Hall of Mirrors and your mount will be in the stables whenever you are ready.

He walked to his left, passing beneath a series of great arches. The view to his left was very familiar and when he looked to the second floor windows his right, he realized that he had spent the night in that room, overlooking the gardens. It seemed like a very long time ago now. Robert soon found Louis XVI pacing next to one of the reflecting pools. The King didn't look with enthusiasm upon seeing him and he immediately dismissed the servants.

"Major Dubé, I have heard disturbing reports regarding your conduct in Paris. Balloon rides, digging up a piece of land in a poor section of Paris and visits to those scientists and absolutely no progress with the real reason I sent you there. Have you followed any of my commands?" The King shook his head sorrowfully as placed special emphasis on the word "any".

Robert thought of an acceptable response as quickly as possible.

"Your Majesty, I don't know who you have been listening to; please allow me to explain. To begin with, I haven't been receiving much support from any of the members of the general staff I've contacted, so I've had to change my strategy a little. I want to create a new fighting force that will accept its members from the military. They will be volunteers consisting of both officers and enlisted men who actually choose to become the elite of the elite. A fighting force so fierce, that opposing forces on the battlefield will know that they must withdraw or die. I will be successful, if I work with the sort people who are committed to being instructed. To achieve that, I will require more room than what is available at the Military School."

"The area where I have been digging is going to be an exercise area for members of this select fighting group. They will practice tactics and martial arts in one location and run to the exercise area. These men will be the most physically fit fighting force in the world."

The King appeared to listen intently to his explanation, so Robert continued.

"The Royal Academy of Sciences and the balloons of Jacques Charles are related as well. I visited the Academy because they are working on a method to map the world so that every location on earth has a specific pair of coordinates assigned to it." Robert withdrew his cutlass and began to draw lines in the pathway to illustrate what he meant. "Using these coordinates we can identify any spot on the planet. This would enable an observer from an elevated position, like a balloon; to report the locations of enemy troops, to our infantry and artillery. Because the observer in the balloon reads from the same map as the artillery commander on the ground, the cannons don't need to be moved to the battlefield, where they would be exposed to the enemy's cannon fire. Because they are in a remote position, they are able to engage more than one enemy location with cannon and the enemy would be unable to determine where the cannon fire is coming from. That is what I have been doing in Paris, in your name; Majesty." Robert dramatically ended his speech with a deep bow, and a prayer that Louis XVI sincerely believed any of this.

The King embraced Robert and kissed him on both cheeks. "I am sad that I doubted you for one moment, Major. Continue your efforts on my behalf and remember that you have my sincere support. I will leave you now as I have granted an audience to the American ambassador, Thomas Jefferson who is waiting for me to receive him in the Hall of Mirrors. I haven't decided how far my throne will be from the entrance but I believe that I have postponed his visit long enough."

The King began to turn when Robert blurted out, "Thomas Jefferson, the third U.S. president; here? He helped write the Declaration of the Rights of Man."

When the King looked at him; extremely puzzled as Robert remembered that uttering words without considering their impact was never a good idea and usually put him in a very difficult position.

"The United States has only had two presidents, Major and currently John Adams holds that office," the king began looking questioningly at Robert. "Thomas Jefferson has been the United States representative to France for these past four years. And what is this Declaration of the Rights of Man you mentioned?" the King said frowning.

"Why don't you just ask if you can take his picture?" thought Robert. "Thomas Jefferson won't be president for twelve years and the Declaration of the Rights of Man will be written by Lafayette after the French Revolution."

"I beg your pardon your Majesty. I believe I was referring to the title of a book written by Ambassador Jefferson."

Seeming satisfied with Robert's answer, the King thanked him for his hard work. Before walking away, he waived his left arm. "I believe these persons also wished to speak to you."

Looking in the direction the King had pointed, he saw Gabrielle and Marie-Therese and Louis-Charles rushing toward him.

Marie-Therese ran to Robert and jumped into his arms.

"Look at you," he said as he lifted her off the ground; hoping that her mother was not present. She and Gabrielle were both dressed in lavender dresses with a yellow border. Gabrielle wore a matching hat as usual.

"You will join us for our afternoon meal, won't you," pleaded Gabrielle. "We have missed you so very much."

Servants were already moving glass covered tables and awnings into position to shield them from the sun, so there was no doubt that the decision had already been made for him. Gabrielle, Robert and Marie-Therese and her brother, sat under the awning covered tables; overlooking the reflecting pools in near where he once sat watching fireworks one evening.

After they completed their meal, Robert renewed his search for an exit strategy; which was again blocked by Gabrielle. While the children ran ahead, she took his hand and asked him to walk with her. Looking around to be certain that they could not be overheard she spoke in a hushed tone.

"There is a spy watching you in Paris. Are you aware of that?" she said smiling, not wishing to expose the seriousness of her topic.

"I hadn't even considered that, until this interrogation by the King," he replied.

"You need to find a way to discover the identity of the person who is watching you," said Gabrielle. "It is highly unlikely that the person, who reported your activity to the King, is actually the same person who is following you. I would guess that this spy supplies information to someone else. You need to be as clever as they are devious. I don't believe intelligence will be a problem for you."

Robert looked into Gabrielle's eyes, hoping to find the answer there. "Do you have any idea who it might be?"

She moved closer to him and squeezed his hand tightly.

"This is Paris, Mathurin. You can trust everyone, you can trust no one. That is why you need a plan to make this person reveal him or herself to you, without feeling as though they had revealed anything. It doesn't need to be complicated. It simply needs to work."

He turned and stared at the reflecting pools for a moment. "I need to return to Paris," as he took her other hand in his. "Will you walk with me to the stables? I will need to retrieve my horse; now."

Gabrielle turned to a servant standing near the tables.

"You there." The servant bowed to the Duchess and looked without expression as he waited for his order. "Run to the stables immediately and bring the Major's horse to the Royal Courtyard, then wait for him there."

The servant turned and ran in the direction of the stables.

"Oh, well that was easy," he said, watching the servant disappear around a hedgerow.

"We'll walk for a while, brother. I have the children to watch, of course." They strolled hand in hand, while the children walked on ahead. As they stood watching children splash the water in the pools, a corporal ran toward them. Saluting Robert he said, "Major, you will find your horse next to the arches leading to the Royal Courtyard."

Gabrielle turned and kissed Robert's cheeks tenderly. "Be safe, brother. The children and I need to see you again."

"I'll be back soon enough, Gabrielle." He retraced his steps around the Hall of Mirrors, passing beneath the arches and found a servant holding Sadeek's reins.

Soon he and Sadeek were leaving Versailles again through the Palace's familiar gates. Sadeek responded to the same urgency Robert was feeling; he needed to return to Paris as quickly as possible. He was never beyond Robert's control, proceeding quickly and without recklessness. They reached a familiar area, where the narrow road quickly opened into a wide field with very few trees. A pair of large oak trees straddled the road in the middle of the field.

The puzzle of how to catch this spy had weighed heavily on his mind since leaving Versailles. He had hoped riding alone would have enabled him to think of a solution, but he wasn't making any progress. Now they found themselves looking out at a large open meadow, under a clear blue sky with a long straight road passing directly through it. This was where he felt Sadeek would have the opportunity to gallop when Robert suddenly realized what his plan would be. Sadeek's eagerness to take advantage of this open area was apparent now and let Robert know that this was the moment to let him go. Now that he was closer to resolving the spy problem he gave his stallion his freedom.

Robert could feel the intenseness in Sadeek's gallop and as he began to move faster across the field, Robert looked ahead and noticed two riders, sitting motionless blocking the road, just before it re-entered the forest. Sadeek was moving very fast and as Robert leaned forward his attention now focused on these two men waiting just ahead. They reached the twin oak trees when he saw a flock of birds rise on his left, but he never noticed the rope which lay across the road and sprang up just as they passed between them, striking Sadeek in the breast.

As horse and rider stumbled and plummeted to the ground; Robert saw a swirling flash of blue sky and green leaves. He felt weightless for a fleeting moment and in the next instant, saw the ground rush up at him as he landed hard on the ground next to Sadeek. He hadn't completely lost consciousness and could hear voices approaching from behind the tree on his right.

"We need to finish him this time," said one to the other as he looked in the direction of the voices, but could see nothing.

With some effort, he wiped a hand across his forehead and rubbed his fingers against his palm. He felt something warm and damp against his skin. Opening one eye, he could see his hand covered in blood, which was pouring from a wound to his forehead. His vision was beginning to clear as the two men became alarming closer. Sadeek was struggling to rise as Robert remembered his military pistol, which he had never fired.

He now saw two men approaching slowly; one of them holding a pistol while the other pulled a dagger from his belt. When Sadeek raised himself to his full height, Robert found that his left boot was still in the stirrup and he was beginning to be dragged across the road. Gripping the pistol with his right hand he pulled the hammer back as the two men exchanged surprised glances while their quarry began to slide away from them. The man holding the pistol was about to utter something, but was silenced when he saw Robert roll on his side, take aim at him and fire his pistol first. The flash of gunpowder was followed instantly by the roar from the pistol as a huge cloud of smoke obscured his view of the man with the dagger. The sound of boots ceased for a moment as one man stared down at his motionless partner and realized that this mission was unfolding exactly like the action on the bridge at Versailles.

Almost immediately however, Robert heard the sound of his boots drawing nearer.

Blood still hampered his vision as he tossed the pistol aside and reached for his cutlass. His foot fell free from the boot in the stirrup and he swept the blade through the smoke until he felt it suddenly stop, as a scream of pain rang out. The other man fell to the field, dropping the dagger he was carrying. Robert was fairly sure it was a severe wound as he had swung his blade with as much force as he could from his back before it found his attacker's leg. Without realizing it, the second man fell just a few feet from where Robert lay. The pain to his leg from Robert's cutlass caused him to momentarily forget the person who had been his quarry. Now his comrade lay dead in the field and he didn't realize that he had now become the hunted, until he felt a blade pressing against his neck.

Robert raised his cutlass until its point rested against the man's neck. He bore the terrified look of someone who had no idea whether he would survive this day. Blood ran toward his shoulder from the blade as Robert looked him in the eye, "Run." The man needed no encouragement as he rolled from his back, raised himself to his feet and hobbled toward the tree line with a gash in his clothing, wet with his blood.

Now, his concern turned to the two men he had seen earlier in the distance. He could hear what sounded like approaching horses. Rolling onto his back, he saw both men approaching fast with swords drawn. He remembered the unfired pistol that the first man had carried and raised his pain racked body from the road. Walking doubled over at the waist he limped until he stood above the man who had meant to shoot him while attempting to ignore his intense pain. The pistol laid on the ground next him and Robert lowered himself to his knees, positioning himself to face the riders. He picked up the pistol from the dirt, propped his arm on the chest of his former opponent and slowly drew the hammer back. This time he could hold the pistol with both hands.

"I wish there was a tutorial for this," he thought.

The closest rider had his sword drawn, seeing only Robert lying prone, across the chest of his fallen comrade. It was too late when he grasped that he was not attacking an unarmed man. He saw a flash, a cloud of smoke and was lifted off his horse as the ball from Robert's pistol hit him squarely in the chest.

The danger from the second rider still remained and while Robert could barely see through the smoke, he remembered that the second rider's sword was drawn also. Armed only with his dagger, he wasn't certain how anyone stand against an opponent on horseback. He was planning his strategy when an object streaked across the road from his left, striking the rider and horse broadside. The black horse landed in the grass while the rider hit the oak with such force that it seemed to reverberate across the field.

Robert looked first at the person lying motionless next to the oak and then and saw Sadeek standing victorious in the center of the road, drawing deep breaths and gazing at the fallen horse and his rider.

Robert started to call Sadeek, but his faithful friend was already headed in his direction. While his horse stood over him, Robert raised himself to his knees and grabbed the dead man's cloak. He tore it open with both hands to verify one thing before they left the field. Attached to his hip was a dagger, identical to those used by the outlaws on the bridge at Versailles.

Using the stirrups to pull himself up, Robert scrutinized the third man. It was no surprise to him that he recognized him as one of those on the bridge who had participated in the attack on the King's coach.

Robert and Sadeek were both exhausted. Before mounting him, Robert hobbled to Sadeek and rubbed his muzzle. For his part, Sadeek raised his head and breathed heavily with a fierce, confident look in his dark brown eyes.

Robert was able to stand now and painfully walked over and picked up his hat. Raising his leg to put it into the stirrup was painful enough. Expending his last element of strength, he mounted Sadeek as every part of his body cried out in pain. He waited for a moment for the dizziness to pass before directing Sadeek toward the man who had slammed into the oak. Robert recognized this one as well. When he landed against the oak, his own sword had dealt him a blow from which he would not recover.

They headed across the field in their original direction, eager to get out of this open area and return to Paris. This return was not as swift as the trip to Versailles, but they were determined to complete it and were soon traveling along on cobblestone streets lined with tall buildings, ignoring the stares from pedestrians and others on horseback. The blood had stopped flowing, but now his head throbbed so much that he couldn't decide which condition was worse.

Henri and Gerard happened to be standing by the door to Lisette's shop when Robert halted Sadeek. Henri took the reins while Gerard stared; attempting to understand what was wrong with Robert as he dismounted slowly. Leaning against his horse and holding onto the saddle for stability, he fought to keep his eyes open.

"Boys, this is very important. You must hide Sadeek. Tell no one where I am or where you put the horse. Do you understand?"

Neither boy could verbalise an answer. They silently looked at Robert's blood caked forehead, seemed to have fully comprehended Robert's directions, nodded and took hold of the reins.

Lisette had seen him from the shop as he spoke to the boys, not aware that anything was wrong. He turned and began to limp toward the door as Henri gently relieved Robert of his grip on Sadeek's reins. One of the ever present women opened the door for him as he shuffled through the doorway. When he raised his head to look for her, Lisette put one hand to her mouth as she tried to hide her shocked expression and ran past the counter, across the floor to him.

"Lisette," Robert said, before everything went dark.

CASTING A NET

When Robert opened his eyes, he found Lisette sitting in her chair next to him.

"How did I get up here?" he asked as he raised his hand to his forehead and attempted to sit up too quickly. He instantly realized that neither was a good idea, as the awful throbbing resumed while the room spun.

"Charise Vasser was here when you collapsed. She ran home and Guy carried you up the stairs. The boys have Sadeek hidden in the stables in the alley and are caring for him. Monique stitched the wound in your forehead. You've been asleep for two days."

"I can't believe this is happening," Robert moaned. "Where is my uniform?" as this time he raised himself slowly.

"I burned it, Mathurin. It was covered in blood. You know, if you can't take better care of your uniforms, the King may stop giving them to you." Although there was a hint of sarcasm in her words, the concern in her voice was unmistakable. But she would not ask him what had occurred. She knew that what he needed now was her care and he could explain when he was ready.

Robert attempted a smile, but even that was an effort. "I'm not too worried about that right now. I'm actually looking forward to a time when I have no uniforms. What I need to determine is why these people are still after me and how they knew I was travelling to Versailles? I know they were part of the same group who attacked Marie-Thérèse. Does that mean they are still after her?

"It may seem trivial but I also have to bother myself with the climbing cube before we install it in the playground. I really need to leave soon so I can complete the work for transferring everything to the site. Would you get my other uniform please? I have some work to do."

Swinging his feet off the bed, he placed them on the floor and quickly grabbed the edge of the mattress as the throbbing worsened and the room began spinning again.

Robert noticed that Lisette was still sitting in her chair. "You're not getting my uniform, are you?"

"You're not going anywhere until you've had something to eat, Major," she said forcefully. "Unless, of course; you feel like riding your horse wearing that nightshirt."

"But I don't remember where Sadeek is," complained Robert.

"Exactly. I just explained where he is and you have already forgotten. Wait here or meet me in my dining room if you want to feel as though you've accomplished something," and she exited down the staircase to the kitchen.

Her bedroom's appearance was similar to the living room. The furniture was very attractive without looking pretentious. A four post bed, which had been his for the night, stood by a window overlooking the alley. The wardrobe, chest of drawers and the dressing table all matched. As he looked more closely, they looked like they were made of cherry. Of course, everything was spotless.

A pair of blue slippers lay next to the bed and putting them on, he rose very slowly and made his way to the mirror by the wash basin. Staring back at him was the reason that he had seen his bloodied hand in the field the day before. A large gash about four inches long stood out in the middle of his forehead, now closed by Monique's handiwork. When he lowered the brim of his hat it would conceal his wound from view, but he wondered if he could conceal from others the level of discomfort caused by wearing it.

Robert climbed cautiously down the staircase to the living room where recently they had met to discuss the possibilities of building a playground.

When Lisette came upstairs from the kitchen, she found Robert sitting in a chair near the window, looking down to the alley below, observing people walk down a narrow pathway between two buildings.

"Can you reach the playground using that path?" he asked.

"Yes, but it is only for pedestrians," said Lisette as she placed a tray on the table. "It's barely wide enough for people to pass each other and definitely too narrow for a carriage."

Robert absentmindedly raised his hand to his forehead and rubbed his wound, with a subsequent fresh round of pain.

"Monique will be very upset with you if you tamper with her stitching, "as she held his hand while she inspected his wound. "We don't always have a doctor to tend to the men when they are injured at work. Monique has a lot of experience at mending men's wounds. She called yours a bad scratch. She will remove the stitches in a few days, but now you need to eat; especially if you intend to return to your work. We have eggs, tea, fruit and some very nice bread."

"Thank you, Lisette, "he said gratefully. Sounding very concerned he said, "Remember, it is very important that no one knows I'm here, it could be dangerous for you as well. I have been told by a friend at Versailles that someone is watching me and then reporting my activities to another person. I was working on a method to discover their identity when I was attacked. This is all related to the King and his family somehow. I just need time to figure it out."

Lisette poured tea for them both and sat next to Robert.

"We don't need to worry so very much about your secret being kept. Our neighborhood can be very secretive when we need it to be. The people who need to know things will; and those who don't need to; won't." She buttered some bread and placed it on his plate.

Robert ate some of his egg and took a sip of tea. "Do you know anything about the progress of the playground?"

Lisette sliced some fruit and put that next to his bread and turned in her seat, frowning at him. "Well Major; let me see. I have been a little occupied taking care of a hard headed officer who collapsed in my shop just the other day. But I have heard that some of your equipment has arrived along with some supplies which according to Charles, were "donated" by the King. I decided not to be concerned about details."

During breakfast, Robert explained to Lisette all that Gabrielle had told him, following his questioning by the King, and then the gruesome events in the field during his return to Paris.

"I find it difficult to believe that it could have anything to do with Captain Petit's bruised ego, "reasoned Lisette. "He sounds like the vainest person in the world, but I feel that there is something bigger involved. Who would direct another person to perform an act such this attack to simply avenge his ego? No, someone must have a larger agenda. I agree however, that you can trust no one," There was a pause from her as she smiled, "unless of course, you collapse on a person's floor and that person sleeps in a chair while you sleep in her bed. I think that is a person you can trust."

The uniform he wore the day he visited her shop after digging in the playground was cleaned and hanging in her wardrobe. Somehow, he felt a little more robust as he dressed himself in his uniform. The women in the shop stopped talking when Robert descended the stairs and walked into the bakery. Monique was checking on something in the oven.

"How are you feeling, Major? You certainly look much better. We were very worried the other day." She wiped her hands on her apron as she stepped closer to inspect Robert's forehead. "Hmmm," she mused. "You know, I really do extremely fine handiwork. You were lucky to have traveled any distance at all on horseback with an injury like that. Are you sure you shouldn't be resting and allowing Lisette to nurse you a bit longer?" she said with a sparkle in her eye.

"I would like that a lot Monique, but in all honesty, I need to act now. I haven't been able to determine who attacked the King's daughter, but I think it's safe to presume that they have found me," as he pointed to his wound. "For my safety and yours, I need to find them. It's very important that no one sees me leave here. Do you know where the boys hid my horse?"

"Yes, I do," she said as she used a long wooden peel to check on the progress of bread baking in the ovens. She removed several loaves of hot bread and set them on the counter to cool. Monique then ushered him past the staircase, which led to a hallway. When she opened the door, they stepped out to the courtyard in the rear of the building. This was the courtyard he had seen from Lisette's apartments. The dirt was a mixture of prints left from pedestrians and a single set of hoof prints leading away from the path toward a neglected part of the courtyard.

"Follow these tracks and you will find your horse, Major. Those stitches will need to be removed in a couple of days. I'm sure we'll see you back here soon," and Monique retreated to the bakery.

Robert followed the hoof prints to a wooden extension of Lisette's building. It was in incredibly sad condition. If there had ever been a period when it had been painted, all evidence had been eliminated by the sun and rain. Its appeal was the fact that no one had any reason to approach it, much less enter. Robert passed through the door less entry way. Its ancient rusted hinges were the only evidence that any doors had ever existed at all. Light streaming through gaps in missing and twisted wood in the walls and roof, revealed several stables. From the farthest stall, he saw a familiar long black tail which moved rhythmically from side to side.

"Sadeek," Robert said almost in a whisper, and instantly he saw the unmistakable form of his Arabian stallion. Sadeek came to him, lowering his head and rubbed his forehead on Robert's shoulder. Henri and Gerard appeared from the stall with straw in their hair.

"You boys slept here?" Robert asked, astonished.

"He looked lonely," explained Henri. "Besides, there is no way to secure a stable which has no doors. We had to stay, Major," Gerard said as he saluted.

"What happened to you yesterday, Major?" asked a concerned Henri, gazing fixedly at Robert's forehead.

"I met some people who didn't appear to like me very much, boys. I can't really tell you very much about it. Still, I appreciate all your help so far and I will need more assistance from you very soon. Can you continue to help me and our friend Sadeek?" They both eagerly nodded their heads.

"Keep Sadeek's presence here a secret. No one can know that we are here. I would like you to use brooms to move the dirt around to hide his hoof prints. Can you do that for me?"

"Yes sir," they said, saluting.

Robert saddled Sadeek and led him out of the stables. "I need to finish the work on your playground. We will see you tomorrow. When this is finished we will take a long ride together."

He put his hat on gingerly, and returned their salutes. Painfully mounting Sadeek, he made his way down Passage de la Bonne Graine, turned onto Rue du Faubourg, and rode past the Bastille until he reached the Louvre. Hitching Sadeek to a post nearest the entrance, he resigned himself to the fact that all tasks today were going to take longer to complete. Every effort he made to accomplish anything quickly would be tempered by the increased throbbing in his head. .

He found the members with their chairs arranged in their customary circle engaged in some passionate discussion. When Méchain saw him in the doorway, he dropped the newspaper in his lap and hurried to greet him.

"Mathurin, we are so glad to see you again. We are engaged in a discussion concerning black holes and we need your input. Also, Lieutenant Maingon has something very important to show you. Please sit next to me."

Aubrey looked sternly at the ceiling and headed through a door to arrange something for their unexpected guest.

The lieutenant first brought a devise to Robert, handed it to him and sat in the wing chair next to him. As Robert examined the device, he held it with one hand and spun it with the other. There were two metal plates of the same size, about six inches square, separated by ball bearings. This was exactly what was needed for the spinning platform.

Lieutenant Maignon sat forward in his chair as he described the devise.

"As soon as I saw your drawings, I was certain that I could get what you needed, Major. We use these to support the steering mechanism of our ships. It was made to endure a lot of stress."

Holding the bottom piece in one hand, he saw how effortlessly the upper portion turned. Robert nodded. "This is perfect. Thank you very much." He gingerly removed his hat, revealing his injury.

Before the members could react to the large wound on his forehead, Robert explained. "I fell from my horse yesterday, but thanks to some very helpful people, I'm feeling much better already." He thanked Aubrey for the tea and cakes. "I do feel a little weakened from my fall, so I can't stay as long as I would like.

I would love to discuss my research about black holes with you and then I'll leave. I have to resolve a problem we're having with the exercise equipment too. The incline station seems to have become a complication."

For the next hour he and the members shared ideas and information about black holes and gravity, singularity and time travel. He felt that this was time well spent, but he had several items to complete that day and he needed to excuse himself. The members all shook his hand, knowing that this might be the last meeting they would have together.

He left the Louvre with the device for his spinning platform stored in his backpack and mounted Sadeek to return to the Bastille. Now that the rotating plate was in his grasp, it was time to visit Sergeant Pelletier at the Bastille.

When he passed through the east gate, Robert rode Sadeek to the carpenter's shop and handed the reins of his horse to a soldier to have Sadeek watered and rested. He could see Sergeant Pelletiere running around his shop as usual. He stopped abruptly when he saw Robert and then ran toward him.

"Major Dubé, I have very good news for you. Everything you requested is ready. Come and see it."

There in the middle of his shop, stood the swing set and the spinning platform like the centerpieces on a dinner table. "This is really amazing that you were able to finish this so quickly, sergeant," said Robert as he inspected the finished work. The swing set had four swings with smooth wooden seats each hung at a different height.

"I still don't see how this will aid soldiers in their exercises, Major," said Pelletiere as he rubbed the cloth on his head to scratch his scalp and wiped his hands on his bristling grizzled beard.

"It will help to strengthen their abdominal muscles, of course," said Robert. "Here, examine this plate which made for the spinning platform.

Pelletiere sounded confused. "Oh, for abdominal muscles; yes of course." He placed the plate on the bottom of the platform and smiled as if he had just solved a great mystery. "This will work perfectly."

"I gave you the most difficult projects to complete and you completed them quickly. This is impressive work, sergeant. I will make sure and include your name in my report to the King. Can they be at the exercise yard tomorrow? It is on Avenue Ledru Rollin in Porte Saint-Antoine.

Pelletiere nodded in earnest. "You would still be waiting for your equipment if you have told that idiot Boré to do this for you. What you see here is a work of art. His work wouldn't be good for anything but a camp fire. Of course, I will have it there tomorrow for you, sir." The sergeant's pride in his work was obvious and he certainly enjoyed an opportunity to belittle Boré as a person who was not the best at his craft. Robert had to admit that this work on items that some would consider to be as common play equipment was uncommonly extraordinary.

"That will be perfect, sergeant. I am very glad that I found the right man to do the work. I will see you tomorrow. You'll have to excuse me for now though. I need to investigate why we are having trouble with our monkey bars. Thank you very much." Robert left Pelletiere to scratch his head as he attempted to understand the remark regarding monkey bars and walked to the stables.

Sadeek had just been brushed. A night in the stables behind Lisette's shop hadn't resulted in a rested look, but now he had regained the regal appearance of an Arabian.

A voice shouted from the courtyard, "We thought we had seen the last of you, Major. Now you stop in my facility without saying hello?" Robert turned to see François walking toward him with his arms outstretched. They hugged each other and Robert smiled. "Hello, François. I'm sorry that I couldn't stay and visit, but I'm feeling a bit exhausted after falling from my horse yesterday," as he removed his hat slowly, revealing his wound.

François looked closely at Robert's wound. "That's terrible, but I've seen much worse. Perhaps His Majesty should have given you more bacon and less horse," the captain said as he chuckled. "You'll be fine in no time. I have to commend you on not giving up on this training task of yours. I saw what the carpenter made for you. I'm sure his Majesty will be impressed."

That's my hope François," Robert said as he mounted Sadeek. "Another few days and I'll be finished with the exercise yard. Presently, I need to find out why the parallel bars aren't finished yet. By the way, I'm sorry I didn't ask your permission to have your carpenter work on my project."

François looked surprised. "Ask permission? It seems to me that a man with a directive from the King shouldn't need to ask for permission from anyone. Besides, it provides us with an opportunity to see each other and it is the only time anyone can recall seeing Pelletiere slow down."

They shook hands and he turned Sadeek to cross the courtyard. Before he exited the south gate, he turned in his saddle and waved good-by to his friend.

His next visit was to Place des Victoires and the shop of Jacques Charles. As always, it was the neighborhood's center of activity as he dismounted and walked to what he knew would be the source of the noise and commotion.

In the center of the large shop, on a large wooden table, lay a metal box about three feet square. One of the Robert brothers was the first to notice their friend and waived excitedly to him to come where they stood. All work stopped as they were obviously excited about showing their newest creation to Robert.

"We call this our chilling chamber," Jacques explained. "I remembered what you said about reducing the temperature of hydrogen gas before pumping it into the balloon so more gas can enter it. It worked very well with a small model, so we hope that it will work as well on a large balloon."

The box was essentially, a large grey metal cube, riveted together; with a single pipe which passed through its center. In the center of the box, was a large basin, through which the pipe passed, before exiting through the opposite side.

"What we found was that if the basin was simply filled with cold water we could make a significant difference in the temperature of the gas as it passed through the pipe, without using our chilling chamber. But we wanted to further reduce the temperature, so we developed this."

Jacques brought Robert to the opposite side of the chamber. Here a stool had been placed and the original seat's shape had been altered which reminded Robert of a bicycle seat. The horizontal pieces normally used to rest one's feet, had been replaced by pedals which were connected by an axel through an inverted "Y" shaped pipe. There was no chain when but attached to a wheel, the pedals turned a belt which was attached to a gear. When the gear turned, a metal shaft spun, turning a fan located under the basin.

"We also found that adding this fan reduces the temperature of the water even more, allowing the gas to be cooled further," Nicholas-Louis said excitedly as he sat on the stool and began pedaling.

Robert continued to stare at the apparatus, but did not interpret it with exactly the same approach that Jacques was presenting it.

"I can see that you are impressed with this, Mathurin," said Nicholas-Louis. "This will revolutionize the way we prepare our balloons. The chamber was my idea, but Nicholas-Louis thought that circulating air would cool the water further."

Jacques presumed that both he and Robert perceived this invention as an enormous breakthrough in technology, but that wasn't the case. Robert saw this as three men feeding a dinosaur. Balloons filled with hydrogen would cease when the Hindenburg caught fire in New Jersey in 1937. He felt he was witnessing the beginning of the modern bicycle and a rudimentary air conditioner, decades before anyone would manufacture anything resembling a bicycle and over one hundred years before the modern air conditioner would be available.

Robert pointed to the stool. "What if you turned a chain instead of a belt and the chain turned a wheel located behind you? Then you could put a wheel here," as he pointed to an area in front of the stool, "with handle bars to steer it and a frame to connect them as one unit?" Robert was convinced that he was witnessing a revolution in travel. The creation of wheeled travel right here in Paris. Beginning first with bicycles, this logically would lead to a revolution in the mobility of all people everywhere. Beginning with two wheels and eventually maturing into four wheeled vehicles, this could spawn the development of aircraft and spacecraft. He could be witnessing one of the most important developments in history, and it was all happening before him in the little shop of Jacques Charles. The implications were overwhelming and he was convinced that they shared in his excitement

Jacques and the Robert brothers all looked at him and blinked.

"Why on earth would anyone want to do that?" questioned Anne-Jean."

"Oh I don't know; a different mode of transportation perhaps?" he said cynically, expecting the rest to understand his proposition.

Jacques attempted to stifle a laugh and then looked at the Robert brothers; who began to roar with laughter. "That is very funny, Mathurin. We have horses, why would anyone want something with wheels? Now stop joking, we have work to do," as he continued to chuckle and wipe a tear from his eye.

They continued to regard his statement with blank stares. "Probably not a good idea," volunteered Robert and the others laughed and resumed work.

Jacques continued with his original subject. "We were glad to see you because this new devise will be operational in a day or two and we wanted to offer you the first ride with gas delivered through our new chilling chamber."

"That would be a great honor," he humbly replied. "When you are ready to proceed, would you please send a message to my quarters? I don't want to miss this. I'm spending a lot of time completing the exercise equipment for my training area. However, the carpenters are having difficulty with the see-saw. Where do you intend to fly from?"

"We will leave from the Champ du Mars as before. Let's plan in two days' time, and we will definitely send you a message."

The throbbing had resumed and now he couldn't wait to return to his quarters to rest both himself and Sadeek.

The sergeant was surprised when he saw Robert and Sadeek enter the parade grounds of the Military School. Sadeek's gait was slow in approaching the stable and Robert's attempt at dismounting was incredibly ponderous. It was the first time that the Sergeant could remember helping an officer dismount. Robert was content to sit on a pile of blankets as he watched the sergeant care for his Arabian.

It was also very unusual that neither the sergeant nor Robert spoke, especially since they were both beholding the one object whose affection they held in common: Sadeek. He was positive that the sergeant's silence was related to the questions he wanted to ask about the conditions of both Robert and his cherished stallion. He knew that the sergeant wouldn't feel comfortable posing a question to an officer no matter how much affection they shared for his horse. Robert decided to answer before he had a chance to ask.

"We both have had a difficult day or two, sergeant. He definitely needs rest and I will see you again in the morning. I had a problem with four men in a field near Versailles. This magnificent animal saved my life."

Robert started to stand from his position on the blankets but only partially rose as the pain in his face showed the sergeant how serious this "problem" was. The sergeant merely nodded and offered his hand which Robert gratefully accepted, picked up his backpack and walked deliberately to the officer's quarters.

He first hung the plans for the playground on the drawing board. It was difficult to believe that removing his uniform could be more painful than it was when he dressed that morning. Robert looked and found a private in the hall and sent him to look for an orderly to draw his bath. He normally would wait for Garnier to order his meal, however his desire for food wasn't greater than the comfort of a hot bath.

Garnier had ordered dinner when he heard of his superior's arrival and placed it on the table. He could barely see Robert through the steam rising from the bath. To Garnier, he appeared to be concentrating on the drawing, but was he actually staring blankly at the wall above it; reviewing the events that occurred since leaving Versailles and the fact that he was no closer now to identifying the person who sent those who attacked him than he was before he received his orders to report to Versailles.

Garnier looked concerned. "Are you all right, sir? You look exhausted."

"I've had a difficult time lately, Lieutenant," he sighed. He was a little distracted by the sounds of carts and horses from the parade ground. "In addition to everything else, the slide has not been finished properly. I need to remedy this problem; but it will have to wait until tomorrow. He slid further into the tub. As this left only the top of Robert's head to address, Garnier asked if there was any reason for him to remain. When Robert said no, he exited quietly.

Robert lay back in the tub, arms outstretched with his head back; staring at the ceiling; fixating on nothing in particular. Eventually, the water began to cool and dressing in the nightshirt he brought with him from Versailles, he sat for dinner.

The search for those who were responsible for the attack after leaving Versailles was the highest priority for him now, especially the person who was directing these actions. The riders had approached from Paris, meaning it took some time for someone to be notified of his departure and to implement a plan of attack. It still didn't answer the larger question: who is the spy?

He had this day met with several people, any one of which might have been able to pass information to someone regarding his plans or whereabouts. That included everyone from the Military School to the Louvre to Jacques Charles, the boys who watched his horse and the residents of Porte Saint-Antoine.

Everyone he had spoken to had been provided with misinformation about how a different piece of the equipment had become a problem in the completion of the playground. Hopefully, very soon the spy would reveal him or herself or he would be forced to devise a different ruse.

"It could be any one of them, or it could be none of them," he thought as he finished his roast chicken. When his glass of wine was empty, he didn't even care if the orderly returned for his dishes or to empty his bath. He only wanted to sleep.

He slept longer this morning than usual. Even the bright morning sun flooding his quarters didn't wake him. He was forced to dress in great haste to arrive at the stables at his expected time as it seemed that something unforeseen made every effort of his delayed. He had to admit that he was simply exhausted even following a sound night's sleep. Sadeek, of course, looked as if nothing had occurred in the field, or he had spent the night in a forgotten stable. He looked eager to be saddled. Robert felt that he could have dropped the reins entirely and his horse would have known where to go. As it was, Robert gave him almost no direction and they arrived at the playground in time to see the swing set being removed from a cart. The driver of the cart saw him approach and before he could dismount was told that the spinning platform would be delivered as soon as the driver could return to the Bastille.

Robert was very hopeful the playground could be completed by days end. All the pieces would be here soon and all but three had already been placed in the ground with cement mixed by Joseph.

As usual a crowd had gathered to watch the playground being assembled and to admire Sadeek.

Finally, the spinning platform arrived and after an effort requiring all the men present, it was lifted from the cart and moved into place. Lisette arrived with some wine, fresh warm rolls and some cheese. The adults sat on some of the pieces, enjoying this meal from the woman now known as Lisette. People were gradually adjusting to refraining from referring to her as the "bread lady."

Lisette and Robert walked from one piece to the other, beginning with the see-saw and continuing clockwise until they reached the monkey bars at the end.

"This is very impressive, Major." She walked to the middle of the playground. "Why is the center of the playground just an open area? How will the children use this?"

"There are some uses I can think of for that area. As for how the children will use it, trust me; they will figure that out on their own."

He became much more animated now and placed his hands on her waist. "Lisette, I wanted to ask you to go somewhere the day after tomorrow. But it is a surprise, so don't ask me for details. I can promise you that it is something that is science related, I know you have never done before and will never forget."

"Yes of course, Mathurin. How could I say no? After all you have done for the children; we should be doing something nice for you."

Robert gave instructions to wait until the following day to play on the equipment so the cement could harden thoroughly. Then he and Lisette walked to where the boys were spending their time talking to Sadeek.

"I will look forward to finally see you do something related to science," as she held his hand.

Robert raised her hand and kissed it. "What I'll surprise you with next, will be all about science, I promise." He mounted Sadeek and turned onto the street and waved to Lisette and the boys.

The Bastille was relatively close and he wished to stop and express to Pelletiere how much he appreciated his assistance. There was so much commotion that no one paid any attention to the mounted officer entering through the east gate. Soldiers were rushing to assigned positions as an artillery officer shouted commands ordering the gun carriages to be brought to face the gates. And François was at the center of it all. It appeared to a drill to defend an attack on the Bastille.

Robert rode slowly against the flow of men and material until he reached Pellitier's shop. He held Sadeek's reins as he stood just inside the shade of the entrance. The sergeant saw him and put down his tools and left the door that he was working on.

"I wanted to stop and thank you for your work on the project, sergeant. You delivered on time and it seems to work perfectly. I really appreciate your efforts," as he extended his arm to shake the sergeants hand.

The sergeant was stunned. Officers were usually quicker to find fault than to thank soldiers for their contributions. Following orders, was part of following expectations, and not worthy of praise; ever. He snapped to attention and stiffly saluted while smiling. When his salute was returned, he gratefully shook Robert's hand.

"Well; you are certainly welcome, sir."

"Relax, sergeant. I stopped here because I wanted to tell you that what you did will bring a lot of joy too many people."

Pelletiere looked like he didn't quite understand.

"There are a lot of children in that poor section of Paris who can play there when the soldiers aren't using it to exercise."

A familiar voice behind him interrupted their discussion.

"What is it now, Mathurin? Do you need a table and chairs this time?"

François spoke from the courtyard in a mixture of mirth and sarcasm. He first shook Robert's hand and then hugged him.

"I hope our work met your standards. I heard that you were having difficulty with your slide."

Robert stopped and involuntarily took a deep breath, pausing for a moment before exhaling, hoping that a facial expression or his stifled reaction to what François' had unwittingly divulged would reveal the shock that just ran down his back.

Robert calmly answered. "No, no François. We managed to solve that problem. How did you hear about the slide?"

"Oddly enough, it was Petit." François said, leaning against the door frame. "He approached me following one of our early morning drills. We only talk officially and he knows that I resent his non-soldering, noble class, entitlement attitude. I'm at a loss why he would suddenly talk to me about your project."

Now, Robert needed to leave to digest this latest information and take time to plan his approach to solving his puzzle now that he had been presented with the final piece.

"I really appreciate all your help, François. We need to have dinner together once I have this exercise yard put together."

François agreed to make time for him and together they walked to where Sadeek stood. They shook hands as Robert mounted his horse and turned toward the west gate.

"So Garnier is the source of my discomfort," thought Robert as they headed to the Seine. "I cast my net and have caught my spy. It makes sense although I never would have guessed that he was the person betraying me"

As he thought more about it, he was certain that his aide must be the informer. Garnier was the only person whom Robert had informed about a problem with the slide. All the others had been told of a problem with a different piece of playground equipment. The officer who delivered the command from the King to report to Versailles was stationed at the Bastille. He must have divulged the information in the orders to Petit and Petit had ordered the attack in the field.

His mobile devise hadn't been left accidentally on the table after all. He must have surprised Garnier as he was examining the contents of his backpack.

Was it simply coincidence that DuPont had picked Garnier as his aide, or was his aide acting for both DuPont and Petit?

That was really a non-issue now. Robert knew that Petit was controlling Garnier, who needed to be eliminated without placing any blame upon himself. It didn't take long for him to settle on a solution, but he would need to enlist the help of someone he knew well and someone he had not yet met.

Before he finished feeding and grooming Sadeek; he had formulated a plan and decided how to implement it. As usual, the sergeant remained close to the stable and didn't converse a great deal. But he did know a great deal about horses and had a great deal of input in that area.

"You two form a closer bond every day that you are together," the sergeant said admiringly. "I would have sworn that you had been a horseman all your life and Sadeek had always been yours."

The following morning, Robert and Sadeek left the parade grounds in the direction of the Hotel des Invalides, but turned south toward Versailles the moment he couldn't be seen from the Military School.

In a few hours, he entered the Royal Courtyard and went directly to the stables to have Sadeek rested. Walking past the manicured hedges and fountains, he saw a member of the palace guard walking toward him.

"Private, I need to speak to the Captain of the Guard and the Duchess immediately. Where can I find them?"

"Sir, the Captain could be anywhere in the chateau. The Duchess passed here not long ago. She was walking in the direction of the Hamlet." The private held his salute until it was returned.

"Private, it is extremely important that I speak to your captain. Would you please locate him and tell him to meet Major Dubé at the Duchess's cottage in the Hamlet?"

As the private ran to locate the Captain of the Guard, Robert walked quickly to the Hamlet and found Gabrielle playing a game with Marie-Therese and Louis-Charles beside the pond next to her cottage. Marie-Thérèse was the first to see him. "Major

Dubé," she shouted, dropping the ball she was holding; running past flower pots and across the lawn to greet him.

"Would you like to play a game with us, Major?" Louis-Charles asked.

Robert knelt to talk to him. "I would like that very much. Can you teach me how to play?"

Each child took one of his hands and led him back to where Gabrielle waited with her arms outstretched. She embraced him and kissed him on both cheeks.

"Mathurin, we were just wondering when we would see you next and there you stood. What is the reason for your visit?" she asked as her violet eyes sparkled in the sunlight

Robert responded by removing his hat for a moment to reveal his wound. She raised her hand and gently touched the area around the stitches.

"My God, Mathurin. What happened?" Her eyes grew wide as she almost spoke in a whisper.

Louis-Charles threw a ball to Robert, hitting him in the chest. He bent to retrieve it which resumed the intense throbbing in his forehead. As he stood, the concerned look from Gabrielle was unavoidable as she witnessed his struggle to remain erect. Tossing the ball to Louis-Charles, he spoke to the Duchess in a hushed tone, barely more than a whisper.

"Gabrielle, I'll explain it all in detail, but I need to talk to your Captain of the Guard about something urgent. I ordered an enlisted man to search for him as I rode in and told him to send him here, so I expect him soon; but I thought it would mean more if the request came from you."

As he tossed the ball back to Louis-Charles, Gabrielle called to one of the servants. A tall, thin man approached her and bowed. "Find Captain de Bela and tell him to report here to Major Dubé immediately. You tell him that I said that this supersedes anything he is currently engaged in. Now go," she said sternly. The servant began to walk in the direction of the palace.

"Did you not hear me, idiot?" she screamed. "I said now!"

Without looking back, the servant broke into a run and disappeared around a line of hedges. Gabrielle turned and smiled, "I believe we can expect to see the Captain very soon." Robert nodded now that the situation was in her control and continued tossing the ball to the king's son while Marie-Thérese chased a butterfly.

He folded his coat and placed it over the back of a chair.

"I believe I am getting closer to the identity of the persons who were responsible for the attack on the bridge. Unfortunately, it seems that they are also getting closer to me. I was attacked by four men on the road returning to Paris. The closer I get to them, the more desperate they seem to become. I think that eliminating me is part of their plan."

Gabrielle's concerned expression immediately changed to a frightened stare. "Do you think it is wise for you to continue this search of yours? I couldn't bear the thought of anything happening to you, brother," as a tear ran down her cheek.

"No, quitting is not an option," he said resolutely. "Even if I stop looking for them, they will keep coming for me. I honestly believe that moving forward is the only smart option."

He was interrupted by the appearance of an officer walking rapidly toward them from the direction of the Queen's cottage. He had an aristocratic appearance and manner with which he carried himself, even when he hurried to the Duchess. Tall, slim with long crafty lips, his smile vanished when he faced Robert. His hair was covered by a white wig. Robert couldn't remember François wearing a wig when he served in this post.

He bowed first to the Duchess and then rigidly saluted Robert, "Captain de Bela, reporting, sir."

Gabriella spoke first, "Major Dubé, this is our Captain of the Guard, Captain Jean Philippe de Bela".

Robert returned the Captain's salute as de Bela spoke. "Major, I came as soon as I heard you wished to see me. What can be so important?" Anything that was positive about his smile had suddenly evaporated in his brash display of arrogance.

The children stood next to Gabrielle and looked to Robert, waiting for an answer to the brash captain's question.

Robert first took Gabrielle by the hand and walked to the edge of the pond, away from the children. "You need to keep the children occupied while I talk to the captain. They really can't hear the subject of this conversation." He turned from her and walked back to the impatient de Bela.

The captain looked puzzled at the delays in speaking to Robert and was about to comment when Robert spoke to him in the gravest tone. "Follow me captain," continuing to walk until he realized the captain remained where he stood, then grabbed his sleeve and pulled him beneath the shadow of the willow.

"Captain, there is one thing that I require from you; and I need it now." The captain looked as if he was considering granting a request from someone who outranked him, but was obviously of a lower social level than his.

Looking down his aristocratic nose at Robert he raised his eyebrows. "And what might that favor be, Major?"

Robert stepped forward so quickly, that any sense of security or well-being vanished along with his condescending air.

"What I need from you, Captain," said Robert's sternly; "to halt this arrogance of yours immediately. I presume that your family is of some importance."

The captain immediately took a step back and glared at Robert. "Yes that is correct Major. I am the son of Duc Philipe-Bertrand de Rochechouart de Bela de Mortemart."

Robert paused for a moment before stepping on de Bela's foot to prevent him from retreating again as Gabrielle approached and stood at Robert's shoulder. She looked at de Bela as if he was a rabbit and Robert was the fox, deciding what to do with his prey. Apparently she was as weary of him as was Robert.

Robert was silent for a moment and glanced at Gabrielle before returning to de Bela.

"I have never heard of your father and I don't care who he is," ignoring the shocked and indignant expression that covered the captain's face. "Listen very carefully to what I am about to say to you, Captain. I am here because I have uncovered a plot to assassinate the King. I haven't determined their identity yet but I will know very soon who this person is." Gabrielle put her hand on Robert's arm to prove where her allegiance belonged, while watching to be certain that children could not hear any of this.

"You have a decision to make, Captain," as Robert spit out the word "captain".

"You may choose either be the hero of Versailles, the officer who singlehandedly foiled an attempt to murder King Louis XVI. Or, you may choose to be known as the dimwitted Captain de Bela who allowed an assassin to walk into Versailles, unopposed and kill His Majesty and possibly end the Bourbon Monarchy. So tell me captain, which would you prefer? Because if you can't control this situation, I wager that the Duchess can. Do I have your attention now?"

"Why, yes," stammered de Bela.

Robert stepped closer to the stunned officer. "Your answer would be "yes, sir"; Captain," he said unsympathetically.

"Yes, sir. Sorry, sir," he said, struggling to regain his composure.

"That's better," replied Robert. "This is what will happen next. You will run to your office and prepare for me an order from the King to reassign an officer to Versailles. Leave the name of the officer blank; that will be mine to complete. When this person arrives, he will report to you and he will say, "I have come to serve the King", and you will arrest him on the spot. You will need to be alert and begin planning now. This could happen sooner than you realize."

"Captain, I am returning to Paris now. I hope that you won't disappoint me more than you already have. I do not wish to further delay my departure." Robert's threatening tone and narrowed eyes conveyed the proper message.

The captain backed up quickly and saluted. "Yes, sir. Immediately, sir;" and managed to step into the Duchess's pond. Up to his knees in water and his ego completely deflated, Gabrielle couldn't help but add to his discomfort. Speaking as if to one of the children she called to him, "I understood that the Major said now, Captain."

The captain stepped onto the grass and began to run with boots full of water, past the Queen's cottage and down a path in the direction of the Palace.

"Well, that was fun," said Robert as he took Gabrielle's hand. "I'm very sorry but I absolutely need to return to Paris to complete this if de Bela is to play the part of the hero."

"Yes, I have never cared for his service or his arrogance," Gabrielle admitted. "The way he treats everyone as if they are not equal to him because his father is someone of importance is shameful. Perhaps if he does well with this, he will be promoted and sent elsewhere." At that moment a servant came from the cottage pushing a silver cart with tea, small sandwiches and bowls of fruit.

"Please join us, Mathurin. To see you for such a brief visit as this is nearly worse than not seeing you at all. I won't protest at all if you decide to leave after you have finished. Besides, I know how long it will take de Bela to run to his offices in water soaked boots," as she smiled and laughed.

Robert removed his hat and placed it on top of his coat. Marie-Thérese instructed a servant to place a chair next to him so she could sit by her savior. He tried not to think how distorted life in the Hamlet could be. It was alarmingly simple to escape from the troubles lying beyond the Hamlet which drove him here. He needed to remain focused on solving the problem and remember that he had this argument regarding life within the Palace compared to life outside its gates with himself once before. As he relaxed in the shade of the willow, a gentle breeze passed by and the occasional sound made by a fish rising to the surface to catch a bug, created ripples in an otherwise still pond, renewing the argument about remaining at Versailles.

"Am I like that that ripple?" he thought. "A life existing for a brief period of time, spreading out in concentric circles until my energy is slowly exhausted, or to hit an obstacle like the bank of the pond and then suddenly expire?

He could have continued debating himself for some time if it were not for Louis-Charles, tossing a ball which hit Robert squarely in the chest, breaking his concentration. They finished their sandwiches and Robert took turns tossing the ball to the children, while speaking to Gabrielle about their shared dislike of de Bela and their hope that he was the right person for the task. He felt that if allowed to, he could remain at the Palace of Versailles, as he was tempted to before; where life was just a little short of reality. But he knew that he had work to complete and as he turned to retrieve his coat, he saw a young, worried lieutenant, hurrying in their direction.

"Major Dubé, Captain de Bela ordered me to give you this with his apologies for not delivering it himself," as he saluted Robert.

"Thank you, Lieutenant," said Robert as he accepted the document. "I imagine it must be difficult for the captain to walk quickly, when his boots are filled with water. You're dismissed."

The lieutenant saluted as he attempted to suppress a grin; without much success.

He felt that this was the perfect time to depart as he watched the lieutenant walk away and spotted the Queen approaching from the direction of her cottage. The King seemed to enjoy Robert's company, but the Queen's opinion of him was another matter entirely. When she reached the Duchess's cottage, he bowed to Her Majesty, kissed Gabrielle's hand, then said good-by to the children of France and briskly walked to the stables.

Sadeek seemed as eager to depart Versailles as Robert. Approaching the stables, Sadeek began to pace and whinney as soon as he saw him. The private in the stables gave Robert a few carrots to for his horse which Sadeek eagerly ate. He became noticeably calmer as Robert saddled him and seemed his calmest when they entered the Royal Courtyard and passed beyond the gates of Versailles.

Their pace was very quick until they reached the spot where the attack had taken place. Sadeek seemed to be looking for evidence of what had occurred, but there was very little to show that a struggle had ever taken place. The grass around the oak tree was still matted where the rider had landed, but any evidence of the violence that occurred on the road itself was now obscured where riders and carts had traveled this roadway in the aftermath of the attack. The bodies of the three men had been removed, but by whom Robert could only guess. There wasn't any reason to remain there if it was solely to solve that riddle and before long their rapid pace resumed as they continued on their return to Paris.

His first stop was Lisette's shop where the usual group of women, were in various stages of several different conversations.

Robert's arrival wasn't unexpected any longer and now he was greeted by them, while those closest to the bakery told her that she had a visitor. She walked across the bakery floor, smiling and wiping her hands on her apron.

"Hello, Mathurin; are you here to buy some fresh bread?" When she got close to him he could smell the flour and spices she had been using to bake her bread. He didn't think there could be a more wonderful aroma in the entire world.

"I'm not sure, is it any good?" The look he received from Lisette and the giggles from the women made him realize that that sort of humor was not well received and this might be a good time to state the reason for his visit. "I just returned from Versailles and I hoped that you would be able to come with me tomorrow so I can show you the surprise I promised. If that is all right with you I will be here tomorrow morning and we will be gone for the day."

Lisette placed her arms on his shoulders and her hands behind his neck. "Of course Major, I have been anticipating the day when I would see this surprise of yours. I will be waiting for you and don't make jokes about my bread or you'll never have another morsel of it. Now go on to your quarters and let me return to work so I can spend tomorrow with you." She pulled him toward her and kissed his cheek.

When he reached the stables at the Military school, he found the sergeant tending his grey horse as the carriage stood in the background. "Even though you spend more time with your Arabian, this horse needs some exercise as well," the sergeant explained. "So when you are gone I take him for brief rides or have one of the enlisted men do that. It keeps him fit and in good spirits."

"Well thank you, sergeant. I don't mean to neglect him, it just makes more sense to ride Sadeek," as he began to remove his saddle and brush him. After he had fed and watered him, he thanked the sergeant for the suggestion to visit Jardin des

Plantes. "It was really perfect and we have repeated the visit. I will see you in the morning."

"Well, you are quite welcome, Major. When I told my wife that I had suggested that you and your friend visit Jardin des Plantes, she said it brought back so many memories; good memories. We would literally spend hours walking on the paths leading to the museums and then we would sit beneath the tall hedges and talk. My wife's favorite part was the different varieties of roses. She would stare at them so intently that sometimes I don't believe she really heard what I said to her. When we bought our farm outside of Paris, she made me promise that I would plant rose bushes. That was one of the first tasks I performed, Major. Now, she takes care of our chickens and goats and horses and when she feels tired, sits next to her roses. I suppose that when I retire, my primary duty will be to enlarge her rose garden until it rivals Jardin des Plantes," he said with a wide grin.

The sergeant smiled and wished him a good night as Robert strode across the parade grounds to his quarters. Garnier handed him the envelope he was hoping to see. Tearing it open, he saw that it was indeed a message from Jacques Charles.

Dear Mathurin,

We plan to fly our balloon using our latest invention tomorrow from the Champ de Mars. Please join us..

Your friend,

Jacques

Following his bath and dinner he thanked Garnier for his time and dismissed him for the evening, saying that he needed to be alone.

As Garnier closed the door, Robert slowly removed the document he carried from Versailles and carefully spread it out on the desk. This would order the person whose name appeared on it to report immediately for duty at Versailles and in turn; be immediately arrested. Robert picked up a quill and dipped it in his ink well. In the space where the name of the person who would follow those orders he carefully wrote:

LIEUTENANT EMILE GARNIER

With Garnier's fate now sealed, Robert first blew out the candles on his desk, extinguished those near his bed and was soon fast asleep.

Robert awoke, continuing his internal debate questioning if his course of action against Garnier was justified. He debated with himself over the ethics of sending Garnier to Versailles, speculating whether he would be satisfied with the results of de Bela's actions against him. He was certain that Garnier's punishment would be severe, but perhaps with the Revolution occurring soon, Garnier might escape in the ensuing chaos.

His decision to proceed with ordering Garnier to his doom was difficult in the beginning, but its logic was impossible to deny. First, it was necessary to place Garnier in a position to deny his ability to report to Petit about his plans. Second, was Garnier's unforgiveable treachery. He had invited Garnier to share meals with him and had taken time to explain his plans for the playground. Garnier had escaped punishment when Robert found him examining his mobile device. While he was attempting to make Garnier feel as an equal in an environment where rank and class distinctions were better at keeping persons separate, Garnier used all of the information Robert gave him, to allow Petit to make plans that would have resulted in his death; if the men on the road to Paris had been successful.

"No, this is definitely the right path to take," thought Robert. He just wished Garnier would bring breakfast so he could take care of this unpleasant business and make his way to Porte Saint-Antoine.

A quick knock at his door, followed by the sound of the handle being turned; signaled Robert that his plan was about to begin, but not before breakfast was served. Garnier poured two cups of tea and buttered the rolls and placed the plate with eggs before Robert. He had finished his second cup of tea including his eggs and rolls when he placed his cup on the table and looked straight at Garnier.

"Lieutenant, I have some very good news to discuss with you."

Garnier lifted his head and gave Robert an inquisitive look. "Yes, sir?"

"Lieutenant, I was summoned to Versailles again yesterday. While I was there, a senior officer met with me about a very serious matter. It seems that they lost an extremely important officer to promotion and wondered if I knew a young, intelligent and dedicated officer whom I would recommend for assignment to the Captain of the Guard. This is a very important position and I couldn't think of anyone more qualified than you, Lieutenant." Robert handed Garnier a document so dispassionately that it caused a chill down the lieutenant's back.

Garnier stared at his plate on the table for a moment. Robert deduced that he was searching for an appropriate response, but it would take a moment for Garnier to realize that there was none.

"Why, yes sir, thank you very much sir. How long do I have to consider this?" he stammered.

"Lieutenant, read your orders. This is not a request, you are ordered to report for duty to Captain de Bela; the Captain of the Guard at Versailles. This is a very important position. It gives you a real chance to be noticed by His Majesty. You should be happy." Robert felt as if he were inflicting some additional discomfort into Garnier's already dismal morning.

"Yes sir, this is wonderful news as you say, major. I will leave here and head to Versailles. I only need to manage some things at the Bastille first and then I will be ready to go.' Garnier seemed to be searching for a remedy to his situation, but Robert was determined to give him no options.

"Lieutenant," he said slowly. "Do you see the word "immediately" anywhere on your orders?"

"Yes sir, I see it more than once actually, sir," as Garnier's voice diminished.

"Lieutenant, do you see anywhere in your orders that you are to visit the Bastille or anywhere before you depart for your assignment at Versailles?" Robert said with an air of finality.

"No sir, no I do not."

"Then, Lieutenant; I would suggest that you pack quickly and procure your horse from the livery and leave "immediately" for your new assignment at Versailles, where you will report to the Captain of the Guard; Captain de Bela. When you report to him, you will say these words exactly, "I have come to serve the King". I will wait for you on the Parade Grounds. Congratulations."

Robert stood and waited for Garnier to rise and then shook his hand and walked him to the door. Garnier exited looking crestfallen.

When Garnier stepped onto the parade grounds from the officer's quarters, he found Robert waiting for him. Neither spoke as they walked across the parade grounds to the stable where the sergeant had already saddled his horse and was holding his reins. His horse was light brown, with a black mane and tail. There was a white spot just above his eyes and the area around his mouth was greyish. He looked sturdy enough to make the ride to Versailles and certainly looked more eager for this trip than did his rider.

Robert looked up at Garnier who seemed very ill at ease. "You already had the sergeant saddle my horse for me?"

"Absolutely," said Robert evenly. "I wouldn't want anything to prevent you from getting everything you deserve. Good luck, Lieutenant."

Garnier saluted from his mount and moved toward the gate with a dazed look on his face. He didn't exactly know what was happening and he couldn't quite figure out what to make of his situation. Upon reaching the gate he turned right and galloped out of sight.

Later he reached Versailles and sought out the Captain of the Guard, Captain de Bela. He saluted and told the captain that he was reporting as ordered. "I am here to serve the King," he said saluting de Bela. His salute was never returned, as he was immediately arrested and was not seen again.

SCIENCE LESSON

At the shop, he found that Lisette and the usual group of women were ready to receive him. Lisette wore a very bright blue dress and was waiting behind the counter when he entered. All the women smiled as he greeted her and held open the door as she walked to where Sadeek was hitched.

After Robert helped her mount Sadeek, they both looked back to the shop window as everyone had, as usual, moved to the windows and waved good-by.

When they arrived at Champ de Mars, he helped her down from Sadeek so she faced the military school with Champ de Mars behind her. Robert held her hands and asked her, "Lisette, do you trust me?"

"I wouldn't be here if I didn't, Mathurin. What were you going to show me?" she said; impatiently.

"I'm going to reveal to you the surprise I promised and it involves an historic scientific experiment I have been involved with. But I want you to close your eyes and take my hand. Can you do that?"

She squeezed his hand. "Yes of course. This is so exciting," as she tightly closed her eyes.

He led her past the trees where he immediately saw that the balloon had been inflated. The chilling chamber had done its job and a large throng of people stood around the basket and the other apparatus. As they walked along the grass, Lisette attempted to guess what role the voices of the onlookers played in Robert's surprise. The murmuring rose in volume as Robert led Lisette to a set of wooden stairs next to the basket.

Robert guided her to the bottom step. "Lisette, there is a staircase directly before you. I'll help you walk to the top. There are only seven steps until you reach the top step and then I'll lift you down. Keep your eyes closed and very soon, you'll be able to open your eyes and see the huge surprise that I have arranged for you."

Lisette sounded as if she was becoming slightly irritated. "This is beginning to tire me, Mathurin. How much longer do I need to close my eyes?"

He didn't want to rush this and risk dropping her into the basket. "It won't be long, I promise," he said attempting to sound reassuring.

When they reached the top step, he lowered himself into the basket before turning around and placing his hands on Lisette's waist.

"Lean forward and place your hands on my shoulders. That's very good. Now I'm going to lower you very slowly."

When he had safely placed her into the basket, he nodded to Jacques, who released the tether and the balloon rapidly began to rise.

Robert gently put his hands on her face and said, "It's all right. You can open your eyes now."

Lisette's reaction was what he had hoped for, as she stood smiling for a moment, her hair blowing in the breeze, until she noticed a goose flying past. Sensing that something was not right, she slowly turned her head.

The Champ de Mars, the very long, very wide grass covered boulevard was now merely a sliver of green. As her eyes widened, she gasped for air as a shock of terror coursed through her body. She turned to Robert, whose expectation, until that moment had been was Lisette's complete enthrallment with this flight. He was entirely unprepared for Lisette's reaction.

"Surprise," he said excitedly; as she looked back at him, a shocked expression on her face. One hand clutched the edge of the basket, while the other covered her heart as she attempted to speak but no words came out.

"Surprise," as he placed his hands on her waist, believing that she hadn't heard him the first time.

"Surprise?" she screamed. "Are you insane? You are going to kill us both. Release me now," and she pushed his hands away until she backed into the edge of the basket, turned slowly and looked up at a cloud and then down at a Paris that was growing steadily smaller. Her screaming stopped as she leaped at Robert and wrapped her arms around him.

"How could you possibly imagine that I would like this, you maniac?" her voice becoming a shrill cry for help where there was no possibility of rescue.

Robert held her with one arm and stroked her hair with the other.

"You wanted me to show you some science, didn't you? This is all about science. This balloon above us was filled with hydrogen gas created from a reaction between iron and sulfuric acid. It was pumped into the balloon with an invention I helped create. Now we are floating above Paris, following the wind and when we land, the people following us will return us to Paris and I will return you to your home."

Lisette had stopped protesting and now looked at him sternly, standing with her arms crossed, waiting for him to explain further; so Robert pressed on, hoping for the best.

Lisette seemed to be recovering from her initial shock and was beginning to relax. Soon she left Robert and stood with her hands on the edge of the basket, occasionally glancing upward nervously at the balloon before she regarded the pattern of the city streets and their designs. It was difficult to imagine how they were all connected until they were viewed from this altitude. Now it looked like all of Paris resembled a series of interconnected watches.

"You can see the Seine below and the Tuileries Gardens to the left and the Champs-Elysées after that," continuing to point to streets he was unfamiliar with until the neighborhoods gave way to trees, fields and villages.

He recognized that they had passed the Seine again and thought they should consider landing soon before they drifted too far away. The city had left them some time ago and now the wind had carried them beyond the town where they destroyed a farmer's grape crop, something he was desperate to avoid.

The land here was very flat, surrounded by tall trees and an abundance of shrubs and uncultivated fields. Robert managed to land the balloon in a field full of tall grass and purple wildflowers. As he helped her from the basket, Lisette gazed around at the fields and bushes and smiled. "Was your idea to place this balloon in a field another surprise of yours, Major? Because from here, it looks like we have quite a walk back to Paris."

Robert feigned a bored expression and lowered his chin while he looked at her. "Riders have been following us on horseback since we left Champ de Mars. It shouldn't be any longer than a day or two. Maybe we can sleep in that hedgerow," he said pointing at the nearby line of tall, dense hedges.

"You know I am very happy that you showed me the scientist in you today, Major," she said as she put her arms around his neck. "But do not make jokes about sleeping in those bushes tonight. Besides, I'm hungry and now it's my turn to treat you," and she returned to the basket and withdrew the bag she had had carried from which she produced a baguette, some cheese and a bottle of wine.

By the time the riders reached them, Robert and Lisette had treated themselves to the bread and cheese and there was enough wine left to share with the riders. Robert recognized them as the riders who had followed him and one of the Robert brothers on their unfortunate flight over the grape famers cart and their descent into a farmer's field. While one rode away to direct the cart to the site for the return to Paris, the second rider remained to assist in preparing the balloon for the trip back to Paris.

"This is a much better spot than the last flight, Major," said the rider. "No ruined crops, broken carts, crushed grapes or angry farmers," he said surveying the scene. "If we are fortunate, we may have the balloon loaded and be on our way before a mob arrives."

Robert and the rider had determined the easiest point for the cart to enter the field and had released enough gas to make the balloon easier to handle, just as the recovery crew arrived. Sadeek had been tethered to the cart and appearing eager to be ridden, Robert helped Lisette mount Sadeek and together they followed the cart back to Jacques's workshop at Place des Victoires.

Robert entered the workshop with Lisette next to him, her arm through his. He was fairly certain that if it hadn't been for the success of their chilling chamber, he might have entered the workshop unnoticed.

Jacques filled everyone's wine glasses and made a brief speech about how the chamber was the result of Robert's idea and today's success was a direct result of that. Then they asked Robert to comment on the day's events. "Well," he began cautiously, as their reaction to his earlier suggestion about the revolution in transportation was still fresh in his mind. "Had you considered that the chilling chamber could possibly be used as a method to cool homes and buildings someday?"

It received the same reaction as his idea about people traveling on contraptions with wheels. Jacques looked at the Robert brothers, a stifled chuckle became a hearty laugh and almost instantly the entire workshop echoed with peals of laughter. Robert was rapidly building a solid reputation as the most hilarious scientist in France.

The moment that Jacques and the Robert brothers had finished their commentary on his idea, Robert and Lisette rode Sadeek back to her shop. Robert led Sadeek back to the stables, where he could see that Henri and Gerard had been very busy cleaning it. The manner in which these two boys approached their responsibilities impressed him very much. They had stopped asking him for money some time ago and now were on the verge of making the stables at least as presentable as it probably had been when it was first built.

When Henri and Gerard noticed them standing in the entrance, they both shrieked with joy, immediately dropping their tools, running past Robert and straight to Sadeek. Turning immediately, they saluted and without waiting for a salute in return, each boy spun around and began rubbing Sadeek's flanks and his muzzle. "We can take care of him now, Major. He is thirsty and hungry and in need of a good brushing." Henri was the first to seize the reins from Robert's hands and as both boys looked affectionately at their stallion, Robert was quickly forgotten as Sadeek was led away to be pampered.

Justified in feeling totally ignored, he was surprised when someone's arm slipped through his. Having approached him from behind as he watched Sadeek returning to his stable, Lisette smiled at him; "Are you going to show me your playground Major or do I have to go there alone?"

Walking through the alley to the playground between tall buildings filled with apartments on either side, the noises from the people living in those cramped spaces escaped through dirty sometimes broken windows, filling the narrow passage with their cries of despair and made him wonder if the conditions inside the apartments could possibly be any worse than the misery suggested by their shouting.

More of the playground became visible as they drew nearer to the street and soon the unpleasant noises heard from the miserable apartments above were replaced by the sounds of children laughing and playing on the equipment made through "donations" of Louis XVI and man hours from the parents of Porte Saint-Antoine.

The children created a stage of boundless energy as they slid; climbed and spun their way from one piece to another, while some chased each other and played impromptu games of their own in the center area that some had questioned the logic of placing it there. Lisette held Robert's hand and looked at him, "You have really created something special here, Mathurin. Porte Saint-Antione owes you more than you know. The least I can do is cook dinner for you."

"This is a big day, Lisette. Let's go where I know the bread is the freshest and I promise I can get a window seat for us. I know the owner."

Their return through the alley to Lisette's shop surprised Robert somewhat. The walls, which had earlier seemed to house so much despair, now seemed to be even grown in their darkness. All of the misery bottled up inside those walls now seemed to shout down on him. Inwardly, he asked what more he could do, but the walls didn't seem to offer a solution to their problem. Maybe his contribution of the playground would be a turning point for some of the sorrow he had observed here.

The path through the alley had been so frequently traveled, that the stones used to pave it had been worn smooth. Robert and Lisette talked as though they were they only persons walking on the path, until they looked forward and noticed two men approaching. They continued discussing their plans for a return visit to Jardin des Plantes, when he glanced at the two men as they passed.

Usually people would at least acknowledge someone's presence and customarily exchange greetings, but these two seemed to be doing just the opposite. They averted their eyes and lowered their heads and were silent at the moment people would usually greet one another. The alley was narrow enough that they had to walk in single file as Lissette walked behind Robert. It was as if the sun had determined that this was a part of Paris where its light wouldn't be allowed to enter, so tall were the buildings and the alley so narrow.

Something about one of the men looked familiar to Robert but he had met so many people in Porte Saint-Antoine that this person must be someone he had already met. But wouldn't they say something if they were known to each other? Lisette continued to talk about Jardin des Plantes while he tried to make sense of it all. Suddenly he remembered what was familiar about one of the men. Even in the shadows he could see the scar he bore on his right cheek where Robert had struck it with a shakira, the day the man had attacked the royal carriage near Versailles!

Lisette saw Robert's face as he turned in the direction of the two men. His expression had changed severely; he had drawn his pistol and was turning to fire. She grabbed the arm holding the pistol, "Mathurin, what are you doing? I know that man."

FIREKEEPERS

Intelligence Specialist Franklin sat behind his desk in his office in the Pentagon. He continued to evolve in his new position involving securing the nation's computers from cyber-attack. Having just completed his morning briefing with military officers assigned to U.S. Cyber Command, he barely had enough time to sit anywhere but in his office and now realized that his hunger couldn't be ignored any longer. Driving home for lunch was not really an option as he would spend the majority of his time in his car before returning for more afternoon briefings. He decided to sit at one on the many benches in the center courtyard of the Pentagon. At the very least, he could hope that his much delayed attempts to vacation in Maine might come to fruition if he invested more time planning. For the moment, he felt somewhat rejuvenated by the warmth of the sun on his face and an uncommon breeze that blew the leaves across the courtyard. His solitude was short-lived however, when the usual rush from some of the 28,000 personnel who worked at the Pentagon, converged on the snack bar.

Acknowledging that his seclusion was broken for at least the next hour if he remained on this bench, he sighed and tucked the magazine his arm. When he returned to his office he had just sat at his desk and turned his attention to reading and planning his elusive vacation when he turned in his seat to find agent Tyler standing in his doorway about to knock.

Tyler was holding his mobile device and had judged correctly that he had once again, managed to interrupt Franklin's thoughts.

"Sir, I know that this is probably a bad time, but this is something I believe you should see."

Tyler's somber expression convinced Franklin that he felt this was sufficiently important to interrupt his reading.

"What is it this time, Tyler? Another one of your amazing dog videos?" jested Franklin.

Tyler set up his devise on the desk in front of Franklin. A video began, showing three men surrounding and attacking a fourth man but the solitary man was having no problem defending himself and eventually was the only one left standing.

"You are interrupting me to watch a video of a barroom brawl?" said an unimpressed Franklin.

"No sir, not exactly," replied Tyler, "keep watching."

Franklin continued to view the fight, as the lone combatant held one of his opponents by his shirt, appearing ready to strike when something in another direction distracted him. As he released his hold on the person's shirt he turned and faced the camera.

Franklin sat straight in his chair and drew a deep breath. "Well, I see that Dr. Dubé is still a busy person. How does he ever find the time to work? What else do you have?" as he put his magazine away and moved closer to the screen.

"To begin with, this isn't a bar; it's a restaurant named "Firekeepers", located on the Onondaga Indian Nation which is a few miles south of Syracuse. The video was taken by a customer about three days before the time machine disappeared from the courthouse in Pasadena. I've contacted the physics department at Syracuse University and it seems that Dr. Dubé went missing just after our interview with him in the chancellor's office."

Franklin rose from his chair and looked from his window at the boats docked in the marina on the other side of the freeway. "And the Onondaga Nation would be a perfect place to hide something from the government," he added. "Can you look into...?"

Tyler interrupted, anticipating Franklins next thought. "We have reservations on a flight leaving Dullas for Syracuse in one hour, sir," as he stood holding Franklin's jacket.

THE OFFER

With one motion, Robert pulled back the hammer on his pistol and took aim at the men. At the same instant, he saw something flying through the air in their direction. Lisette's intervention was about to have consequences in Robert's decision making. He immediately must choose between firing his weapon or attempt to knock down the knife that going to be upon them in seconds.

The passage was too narrow for him to push her away from the knife's flight. At best he could attempt to deflect it and he chose to strike at the knife. Stepping forward, he swung his pistol in the knife's direction and managed to make contact with the barrel of the pistol. He heard a scrapping noise as it hit the stone wall of the alley. Sweeping his arm to his right, he brought his pistol to bear where the men should have been, but Lisette's distraction had given them the time they needed to reach Avenue Ledru-Rollin and they were probably now walking down the avenue past the playground.

He turned to Lisette to tell her that he was going to pursue them, when he saw her lying on the path. The knife had deflected off the wall, lodging itself in her back just beneath her shoulder blade and now the pursuit of anyone became secondary to Lisette's condition. She was semi- conscious now, but he would need her help if he hoped to move her from the alley. He tore away part of her skirt and dressed the wound around the knife in an attempt to stop the bleeding.

"Lisette, I am going to lift you and you need to put your arms around my neck. Can you do that for me?" he asked and received only a feeble moan from her. He lifted her in his arms, somehow managing to keep pressure against the wound. As he stepped into the street, people and animals, time and sound all seemed to stop. He heard no one speak; there was no rapid movement as everyone turned to see him cross the avenue with her in his arms. Her arms were wrapped as tightly around his neck as she could manage and his uniform was stained with her blood.

Robert encouraged her to hold as tightly as possible while he searched for someone to help locate a doctor. One of the children from the playground screamed when she saw the severity of Lisette's wound and its evidence on Robert's uniform. That shocked everyone to reality and Robert soon found Guy Vassar and Charles Montagne standing next to him, looking at him in search of directions and explanations.

"We were attacked in the alley," he explained. "She's badly wounded and I have managed to slow the bleeding, but she needs a doctor now."

Guy and Charles quickly glanced at each other and then looked gravely at Robert.

"Mathurin, doctors don't come here often and even then they usually arrive too late. The condition of the poor doesn't offer an abundance of incentives for doctor's to devote much of their attention on us. We rely mostly on the abilities of midwives for our needs, like the stitching of your wound by Monique. It could take hours for a doctor to arrive," Guy said as he placed his hand on Robert's arm.

A crowd had gathered and he could see the crowd separating as someone was moving to the spot where Robert held Lisette. He looked up to see Monique frantically pushing people aside as she made her way to her friend's side and immediately examined the knife wound. "You did well to leave the knife in the wound, Major. But she needs a doctor. This is beyond my capabilities. It could take hours......"

Robert stared at Monique and then at Guy and Charles. "I don't have hours. She doesn't have hours. We don't have hours," placing particular emphasis on the word hours. "Look at me, stop talking," speaking so calmly it surprised him. "It will be fine. Get me the cart and take us to the Bastille."

They looked at Robert as if he was out of his mind. He was determined to stop their resignation to Lisette's fate.

"But we don't have a cart," Monique attempted to explain, with tears in her eyes.

"I don't mean your cart," snapped Robert. "I mean his cart," as he nodded to a cart whose driver was standing on his seat in an attempt to discover the nature of the commotion. "That cart there, Guy. Stop him, it will be our ambulance." Guy and Charles both sprinted to the cart and above the protestations of the driver, held the team while Robert walked toward the cart. The driver had produced a club which he intended to use to defend his property, but dropped it when he saw the blood stained officer carrying Lisette, whom he immediately recognised as the bread lady and then willingly offered his assistance. He rearranged some sacks of grain to give Robert a place to sit where he could give more support to Lisette and keep pressure on the wound. Robert propped himself against the sacks while people from the crowd helped raise her until she sat in his arms. He held her tightly against his chest while Monique held her hand and spoke softly to her.

"The Bastille, quickly," Robert shouted as he stared at the discomfort on Lisette's face.

The driver proceeded as fast as he could and barely slowed when challenged by a guard at the Bastille's gate. "Private," yelled Robert, "where is the infirmary?"

The sentry saluted briskly, pointed across the courtyard and the driver whipped his team to cover the distance as quickly as possible, until he halted at the entrance to the infirmary. Robert lowered Lisette into the arms of Monique and some enlisted men before he held her and turned quickly toward the entrance, expecting to meet someone who would be willing to help.

He came upon two orderlies, who sat across from each other playing cards. Before they could speak, he shouted, "Where is the operating room?"

"Through those doors, sir. But we don't administer care to civilians. It's only open to military personnel. You'll have to take her elsewhere."

Robert turned and walked to the doors to the operating room and kicked them open. Shouting over his shoulder he said, "Well, they're open now. Get your doctor up here immediately. He has a patient."

He located the operating table in the center of the room and gently placed Lisette on her side and directed Monique to keep her still, opening curtains and lighting candles, before returning to check on the progress of the orderlies.

One orderly saw the determined look in Robert's eyes and held his breath, while the other appeared unconcerned and continued to shuffle the cards. His eyes widened as he saw Robert's left hand withdraw his dagger from its sheath and his cutlass with his right. The dagger came straight down, piercing the deck of cards and the table. As the second orderly withdrew his hand, he found a cutlass pressed upon his neck and Robert's boot on his chest. A second later he was lying on his back, with the blade of a cutlass under his chin, staring at a very determined grim looking officer. "Get the doctor now. I will not ask again."

"Yes sir, yes sir," said the startled orderly as he scrambled from the floor and raced through the doors.

He looked at the first orderly who now stood in a corner. "You there, do you know how to prepare for an operation?" demanded Robert.

"Yes sir," he answered without hesitation. "But the doctor," his voice trailed away when Robert's glare bore down on him. "Yes sir, immediately sir," and he ran into the operating room.

Robert followed him and as the orderly prepared the operating room for the absent doctor, he and Monique changed the dressing and continued to apply pressure to the wound while they waited agonizingly for the doctor to arrive.

When the doctor entered the operating room he looked very irritated. However, his irritation was no match for Robert's unyielding look and he decided it would be in his best interest to consider the temperament of this officer. He walked to Lisette, examined her wound and looked at Robert with a stare that was empty and cold, "She is a civilian, one of those peasants from Porte Saint-Antoine. I have no time for this. Deposit her remains with the rest of the trash from that district," and turned to leave.

Before the last words had left his lips, the doctor heard the unmistakable click of the hammer of a pistol being pulled back, and felt the cold round barrel of Robert's pistol rammed against his temple.

"Doctor, this woman is the only person who can identify the man who recently held a knife to the throat of the King's daughter. She must survive, so I can bring this man to justice. So doctor, I will make you an offer that you cannot refuse. You save her life, or I pull this trigger. At this moment, her life is much more valuable than yours."

"I always loved that movie," he thought.

"Yes, yes; just lower your weapon," the doctor said indignantly with his hands raised. "I didn't realize that this wasn't the result of some common street violence. We see too much of that sort around here," as he examined the wound and bent low to examine Lisette's mouth. "Her breathing is not labored and there is no sign of blood around her mouth. That's a good sign because she probably isn't bleeding internally and the knife didn't puncture her lung. You did a very nice job dressing the wound and she hasn't lost too much blood. What you did probably saved her life, Major. I need to get to work on this now, however. Where are your quarters, Major? We can notify you when we are finished."

"For now doctor, my quarters are here," as he returned his pistol to its holster and sat uneasily on the edge of the sole chair in the room.

"You can't stay here, there are rules," he informed Robert, who immediately rose from his chair.

"Oh, never mind," as he quickly relented. "Get the orderlies would you please?"

Robert walked through the operating room doors and reappeared moments later with both orderlies before him, their mouths wide open.

The doctor looked at them and back to Robert. "Let me guess, he made you an offer you couldn't refuse?" Both men nodded dumbly. "Get this room ready for an operation and after that, fetch a cot for the Major and place it in the recovery room. He will be staying here for some time."

One orderly cleaned a tray next to the operating table with alcohol and placed instruments on a white cloth while the other administered a liquid to Lisette. "Opiates," the doctor said without looking at Robert. "Withdrawing the knife is going to be extremely painful; it will help to ease the pain." The doctor washed his hands in a basin and leaned over to speak to her. "I need you to be brave, young lady. I have to remove the blade from your back and it will be very painful. Claude gave you something for the pain which will help."

Lisette struggled to turn her head to face the doctor. The doctor hesitated for a moment and turned to Robert, "She wants you to stand here," indicating a spot next to the operating table where she lay.

Robert rushed across the operating room and Lisette immediately reached for his hand, squeezing it very hard. The doctor looked seriously at Lisette as he gripped the dagger with one hand, and placed his other near her shoulder blade. When he removed the blade, Lisette let out a gasp but nothing else, and then she released her grasp on Robert's hand.

The doctor took quite some time cleaning the wound and then stitched it closed. In the end he looked at Robert as he washed his hands. "Your witness is an extremely brave woman, Major. I have heard men scream when I treated them for lesser wounds. She will be in the room across the hall for now. Your cot will be next to her bed"

The doctor signaled to the two orderlies to bring a stretcher next to the operating table. The orderly who lost his deck of cards to a dagger earlier, looked at Robert with no malice and nodded toward the operating table. Positioning himself next the operating table, the orderly told him to support Lisette's torso while he readied himself to lift her from her shoulders and the second orderly would support her legs. He counted to three and without wasting time or effort, lifted her onto the stretcher and carried her across the hall into a recovery room. They repeated the procedure, she was placed her in her bed as comfortably as possible and a cot was placed next to Lisette.

The recovery room was far from glamorous and certainly not what someone from the 21st century would have expected. It resembled a large dark box, with a small window, overlooking the Bastille's courtyard, but the room was positioned in a corner of the Bastille's walls at such an odd angle, that the room benefited more from the light provided by candles than sunlight. As this seemed like the best he could hope for, he instructed the orderlies to leave and bring a bottle of alcohol to clean her wound. The doctor entered the room and asked Robert it there anything else he required. "Please tell Captain Rigaud that I am here. That is really all I need. Thank you very much doctor."

The last thing he remembered was sitting on the edge of her bed listening to Lisette's deep, peaceful breathing, but hours later he was awakened by the sounds of someone's presence and woke up on his cot. Monique smiled at him as she sat on the edge of Lisette's bed. She had returned to look after her friend and to allow Robert some time to himself.

Robert left the recovery room to seek out François while Lisette slept. During the following several days they would meet in François' office or in the officer's mess where Petit's errant shot still scarred the ceiling. They discussed a variety of subjects and eventually Petit became a topic for discussion.

"News arrived for Petit which visibly upset him. I thought at first that it might have been unpleasant news about his family, but I know now that it came from Versailles. Whatever it was, it put him in a fouler mood than usual, and then he started mumbling something about seeking revenge, but no one here really takes him too seriously; so I didn't give it too much thought. This business about the attack in the field near Versailles puzzles and worries me, Mathurin. Part of me wants to believe that he is capable of arranging this attack but he always seems so disinterested in everything but himself that I wonder if he would even be interested in the effort it would take. I feel that you should be extremely cautious in ensuring your safety."

Robert placed his boots on the floor and leaned forward in his chair. "Are you familiar with a Lieutenant Richard, François?"

"Pascal Richard," he answered; his interest piqued. "A new officer, he seems like a good man, competent, intelligent; from a good family. May I ask, what is your interest in him?"

"He delivered orders to me at Lissette's boulangerie which sent me to Versailles on the day I was attacked. Whether or not he was sent by Garnier, he knows where she lives. Even if his involvement in delivering the order was innocent, he's dangerous because of the knowledge he possesses. Would it be possible that he is ready for a new assignment?" he said to François.

"Yes I quite agree, Mathurin. I seem to remember reviewing an order for one of our officers to report to our outpost near Mons, by the Austrian Netherlands border. He may be absent for a month at least."

Robert nodded. The following day, Lieutenant Richard received his orders to report to a post near the border separating France from its northern neighbor and Robert watched as the lieutenant and his information left Paris. By the time the lieutenant returned to the Bastille, Robert hoped to be researching black holes in Syracuse.

When he returned to Lisette's room and sat quietly on his cot, she opened her eyes slightly and looked at him as if through a haze, "Mathurin, I don't remember very much from our walk in the alley, but my shoulder hurts so. First, you receive the wound on your forehead and now I find this one in my back. If we manage to survive this ill luck of ours, will you promise me something?" as she placed her hand on his cheek.

Robert moved from his cot and sat next to Lisette. "Yes, of course, Lisette, whatever you want. Just ask me."

She attempted to sit up, but it was clearly too painful, so he piled all the available pillows together behind her. "Promise me that we will find a more productive way to spend our time together. I am growing weary of this habit we seem to be forming where one of us is always recuperating."

Robert nodded. "Yeah, it's a good habit to break, definitely." He realised that this was the first time he felt relaxed since the attack in the alley. Now he was thinking ahead to moving Lisette home from the Bastille, which wouldn't be for a few days at least according to the doctor. The wound was far too deep for her to move until she had more rest. He knew that he could rely on François for assistance in obtaining a carriage when the time arrived because even if Sadeek was here at the Bastille, she could never be moved on horseback.

His thoughts were suddenly interrupted by the sound of someone calling to a person who gave no reply. As the noise came closer, he could tell from the sounds in the hall that several people were approaching in the direction of Lisette's room. Robert reached for his pistol and cutlass, not knowing who or what to expect.

"It's the door on your left," shouted the person in the hallway. The door opened slowly and an orderly stepped inside, followed quickly by a brilliant purple dress with a matching umbrella and Robert saw all that he needed to know who was entering.

"Hello, Gabrielle; what a nice surprise," he said a moment before she crossed the threshold. The Duchess as usual, flowed into the room like a breeze; nearly flattening the orderly against the wall and paused to smile at Robert while she held the hands of Marie-Thérese and Louis-Charles.

Robert hugged all of them while Marie-Thérese seemed content to leave her arms wrapped around his waist. He looked at Gabrielle as he patted Marie-Thérese's head, "I've never seen her silent before. It's a little unusual."

"I told her that she must be very quiet in a hospital so patients can get well, especially your friend," as she looked at Lisette. "She wants your friend to get well so badly that she promised to remain silent until she recovers. I'm not certain how long that promise will last," she said smiling at Robert.

Marie-Thérese walked over to the side of Lisette's bed and held her hand. "You are Major Dubé's friend are you not? You must be better now, because I promised I wouldn't talk again until you were well. He saved both our lives from some very bad people. That makes us like sisters, doesn't it? I would like it very much if we could be friends and you and the Major could come and visit us at Versailles." Continuing to hold Lisette's hand, Marie-Thérese raised her eyes to Robert, "She is very beautiful my savior; are you going to marry her?"

Lisette raised her hand to her mouth, attempting to stifle a giggle while she glanced at Robert.

Robert looked uncomfortably at them both, while Louis-Charles seemed content to remain on the cot. "Remember Marie-Thérese," he said, "This is a hospital and you really need to be quiet."

Lisette stroked Marie-Thérese's hair and attempted to sit up a little more but it was far too painful. "Why don't you tell me all about where you live? I have never visited Versailles, but I would love to see it someday. Can you sit and tell me about your life at Versailles? I think that the Major and your Duchess are about to leave us as it appears that they have something of importance to discuss." Lisette looked at Robert as Gabrielle nodded and turned her head toward the door.

Robert looked at both women, wondering what sort of hidden code they had just displayed, understood only by them. He and Gabrielle walked into the hall as her serious expression conveyed to him that this would probably not be welcome news.

"My brother, I have come to tell you that you are in grave danger. Your aide Garnier was arrested for plotting against the King. He revealed that he reported your activities to Captain Petit, who was probably responsible for the attack against you in the field near Versailles. Petit was recalled to Versailles to be questioned about his involvement but he was shown to be innocent. When I heard about the attack against you and your friend, I came to Paris as quickly as I could."

"I'm a little confused, Gabrielle," interrupted Robert. "What do you mean when you say that you heard about the attack? How would someone inform you about what happens to me in Paris?"

"This is Paris, Mathurin. I don't know exactly who informed whom, only that while someone scrutinized your activities to bring you harm, you apparently have someone observing you for your protection as well."

"Petit still considers you to be his biggest source of embarrassment in his military career and won't stop until one of you is eliminated. He has convinced enough officers that you were responsible for the attack on our coach and deserve to be arrested. The King would stop him now if he could, but Petit will act first and worry about the consequences after. By the time the King hears of it, it will be too late to save you. Petit is on his way, my brother. You can't stay here any longer. I have managed to delay his departure from Versailles as long as possible, but he will soon return. It is time to protect yourself and those you love," as she nodded toward the door to Lisette's room. "Now, it's time for me to properly introduce myself to your friend."

She reentered the room and walked straight to Lisette's bed. "Hello Lisette, my name is Gabrielle."

Lisette was mildly astonished to have someone of the Duchess's station act so familiar with her.

"She's very beautiful, Mathurin," Gabrielle said smiling as she sat and held Lisette's hand. "Are you going to marry her?"

Robert looked sternly at the Duchess. "Gabrielle, this is a hospital and we need to be very quiet so the patients can get their proper rest. Where is your coach right now? We should leave immediately after what you just told me."

Lisette looked at them both with a questioning gaze and Robert knew that he needed to explain further to her.

Robert knelt next to her bed and looked her in the eye. "Lisette, Gabrielle has traveled from Versailles to supply me additional information about the people who attacked us. I am so sorry to have to tell you this, but we need to leave the Bastille, now so I can put us where we are both safe. There is a coach in the courtyard waiting for us"

Lisette struggled to sit forward to get out of her bed and looked up at Robert. "I will definitely require your assistance with this, Major," she said despondently.

Robert began to lift her, but she said no. Lisette moaned feebly but her back stiffened with inflexible will and he helped her to stand and she walked down the corridor while she leaned against him. Gabrielle instructed a servant to hold the door open as they left the room and began their walk toward the entrance. "Run to the coach and make it ready," Gabrielle told the servant.

Entering the courtyard, Robert noticed a guard of six cavalrymen surrounding the coach, all mounted on powerful looking horses. The sun shone brilliantly off the hilt of their swords and they looked so formidable that he was certain if Petit hadn't abandoned his post in the first place, these cavalrymen would have had little problem dispatching the outlaws on the bridge.

He helped Lisette into the coach where she sat with Gabrielle and the children. "I need to sit with the driver until we get to your shop. Then I'll put you into your own bed." Lisette smiled slightly and closed her eyes. Gabrielle sat next to her and placed Lisette's head on her shoulder, while Marie-Thérèse sat on her other side and held her hand and Louis-Charles sat quietly opposite the Duchess. Robert quickly climbed and sat next to the driver who looked briefly at the splattered blood on this major's uniform before raising the reins and commanding the team to move. Soon the royal coach, drawn by a team of six grey and black horses was moving toward the gate in the direction of Lisette's bakery.

The Royal coach certainly had some distinct advantages. It was large and built for comfort. It afforded the best possible ride for Lisette. Conversely, it was probably the most recognizable coach in all France and its cavalry escort didn't make it any less conspicuous. Pedestrians and anyone sitting on a horse or driving a cart or carriage, immediately gave way when they realized who might be traveling in it.

Robert instructed the driver to waste no time in reaching Lisette's shop as they exited through the west gate. Arriving at Lisette's shop, everyone disembarked from the coach and he instructed told the driver to keep circling the streets until he was told to stop. He wanted to draw as little attention to any connection between Lisette's shop and the royal coach.

The women in the shop had never witnessed anything like this before. The door opened briskly as two members of the armed escort entered the shop, followed by Gabrielle and the children. Robert and Lisette followed slowly with two more members of the escort behind them. Two guards stayed on the street, like sentinals guarding the door until Robert told them to move their horses into the stables and then remain inside the shop. Robert motioned to the driver, who began his task of riding around the neighborhood with the two remaining guards until he was needed.

The few women who were engaged in a discussion, stopped when they saw Robert enter, wearing his blood stained uniform, as he helped their friend walk across the bakery floor. He disappeared up the staircase and for a moment Gabrielle waited beside the counter with them. She looked at them all and politely and quietly said, "No one must know of this, do you understand? Your friend's safety depends upon it" They all understood, some nodded mutely while others murmured in agreement. "Good," said Gabrielle. "Now will someone please fetch Monique? Lisette needs her." And with that, she turned and crossed the bakery floor and continued up the stairs to Lisette's apartments.

She looked very relieved to be in her own bed, as Robert pulled the covers up to her chin. Lisette latched onto his hand and would not release it. He looked seriously at Marie-Thérèse and motioned for her to come to him. He whispered in her ear,"I need you to do a favor for me please," and she ran past Gabrielle and disappeared through the doorway. A quick series of the sounds of light footsteps descending to the shop below gave some indication of what Robert had asked her to do.

Marie-Thérèse confidently walked straight into the bakery while engaging everyone in the room with a broad smile. Those who realized that she was the daughter of Louis XVI politely curtseyed. Others, who didn't know or weren't sure what to do, simply looked at this young girl whose elegant dress in all probability, exceeded what most in that room would earn in a lifetime of toil in this section of Paris.

"Who are you?" timidly asked one of the women who seemed the least sure of herself.

In a clear and confident voice she answered, "I am Marie-Thérèse, the daughter of France." Those who hadn't curtseyed before did so now. "Please, I need your help. Major Dubé needs someone to saddle his horse. He desperately needs to leave here soon." When they had recovered from the shock of a polite request from a member of the royal family, one woman spoke to her child who ran through the back door and shortly returned with Henri, who still had some straw in his hair.

"Gerard is saddling the Major's horse now," he offered speaking apprehensively. "Sadeek will be ready to travel as soon as the Major is." Henri delivered the message and then rushed for the door leading to the courtyard and the safety of the stables.

Monique soon entered the shop, silent and resolved; with an intense look; she immediately proceeded past the servants and cavalrymen and went directly upstairs.

When he saw her enter the bedroom, Robert motioned her to his side. Lisette had fallen into a deep sleep and had relaxed the grip she had on his hand. "Monique, I need you to stay here until I return. Her dressing may need to be changed, you be the judge of that. I'll return as quickly as possible." Lisette's eyes opened for a moment as he slowly pulled his hand from hers, but she closed them as Monique took her hand.

The sentries standing guard at the shop entrance opened the door quickly when they saw Gabrielle and the children approaching. The women in the bakery stood and curtsied as Marie-Thérese and Louis-Charles walked past and were then surprised when they turned and said good-bye. Robert stood on the street until he saw the coach approaching and signaled to the driver to stop in front of the shop. A coachman placed steps in front of the coach door and held it open for the children and Gabrielle.

Gabrielle helped the children into the coach and turned to Robert and hugged him and kissed his cheeks. Before stepping into the coach, she paused and looked at him seriously. "You know what is going to happen, don't you?"

Robert felt a need to be evasive with his answer until he knew exactly what she was asking. "I'm not sure what you mean, Gabrielle."

"You know what the future will bring to us, don't you Mathurin?" she said softly as she looked him in the eye.

Robert considered the question before him very thoughtfully before answering and returned Gabrielle's question.

"I will be completely honest with you, Duchess. Your country is about to descend into total chaos, due largely to the actions of the family you serve. The way the people have been mistreated for generations will reach a point where nearly everything you are familiar with will fall apart. When the Revolution has run its course, Marie-Thérese will be the only member of the royal family to survive. It will become a game, where the King makes promises to the Assembly and then reverses himself after listening to the Queen. After they are removed from Versailles to Paris, their attempt to escape France will end at Varennes. The outcome will not be good. You will have moved to live in Switzerland while Françoise finds safety in the Netherlands. The two of you will never see each other again. That is really about all that I can tell you for now. Have a safe return to Versailles, Gabrielle. I have my own person to keep safe."

Gabrielle usually gave Robert a gentle hug and kiss. She had a sense that this could very well be their last meeting together and gave him an embrace and kiss that she wanted to last forever. He held her hand as she stepped into the coach, while the coachman waited obediently. The coachman closed the door and Gabrielle left bearing the look of one resigned to the fact that while she was totally committed to these children, she wouldn't be able to keep them safe from the events that lay before them. She looked one last time at Robert as the escort took up their positions, two in front of the coach and four guarding the rear; she leaned back into her seat; resembling his first glimpse of her when the coach neared the bridge at Versailles. Then the coach began to move slowly forward down the narrow street toward the Seine and home to Chateaux de Versailles.

He stood watching for a moment and noticed the women looking at him through the shop window. He stepped back into the shop and addressed them all. "I really need to stress the importance that none of you talk to anyone about Lisette returning home from the Bastille or who brought her. It's very important that you understand that."

All women present acknowledged their understanding either with a nod or a simple "yes". Josette, Claudette and Charice told Robert that they had already instructed everyone in Porte Saint-Antoine to watch for strangers and to be very guarded about their conversations regarding him or Lisette.

He felt reassured knowing that there was an active plan to protect her. "Good, I need you to be the eyes and ears of the neighborhood if we are to keep her safe." A knock at the door revealed Henri standing in the street holding Sadeek's reins.

Excusing himself from the women in the shop, he opened the door and took the reins from Henri. "Thank you, I'll return soon and we'll need to hide my horse again, Henri. Please be sure that you and Gerard are prepared."

Henri rubbed his hand on Sadeek's flank. "Don't worry, Major. We know exactly what to do."

Turning Sadeek around, Robert directed him toward the Seine as quickly as possible. His stallion sensed Robert's urgency as he had him at a gallop whenever the streets weren't congested. He was concentrating so much on reaching his quarters before Petit's return that he was barely aware how near he was to the Military School until he passed the Hotel des Invalides on his right, before startling the sergeant when he raced across the parade grounds, halting abruptly in front of the stables.

"Sergeant, I need your assistance in two matters", he shouted before his boots touched the ground.

The sergeant became immediately concerned as he had never seen Robert as rushed before and was shocked to see him standing before him in his blood stained uniform. He had seen such things when he was a younger man tending horses before men went into battle and when they returned, but this was different. "Yes sir," was all he could utter as he waited for what would follow.

"First, make the phaeton ready immediately. I will return from my quarters very soon and I will need to leave then. Are you clear with what I just said?"

"Yes sir," said the sergeant as he watched Robert, who barely waited for his reply before turning to ride Sadeek to the officer's quarters. He left Sadeek unhitched outside of the officer's quarters, confident that his horse was intelligent enough not to wander from the spot where he left him, ran up the staircase and saw a private who had the unfortunate circumstance to be found walking in the hall.

"Private," he shouted; loud enough to be heard by anyone on the floor.

"Yes, sir," he said as he saluted stiffly.

"Private," Robert began, "I will need a bath drawn for me and a dinner bought to my quarters now. I am to travel to Versailles on His Majesty's business, so be quick about it."

"Yes sir", replied the private as Robert walked away.

The door had barely closed before he removed his blood stained uniform, folded it and placed it on a chair in the center of the room. He changed into one of his clean uniforms and then carefully deposited the remainder of them on top of his ruined uniform. Quickly gathering his few belongings and placing them in his backpack, he walked down the hall, encountering the terrified private.

His cold stare stopped him in his tracks. "Private, I have looked everywhere for you. I told you that I want to have a bath and eat dinner before I leave for Versailles, not when I return. Can you tell me where my bath and my dinner are?"

The private looked shocked to the extreme. "Oh, yes sir; immediately sir," and he raced down the hall. As soon as the private disappeared, he exited the officer's quarters and rode to the stables, where his grey horse had been hitched to the phaeton.

"Sergeant, when we first met you said that you and your wife owned a farm outside of Paris. Is that right?"

Oh yes sir," the sergeant with an air of pride. "My wife and I own a small farm not far from Paris. We raise some crops and chickens and livestock…"

"Sergeant," Robert interrupted, "I need to know if you would have room for Sadeek. I must leave for my home and I would love to have someone like you, who appreciates him be the one to care for him. This second part is very important. If anyone asks you where I have gone, you will tell them that I left for Versailles riding Sadeek. And promise me that you will move him to your farm before some officer comes and claims him. I want him to be yours. Do you understand?"

The sergeant looked affectionately at Sadeek, already protective of both his stallion and Robert. "Who would come looking for you, Major?"

"You'll know when they arrive, sergeant. I need to leave now," as he leaned over and stroked Sadeek's muzzle one last time.

Robert climbed into his phaeton, glanced over his left shoulder at both the stables and the sergeant as he held Sadeek's reins while his head bobbed up and down. The sergeant saluted Robert for the last time as he headed for the gates of the Military School. Turning right in the direction of Versailles; he turned left toward Lisette's shop when he was confident that he couldn't be seen from the Military School.

As Robert was crossing Pont de Sully, Lieutenant Petit, accompanied by four cavalrymen, galloped onto the parade grounds of the Military School. The sergeant stood and watched closely as they dismounted outside the officer's quarters. All five men, with Petit in the lead; disappeared through the entryway.

Petit was the first to reach the top of the stairway and hurried down the hall to Robert's quarters as he withdrew his pistol. "Major Dubé, open this door. You are under arrest," he shouted, pounding on the door with his free hand. All had drawn their pistols and when there was no answer Petit struck the door with his shoulder, without any effect. After the second attempt, the trooper on his right reached forward, turned the handle and the door opened easily. Petit seemed unfazed and charged into the room brandishing his pistol. Seeing movement on his right, he quickly turned and took aim at the figure of a man who was partially obscured by steam rising from the tub.

"Dubé, stop right there. You are under arrest," he shouted again as he closed the distance to his prey, confident that the end was near.

A startled private turned and faced Petit, "The Major isn't here just now, sir. He ordered me to draw his bath and to get a meal for him; he is preparing for travel to Versailles." The only evidence that he had ever occupied the room now lay on a chair in the center of the room. Petit stared at uniforms stacked on the chair; hating them as thoroughly as the person who wore them; when sunlight broke through the windows and fell upon the chair and its contents, mocking him.

Visibly angry, Petit pushed past the other cavalrymen and stormed out of Robert's former quarters. There were the usual assortment of troops and carts on the parade grounds, but he noticed one person present who was in a perfect position to observe the activity of everything that entered or exited the Military School. He rode directly to the stables and found the sergeant working on a wagon which had been left in front of the doors to the stables.

"Sergeant!! "shouted Petit from his horse.

Looking up slowly as if he was uncertain where the voice was coming from, the sergeant stood at attention and slowly saluted.

"I am looking for Major Dubé. You would have seen him leave here wouldn't you?"

"Why yes sir, I definitely would have," said the sergeant as he wiped his brow with a towel in one hand and shielded his eyes from the sun with the other.

"Well?" said Petit, waiting impatiently for more details.

"Well what, sir?" the seemingly very confused sergeant replied.

"Where is he?" Petit demanded.

The sergeant scratched his head and looked blankly at Petit. "I don't know exactly, sir."

Petit's face was a brilliant shade of crimson. "You just told me that you knew where he was, idiot."

"No, sir," the sergeant calmly replied. "I said that I saw him leave. He ordered me to saddle his horse and left the grounds just before you entered. He exited through the gate and turned right. Now if I had to guess where he is, I would say that he is on the road to Versailles."

"Versailles," Petit shouted to himself. As he galloped toward the gate with his troopers close behind, the sergeant grinned, pulled some carrots from the pocket of his apron and walked around the wagon to give Sadeek a treat.

"It was a practical decision to leave Sadeek with the sergeant," thought Robert. He needed to be as inconspicuous as possible now and nothing drew more attention than his Arabian stallion. Not one person even glanced his way as he drove his plain phaeton, drawn by a plain, though sturdy grey horse to a simple bread shop in Porte Saint-Antoine. The stable behind Lisette's might be suitable for his small carriage, but it pained him to leave a horse like Sadeek there for the day or two when he lay in Lisette's apartment recovering from his injuries. Leaving him there permanently, when he could be living on the sergeant's farm would be almost criminal. His most difficult task now would be explaining to Henri and Gerard that Sadeek wouldn't be staying with them any longer.

He was able to slip into the courtyard unnoticed. The exterior was still as miserable looking as ever, but Henri and Gerard had been very busy transforming its interior. Its appearance was completely changed. They had swept the floors and placed hay and feed and water in separate areas. An unused ladder had been uncovered which led to a loft that they cleaned and supplied with two cots and a table with chairs. A skylight, hidden by years of neglect, had also been discovered and once opened, supplied their loft with sunlight. The two boys seemed shocked when they saw the carriage in the courtyard instead of the stallion they had expected.

Henri was the first to speak. "Where is Sadeek, Major? Gerard and I were waiting for him because we know that it is time for his carrots," as they looked curiously at the grey horse, still hitched to the phaeton.

This was the moment he was dreading, explaining the truth to these boys who had been so dedicated to Sadeek's welfare; he was convinced they would be devastated.

"Boy's things have changed. I had to leave Sadeek with a sergeant at the Military School. He owns a farm where Sadeek can happily live and run with other animals. But I still have the grey horse which desperately needs both a home and someone to give him a name." Robert stared at the expressions on the boy's faces and waited for the worst possible reaction to the horrible news.

Gerard paused for a moment before he walked to the entrance and took the reins from Robert. Henri stepped quickly and began rubbing the horse's muzzle and rubbed his neck.

"He needs water and carrots, Major. Leave him with us, we know just what to do," as they led him into the stables and began the process of unhitching him.

When he entered the shop through the rear entrance, he saw the usual gathering of local women; who were talking and helping Lisette by baking bread for her until she regained her health. They all smiled as he greeted them with a wave, speaking briefly each of them before carrying his belongings up the stairs to Lisette's apartments.

Monique was still sitting with her as she slept. She laid Lissette's hand softly on the blanket, rose from her chair and spoke to him quietly by the staircase.

"Major, she is resting now. I changed her dressing and she had a little tea. Her wound seems to be healing fine but she needs to sleep. How will we contact you when she makes more progress?"

Robert put his coat and hat on a chair near the doorway. "You can find me here now. I feel responsible for her injuries. I will remain here until she's recovered. Oh, and you can stop referring to me as Major. It's a complicated story, but please call me Mathurin from now on."

Monique had appeared confused earlier. Now she understood why he had departed earlier and returned with his belongings. "I think that you may be a bigger part of her recovery than you realize."

Monique turned to descend the stairs but before she left Robert had one question for her. "Monique, may I ask you something?"

"Of course, Mathurin," she said with a smile.

"Whenever I come here there is always a room full of women who don't seem as if they are here to buy or bake, but simply to talk. What is it about the bakery that I don't understand?"

Monique continued to smile. "This more than just a simple bread shop, Mathurin. What you have discovered is the real center of power in Porte Saint-Antoine. Actions may be carried out by the men of our neighborhood; but decisions are made and secrets kept by the women who meet here." She took his hand and held his arm with the other. "You can feel safe here, Mathurin. Your secrets are ours now," and she turned to walk down the stairs to the bakery.

He took his clothes to the wardrobe and hung his uniform for what he hoped would be the last time. He dressed in the simple brown shirt and grey pants that he hadn't wore since the King gave him his commission in the cavalry. The only item of clothing he intended to keep was his riding boots. Tall, black and rugged; they really didn't match any clothes he had; he just liked the way they felt. The rest of the uniform already seemed like a part of his life which he had long since abandoned. Now he was dressed as a simple working class laborer, caring for a woman who had been struck by a knife which had been intended for him.

Within the next several days, Lisette was able to rise from bed and walk gingerly around her bedroom. Robert spent evenings asleep in the chair next to her bed, while during the day he would get tea and meals and change her dressing when Monique wasn't present. When she had someone who would sit with her, he would spend time in the bakery, where he discovered a hidden talent he had for baking breads; especially Tuscan Garlic bread. Thinking it probable that Petit was attempting to discover his location, he made certain to limit his movements outside of the shop. He would take Henri and Gerard on occasional carriage rides through Porte Saint-Antione and sometimes they would help him deliver fresh bread to the poor children in the neighborhood.

He knew that the two boys who had become such an integral part of caring for Sadeek amongst other things, lived somewhere in the vicinity, but they never appeared willing to volunteer any information about their homes and because one of them was always in the stable he never felt the need to know. He always rode through the streets of Paris in his phaeton with his wide brimmed hat on and the carriage top always drawn forward; even though it could be folded back on sunny days. He felt that the need to resemble one of the ubiquitous carriages traveling the thoroughfares of Paris was achieved in this way.

He also had developed a habit of practicing his katas outdoors where he could to enjoy some sunshine and fresh air. He found that some of the children wanted to emulate him and before long, he was conducting impromptu karate classes. He began teaching in the courtyard outside the stables, but as the number of children increased, he moved his instruction to the playground. There he would teach the fundamentals of martial arts to these students of his, until a crowd began to form and then he would put his hat on and melt into the crowd.

After Lisette felt well enough to leave the shop, she and Robert would ride in the phaeton to Pont Neuf and stop where the statue of King Henri IV overlooked the Seine, watching the boats travel past the tree lined embankment. In a short time, Lisette felt well enough to walk in Jardin des Plantes with Robert, while he continued to maintain a low profile.

One day, as they were returning from a ride to Jardin de Luxembourg they both noticed a great sense of agitation from the people in the streets. Pedestrians were talking with a very animated manner and when they entered her shop the women looked at them in a grim silence. This was the first time he could recall complete quiet in the bakery.

"What is it?" asked Lisette apprehensively to a room full of silent women.

"Necker has been sacked," said Josette in despair. Lisette gasped as she and the women realized what the implications of this meant.

Jacques Necker was the Minister of Finance and considered by the common people to be sympathetic to their condition. For him to be fired by the monarchy was clearly the limit for some as it meant that now everyone in a position of power favored the nobility. There had been a longstanding hostility toward the nobility, holding them responsible for the woes of Parisians, providing a base for revolutionary antipathy toward all nobles. Suddenly, their precarious position was about to become unbearable. Some in the room looked as if they would soon be deciding on what action to take in the wake of this terrible news.

From Robert's perspective, this was infinitely more serious than anything these people realized. This was July 12th and in just two days the Bastille would fall, plunging France into complete chaos, eventually involving all of Europe.

Lisette's wound was healing rapidly and he could choose now to return to Syracuse and his position at the University, but being a witness to one of the most important events in world history was an opportunity that could not be ignored.

REVOLUTION

On the 13th of July an angry mob broke into the Monastere Saint-Lazare, a property owned by the clergy, where it was rumored that food and guns were being hoarded.

The morning of the 14th of July began like any other. It was sunny and warm, there were a few clouds drifting over Paris' neighborhoods. While the sky's appearance was pleasant to some people looking up from the Parisian streets, the disposition in certain neighborhoods below had grown radically different. The residents of the area surrounding the Bastille had complained to the Assembly of Electors about the warlike preparations targeting their neighborhood being readied by de Launey, Governor of the Bastille

Robert hadn't slept well in his chair and had risen early to make breakfast. Lisette's wound was healing rapidly and Monique had removed her sutures, but the soreness in her shoulder couldn't be disregarded. She still required assistance rising from her bed, but was now able to negotiate the stairs alone and was welcomed this morning by a breakfast waiting for her when she descended to her dining room. He had cooked an omelet with vegetables, rolls and fruit and poured tea for her. They talked briefly over their first meal of the day before he announced that he had to drive his carriage to the Hotel des Invalides.

Riding in his phaeton, he crossed Pont Neuf, knowing that he was traveling to witness an event in which most who gathered near the École Militaire, weren't even slightly aware that they were about to be participants. He stopped his grey horse on Avenue des Tourville, surprised by the number of people who stood in the street as if waiting for direction. That direction came from the newly formed militia and as he sat in his carriage, hoping that someone from the nearby Military School wouldn't recognize him. Suddenly the mob surged forward and stormed the Hotel des

Invalides, where they seized about thirty thousand muskets, but found no gunpowder or musket shot.

Robert returned to Lisette's, as the mob now numbering 6,000-7,000 subjects, made their way through the streets, armed with muskets, sabers, pikes and pitchforks and marched to the Bastille. He spent some time talking with Henri and Gerard while they unhitched the horse, placed the phaeton in the stable and brushed the ground to remove traces of hoof marks.

Within the walls of the Bastille, there were only seven prisoners, but nearly thirty thousand pounds of gunpowder, which the mob wanted badly. The governor of the Bastille refused to surrender either the gunpowder or prisoners to the mob and then ordered his men to fire on the crowd, killing several of them.

By now, the officers which Captain De Launay, the Governor of the Bastille had hoped would arrive to support him, switched sides and brought with them more troops and supplies to aid the revolutionary cause. As the initial salvos began to fall on the walls of the Bastille, they soon realized that their cannons were better suited for use on the wooden gates and began to target them.

Robert had decided to walk to the Bastille and watched, standing upon a low stone wall near Rue de Charenton which offered him a clear view of the ancient prison, as the revolutionaries began to focus their cannons on the Bastille's gates. The battle between the crowds surrounding the Bastille and the troops inside its walls had reached a stalemate when suddenly, the south gate inexplicably opened and the crowd flowed from all sides, like the sea into the fortress. Captain de Launay, the governor was seized by the mob, dragged out into the street and beheaded.

Robert smelled the gunpowder from the constant musket fire and cannon which hung in the air. The security of the gates should have been Petit's responsibility Robert thought. Had he been ordered by de Launay to open the gates, or was he solely responsible for opening them? He thought it must be the latter. Any decision to open the gates by de Launay would have been the result of negotiations with the revolutionary forces. For them to open unexpectedly could only mean that Petit was somehow involved.

Following the surge of the revolutionaries into the Bastille, they began removing the officers and troops to be held somewhere in Paris. He walked through what was quickly becoming a war zone and saw three men holding and abusing an officer. The only reason he gave this any attention was to be certain that the officer they were restraining wasn't François. He saw now as the smoke cleared that the center of their attention was Captain Petit. These men were obviously drunk and had no real idea of what to do with him, but may have been inclined to subject him to the same fate as de Launay. Pulling his pistol from beneath his shirt and stepping over the rubble, he advanced between the three men and shoved them away with his left hand as he aimed his pistol at Petit's head. The three men protested for a moment, but didn't wish to be a party to this obvious personal vendetta and watched as Robert pulled Petit into the building through an entrance whose door had been shattered by cannon fire. He shoved him into a room that had been raked by guns firing from the Bastille. Near the corner of the room lay a civilian, dead from his wound, a sword lying at his side.

"Now Petit," Robert said as he pressed his pistol against Petit's heart, "you are going to tell me why you have been pursuing me since the attack on the bridge near Versailles."

"You have no idea what you have done," Petit sneered through his narrow lips. "Single handedly, you have undone months of planning intended to save our nation. All of your adventures and intrusions have caused what you witnessed in the streets today. This country is now headed in the wrong direction. You aided those meddling priests and stopped the men from performing their duties on the bridge near Versailles. You thought you so clever, didn't you? Traveling the countryside with your guide and acting like you were nobility, while you carried those filthy letters of yours. We had you followed since you left Cholet but missed our opportunity to strike at Le Mans."

"Are you insane?" shouted Robert. "I delivered letters to a few priests as a favor to a friend and saved a little girl from a man with a knife at her throat. I had no idea who the girl was until after I rescued her."

Petit's face was cold and austere. "Those priests are traitors," he spat out as he whirled his head from left to right. "They serve the church and looked forward to the chaos so they can control all France!" he ranted. "Those men on the bridge were patriots who wanted to create a dramatic change in the manner in which the majority are governed and turn control of our country to the people. We would have succeeded if I had intercepted you after you departed from Le Mans," as he began to shout. "But you sent us in the wrong direction as we searched for you on the road to Brest and then I missed you with my shot as you stood next to the royal coach."

"You're wrong Petit. Those letters were written for priests who desired to quit France if conditions deteriorated. They never wanted any sort of power. Those men of yours at the bridge were some sort of military, weren't they?"

Petit seemed startled at Robert's accusation. "I saw the daggers, Captain," said Robert. "The men on the bridge, those men I encountered on the field near Versailles, all carried the same dagger as the one I was issued from the military compound near Versailles."

"They were," yelled Petit scornfully. "Our mission was to abduct the King's daughter and hold her until he agreed to abdicate in favor of a republican government. We knew that having lost his son recently, he would choose to relinquish his power than risk losing Marie-Thérèse and then the people could decide upon their own government. Now you have simply perpetuated what the majority of France's people have endured for generations to continue."

"You're delusional if you think that anything you and your little group, or I would have any effect on the condition of France. Tell me captain, when the mob had the Bastille surrounded, how did it happen that the gate suddenly open?"

Petit smiled for the first time and looked very satisfied with what he was about to say as he focused on Robert with his venomous little eyes. "Your friend, Major Rigaud was commanding an artillery crew defending that gate. Governor de Launay ordered one of the gates opened, so I ordered the one closest to him be opened so his battery would take the brunt of the assault on the fortress. But at the last moment the governor relieved Rigaud of his assignment, and guarded that entrance himself. The governor was seized by the mob, who beheaded him instead of Rigaud, who I understand managed to escape. So what is your plan now, Major? You may think that you are in a position to dominate me, but let me tell you that are not the one who is in control here. Who are you to decide my fate?"

Petit's statement reminded Robert of the debate he once had with Ron about getting involved in the treatment of his father's disease. He paused for a moment to reflect how similar the debate with Ron concerning the ethics of intervening in his father's condition, reminded him of the current situation with Petit, allowing his concentration to be broken. Petit exhibited his complete arrogance and distain for Robert by mistaking his distraction for a lack of commitment on his part. He cast a defiant glance as he walked toward the doorway and smirked, "I knew you weren't capable of harming me."

This episode however, was going to end on Robert's terms, not Petit's. He violently grabbed Petit by his collar and slammed him against the stone wall. Judging by the expression of Petit's face, he grasped that the situation had not been altered in the slightest.

"Change coats with him," demanded Robert pointing to the motionless man lying on the stone floor.

Robert kept his pistol aimed at Petit while he rubbed where his head hit the wall and defiantly stripped the coat from the dead man before removing his own. He draped his coat over the dead man and stood holding the man's coat, facing Robert and expecting the worst. Petit glanced at his coat when Robert's fist landed squarely on his jaw; followed quickly by the barrel of the pistol slamming upon his head. As Petit slumped to the floor, Robert raised his pistol and fired a shot into the ceiling. Pieces of wood and plaster showered them both, as he dragged Petit into a corner and put the unknown man where Petit had fallen. He picked up the blood soaked sword, tossed the dead man's coat on Petit and carried the sword with him. The three men were still standing where he left them, now curious about what had occurred inside the building.

"It's over with that one," he said as he returned his pistol to his pocket. He threw the sword into the street. "There's nothing to see in there except a dead man. He left you his sword. You'll be better off looting the Bastille." They understood from his tone and serious look, that this was not really a suggestion and ran off to join the melee as one of them paused to retrieve the sword.

Smoke from musket and cannon fire now mixed with the flames from some structures burning inside the Bastille, although now that the hated symbol of the Monarchy had fallen, the air was filled with cheers from the victors and pleas of those who were taken prisoner. Robert made his way around the troops and civilians all occupied with the elation that comes from a sense of great accomplishment. Now they were all related in this latest circumstance and willingly or unwillingly they would be integral pieces involved in what direction it would take.

When he finally reached Lisette's, the mood of those in the shop was one of great excitement. Lisette stood on a chair in the bakery, stepped to the floor, ran across the room and threw her arms around him when she saw him.

At the Palace of Versailles, King Louis XVI was returning from hunting and was met by a Duke who carried the news from Paris. The King asked, "Then it's a revolt?"

"No sire," replied the Duke, "it's a revolution."

JUDGEMENT

While the lives of everyone in France, whether in Paris or the countryside, were heavily invested in the recent events that some had expected, no one had any premonition of the effect it would have on their country or Europe. Most were however, surprisingly accurately informed about the current circumstances in distant parts of France. Monique informed him that many chateaus had been set ablaze and others had been plundered. The seigneurs were being hunted down like wild beasts. Peasants were breaking into their homes and taking all of the records of titles held and taxes owed and were burning them. All of this was being added to the funeral pyre of the nobilities' entitlements.

On the morning of July 15th, Robert woke from an evening's sleep in the chair next to Lisette's bed. As she slept soundly, he made his way to the kitchen to make breakfast for her. He was concerned about the riots which were spreading into their neighborhood and the possibility of her shop becoming a target for looting as food became scarcer.

Claudette and Charice, thought it best to avoid the area nearest the Bastille, but were curious nevertheless and convinced Robert that he should escort them to the sight symbolizing the establishment of the French Republic. As they neared the Bastille, they could only sense the smells of yesterday's action. The rain was heavy that day and while it washed some of the remnants of the struggle that had settled on the streets, the smell of powder from cannon fire and musket fire still hung heavily in the air. When they continued down Rue de Fauborg Saint-Antoine, crowded with people, they could see some of the results of the storming of the Bastille. The day following the fall of the Bastille, began with its spontaneous demolition. Claudette, Charice and Robert stood on the periphery as massive stones tumbled into muddy ditches while citizens of their new republic flooded into the Bastille to participate in razing it, in one of their first signs of freedom and to visit the dungeons and loot it for its books and archives.

Robert enjoyed the sensation that he felt there was no need to conceal his identity any longer. The Revolution had begun and his need to be cautious about being recognized outside Lisette's shop was over. After serving breakfast to Lisette, they talked in her kitchen before the familiar group of women assembled upstairs, presumably to discuss plans for their neighborhood's future. He had the impression that these were topics which had been waiting for Revolution to start and he seized upon this as an opportunity to leave.

Henri and Gerard were busy sweeping the stables when they saw Robert exit through the rear door and head straight in their direction. He was walking quicker than he had recently and he was without one distinguishing feature whose absence excited the boys very much. Robert was beaming and wearing no hat.

"Get the horse ready and hitch him to the carriage boys," he said loudly. "And we won't require this either," as he cheerfully lowered the top of the phaeton.

They quickly harnessed the grey horse to the phaeton and presented themselves to Robert. "Quickly, Major. Gaston is in a hurry to see the city."

This was the part the boys loved best because they never tired of waving to people they knew as it made them feel important to be seen riding in a carriage with the top down on a sunny day. They repeated this during the next two days as Robert wanted to explore parts of Paris that he hadn't seen before. The boys were curious about the Bastille, but he was adamant that he wouldn't go in that direction. Although he felt certain that they did visit what remained of the Bastille when they sprang from the carriage with the excuse that they were going home; thinking that he wouldn't realize it was a ruse.

On what he thought was perhaps his last day in Paris, he made breakfast for Lisette. His goal now was to serve a morning meal to Lisette and pack all of his belongings into in his backpack. He was going to leave his uniform behind except for his prized riding boots. He placed his key fob in an easily accessible pocket before he walked into the stable with Lisette to say goodbye to Henri and Gerard.

Preparing to leave Paris was becoming more difficult than he had anticipated, but there was really no reason for him to remain any longer. He determined that leaving the key fob in the front pocket of his backpack, would be the most convenient place for it. He held her hand as they walked into the kitchen from the stables to say goodbye to the women who had labored baking bread while Lissette recuperated from her wound.

From their view of the street, some of the women closest to the window became aware of increased activity outside. His curiosity about what they saw and apprehension about circumstances outside of the bakery that might affect the boulangerie brought him to the window also. Overall, he wasn't excessively concerned as the women had guaranteed the safety of the shop and everyone in it.

But something was definitely unusual as people in the streets stood like trees and stared in the same direction down La Passage de Bonne Graine as if they were watching the same approaching storm. Pedestrians then began to step aside only wide enough to allow this unseen maelstrom to pass, as a group of men emerged from the crowd.

This group approaching the shop bore a different appearance than the general population however. They weren't roving looters or uniformed soldiers. These men were focused, heading directly toward the shop's entrance, as if none of the other buildings even existed. One man led the group and as he entered Lisette's shop the other men spread out behind him. Their leader stared only at Robert without saying a word. As he waited to declare his intent, more commotion came from the rear of the bakery as additional men rushed in and stood behind Robert, waiting for orders.

"Mathurin Dubé, you have been denounced as a British spy and an enemy of the Republic," he announced. "You are to be taken immediately from this place for trial and punishment."

The women were confused and incensed. While this was no group of rioters, they weren't regular army personal either. As the chaos in the streets spread, there was no real way to tell who was in charge or where their allegiance lay. The security that they seemed to have controlled in their neighborhood until now had entirely evaporated. There was nothing in appearance to separate these men from the mob on the street, except these men were armed. The women protested, but the militia simply said they were following orders from the local magistrate. No amount of pleading or insults would deter these men from seizing Robert.

Before they could complete their objective, Robert considered taking the fight to them and possibly making his way upstairs to his backpack and his key fob. But he decided that the chances of injury to the women from these armed men, was not worth the risk. He put his arm around Lisette's waist and drew her close to him. "Look in the front pocket of my backpack," he whispered. "In it you will find a small, smooth, black object with buttons on it. Find out where they are taking me and bring it to me."

Just as he finished giving her the message, his arms were pulled from her waist and his hands were bound tightly behind his back.

Lisette placed herself defiantly in the doorway. "Where do you think you are taking him?" she demanded. The other women all moved and stood with her boldly glaring at the militia, something that these men had clearly not been prepared for.

The man in charge seemed to have a grasp of what was at stake here. "This man has been denounced as an enemy of the people and will to be taken to trial," he chuckled. "The sentencing will take place at the people's courthouse on Rue de Faubourg. You can watch with the rest if you like. It will go better for him if I don't have to report to the magistrate that force was required."

Lisette looked at Robert who motioned with a shake of his head to move to aside. The man shoved Robert through door and paused in the entryway before Lisette. "I hope he just said goodbye to you," he said with a sneer. "You won't be seeing him again."

Robert was rudely pushed into the street toward a waiting cart, already occupied with others who were bound like him. Roughly thrown into the back of the cart, he struggled to stand without the use of his hands as the cart moved from side to side over the streets uneven surface. No one in the cart spoke as it moved slowly down the narrow pathway. People stopped and stared and the cart's unfortunate cargo, while some shouted insults and others took an opportunity to throw whatever was available at Robert and his companions. The people, who recognized him, looked on with similar helpless expressions and then turned away.

They traveled a short distance when the cart suddenly stopped before a building and people surrounded it, forming a gauntlet to its entrance. The building stood four stories tall with nine grey dormers across its roof. Buildings on either side were a few floors taller, blocking his view of the partly cloudy sky. This was the only building on the street which had a roof over the entrance, suggesting it once was a theatre before being converted into a supposed hall of justice. It lacked the importance of a municipal justice building as the remainder of a faded sign above its roof was all that lingered of what had at one time identified it. The occupants of the cart were emptied hurriedly onto the street and pushed through the gauntlet like cattle, from side to side past a large entrance with two doors; where a pair of somber looking armed sentries stood guard.

As they flowed into the building, Robert was quickly separated from the rest of the captives and nearly dragged into the only open space on the building's expansive floor. There were only two parts of this so-called court that seemed as though any amount of planning had been spent in its arrangement. One was an elevated gallery where a solitary man sat behind a large desk in a partially shaded portion of the room. On the floor about thirty feet from where Robert stood alone, sat ten men behind a long wooden table. He was unable to tell whether they were merely disinterested or simply drunk, but the mood of the crowd seemed bent on exacting some sort of revenge and judging from the disposition of the militia leader; it really didn't matter who was sacrificed in order to satisfy their hunger.

The remainder of the building made no sense at all. The floor and the balcony were filled with people who were squabbling and shouting at one another in the fiercest sort of contest to see who could be the rowdiest. There wasn't a single person who wasn't engaged in some verbal battle and the shouts from the crowd were deafening.

The man who had dragged him into the room released his grip on his arm, leaving Robert to stand alone as the man behind the desk slammed a gavel and order was restored in the massive room.

When the roar in the room been reduced to a murmur, the man in the shadow spoke.

"Mathurin Dubé, you have been denounced as a British spy and an enemy of the Republic. How do you respond to these charges?"

He opened his mouth to speak but before he could respond to the charges, an old woman whose face was covered with her matted grey hair screamed, "Kill him," as the rest of the crowd yelled in agreement.

"Silence," demanded the magistrate; as he continued to bring his gavel down upon the desk. "The accused will answer the question."

"It is completely false, sir," as he shouted to be heard above the rants of the mob. "I relinquished my British citizenship to become a citizen of France and served my country as a major in the cavalry. Show me my accuser, so that I may defend myself. I will show you who is telling the truth and who is bearing false witness. I demand to face my accuser."

"The accused does not have the right to ask questions or to make any demands of the court," responded the magistrate. "Isn't it true that you deserted your post at École Militaire?" Screams of guilty and demands of several methods of punishment poured down from the gallery.

"No, no your honor; that statement is absolutely untrue. I left the Military School to continue searching Paris for the man who is responsible for the attack on Marie-Thérèse; the daughter of France." This statement seemed to placate the crowd until the grey haired woman managed to push her tangled hair to one side long enough to shriek, "He is a servant of the Queen. Kill him," spawning a renewed round of chaos from the mob.

From the edge of this insanity he saw Lisette maneuvering herself closer to him, providing him with a sliver of hope. "Enough," yelled the judge. "We will now vote on the accused's guilt," as he looked at the table, where the row of disinterested looking men sat.

The man at the extreme right looked at the ceiling and yelled "Death," which was followed in unison by all at the table. In less than one minute, his fate had been sealed.

The magistrate now spoke amid cheers from the crowd. "The accused has been found guilty and will be removed to the

Conciergerie where he will face execution tomorrow. Now take him away."

The impassive tone of his voice shocked Robert. "How is this possible?" he thought, as Lisette began yelling at the crowd and the judge before she suddenly rushed toward Robert. Sentries attempted to restrain her, but the judge waved his hand to indicate that she be allowed to visit him one last time. She threw her arms around him, abandoned to her grief and dissolved into tears. "I'm so sorry. They wouldn't let us leave the bakery before they made us come here. I never had a chance to get the black item from your pack. Oh my God, Mathurin; what have I done?"

Robert was trying to think of something comforting to say to her and still formulate an escape plan of some sort, as he expected at any moment he would feel someone coming to drag him off to another cart full of miserable offenders. He was distracted by the sounds of people who were yelling and fighting in the crowd as five bound and struggling men were being pulled and pummeled by a group of the meanest looking guards he could have imagined. As they reached the center of the floor they were made to stand and face the magistrate with their backs to Robert.

Despite the immediate problems facing him, he couldn't help but be curious about this group of unknowns who were undoubtedly about to share his doom. As he studied the profiles of the five men, he recognized some them as those who had attacked the royal coach on the bridge near Versailles. All of his fortunes and misfortunes seemed to have hatched from that occurrence, all the result of chance; and now the irony of ironies would join them to perish together.

He recognized first the man with the scarred face as the one who attempted to assassinate Lisette and had held a blade against the neck of Marie-Thérèse. Two others had been launched into the lake when he had struck them with his staff, and the man who painfully limped into his position was having difficulty standing, as the sole survivor from the attack in the field near Versailles. The final man was not as much of a surprise, now that the identities of his comrades were known to Robert. The last prisoner was Captain Petit!

The attention of everyone was focused on the magistrate as he spoke from the shadows. "You men are here to answer for crimes committed against the Republic and its citizens. You are accused of murder, thievery, and assault for your own gains." He immediately turned to the ten members of the jury for their turn to pass judgment on the prisoners as they were expected to stand at attention. Petit stood stiffly, while the man, whose leg had been struck by Robert's cutlass, knelt on the floor. The other three feigned any sort of respect for the court and seemed unperturbed with the impending decision, which was issued no slower than Robert's had been. "Death, death, death," and so on; as if it's meaning in some way was diminished with repetition.

"The decision has been reached," the magistrate announced. "Your crimes have been considered and now you must be held accountable for them. Your sentence will be carried out immediately. Escort the prisoners to the courtyard," commanded the judge. "In addition, new information has been provided to this court regarding the charges against Mathurin Dubé. As a result, he is exonerated and is free to leave without delay," as his gavel struck again.

Petit looked like he had been struck by lightning. As one of the guards reached for him, he spun around and fell at Robert's feet. "Major, please tell them to release me. They've acted on your behalf, you can save me. Please, help me; I beg you"

Robert contemplated that all of these men had been given a second chance to leave him alone and yet they were relentless in their goal to eliminate him. Robert looked at the pleading officer who had shot at him on the bridge and attempted to shoot him in the Bastille. He was responsible for the attack in field near Versailles and the attempt on Lisette's life.

"You said it yourself, Captain," he replied with a gloomy prophesy. "Who am I to decide your fate?"

The anguish on Petit's face was absolute as he realized that he had completely lost the game. The guard pulled him to his feet and he was made to follow his unfortunate fellow prisoners.

Feeling puzzled, Robert looked at Lisette who was absolutely beaming. "Lisette, can you tell me what just happened? One second, I'm about to be taken away to be hung and people are screaming to kill me; especially that grey haired witch over there. Now she's smiling at me and it seems like they've forgotten I'm even here. Hurry, untie my ropes so we can leave here before they change their minds."

He stopped talking as he heard the sound of someone approaching from behind and was convinced that his nightmare was about to resume.

The footsteps approached directly behind him and stopped as a loud familiar voice spoke out, "Holy cow. Well, sucks to be them, eh my friend?" said a familiar voice. "Etienne, cut Mathurin's bonds please."

Robert's breathing stopped for a second as he felt a tug on his bonds, followed by the release of tension and the sound of rope falling to the floor. He cocked his head and looked at Lisette in disbelief and smiled. Turning slowly with both arms around Lisette, he faced a large grinning man he was well acquainted with.

He inhaled and smiled broadly, "Lisette, I want you to meet my friend Bernard Badeau. He rescued me when I was lost in La Rochelle, saved me from a knife in the back in Versailles and guided me all the way to Paris. We have also shared some of the worst meals ever cooked. And the man who just cut the ropes from my wrists is his cousin, Etienne."

Etienne, even larger than Bernard, simply smiled and bowed to Lisette. "Bernard, this is Lisette Rousseau. "

"Yes, the Bread Lady," interrupted Bernard as he stepped forward and gently kissed Lisette's hand. "We've never met, but I am well aware of her reputation for all the good she does for the poor in Paris."

"Bernard," Robert said as he paused and inhaled deeply. "I never expected to see you again. What happened since we last saw each other? I thought you had returned to La Rochelle long ago. How did you manage to become my guide who once again saves my life from someone who wanted to stab me in the back?"

"My friend, that really involves two questions," said Bernard thoughtfully. "Let's begin with our friend, Petit. His behavior didn't improve after the incident in the Hercules Salon and again when we were with François in the officer's mess at the Bastille. Apparently you met him again at the Bastille, when it fell?

"You're correct about my encountering him again," Robert confirmed. "After the gates to the Bastille had been breached, some of the officers were taken captive by citizens. I found Petit who had been taken by three men who were about to do away with him. My intent was to eliminate him myself, but something caused me to change my mind at the last moment and I knocked him unconscious and left him lying on a building floor."

"Well, you should have finished him when you had the opportunity," said Bernard bluntly. "If you had, we wouldn't be having this conversation. If a different magistrate had spoken to his accomplice, you could be in a cart bound for prison. Petit regained consciousness and followed you to Lisette's and then sent the man who had held the knife to Marie-Thérese's neck to visit me with instructions to denounce you. I recognized him immediately and was concerned that he might have identified me as your guide, but that day on the bridge his eyes were focused only on you and I don't believe that he ever looked in my direction."

"My friend, these men who worked with Petit were the worst sort of scoundrels. Petit was an idealist. His goal was to replace the Monarchy with a Republic by forcing the King to abdicate. His scheme was to kidnap Marie-Thérese and hold her hostage until the King agreed to abdicate. He reasoned that because his son had died recently, he would abdicate before he would risk losing another child. He sincerely believed that his scheme would work and that these men wanted the same result as he did. Had fate not placed us at the bridge, the outcome would have been completely different"

"His accomplices were actually working with Petit in the hopes that they could convince the King to pay a huge ransom for his daughter and then decide whether to return her safely or not. My guess is that they would have simply discarded her once the ransom had been paid and possibly done away with Petit and his idealism as well. While they pretended to support Petit, they preyed on their fellow countrymen, committing murder and robbery on countless innocent people."

"I told the man whose face was scarred from your shuriken that I would see to your prosecution; but I would need them to attend the trial so they could testify against you. It was really the only way I could be sure to capture them all at once. We used you as bait, my friend and I apologize, but I felt it was the only way to succeed."

Robert crossed his arms and tipped his head as he looked closely at Bernard. "Are you saying that this is all simply of a play of some sort?"

Before Bernard could provide an answer, the sound of a loud drum roll emanated from the courtyard where Petit and his accomplices had been taken earlier. The drum stopped abruptly, followed a moment later by a command and the roar from the volley of a dozen muskets. Bernard looked in the direction of the courtyard door and said nonchalantly, "No not really. Our friend Petit and his group won't be bothering you two or anyone again."

Robert and Lisette looked confused at Bernard's last statement. "Your name was on their list also, Lisette. The attack in the alley was never about you, Mathurin. Lisette vaguely knew the man with the scar and then you two met and their fear was that she could identify him; hence the need to eliminate her. When I heard what had happened, I sent word to the Duchess through someone I know at the Palace."

Bernard felt that they needed a change from standing in the middle of the floor and the eyes of the inquisitive. "Come, my friends, let's have a seat at my desk where we can be away from all these people who would be better served by finding a wiser way to spend their time. However, compared to what most of these people have endured for so long, a bit of theatre, no matter how macabre, is a respite from their daily lives and provides them with a diversion from all the uncertainty that this Revolution will bring."

As they crossed the floor to a staircase, the haggard, grey haired woman held her limp hair aside with one hand and waved with the other, offering an expansive smile while exposing her few remaining teeth. They climbed the staircase to Bernard's desk and he began to explain his new position to Robert and Lisette.

"My rise to becoming a magistrate in the new Republic began when we parted company at the Military School. I immediately became suspicious of that weasel Lieutenant Garnier the moment we rode away in your carriage. I was still reflecting how quickly we had progressed from two travelers who had experienced so much, to being paid for my services and now being escorted by your aide, that I hadn't really given much thought to my immediate plans or destination. Should I return immediately to La Rochelle or should I remain as a tourist in the City of Lights?"

"I found it very unsettling that his first suggestion was for me to see the Bastille. He seemed determined that I should accompany him to a prison. I'm in Paris; why on earth would I wish to be inside that place again? The more he insisted that he should take me there, the more I resolved to part company with him. Before we left the parade ground, he had repeated his suggestion that I make the Bastille my destination four times."

"As we turned onto the street, I noticed a huge gathering on the Champ des Mars. The cart was moving slowly enough that I was able to grasp my belongings and run across the street in the direction of the crowd. Garnier yelled at me to stop like I was a criminal, but I continued to run through the trees and was able to lose myself in the crowd. I never saw him again."

Robert sat back in his chair as he accepted a glass of wine from Étienne. "You were very perceptive, Bernard. Garnier was supplying Petit with information about my movements. I knew that someone was betraying me. When I discovered it was my aide, I concocted a scheme to have him arrested for plotting against the King."

Bernard sipped his wine and looked inquisitively at Robert. "I heard the rumors about his arrest. That was your idea? Very clever. Do you think that Colonel DuPont was involved with Petit also?"

Robert had raised his glass to his lips, but placed the glass back on the table and considered Bernard's question. "You know, I think that DuPont is simply someone who hates being assigned to the Military School. I'd be surprised if he was even aware of any of this."

"Small matter, actually," said Bernard indifferently. "His name is on another list."

"What happened next, Bernard?" asked an impatient Lisette.

He looked at her as she relaxed in the chaise lounge next to his desk, a glass of wine in her hand and smiled at them both. "Well my friends let me continue."

"I made my way through the crowd to listen to the speakers. They were complaining about the conditions of the common people in the cities and in the countryside. The speakers discussed poverty and starvation in Paris and amongst the farmers. When the speaker asked if anyone had witnessed examples of this, I nodded and raised my hand. He asked if I would be willing to share any of our experiences about the people we met on our travels to Paris and a moment later I found myself on a stage sharing what we had experienced with these people whom I had just met. The crowd encouraged me to address them further and it was then I realized that I truly like to speak."

"Really, now who would have guessed that?" Robert said sarcastically.

"Go on," Lisette said as she smiled at her new friend.

"When the speeches concluded, I began conversing with some of the people who were sitting on the stage. One of them was Jean Romilly, co- owner of the newspaper; Journal de Paris; who was very interested in what I had to say. He invited me to dinner with his party and we discussed my reasons for being in Paris. I told him that my arrangement with you had just concluded and I had neither plans nor accommodations. He was kind enough to offer me both a place to stay in his home and a position at his newspaper."

"I began working with Jean, helping to gather news and speaking in public about the pitiful conditions of the common people and helping to promote the Journal de Paris." Bernard paused and placed his large hands on Robert's shoulders. "My friend, are you aware just how much money you gave me the day we parted ways? I only expected enough to pay for my return trip to La Rochelle and to have a little extra left over. What you gave me was enough to become a partner in the newspaper."

"Soon, I was meeting very influential people, who were surprised to learn that I had served as a magistrate in La Rochelle and suggested that I become more involved in studying our country's public policy. They felt that France was going to face many challenges, some known and some unknown in the near future and people would be needed to fill positions of authority very quickly So, when Necker was dismissed, a de facto leadership committee headed by Adrien Duport was formed to raise a militia and fashion a court system and they asked me to serve as a magistrate."

"Wait," said Robert as a puzzled look swept across his face. "You never said anything about having been a magistrate. When did you serve in the court system?"

"Well, I sometimes delivered documents for the various judges in La Rochelle and Etienne's brother; my cousin Marcel; is a lawyer, so it's nearly the same," he said, trying to sound convincing.

Robert looked at Lisette looked at each other and shrugged.

"After the Tennis Court Oath, it appeared to some people that we were going to need a new form of government very soon and with it, a new legal system. Some of them asked me to be ready to assume the role of a magistrate, should the revolution become a reality."

"Now, I feel that I can do some good for citizens and the Republic by being fair and impartial in my decisions. My life is very exciting and rewarding and I owe it all to you, my friend. I feel that I can accomplish so much and rise in stature and responsibility. I could follow my brother André to Switzerland, but now why would I even consider that? I do hope at some point conditions here will change enough that he will feel it is safe to return."

"I also met a journalist named Jean-Paul Marat, a powerful writer who attacks the enemies of the Revolution. Camille Desmoulins and François-Noel Babeuf are also very important powerful writers who advocate for the rights and protection of the poor and against the nobility who created this state that our country is in now and all have bright futures."

Robert hesitated to respond to his friend's mood with the latest news but he felt a need to offer some advice to his friend and at the very least; inform him of which the direction the country would proceed. All three men he mentioned would join the countless number of victims of the Revolution. Marat was assassinated in his home and Desmoulins and Babeuf would both be executed as victims of the many struggles for power.

"Bernard, do you remember when I cautioned you against accepting the titles and other benefits from the King? Don't allow your exuberance with your new position to cloud your judgment. France's new condition will bring a lot people to power whose influence will result in a great loss of lives. You will be much safer by remaining on the periphery of this whirlwind instead of being drawn to its epicenter."

Bernard nodded and appeared more agreeable than he was when Robert attempted to give him advice at Versailles.

"And what about your plans, my friend? It looks to me like you have ended your military career, judging from your clothes. You would do well here with the new Republic. Would you consider that?" his eyes glittering

It didn't take a lot of consideration from Robert to answer. His goal when he left the Nation was to return to his position at the University. Two months of delay in France hadn't changed that.

"No Bernard, I can't remain in Paris any longer. I need to return to my research position at the university. I do have a huge favor to ask of you though. Lisette and I may be traveling through France and we will need papers to allow us to pass unimpeded. Can you give us papers that will allow us to pass through the various checkpoints?"

Bernard laughed heartedly. "Is that all my friend? Let's sit at my desk and I'll prepare all the papers you will need to pass safely without question."

Etienne brought several papers covered with names of those who were accused but had not been informed of the charges against them. "My friends, would you excuse me for a few minutes? The next group of people to stand before my bench will be here shortly and I need a few minutes to read information regarding their arrests and their punishments."

He knew his departure was imminent and Robert was reminded of the time when he was about to leave La Chapelle-Thérmer and wanted to explain to Genevieve who he really was. He was now faced with this similar situation and didn't want this to become another missed opportunity that he would regret later.

"I believe that I'll return to Nantes," offered Lissette. She sounded very tired and slowly looked from the floor in the direction of Bernard's desk. "I still have family there and we own property nearby. It's been so long since I've seen it that I don't remember it in detail, except there was water nearby and it was very peaceful. There won't be much for me here soon and from what you say it will be safer there."

Robert started to explain slowly. "That's not entirely true, Lisette." "It will be peaceful there for a while, but Nantes will become part of the worst violence of the Revolution. Two or three hundred thousand will die when the Revolution comes to that part of the country. Maybe you can go to Switzerland and stay with Bernard's brother, Brother André."

Robert began the next segment of the conversation very seriously. "There is something else that I'd like to tell you, Lisette. I want you to know that my name isn't Mathurin. That name belonged to my ancestor who left France in 1650. My first name is actually Robert. I'm a research scientist in theoretical physics, a discipline which doesn't exist in this time, for Syracuse University, which is located in a city that doesn't yet exist, and I was born in the year 2002." He divulged everything as quickly as possible, expecting her to react to his disclosure by running away.

"Is that all?" Her composure surprised Robert. "I knew there was something different about you, Robert. Is there anything else I should know?"

"That will do for now," he answered. "I do have a question for you though." Lisette tipped her head as she tried to guess what his question might be. "Lisette, do you trust me?"

Lisette paused for a moment, although she had decided on her answer before the question could be raised. "I'm not sure, Major. Are there balloons involved?"

Robert remembered the last time he asked that question was just before he surprised her with a ride in Jacques Charles' balloon. "No, I promise you that there are no balloons," he said definitely.

"Then yes, of course I trust you," she said in all earnestness.

Bernard looked from his list at his friends and appreciated that despite all of the turmoil in this hall of justice, the city of Paris and all of France; two people were able to find a reason to smile and laugh. Then they both turned and looked at Bernard as he signaled them to return to his desk. "I have prepared your documents for you. With these you will be able to travel anywhere in France without delays," he said handing one to both Robert and Lisette. "I asked Étienne to get some tea and cakes for our little celebration. It isn't everyday a condemned man is granted his freedom."

Étienne carried a tray filled with a variety of cakes and tea to Bernard's desk'. While they ate and drank, Bernard entertained Lisette with a detailed description of when he discovered Robert wandering in La Rochelle, how they escaped from Le Mans, their fight on the bridge and what they experienced at Versailles. Lisette listened intently to everything Bernard said, convinced that with a skillet in his hand; he was definitely a force to be reckoned with.

As they placed their tea cups on the desk, Robert and Bernard realized that it was for the last time. They avoided looking at each other until Robert said, "Bernard there is something else you can do for us before we leave."

Bernard walked with Robert and Lisette through the constantly swirling mass of people in the former warehouse, until they exited through the twin doors, still guarded by the pair of sentries. Earlier he had passed through this doorway expecting the worst. Now, he was leaving accompanied by Lisette and with certainly much more hope than he had earlier. They all shook hands and embraced for one last time as Bernard wished them both good luck and Robert reminded him to heed his advice. When they crossed Rue de Faubourg, he turned toward the place where he had narrowly escaped death to look for his friend but Bernard had already returned to his place as magistrate in the new Republic.

The mood of the people they passed they passed in the street was decidedly varied. There was the look he had become accustomed to; hungry, desperate and exhausted. The majority however, seemed elated in the wake of news that the Bastille had fallen. Some were shocked, faces filled with hopeless perplexity, lined with soot and dampened with sweat, following their involvement in the beginning of the Revolution and the eventual cost of human capital. Whatever their individual perspectives were concerning what occurred in the past two days, they were all bound by what lay ahead. The smell of smoke from the previous day's fires still hung ominously over Porte Saint-Antoine as a reminder to everyone.

Walking up the street, Robert and Lisette saw Henri and Gerard standing outside of the door to her shop. They both turned and ran inside when they saw them walking around other pedestrians and moments later the ever present women streamed into the street and rushed to meet them.

The women had been waiting expectantly since notice of Robert's vindication arrived with Henri and Gerard. Children weren't allowed in the building where the trials were conducted but they somehow found a way to observe from the shadows and ran swiftly to the boulangerie when they heard about Robert's acquittal and the thunderous noise of the muskets in the courtyard which signaled the finality of Petit's sentence. It seemed odd to Robert to enter the boulangerie, absent the customary smells from the bakery or the constant movement involved in preparing bread to be baked.

Henri and Gerard had disappeared amid the celebration and Robert needed to have a discussion with them. Leaving the women with Lissette he exited quietly through the rear entrance and walked to the stables where he saw a familiar scene of two boys pampering a horse.

"Boys, I need to talk to you about something very serious." Henri and Gerard ran and came to attention and saluted. "Yes, Major?"

Robert sat on a stool that had recently joined their newly acquired furniture. Like the location of their home, he decided not to question them about it. "The reality is that I am returning home and the phaeton and the horse..."

"Gaston, Major," Henri quickly corrected.

"Yes, Gaston," accepted Robert. "I want to leave the carriage and Gaston with you because you two love horses and are very responsible. I need you to promise me that you will care for Gaston as you would have Sadeek. The two of you will be partners in caring for him as well as the carriage. This is a new Republic and you will do well together."

"Henri and Gerard accept your orders, Major Dubé," as they saluted stiffly.

"One other thing, boys. I am not serving in the cavalry any longer, so there is no reason to salute me or call me Major. My name is Robert."

They paused for a moment, before rushing to him and shaking his hand. "Thank you Major Robert. We will take very good care of Gaston."

He turned and walked across the courtyard where there was no longer a need to hide the hoof prints left by Sadeek or Pascal and proceeded immediately to Lisette's upstairs apartments.

Lisette meanwhile had lingered behind in her bakery. . As her friends spoke to her, she passed between the counter like countless times before, running her fingers across the counter. Steeping onto the stone floor of the bakery, she examined her fingertips and stood before the area where dough was kneaded. She placed her hands palms down on the counter and moved them across its surface, collecting all the flour and spices that had spilled there. She vigorously rubbed her hands together, until friction warmed her hands and then raised them until they touched to her nose, closed her eyes and inhaled deeply all the aromas she was so familiar with. She suddenly realized that she had never noticed that even when the ovens were baking bread, the stone walls were always cool. She walked around the area where the ovens were located with her hand pressed against the wall, noticing also how much smoother they were than she had remembered, and paused briefly in front of the bins where her various typed of flours and spices were stored. This was the reason that patrons from the wealthy arrondissements came to Lisette's shop for the breads they could not find elsewhere.

Lisette baffled her friends when she gave instructions about which types of breads should be baked in what order and when to deliver bread to the poor before she turned to climb the stair to her apartments. She had never noticed before how uneven and creaky the steps were in places. Robert had hurried to the wardrobe, had repacked his belongings for the third time and now stood with his riding boots hanging over the edge of his backpack while clutching the key fob tightly with his left hand.

"Well Major, it looks as if you're in a hurry to be somewhere," Lisette observed.

Robert took a deep breath and glanced at her. "I am definitely ready; although I'm in no hurry. But if the recent past has taught me anything, it's to not waste time. I hate to say it, but I should leave soon," he said looking downcast.

"Me also," said Lisette as she surveyed her apartment before walking deliberately to a small desk next to her bureau. Opening the drawer, she withdrew several documents and rolled them carefully into a tight cylinder before securing it with a ribbon and placing them in her bag. She strode across the room to where Robert stood and held his hand. "I have everything I need."

Robert didn't hesitate for one second. "Here is a little more science for you," as he pressed the button. Instantly they appeared in the time machine in Sarah's outbuilding on the Nation.

LETTER TO A FRIEND

The first thing he confirmed was that Lisette's hand had remained in his. He was about to say something to her when he became acutely aware of a very familiar aroma filling the room and his senses. It was the unmistakable smell that could only be from bacon, including the sounds of sizzling and popping from the noise of his favorite food simmering in a large skillet. But who was cooking it?

Lisette's senses were also occupied as she busily examined all that she was encountering in her first few moments in the 21st century. She had anticipated some things would be different, but was truly amazed by the brilliance of a room in the absence of candles, with light emanating from small windows in the ceiling and large objects that to her resembled very tall candle stick holders from which light also streamed.

Robert quickly turned and saw Ron standing in the kitchen, tongs in hand next to the source of the unmistakable aroma. "Well, it's about time we saw you. Where have you been?" Ron looked slightly annoyed as he continued to turn the strips of bacon agonizingly slowly, extremely aware that it was torturing Robert.

Ron looked at Robert as he stepped out of their time machine, walked to him still holding the tongs and stood before him with the palms of his hands open in a mystified pose. Leaning forward he whispered in his ear, "Dude, I don't know how to tell you this, but there is a woman on your arm."

Smiling, he turned his gaze to Lisette and then back to Ron, "This isn't just a woman Ron. I'd like you to meet my wife, Lisette."

"You have been busy haven't you? I think it's great that we returned to visit and you had time to marry and go to a costume party while I waited for you to deliver my documents!"

Robert looked at the clothes that both he and Lisette were wearing and realized how out of place he looked now, when a few moments earlier his appearance would not have attracted attention from anyone.

"Ron, these clothes are what the common people in 18th century France wear."

Ron looked puzzled. "Wear? Don't you mean what they wore?"

Clearly he felt that he owed Ron an explanation. "When I left from this house for France, my intent was to deliver your documents personally. However, I experienced one our huge technical problems. I meant to visit you in Paris; but I missed your time period by approximately 270 years and I literally had a front row seat for the French Revolution. The package I sent to you was from the coordinates you gave to me, but in 1789 it was just an empty lot."

Ron began removing strips of bacon from the pan and placed them on a plate. "My father and I intended to go to Pasadena, so I could show him the Cal Tech campus. We really never had time for that previously. I used our machine as the receiver and expected to arrive either in your office at S.U., or in your apartment, enter the coordinates for CalTech and then transport to California. Instead we find ourselves in this tiny house in the middle of nowhere and your security devices made it impossible to do anything, including returning to Paris. We wandered around until your friend Nathan found us. Now we're stuck in this house because we're hiding from another acquaintance of yours."

Robert walked slowly into the kitchen attempting to remember a time when the words friend and Nathan could be used in the same sentence, picked up a piece of bacon and slowly put it into his mouth. His puzzled look revealed to Ron that he was baffled as to who this "friend" could be. When Ron mentioned Franklin's name his reaction was so sudden that Lisette couldn't help noticing.

"Who is Franklin?" she asked cautiously.

Robert thought for a moment before answering. "He is sort of this century's equivalent of Captain Petit."

Lisette rolled her eyes toward the ceiling as she pushed her hands through her hair and sighed heavily.

"Are Franklin and Captain Petit a problem?" asked Ron, feeling as if he was excluded from a topic of some importance.

Robert looked at them both and realized that he had even more to explain, however given this recent information, he thought their time would be better served by making plans to leave now. He glanced quickly at Ron, "After you left for Paris, agents from the Department of Defense arrived at our office and confiscated our machine. I eventually stole it back from them and then hid it here. If Agent Franklin manages to reclaim it, you may not make it back to Paris. Captain Petit was a French officer who tried to kill me himself or to arrange it several times, but his arrogance betrayed him and was himself executed. It's an incredibly long story and trust me I will explain later, but believe me when I tell you that we need to leave, immediately."

As he finished speaking, the door opened, he turned quickly expecting Franklin to walk through the door and was very relieved to see Nathan entering the house.

Nathan walked to Robert and shook his hand, while he smiled at Lisette. He was about to introduce himself when she extended her arm and shook his hand, "Pleased to meet you Nathan. My name is Lisette Dubé."

Nathan was pleasantly surprised to meet this charming new addition to these guests who appeared in this house without entering it. He stopped for a moment to consider how unusual that this was becoming routine for him. "Very nice to meet you Lisette," he said before turning to Robert.

"You have a considerable problem, Robert. Agent Franklin arrived here about two weeks ago, demanding to be told where you were hiding and claiming that you were in possession of stolen government property." Nathan nodded toward the time machine. "I guess that's what they're looking for?" Robert nodded in agreement.

"We reminded him that his government is in possession of land they stole from us and while he is on Nation land; he was in no position to make any demands," as his head swiveled quickly toward the kitchen. "Hey Arnie, is that bacon I smell?"

Arnie responded by smiling and holding a crisp strip of bacon with his tongs.

While everyone else had been distracted by the discussion surrounding Franklin and Petit, Lisette had joined Ron's father in the kitchen and they were now in the process of making bacon sandwiches.

Meanwhile, Nathan resumed briefing Robert about the situation developing outside.

"In the beginning, dealing with Franklin was like a game. He arrived with U.S. Marshalls demanding access to our property without a search warrant. That didn't end well for them and they were escorted from the Nation, after a Federal District Court judge ordered him to leave. Since then, he's learned that he needs to be granted permission to be allowed on Nation land in any official capacity. He has been very persistent, though. Every day he tries some new tactic to meet his goal and he tries very hard not to look angry when he is rejected. It's pretty funny actually."

"Anyway, the elders are growing tired of his arrival every day and want him to return to D.C. permanently. They're inclined to let him look in here, but Sarah remains adamant about not allowing that unless you say it's OK."

Lisette handed Nathan a plate containing a bacon sandwich. As she walked away, Robert looked at Nathan's plate and at the departing Lisette and again at Nathan, who shrugged and bit into his sandwich.

Robert approached the window and cautiously peered toward the road. He was familiar with Nathan's pickup truck, but not with the black vehicle parked behind it. Looking toward Sarah's house he saw a group of people talking and alarmingly, they were headed in his direction. Several members of the group were very animated as they spoke; two weren't at all. They wore dark suits and both were unmistakable; Franklin and Tyler were approximately one hundred feet away.

He knew that without permission from the Nation, they may as well be one hundred miles away; but the information that Nathan had just disclosed didn't make him feel completely at ease. "Ron," Robert shouted. "Enter your coordinates in the machine. We need to leave this second."

Ron recognised the agitation in Robert's voice and he knew that ignoring it would not be wise. Robert walked quickly to the machine, entered his PIN and scanned his fingerprint.

"You and your father will go first. I have six UPS's divided into three pairs. You'll use one pair when you go and then Lisette and I will use the other two. These people outside stole our machine once and lost it, but they won't repeat their mistakes. If they take it again, we will have huge problems to deal with. I need to bring the machine with us and it will take some time to be rewired."

Ron and his father placed their sandwiches on their plates while his father took one last bite, before returning them to the kitchen. As he entered the coordinates into the machine's computer, he turned to Robert. "Are you sure you don't want to go first, just in case?"

Robert was adamant. "No, there is something I must do first. It is necessary that you go first, and you need to go now." He turned to Nathan, "Can you please find me an envelope, paper and pen? I need to write a letter to a friend."

At this point, Nathan knew better than to ask why and began searching through Sarah's desk. As he turned to hand them to Robert, he saw Robert and Lisette standing next to the machine, while Ron and his father calmly waited to depart. Arnie had taken just a moment to return to the kitchen and now held the plate with his bacon sandwich. Robert remembered the expression of satisfaction that Genevieve bore when she had gained control of his bacon before he left La Chapelle-Thémer. Just as he was about to energize the machine he called to Ron, "Hey, are your ceilings tall enough for this machine?"

Ron thought for a moment. "Yes, I believe so, but why..?"

"Move furniture if you need to. We'll be arriving shortly." Robert energized the field, Ron and his father vanished as he glanced at the astonished appearance on Nathan's face.

Nathan's arms hung at his side, as he held an envelope in one hand and a pen and paper in the other. Robert leaned forward and spoke calmly as he removed the items from Nathan's hands. "Perhaps you should eat something, Nathan," he suggested.

Lisette stood with her head tilted slightly and the index finger of her left hand resting on her cheek. "Robert, you will have to show me this again."

"Oh, you'll see this again very soon." He had finished his writing, folded the letter carefully and placed it into the envelope.

"Nathan, please delay them for five minutes and the give this to my friend waiting outside." He handed Nathan an envelope and when he turned it over in his hand he saw that it was addressed simply "Agent Franklin".

While Robert busied himself with the task of altering the wiring of the machine, Lisette had discovered the nuances of plumbing and light switches.

As lights turned on and off, followed by the sounds of water flowing from the kitchen sink, Robert stood and addressed Nathan. "I'm finished and we're ready to leave. If you have a use for these UPS's your welcome to them. You may want to remove the "Property of Syracuse University" stickers though."

"Lisette, it is time for us to leave;" he said hurriedly as he approached Nathan and held out his hand. They shook vigorously, and each placed his free hand on the others shoulder.

"It is a shame we have to leave so quickly Nathan. I would have liked to spend more time with you."

"If you return someday we could go out for coffee;" he touched his nose and grimaced, "but not at Firekeepers."

Robert helped Lisette enter the machine and nodded at Nathan. "It will be my pleasure and my treat." He pressed the button, two pairs of the UPS's glowed for a moment and suddenly Nathan was alone. After allowing himself a moment to grasp all that he had just witnessed, he opened the front door and regarded the group standing a short distance away. Franklin gave the impression that he was the most eager to hear any news.

Ignoring the stares of Franklin and Tyler, he approached Sarah and whispered his entire report into her ear. "He says it's OK," and he smiled as he returned to the house.

Sarah looked straight at the distant hills and avoided eye contact with the federal agents. "You may inspect the premises, Agent Franklin; but touch nothing."

Franklin and Tyler walked deliberately across Sarah's lawn, while the members of the Nation appeared to be bored with this latest incursion. Franklin expected that he would soon finally retrieve his prize. Because what Sarah didn't know was that the Nation's sovereign status meant nothing to him. Retrieving the time machine was his justification for any lengths he would take to achieve his goal. If he found the machine again he would not allow anyone obstruct him from seizing it permanently.

Sarah and the others grinned as if they knew that his aspirations had already been derailed.

Franklin reached the house first and looked at Nathan who regarded him impassively. Franklin reached for the door handle but entry was quickly blocked by Nathan. He wasn't about to allow someone from the federal government and an enemy of his friend, to be allowed access to Sarah's property without permission.

Nathan looked to the elders, who turned to Sarah; who in turn nodded to Nathan. He did not want Franklin to enter first, so he stepped in front of him, opened the door and was painfully unhurried as he slowly walked through it.

"He wanted you to have this," said Nathan, mocking him with satisfaction beaming from his face as he handed the envelope to Franklin. Franklin looked at the six UPS's arranged around an empty space in the middle of the living room. There was in indentation in the carpet where something had rested.

"It certainly looks like the approximate dimensions of that time machine," he thought. Franklin looked for a moment longer at the carpet realizing that his prospects were suddenly not as promising as they appeared earlier and tore open the envelope quickly, like one would pull a bandage from a wound.

Dear Agent Franklin,

I have some bad news, and some really bad news. First, the bad news is that both we and our time machine have left. Second, the really bad news is that we are somewhere that you will never be able to reach either us or the machine.

Have a nice trip back to D.C.

Sincerely,

Robert Dubé PhD.

Franklin slowly and deliberately folded the letter and returned it to the envelope. He looked at Nathan who offered him a plate. "Bacon sandwich, Agent Franklin?"

Saying nothing, he brushed aside the plate, heading toward the door and walked stoically past the elders and Sarah as Tyler tried to keep pace.

Tyler caught up with him as they neared the government vehicle. "Sir, may I ask what was in the letter?"

In a voice born with resignation, Franklin walked straight to their car, looking neither left nor right, ignoring everything but his thoughts. "Have fun in Maine," he spat out dejectedly. He backed the car off Sarah's property and as he drove in the direction of route 11A his mood seemed to brighten. "Tyler, let's stop at the Dinosaur BBQ before we return to D.C. We may as well end this day on a positive note"

HOME

Robert and Lisette exited from the machine and stepped into a sea of white. Ron and his father were resting upon a large white sofa, which sat upon a white tiled floor with white walls. The room was lit by recessed lights in the periphery of the ceiling, totally fascinating Lisette. A pair of black lamps rested on glass tables provided the only contrast in shades.

It was obvious from their view that they were well above the street level as the dark grey rooftops of Paris buildings extended to the horizon. Lisette walked to the open door and gasped as she grabbed the doorframe. "The Seine. Is that the Seine?" as she pointed to the river below. "And what is that?" as she pointed to an object in the distance. "That's Champ de Mars, but that wasn't there before," she stated with her arm still pointing at a dominant structure in the distance.

Ron rose from his chair and walked to the doorway with a confused look on his face. "You're from Paris but you don't recognize the Eiffel Tower?"

"This is going to take some adjusting by all of us," suggested Robert "We left Paris in 1789. The Eiffel Tower was erected in 1889."

Pausing to process Robert's statement, Ron nodded, and then pointed to the balcony which extended along the entire length of the building. "This building is ten stories tall and we live on the top two floors. Let me show you my favorite part."

They walked along the teak floor of the balcony, the Seine ten stories below on their right and a wall of glass on their left. Lisette could not stop staring at the Eiffel Tower; or loosen her grip on the railing. The balcony led to a terrace with hardwood floors, an oak table and chairs and plants in large terra cotta pots as well as planters. "We can just sit and gaze as life on the Seine passes by below and watch as planes pass overhead. In the evening they light up the Eiffel Tower; it's simply the best."

Lisette was silently observing the sky, trying to make the connection between the unusual cloud like streaks forming an odd pattern across the sky and the objects they emanated from.

Robert watched as she leaned back further in her chair, straining to watch the jets pass by. "It's called an airplane, Lisette. We'll fly on one of those soon enough. Some things haven't changed in twenty years, apparently."

"They're about to change radically, now that you're here," Ron said as he leaned forward and smiled. "Remember when we were building our time machine and you said that perhaps people wouldn't be as interested in traveling between different periods in time as they would be in traveling quickly between different destinations in the same time period? I joked that you couldn't decide between earning an MBA or a PhD. Well, when we arrived in Paris I found that plane travel has become moderately quicker in the past two decades. However, no matter how fast or high they travel, there is still a limit as to how long it will take for someone to reach their destination. Plus, the world's population has increased dramatically and there is a limit on the number of available aircraft that can fly at once, take off and land from a limited number of airports; with a limit on the number of passengers one plane can carry. So I took our idea and created a new, absolutely unique business. We offer our machines to individuals and businesses who want to travel anywhere on earth instantly. They're not for sale, we produce and lease them."

"It seems ironic that I was able to solve our problem regarding traveling back in time to the desired date and now people simply want to arrive at their destination quicker."

When Robert looked at Ron with an inquisitive stare, he decided to explain.

"The one aspect we neglected to include in our calculations was rotation. Everything spins, the earth, the solar system, the universe; atoms, electrons; everything and all of these objects spin relative to each other. Once I added that constant to our time machine's computer, traveling back in time became as accurate as traveling in forward in time. But as I said, few people are interested in that now."

"Our business address is in the La Defense business district, which we will visit tomorrow," as he handed Robert one of their business cards. "We should also do some clothes shopping for you two. You may not attract much attention dressed that way in the 18th century, but you'll really stand out now. We have one of the bedrooms made up for you on the first floor that overlooks the Seine."

"First floor?" said Robert surprised. "You mean the entire floor? I presumed that you meant part of it, not all of it."

Ron smirked. "We have two floors, seven bedrooms and seven bathrooms. We even have room for our machine, although it really doesn't match the décor. We never realized that we could afford property like this, but I slightly miscalculated when I originally purchased my father's stock. I had estimated that my father's worth would be $100 million after 20 years. As it turned out, I underestimated its growth potential just a bit, misplaced a decimal point and found that his worth is closer to $100 billion. That was quite a surprise."

"Something I'm curious about Ron, are the coordinates for your home. I understand that things have changed since 1789, but I know that I was not this close to the Seine when I sent your package to you."

"That was our first apartment when we arrived here. It was convenient for a while, but our business began to show a profit and when I realized what my father's net worth really was, it just made sense to move here. I planned to keep it until you arrived; but now there is no reason to hold onto it. By the way, you and Lisette should start to look for something like this for yourselves. My business partner should live in a home that reflects his accomplishments."

Arnie was stretching out on his chaise lounge, hands behind his head; smiling and looking up at the blue sky and winked. "Lunch is on the way," he announced to everyone as he put away his electronic device. "You'll love this," he said and resumed gazing at the sky.

"By the way Lisette, you look a bit perplexed," Arnie observed. "Is something on your mind?"

"I am sorry sir, but there are two questions that I have." She paused for a moment to gather herself. "First, please explain to me what exactly is this airplane? Second, how can you live up here in the clouds while all the suffering and needy people live beneath you?"

Ron's father observed a jet descending as it prepared for a landing at Orly airport for a few seconds before answering. "In the first place Lisette, please don't call me sir. My friends call me Arnie."

"Now you see those clouds up there? What you were watching are called contrails, formed by water vapor from the exhaust of an airplane's engines. An airplane is sort of like a ship with wings that transports people from one point to another; called airports. It would be fun to visit Orly airport where you can watch them land and take off."

"Second, you won't see the conditions that you remember from the Paris you knew. People who have what you see here usually achieved it through hard work, not because of birthright. People are given opportunities to better themselves without being advanced or held back by their family history. These boys attended one of the finest physics programs in the world and constructed something that others said couldn't be built. And now, they are going to create something truly astounding. Not everyone has what you see here, but most aren't living in the sort of misery that you experienced in your time either. You'll see that also."

"For now, let's concentrate on lunch," as he waved to someone behind them. "This is Yvonne, our chef. Our day isn't complete without one of her creations served on our deck. Her dinners are a special event too."

They sat on the deck, gazing at the Eiffel Tower, the Seine and a partly cloudy sky as they were served, bread, seared beef and roasted potatoes, a salad with some cheese and ice cream; a first for Lisette.

The following day began with a visit to clothing stores at the Carrousel de Louvre mall. While they were both familiar with Pont Royal, Lisette wasn't accustomed to travel by car or passing through underground tunnels. Shortly after crossing Pont Royal, Lisette was adjusting to her first ride in a car, enamored by its speed and electric windows. As a breeze swirled about them while she repeatedly opened and closed her window, Robert realized that they were descending beneath Pont Royal and driving into an underground parking lot. He was concerned that she might be apprehensive but was relieved when she treated this excursion as her latest adventure.

The Louvre was very familiar to both Robert and Lisette as they viewed it from Pont Royal prior to entering the tunnel. However shopping in this underground center was entirely new to Lisette and like the experience of driving in a tunnel, she marveled at it. What amazed both her and Robert however was the addition of an enormous inverted glass pyramid. Something that didn't exist in the Paris they remembered; it was suspended from the ceiling by its base, its apex ended a few feet from the floor, nearly making contact with the apex of a small marble pyramid. When they examined it further, they saw that it was made of square glass panes interconnected internally by wires. Looking at the ceiling offered a marginal view of buildings, but Robert could tell that he was far from the parts of the Louvre which had been home to the Royal Academy of Sciences where he had begun his experiments measuring latitude and longitude.

While shopping for clothes not new to Robert, Lisette had never experienced anything like this. Fortunately, Ron asked his chef, Yvonne to accompany them and offer her opinions. Ron and Robert's clothes selection did not take long and they eventually found enough garments to satisfy Lisette and Yvonne. "She certainly likes colors, this one, and she has excellent fashion sense," commented Yvonne as she presented her purchases to Robert while enjoying espresso in one of the restaurants.

Their shopping completed, they drove through Paris and visited some of the locations that were familiar to them both. Lisette was very happy to see the view from Pont Neuf and to drive past Jardin des Plantes. Her former address on Passage de la Bonne Grain; somehow looked wider and brighter than it had over two centuries earlier. A different business occupied the spot where her bread shop had been located and coincidentally the exterior was still dark green, the name of the company appearing in gold letters just as "BOULANGERIE" had when she occupied it.

The stable was now no more than a memory and had become a parking lot for the more recent tenants of the surrounding buildings. Robert expected that if anyone could have made a profit from a small grey horse and a phaeton, Henri and Gerard would have managed to. The alley that had led to Avenue Ledru Rollin didn't appear as desperately depressing as it had when it was possible to pass through it to reach a playground. It was still only wide enough for pedestrians, but not too narrow for the occasional motorcycle, as tire tracks had now mingled with prints from shoes and sandals.

Robert supposed that seeing her former home might sadden her, but she was surprisingly interested in the property and said that she intended to return very soon to see more of both it and the neighborhood. As they returned to Ron's, he and Robert put all of their new clothing in their room while Lisette rode in her latest fascination; their elevator.

The following day, after enjoying breakfast on the terrace, Robert, Ron and Lisette drove to the La Défence business district where she had her second experience driving through a tunnel as their car approached an area of immense buildings. They walked slowly through an extremely wide plaza surrounded by buildings, with such an extensive use of various shapes and designs; that Robert and Lisette unhurriedly studied them all. Some were four story affairs as long as two city blocks. Others taller structures towered over them, rising forty or more stories high. Nearly every one used mirrored glass for its outer shell, they were all unique works of art.

Ron turned and encouraged them to continue to move toward the reason they were in La Defense. His attention was focused on a building in the center of the mall; not larger or grander, but dominant just the same.

Ron saw what had captured their attention as they resumed walking. "That is Grande Arche de la Défence. I've never been on its roof but they say that you can see the Louvre from there."

It was a truly fascinating structure that resembled an enormous hollowed out cube, whose walls measured over three hundred fifty feet tall and sixty feet wide. It appeared to be solid stone as they approached the front, but its sides were constructed entirely of glass.

"It's amazing and inspiring," admitted Ron. "What isn't covered in glass is clad with white marble and granite. There are days when I am walking to our office and I may not be aware of these other buildings but you can't avoid this. It's as though it demands to be noticed."

As they continued past the Arche, Ron pointed out more buildings in the distance. "The area we are located in is largely devoted to science industries," Ron explained. "Banks and military contractors are located further away."

Ron walked straight toward a cube shaped building constructed of shimmering black glass which appeared to be one seamless solid sheet of glass. "And that is our business," said Ron with an inescapable sense of pride. The name "MERCURE" in pulsating bold red letters, flashed from left to right across its face, disappearing as it reached the corner of the building and reappeared in violet letters moments later.

"Mercury," Robert said quietly, as the name vanished again.

"Yes, Mercury," Ron explained. "I was searching for a recognizable name that stood for speed and then one night, there it was. My father and I had left Paris for a weekend in Ploeumer on the Atlantic coast. We were walking along a path next to the highway as the sun was setting. The view was nearly perfect because it was a small town without big city lights to interfere. Out on the horizon I saw two planets and I told my father that one of them was Mars, when a boy about 12 years old yelled to us from his swing set that it was Mercury. When I tried to correct him, his father stepped out from their house and said that his son was actually correct. His father was the local science teacher at Collège Charles de Gaulle. He invited us to sit with him in their yard, looking out over the ocean and explained that Mars and Saturn are visible on the horizon also, but we were definitely observing Mercury. We sat in his yard, facing the Bay of Biscay, surrounded scrub grass and listened to the surf roll in as the waves crashed on the rocky beach. He said he loved that location because the he could observe the sky, uninterrupted for hours. He invited us to stay for dinner, left us for a moment as he went into their house and in a moment returned with wine for us all. We sat on tables and looked at the stars and enjoyed a dinner of lobster and pasta with mussels."

"Anyway, I thought that was perfect. Mercury was the…"

"The Roman god of speed," interjected Robert.

"Yes, and the god of commerce and financial gain," continued Ron. "It seemed perfect. The name combined speed and business; plus Mercury sounds so much better in French. Let's go inside and you can hear it for yourself."

Various works of art were spread out amongst the buildings, but one appeared to be entirely out of place and vaguely familiar to Robert. While Ron continued talking, he walked directly and with purpose, stopping before one in particular and glared at it while reading a plaque attached to its base. Lisette had seen this look before and knew that this was definitely not a face he wore when he was content.

"Are you joking?" he yelled with his arms crossed, startling some of the people who were crossing the plaza. He turned quickly to look in Ron's direction as he had paused for a moment, then lowered his shoulders and glanced at the ground before changing direction and walked to where the offensive statue was positioned.

"This plaque says that two French physicists invented the first time machine," complained Robert as he began to shout. "The world's first, the only problem is that the date was fifteen years after ours was built. French physicists are so wrapped up in their mathematics; they wouldn't have been able to accomplish this before us."

Robert was so vocal about his dissatisfaction with this statue that some people were beginning to gather to listen to his rant.

"I know, I was as surprised as you when I first saw it," Ron said nearly apologizing. "I hoped it was a mirage. They apparently sent a cantaloupe or something into the future and that was the extent of their experiments. I try not to pay any attention to it."

"Fruit? They sent fruit into the future and someone erected a statue to them?" Robert shouted, desperately irritated. "Why not send a fruit salad? I'm pretty sure that would have been worth a Nobel Prize."

Ron was doing his utmost to separate Robert from the statue and the crowd gathering around him. "That's about it really. As far as I know they accomplished nothing else after that. Let me show you what we are working on and you will soon forget all about this ridiculous statue."

Robert's mood seemed to brighten as Lisette put her arm through his. "Come Major; let's look at your new business and our future."

Passing beneath the mirror covered ceiling, Ron walked with them through their lobby and escorted them past security. Lisette was accorded another thrill when she saw her first escalator as Ron presented the second floor of the building and their offices.

Immediately as they stepped off the escalator, they strode onto dark grey tiles leading to a large flat black metallic desk that looked like it was floating, where a woman with a polite expression and bright brown eyes; sat and addressed Ron. "Good morning Dr. Maxwell. May I get something for your guests?" as she acknowledged Robert and Lisette.

"Actually, Danielle, these are not our guests. I would like you to meet Dr. and Mme. Dubé."

Danielle paused for a moment and drew a deep breath and raised her hands to her mouth before fixating on Robert and Lisette. "Oh yes sir, I was wondering when we would have the honor of meeting you. Is there anything I can get for either of you?"

Lisette shrugged her shoulders, "Some coffee with cream and sugar perhaps? And please call me Lisette," as she extended her arm and shook Danielle's hand.

Robert answered as sort of an afterthought, preoccupied as he gazed about the room, distracted by two gleaming wooden office doors. "Some bacon if you have it."

"I want to show you the reason why we are here," as Ron placed his thin arm around Robert's shoulder and walked with him across the black tiled floor to the entrance to his office. He stood before the door on the left, on which a golden plaque with bold black letters read,

ROBERT A. DUBÉ PhD.

Ron rested his hand on his shoulder. "I had your name put on your door first. I always knew that we would be working together eventually. I just wasn't certain which decade it might be"

His door swung open effortlessly as he stepped into the grandest office he could have imagined. It wasn't simply the amount of space it provided, but the variety of tools he now had at his disposal. Two of the interior walls were video screens, entirely for display of data from his computer with a comfortable chair that could be positioned to face either screen. A platform as large as a newspaper rested upon a chrome post and moved with his chair so he could work while sitting or standing. It was transparent and he was certain that its purpose was connected somehow to the displays on the walls, but wasn't positive how to engage it until he ran his hand along its edge. A tiny button was located on its side and when pushed, the platform became illuminated, the upper half was clear and the lower portion was a keyboard. He typed "Mercure" with his keyboard and it instantly was displayed on the wall. Any impressions he made on the upper half on the platform appeared on the wall and any motion above the word "MERCURE" affected the display on the wall. Placing both hands above the platform, he spread his fingers and moved them away and the letters moved also. When he returned his hands together, "**MERCURE**" looked as it had before.

"We've come a long way from our projectors at Cal Tech. Also, I remembered that sometimes you liked to work standing," Ron said as he stood next to the platform. "I haven't tried it myself, but I'm pretty sure that you can sleep in it too, plus you can disconnect the platform and carry it with you. You may enjoy this part of your office also." Ron turned toward the two remaining walls and said, "Walls, clear." Immediately, both exterior walls became totally transparent and his office now offered a view of the plaza and a portion of Arche de la Défence.

"There's a Starbucks in the lobby. We'll need it, because now that you're here we have a lot of work to attend to."

Unlike his office window at Cal Tech, there were no palm or eucalyptus trees, no landscaping or pools were visible from this office window. He missed those amenities, but that was not what really bothered him. His office window looked straight down upon the accursed tribute to time travel that in his estimation was an insult, as that machine should never have been acknowledged.

Lisette considered that hated monument to be an obstacle as enormous as all the surrounding buildings of La Defense and that unavoidable display would always be a focal point, staring back at them. Lisette had learned that his silence usually meant that he was planning, not simply agonizing over something unpleasant. Before she could think of anything comforting to say, he grinned. "I have this one figured out."

In the evening, they returned to Ron's home and Robert and Lisette took a long walk next to the Seine. She was so excited to see some of the familiar landmarks as well as the modern buildings and her new fascination, autos. They were both pleased that the Seine was really unaltered from what they had been used to. Boats still plied the waters of the majestic river and there was an unmistakable vibrancy resonating now as it did in 1789. Some bridges were new and boats were now equipped with motors, but while Robert was interested in how little had changed since his brief visit in 1789; Lisette was ecstatic that there was enough of the old life here to make her feel that she was still home.

A SLIGHT CORRECTION

Dr. Lenderman, head of Syracuse University's physics department was infuriated as he burst from his office and stomped to the desk of his secretary, Mrs. May. As she was accustomed to his frequent displays of frustration, her reaction did not reflect any sense of urgency. She slowly raised her chin and looked over the top of her reading glasses as he stood at the very edge of her desk, red faced and holding his appointment pad in her direction with his outstretched arm.

"Can you explain this to me, Mrs. May?" placing his devise directly before her, somehow believing that it would hasten her response.

"Explain what Dr. Lenderman?" she responded in her usual composed manner while she pushed her glasses on top of her head and folded her hands in her lap.

"Why this appointment with Dr. Dubé, of course. Why would you do that?"

Mrs. May now stood to her full height and looked down at the department head. "He said he wanted to see you to "bring you up to date with his progress." You usually expect people to make an appointment to see you, so there it is."

"You know very well that isn't what I meant. Our research assistant went missing weeks ago. We've check his apartment, asked his parents, called Cal Tech; even checked with that law student friend of his; Gina Abramson, and yet he is nowhere to be found." He began a serious rant at this point. "He leaves his position at this institution with no explanation and then has the temerity to simply call and make an appointment; for which I might add he is late."

He paused for a moment to regard Mrs. May, who was now staring over his shoulder and silently pointing with her index finger toward his office door.

Dr. Lenderman turned to see what her attention was focused upon and saw his missing research assistant accompanied by a beautiful woman, standing in his office doorway.

"Here I am Dr. Lenderman. Precisely on time and do I have something to show you. Won't you come in, please?" Robert turned slightly and gestured toward the Dr.'s desk.

Turning his appointment pad off, the Doctor glanced at Mrs. May. "No calls, Mrs. May, please," and walked to his office door. "How did you do that, Robert?"

"Nice to see you as well, Dean Lenderman. I would like you to meet my wife, Lissette."

Robert began closing the office door, looked at Mrs. May and winked before it shut.

Dr. Lenderman wasn't upset any longer. He was rooted to the floor of his office, staring alternately at Lisette and a twenty foot long, rectangular shaped object, which now became the focal point of his office. He mutely shook Lisette's hand when she offered it to him; taking some time to release it.

"Is this what I think it is, Dr. Dubé?" as he stepped closer to the time machine; staring at it while speaking to Robert. "You brought your time machine to my office? This is incredible. Where have you been? You really need to contact your mother in her department by the way."

Robert sat in a chair facing Dr. Lenderman. "Let me tell you what is happening now, Dr.Lenderman. You are looking at the time machine which Dr. Maxwell and I developed while we were at Cal Tech. After arriving here, I used it to travel to 18th century France where I was involved in several adventures, but now Dr. Maxwell and I have a business in Paris; 20 years in the future. This time machine will be our gift to the university, just as we discussed earlier."

"I appologise for leaving without notifying you, but the government stole this machine once and came here searching for it. Remaining here longer without taking some immediate action could have allowed them to regain control of it and used for whatever the government feels would best serve its interests.

"I am here to propose this; we will have a presentation on the Quad in front of the physics building, where you and Dr. Fleming from Cal Tech will each give a speech about our accomplishments in time travel."

Robert reached into his backpack and produced a thick binder and placed it in his hands, titled: **"Time Travel: Theory, Practicality and Movement beyond the Point of Creation."**

"This is a paper which Dr. Maxwell and I have authored and will present. The machine will be disabled by that time and will be permanently attached to a pedestal, covered in a clear bubble, including a plaque describing what Dr. Maxwell and I accomplished, crediting the University and Caltech for allowing us to conduct the research leading to the creation of the first time machine. This is a list of people we wish to invite and you may add whomever you feel should attend. We will do this in two weeks from today."

"As for us," as he took Lisette's hand," I am going to walk over to see my mother at the School of Management, and introduce her to Lisette."

"You realize, Dr. Dubé that research papers are usually subjected to rigid scrutiny by your peers before being accepted as fact," the Dean said in a guarded manner. "I'm not certain that a presentation on the Quad will legitimize your claims. Personally, I believe you, but the rest of the scientific community can be a skeptical group and may not be so quick to recognize your accomplishment. You should be prepared for that"

Robert spoke respectfully and thoughtfully. "Yes sir, I completely understand your concerns and can assure you that no one present, will doubt the accuracy of our research at the conclusion of our presentation."

Two weeks later, on a brilliant sunlit central New York day, Ron and Robert stood on a podium located directly in front of the Syracuse University physics building. Drs. Lenderman and Fleming both spoke before a select group about the challenges theorists confront in the field of science and then introduced Ron and Robert to the attendees and welcomed them to the lectern to address the gathering, including Robert's parents, his mother's family and Lisette, Arnie, Sarah and Nathan, and Gina Abramson, in addition to those in the scientific community whom the university had invited.

Following their presentation, Robert and Ron looked out onto a sea of skepticism. Rather than exhibit any sense of doubt, they looked at each other, smiled at their audience, reached into their pockets and pushed the buttons on their key fobs. One second later, the previously silent group was now buzzing as the sole occupant of the podium was now the lectern.

"Well, how do you suppose they're all getting on?" asked Ron as he busily entered co-ordinates into his computer in the Mercure conference room.

"Except for our friends and families, I hope they're trying to figure this out," replied Robert, smiling. "Do you have everything entered into the computer?"

"Yeah, it's all there," as he glanced at him from his keyboard. "Are you ready for our entrance?"

"One more thing," said Robert. Turning to the wall he said, "Danielle, please." A moment later, the wall was illuminated, filled with Danielle's image.

"Oui, Dr. Dubé?"

"Danielle, we will be entertaining the group of people we spoke about earlier very soon. Would you have everything delivered now? We will be returning with our guests in just a few minutes. Merci, Danielle."

"You are quite welcome Dr. Dubé," replied Danielle and the screen turned dark.

"I'm finished, are you ready?" Ron said as he verified his computers data.

"Absolutely," said Robert smiling. "Our guests must be wondering exactly what is happening about now. Let's continue with our presentation."

They reached into their pockets for their key fobs, pressed their buttons and an instant later stood facing each other from opposite sides of the podium in front of the S.U. physics building. There was definitely some confusion among those in attendance. Some guests stood in place while others had begun wandering near their seats. The murmuring stopped as the guests suddenly realized who had returned to the podium as they now expected answers to this unorthodox presentation.

Robert and Ron waited until everyone returned to their seats before pressing their key fobs again. As they walked toward the center of the podium, they alternately vanished and reappeared one step closer to each other. When both reached the lectern, the oscillation ceased, they shook hands and faced their guests and the onlookers, whose numbers were steadily increasing.

Ron spoke first. "I realize that a practical demonstration is a bit unusual when presenting a scientific paper. Generally it is submitted and then scrutinized before being accepted and even then; there may not be a complete consensus. However, you have just witnessed the first demonstration of the ability to rapidly transfer from one time period to another. As we walked toward each other, our right step took place in our real time, while our left step was taken in Paris, France; twenty years in the future, hence the demonstration of our appearance and reappearance."

As conversation among the attendees resumed, Robert spoke. "I'm sure that you all have doubts and reservations about what you have seen and heard. This demonstration is far from concluded, however. You may have noticed the columns surrounding the area where you are seated and the platform that the chairs are resting on. I guess that there is no better way to explain our research to you, than to show you what we mean, Allons-y."

Robert and Ron stepped from the platform and sat with their families. They leaned forward in their seats, looked at each other, smiled and pressed their buttons again.

If the guests were stunned when Robert and Ron vanished from the stage earlier, they were thunderstruck now.

No one moved when they found themselves in a darkened room while their hosts stood and faced them before a wall illuminated first with the word "*MERCURE"* in bright red letters, followed by alternating pictures of La Defense.

"Welcome to the home office of Mercure S.A," Ron began. "This is our main conference room and as some of you may have guessed from the images behind us, we are located in the La Défense district in Paris, France. We are a company which utilizes the technology we developed at Cal Tech and at Syracuse University where we produce and lease our machines to individuals and companies. We are presently twenty years into the future from where you were just a moment ago. You will find copies of our technical paper beneath your seats. Please take some time to enjoy some refreshments and then return to your seats and we will answer as many of your questions as possible. By the way, all of the breads you see here were baked by Lisette and you will discover that they are excellent."

Facing the exterior wall Robert said, "Window, clear," and every body's attention was drawn to the previously dark wall which now offered an expansive view of La Défence.

Danielle stood at one end of a long table in front of the window, filled with coffee, tea and juice in one area and other areas for hors-d'oeuvres. Robert and Ron mingled with their guests as caterers kept glasses and plates filled before they entertained them in a session devoted to answering questions about their scientific achievement.

Following a chartered bus tour of Paris, the group returned to Mercure S.A. and its conference room. Ron addressed the group, "We hope your understanding of the possibility of time travel and its possibilities and technical details. We appologise for not being able to fully disclose all of the details but some relate to our business and are proprietary. We have now reached the point in our presentation where we need return to the University. You will find umbrellas on you chairs as we knew the weather forecast called for a light rain at about the time we returned to Syracuse which should surprise no one." He sat next to Robert, pressed his key fob and a moment later all were sitting again in front of the physics building with their umbrellas open under a light drizzle before and some very startled pedestrians.

Now Dr. Lenderman and Dr. Fleming directed everyone's attention to a large bell shaped object which was positioned next to the podium. Lisette and Arnie both stood next to the focus of their presentation, hidden beneath the enormous white cloth. With a nod from Dr.Lenderman, Lisette and Arnie each pulled on the rope attached to the cloth and it fell to the ground, exposing the time machine beneath its' great clear cover. Protected inside the dome, a plaque was firmly attached to its' base crediting Robert and Ron with creation of the first functioning time machine.

Following the reception in Hendricks Chapel, everyone on Robert's list was invited to dinner at his parent's house, consisting of tandoori chicken and naan. After touring Camillus with Lisette, they returned to Ron's home overlooking the Seine.

In the morning he and Lisette left for his office in La Défence. Robert purposely entered their building from the side opposite Le Grande Arche that day, completely avoiding the plaza in front of their building. Lisette was at his side, wondering what could possibly have caused his mood to brighten so much. The instant he entered his office, he walked immediately to the wall facing the plaza and said, "windows clear", and his office was immediately bathed in sunlight. Smiling, he looked down onto the plaza and where the offensive statue had once been situated, a considerable crowd was gathering to appreciate an imposing granite and steel sculpture by the famous artist, John Van Alstine.

Robert's sense of satisfaction was now complete.

THE BREAD LADY

A sleek, black Peugeot turned right from Avenue Ledru-Rollin, proceeding slowly down the narrow street until it stopped before the address that had been received by its' computer. Leaving the car in 1st gear the driver applied the hand brake and removed his leather driving gloves. Looking forward he saw a woman dressed in shades of mauve and white leaning against the brightest red BMW convertible he had ever seen. As she turned, Robert smiled at Lisette and wondered if there were any brilliant colors that she didn't care for, but foremost on his mind was why she had asked him to meet her in front of her former bread shop on Passage Le Bonne Graine.

This street certainly produced numerous memories; the French Revolution, Garnier's betrayal, the fall of the Bastille and being saved by Bernard. Spotting the entrance to the alley which led to the neglected stables where his horses were sheltered prompted him to speculate about the fate of his young entrepreneurs; Henri and Gerard. The start of his new life in numerous respects had its origins in this narrow street, while the old and present Paris were forever intertwined, creating his life with Lisette which also began here; four centuries earlier. Hopefully, Lisette could explain why they had returned to her old shop.

"Robert, I am so glad you came," Lisette said, very excited as she smiled and kissed him. "I would like to tell you why we are here."

Before she could begin, Robert's attention was drawn to a man in a dark grey suit, who was quickly exiting through the door of the business that now occupied Lisette's former boulangerie. The man was tall and thin with a long mild face. He had a slight stoop when he walked and headed directly toward them, using both arms to cradle a brown leather briefcase with papers protruding from it as if he had left the premises in a hurry.

"I may be mistaken, but could he have anything to do with your explanation?" he asked motioning in the man's direction.

Lisette turned and smiled and when the man reached them she took a step forward, shook his hand and turned to Robert.

"M. Lévesque, I would like you to meet my husband, Dr. Dubé. Darling, I would like you to meet, our avocate, M. Lévesque, who will help us with a legal matter."

"Very nice to meet you, M. Lévesque," said Robert as Lévesque attempted to shake hands while wrapping his left arm around his bulging briefcase.

"I mean no disrespect to you, M. Lévesque," Robert continued. "Our company has a lawyer. Lisette, why do we need M. Lévesque's help?"

Before the lawyer could answer, Lisette explained, "I needed someone experienced in real estate law. I asked your corporate lawyer, M. Gravé, who recommended that I speak to M. Lévesque about the matter concerning my property in Nantes." Nodding in the direction of her former shop, she continued. "Do you remember those papers I gathered just before we left here after your trial? Those papers prove that my father owned that building and when my parents died, I inherited the bakery and the building. There were also papers which I accidentally left behind that proved our title to land near Nantes. My father left the documents in a compartment he built into the wall, but the owner of the business refuses to allow me to gain access to them. That is why I spoke to M. Lévesque."

M. Lévesque realized that this was his opportunity to speak and stepped closer to Robert, looked at him with his gold brown eyes and enthusiastically shook his hand again. "This is indeed an honor to meet you Dr. Dubé, allow me to explain."

Robert stopped leaning against his Peugeot and stood straight, "M. Lévesque, you would be doing me a favor by calling Robert."

Lévesque seemed startled for a moment before pausing to offer an explanation. "Yes, of course, Robert. The owner of the shop, a M. Marchand; was given the choice of allowing us to examine his shop to retrieve the title to Lisette's land and be given a clear title to the building, or being served with an eviction notice and all the legal proceedings that accompany it."

Feeling only moderately more relaxed with this information, Robert stood next to Lisette and placed his arm around her shoulder, "Well, what was the result of this meeting, M. Lévesque?"

At that instant, their conversation was interrupted by the sound of breaking glass as a small chair smashed through the building's front window, landing unceremoniously in the street. This was followed by a volley of insults and other various breakable objects.

M. Lévesque stood with his arms wrapped tightly around his briefcase and turned toward his clients, "Quite well actually," wincing as additional pieces shared the same fate as they lay shattered in the cobblestone street. "I believe he's extremely excited with your most generous offer," he stammered in an unconvincing voice.

"I see," said Robert clearly unimpressed. "What sort of a business does this Marchand own and why is any of this a problem?"

"The problem," Lisette began, "is the documents I need are behind a wall that M. Marchand built after he opened his business. To retrieve my documents, would require him to tear the wall down, an action which he refuses to even discuss. His business is in interior design, internationally known as I understand and he just built a really beautiful bookcase in front of the wall where the documents are located." Lisette was getting the distinct impression that her husband was tiring of this conversation.

"Let me be sure that I understand this correctly," said Robert as he ran his hands through his hair. "Your documents prove your ownership of your land in Nantes and that building and you need to demolish the wall of an interior designer to get them and he isn't ready to comply. Is that right?"

Lisette and M. Lévesque both nodded as Robert looked into the briefcase containing the papers waiting for Marchand's signature.

"Is this it?" he asked; pulling a document from the briefcase with colored tabs affixed to its edges. "Is this what he is having difficulty signing?"

"A copy of it actually," said Lévesque. "The original is probably in his shredder by now. Still, if he signed this ....."

His sentence wasn't finished or was at least ignored by Robert as he strode across the street and stepped into the interior designer's showroom with a copy of the agreement in his hand.

Curtains gently moved in the light breeze where there had once been a large window. In his mind he saw stacks of bread displayed in that same spot which now was littered with shards of glass. As he regarded the counter where Lisette used to knead her dough, a worker with sawdust coated overalls observed him curiously from a doorway.

"I'm here to see M. Marchand, and it's urgent. Tell him Dr. Robert Dubé needs to speak with him immediately."

The worker wiped his hands on his apron and eyed Robert suspiciously. "I believe he is in the office, Dr. I will tell him you are here."

"There is no need for that," he replied quickly. "Where is his office?"

The worker pointed slowly in the direction of the staircase. Moving rapidly, nearly running; he passed where ovens had once baked Lisette's breads and climbed the stairs two at a time until he stood in Lisette's former living room. Here, he once held a meeting to ask for help in constructing a playground for the children and upstairs he and Lisette had taken turns helping the other convalesce following attacks ordered by Petit. He looked straight at a spot next to the window where some time ago he looked down onto a stable and courtyard, now occupied by a dark wooden desk and a man busying himself with gathering and stacking papers next to a shredder. Against the wall where Lisette's father had once built a compartment for storing his personal papers, a beautiful bookcase now stood; recessed into the same wall.

The sound of Robert's shoes against the polished wooden floor startled him slightly. A pallid man in a dark blue suit glared menacingly at Robert.

"This is an outrage," he screamed. "How dare you enter my office without my approval?"

Robert ignored Marchand's protestations and immediately disconnected the power to the shredding machine. Marchand's face became crimson with anger as he glared at Robert.

Looking more closely at Marchand, he seemed even more slender and delicate, accentuated by his smooth bald head and sea blue eyes. His ominous, self-absorbed composure was exactly the demeanor that many take great satisfaction in purging.

"Relax M. Marchand. I'm here to help you," he said in a voice that suggested his motives were exactly the opposite.

"Do you know who I am?" he asked Marchand quietly.

"Yes, you are the husband of that impossible woman," he screamed.

"M. Marchand," he continued, "do you know what business Mercure is involved in?"

Marchand grew very thoughtful, "Why yes, they are involved in a form of transportation," as his eyes widened and he involuntarily inhaled deeply, "and you are Dr. Dubé."

Robert sat calmly in a chair and tossed the document in front of Marchand. "You told my wife that the documents she seeks are now behind the wall you claim that was built for your bookcase," as he pointed his thumb over his left shoulder." The only problem Marchand; is that I have visited this building before and my recollection is clear when I say that you actually recessed the bookcase into the wall. You found my wife's documents when you were building the bookcase and thought you could claim her land in Nantes." Marchand sat back in the chair and looked painfully at him.

"I'm here to help you make the right decision M. Marchand. Your two options are these. You may operate your business here and be granted the rights to the building after you surrender my wife's documents, or you can own the building and continue your business exactly where you are."

Marchand looked both concerned and confused.

"The difference between the two proposals is this, Marchand. Mercure is actually involved with time travel. Your choice is to operate your business as it is and give me the documents, or we will travel together to the year 1789; where I will abandon you after spreading a very nasty rumor with a friend of mine at a Paris newspaper that you are a spy for Marie-Antoinette. That will allow you a very personal, one time affair with Mme. Guillotine. While you are absent we will take what we need anyway."

Unsure whether this fight was winnable anymore he paused and in a timid and irresolute voice, Marchand picked up several pages of yellowed, parchment like documents and handed them to Robert, "Take them, just leave me."

"Stay where you are, Marchand," Robert said with contempt. "Our lawyer will be here directly to clean up your mess."

Lisette and M. Lévesque were very curious when they saw him exit the building and walk to them, holding papers he had rolled up in his hand.

"These are yours, I believe," he said lightheartedly, handing the faded documents to Lisette. Turning to M. Lévesque he said, "Marchand is waiting in his office for you. He has some papers he wants to sign."

"How did that happen?" inquired Lisette.

"It was pretty simple. He never built that wall where your father placed the deed. He discovered them when he actually tore down the wall to install the bookshelf. He had the documents the entire time. I simply made him an offer…"

"One he couldn't refuse, like the offer you made to that miserable doctor in the Bastille? I would have given anything witness that," said Lisette.

Robert simply nodded as M. Lévesque glanced first at Lisette and then at Robert, appearing to have understood what he heard regarding the Bastille.

"You will excuse me, Madame and Monsieur? I believe I have some business to tend to," said a smiling Lévesque. He shook both of their hands and strode to the former bakery, ignoring both the debris in the street and the pedestrians who avoided stepping on the pieces of smashed pottery at their feet before glancing at the smashed window.

Lisette was happy beyond measure as she read the documents proving her ownership to the family land she hadn't visited since she was a girl.

"We must visit this place, Robert. I want you to see where I came from and tell you what ideas I have for its use," she said breathlessly.

"Fine, when would you....?"

"Now, right this minute."

As her enthusiasm made any disagreement futile, he contacted Danielle and arranged for someone to retrieve his Peugeot and deliver it to their home.

Reaching for his keys, Robert hurried to the driver's door of the BMW; but Lisette was quicker and slid behind the wheel of her car, smiling at him over her left shoulder.

"Are you ready?" she said impatiently as he stood in the street, realizing that this was yet another unwinnable battle. He sighed and contemplated his options, then decided it was better that he climb into the passenger's seat and buckle his harness.

Lisette had acclimated herself quickly to all new Parisian surroundings. Her favorite was clearly driving a car, especially her bright red convertible. She treated road signs like they were decorations, pedestrians like objects whose sole obligation was to get out of her way and regarded traffic laws with complete indifference. Robert thought she was the worst driver he had ever seen, meaning she was perfect for Paris. After turning onto Rue de Faubourg and then rounding the corner onto Avenue Ledru-Rollin, they were very quickly launched onto the highway for their three hour drive to Nantes.

The highway wound its way toward the coast, passing Le Mans first and then Angers. Robert briefly explained to Lisette what had occurred when he and Bernard stopped in those communities but spent the majority of his time warning her about other vehicles, never certain if she heard what he said. He hoped to see the cathedrals he had visited long ago, but the highway was always either too far from the center of the cities or the landscape was a heavily wooded blur.

When they reached Nantes, his ordeal as Lisette's passenger had only just begun. Darting in and out among trucks and cars was torment enough on a highway, but the experience was that much worse when she attempted to locate her family's property from a childhood memory that didn't include modern shops or apartment buildings or traffic lights and road signs; which she ignored anyway.

Exiting from the freeway found them on the customary narrow village streets as Lisette's speed actually increased while she sped down these streets looking for something recognizable. Robert saw cars that were either parked on sidewalks or about to be; as drivers attempted to avoid the vivid red convertible speeding toward them. Near the town square Lisette recognised a church at the last moment and they immediately turned sharply left.

Roundabouts, stone covered streets and walls of rock as tall as Robert, quickly gave way to wide paved roads and fields.

Streets narrowed again as the buildings were gradually replaced by shrubs and tall trees, including some that reminded him of small palm trees. Eventually, they reached a fork in the road where road signs of various designs pointed out directions. To his great relief, Lisette slowed for a moment as they neared the sign post and she read them intently. He relaxed for a moment and made the mistake of leaning forward in his seat, only to be thrown back the instant she yelled, "Breton" and she began to race down the road taking the left fork as dogs ran away and birds flew. The road became narrower still and to make matters scarier, visibility was limited as both sides of the road consisted of tall hedgerows.

The pavement was becoming uneven, eventually changing into a dirt and gravel road until he could see water ahead and fields on both sides. Lisette came to a stop at the bank of a wide river by a marina near the remnants of an ancient stone wall.

Robert exited quickly from the convertible, feeling much more comfortable walking on firm ground as she led him to the riverbank. "This is my family's land and that is the Erdre River. We used to raise crops in that field until we moved to Paris. I still remember playing at the water's edge and standing with my feet in the water."

Robert had already removed his shoes and socks and waded into the water. He estimated the width of the river to be less than one quarter of mile wide here. Facing Lisette as a gentle current moved slowly against his legs, he could see that the land closest to the water was level and surrounded by a heavily wooded area.

Lisette waded into the water, stood next to him and surveyed the land where her family used to plant crops. "I can put this land to good use," she said surveying the field as if she was constructing a vision in her mind. "Isn't it funny that this water feels so much colder to me now than it did as a child?"

"Do you remember when I convinced you and Ron to create a foundation to help children escape poverty for just awhile? You two created Mercure Foundation for this very day," as she waived her arm across shore in the direction of her land, as she explained her plans to it. "My family once farmed this land and raised crops. This is where we begin to raise good citizens."

They walked back to the shore across the stone covered river bottom and returned to the spot where they left their shoes, walking barefoot to Lisette's convertible. Robert was very relieved when Lisette asked him to drive for their return trip to Paris while she explained the details of her plans for the use of her family's land.

Over the next several months, Lisette invested a great deal of her free time in her new project. Sometimes she could be convinced to use one of Mercure's machines to transport them to Nantes, often he lost the argument. While she received a new car to drive, her purple Bentley GT was still driven in the same reckless aggressive manner, however Robert felt moderately safer in a larger car.

Surrounded by trees, Lisette transformed her property on the Erdre River into a very peaceful refuge for France's poorer children. She made room for disadvantaged children from all over France, who during the summers could come and play in the fresh air and discover the result of their hard work when their crops were harvested from the rich soil, as well as receiving lessons in civics. Regular lectures by a pair of certain well known scientists, was one of the highlights of the children's visit.

The outcome of their labors in the fields, growing herbs and vegetables and wheat were three good meals per day, including fresh baked bread from their own bakery.

Robert and Lisette worked closely together during the planning and construction of her compound. As it neared completion she asked him to "mind his own business in La Défense" as she wanted the final product to be a surprise.

Two weeks later, she asked him if Ron and Arnie would accompany them to see what Mercure Foundation had helped her accomplish on her family's land. Robert was very happy for the opportunity for a leisurely drive to Nantes and it gave afforded him the opportunity to explain his adventures in 1789 to Ron. However, he wasn't struck with the full impact of Lisette's reasoning until he slowly approached the entrance to her property and turned sharply to his right.

Two stone pillars on either side of the entrance, supported an arch over the unpaved drive with the name "Camp Mercure" in brilliant red letters against a green and yellow background. A narrow view of the river presented itself immediately as the road descended, following a long tree line on their left and a wide field on the right where children were seen tending to their crops. When the tree line ceased, their view of the river expanded before them, revealing an athletic field for soccer and a basketball court and a swimming area in the river.

They were still some distance from the river when Lisette asked him to park the car and walk with her. Robert parked his Peugeot in the gravel covered parking lot and she held Arnie's hand as they all walked toward a stand of tall trees.

"This is something we should all be proud of," she said calling out to Ron and Robert. They continued walking toward the river and a group of one story buildings, made of a beige colored rock with dark grey roofs and shutters. Two of the buildings were sleeping quarters for the children and one was an open pavilion built on the shoreline where a deck extended over the water for docking of canoes and for swimming. The last structure was very familiar looking as they approached it and he saw a store front reminiscent of an 18th century bread shop, built near the water's edge with a green store front and "BOULENGERIE" prominently displayed over the door in bright gold letters.

"This is really amazing," said Robert as he felt that he had taken a step back in time. "I feel as if I should be wearing my major's uniform. All that is missing is the way you looked at me the first time I entered your shop hoping to speak to the Bread Lady. My life almost flashed before my eyes."

"That should teach you not to arrive unannounced, Major," she said with a smile.

Lisette spoke with an obvious sense of pride. "We tried to match my old boulangerie as closely as possible. Some of the equipment is so different, so modern, but I was surprised how little has changed. We used to buy our vegetables fresh at the market, now they come fresh from our fields. The children add ingredients we used in Paris to the dough they knead themselves in the same way we did. The ovens are still made of brick and we fire them with wood, I didn't care for gas ovens."

She walked next to a child who was rolling dough into rolls and she pushed some of the flour and spices together and rubbed her hands faster and faster until the friction warmed her hands. She first raised them to her face and inhaled deeply before placing them on Robert's face and nodded to Arnie and Ron to do the same. He could feel the warmth of her hands and the smells of her spices. Lisette gazed at him with a broad smile, "It's like we never left Paris. This was one of the last my last sensations before we left. This is the best present you could ever give me, Robert."

A NEW LIFE

Robert now possessed considerably more than anything Louis XVI could have ever bestowed upon him and he was able to use his wealth he earned from his business to improve the lives of disadvantaged people, rather than creating wealth on the backs of peasants. Both the business world and the scientific community respected the reclusive physicist.

He and Lisette bought an incredible home close to Ron's penthouse and most importantly, its kitchen was one that his mother approved of. He wanted a home with both a lawn and garden, not easily available in the 16th arrondissement of Paris. The house they selected had seven bedrooms with seven bathrooms and terraces on different levels that afforded a view of the Eiffel Tower. A long rectangular pool with manicured hedges on one side, surrounded by beautiful flowerbeds, sprawled beneath the branches of a chestnut tree, making it one of their favorite places where they could sit and relax.

Lisette loved the windows which reached from floor to ceiling and the expansive, open design of their rooms. Abundant sunlight highlighted the various designs of the highly polished wood floors.

Brilliant white cabinets formed three sides of their kitchen, with one very large window positioned above the sink, overlooking their back yard. They never tired of admiring the patterns and smoothness of their grey and blue and white granite counters. A large maple cabinet with louvered spaces for plates was attached to the wall near the window. An island made of maple with a matching granite countertop stood in the center of the kitchen with seating at one end that accommodated five people comfortably.

The kitchen was bathed in light from a mixture of lamps recessed into the ceiling and additional small lamps which hung above the island.

Their kitchen seamlessly merged with the dining area and was lit by two crystal chandeliers. An adjacent lounge area with large arched doors opened out onto a terrace overlooking their yard. They truly loved their home and found it to be their favorite place in all of Paris. They were always comfortable and relaxed whether they were entertaining guests or spending time alone.

Through it all, he still had one lingering regret from his time in La Chapelle-Thérmer. Leaving their village without revealing his true identity to Genevieve had continued to bother him. Several times he considered travelling back in time to explain it to her, but always stopped when he considered the risks, even if Ron's calculations had truly solved the problem of accuracy.

He also was apprehensive about what he might find in the past. The Vendée Revolt in 1793 was a period of great violence following the Revolution in which nearly two hundred thousand people, both civilians and military; lost their lives. Could that violence have swept La Chapelle-Thérmer away or flowed around it like a wave, unable to reach those who survived on higher ground? His desire to visit La Chapelle-Thémer once more was tempered by some of these potential risks and fears.

Visiting museums had become one of Robert and Lisette's favorite leisure activities and they thought that the Musée Marmottan Monet was the best. Located on Rue Louis Boilly, only a twenty minute walk from their home, it featured impressionist and post-impressionist painters. Works by Monet, Degas, Manet, Gauguin and Renoir were regularly on exhibit.

From their home near Avenue de Saint-Cloud they walked beneath trees down a narrow street, heavily wooded on both sides; until they reached a two lane street covered in brick that was popular with both pedestrians as well as with those who passed them on their bicycles.

An area with boulevards, traffic and tall apartment buildings were reminders to them that they lived in one of the world's major cities but their trek's tranquil nature returned as they continued along a one way street with an abundance of trees on their left that followed a long narrow sparsely wooded park on their right, insulating them from the distant sounds of traffic.

They knew that they were near their destination when they reached the Square des Écrivians Combattants Morts pour la France. In a city known for its expansive parks and statues, this was dedicated to French writers who died during World War I. Absent of any statues or monuments; it was a small square with beautiful flowerbeds filled with roses, bushes and trees. This was where they lingered sometimes before crossing Boulevard Suchet to Rue Louis Boilly and entering through the museum's tall green doors.

On one of their many visits, they were especially pleased to find an exhibit featuring artists whose paintings portrayed scenes from the countryside. He enjoyed paintings by Corot, John Constable, Pissarro and especially, Monet's Sunrise. There were also works by lesser known artists arranged by the various regions of France. While Robert was admiring the masterful way Pissarro captured the image of a village on canvas, Lisette had moved on to other paintings, but had stopped before one painting in particular for some time.

"Robert, you should really see this one. The person in in this painting looks remarkably like you," she said pointing to a young man with his arm around the shoulder of a small girl standing in the courtyard of a village church.

He immediately recognised the church as Brother André's in La Chapelle-Thémer and Genevieve as the little girl in the courtyard who incredibly, had valued Robert above bacon. Genevieve had remembered the picture they posed for and Brother André had fulfilled his promise to obtain art supplies for her from La Rochelle and like everything else she had undertaken, the attention to detail was incredible; including the lone miserable bush in the church courtyard.

A small electronic sign beneath each work provided information about it. He found it difficult to conceal his disappointment because beneath Genevieve's it read only:

Artist: unknown

Title: Unknown

Region: Unknown

Date: Circa 1800

Genevieve had indeed survived the Vendée Revolt and preserved her Oncle Mathurin in a masterful painting. Lisette could tell from Robert's posture that he was considering some action. "Excuse me Lisette," as he turned and crossed the gallery floor toward the gallery director's office and returned shortly. He immediately looked at the screen.

Artist: Genevieve Dubé

Title: Mon Oncle Mathurin

Region:La Chapelle-Thérmer, Vendée

Date:circa 1800

Still, it was clear from his expression that he was not entirely satisfied with his editing. As he studied it, he remembered his wish to reveal his real name to Genevieve and proceeded again to the director's office; this time without saying a word to Lisette. A moment later she noticed a change in the display beneath the painting.

Title: Mon Oncle Robert

He rejoined Lisette this time with a more peaceful expression and spoke while he looked at Genevieve's painting.

"We have just purchased this piece and donated it to the museum where it will remain permanently on display."

Now he had a look of satisfaction, certain that admirers of her work would at least be aware of her name and hoping that on some level this action would substitute for not disclosing his actual identity to his talented niece.

When they left the museum they customarily turned to their right to begin their walk home. Today however, Robert was more intent on extending their excursion and held Lisette's hand as they turned to their left and crossed Avenue Raphaël to Jardin de Ranelagh.

Robert and Lisette sat on the lawn beneath one if the many varities of trees, watching the children ride the carousel and the numerous people who lay on blankets in the sunshine. A group of school children entered the park as their teacher led them from an excursion to Musée Marmottan while they held their drawings and pencils and crayons.

Lisette and Robert sat and talked, watching the children play and draw. One by one the children left their materials on the lawn for their teacher to watch over, until one girl sat alone. She hardly noticed that her classmates had moved on to other interests as her attention was focused solely on her drawing of the trees.

Excusing himself, Robert walked to where the teacher stood and spoke to her for a moment. Their conversation was very animated but brief. He continued to walk to the ice cream stand and engaged in a chat with the vendor before returning to Lisette with ice cream for both of them.

Lisette knew there was a story behind the ice cream cones. "Their teacher tells me that her class is from a local school about five minutes' walk from here. Today was their field trip to the museum and they were about to return to classes before I offered to buy ice cream for all the children."

Soon the teacher formed the children in a line and they marched to the ice cream stand. When the teacher informed them about the surprise courtesy of the man and woman sitting under the tree they turned and waved to Robert and Lisette who waved back. After they had finished their treat they all approached Robert and Lisette and thanked them before returning to their school except for the girl he had first noticed.

She concentrated even more on her work and eventually placed her pencils and crayons on the lawn and approached Robert and Lisette as she held her drawing paper. She handed them her drawing: an extremely accurate depiction of a couple sitting with their ice cream under the trees. Their teacher called them to form their line and reminded them to acknowledge their gratitude for their treat once more before marching across the park toward their school.

They were extremely impressed by the detail of the little girl's art work. As the class eventually became lost from sight, Robert sat brooding on the lawn, closely examining the drawing from the little girl. Picking up a stick he tapped it on his shoe before tossing it onto the lawn.

"There is someone I would like you to meet," he paused as he turned to look at her. "Lisette, do you trust me?"

"That depends, Major," she said grinning. "Does it involve balloons?"

Robert chuckled as he stood, "No, Lisette; there are no balloons."

Lisette rose to her feet.

"Then, yes of course I trust you. Now let's go home. I want to bring bread with us when you introduce me to your niece."

THE END

RESOURCES

Angers, France	Wikipedia
Angers Cathedral	Wikipedia
Anjou, France	Wikipedia
Bourgeois, sans-coulottes and other Frenchmen	Morris Slavin and Agnes Smith Wilfred Laurier University Press 1981
Bastille	Wikipedia
A Brief History of the Tongva People: The Native Inhabitants of the Puente Hills Preserve	Rosanne Welch PhD.
Cathdédrale Saint-Maurice d'Angers	Les Vitraux de la Cathédrale Corpus Vitrearin ISBN 978-2-7351-0722-196
Cholet, France	Encyclopedia Britannica
Contesting the French Revolution	Paul R. Hanson 2009 Blackwell Publishing
Declaration of the Rights of Man and of the Citizen	www.constitution.org
From French Nobility Renaissance to Absolute Monarchy	Russell Major; Johns Hopkins Press 1994 ISBN 0-8018-5631-0
The French Revolution 1787-1804	P.M. Jones
French Royal academy of Sciences	Wikipedia
Biography of Gaspar de Portola	wwwsandiegohistory.org
Grand Tours and Cooks Tours	Lynne Whitey ISBN 0-688-08800-7

Hahamog'na	www.KCET.org
History of Pasadena	Wikipedia
Jean Charles de Borda	Wikipedia
Jean-François de Rozier	Wikipedia
Latitude	www.merriam-webster.com
Le Mans, France	Wikipedia
Le Mans Cathedral	Wikipedia
Le Marais, Paris	Wikipedia
The Life and Times of Padre Serra	William Byrd Press
Longitude	Wikipedia
The Making of Revolutionary Paris	David Garrioch University of California Press
Mathurin Dubé- A Hero of Riviére-Ouelle	Marie-Paul Dubé
Mexican Cession A Continent Divided: The U.S. Mexico War	Center for Greater Southwestern Studies
Mission San Gabriel Arcángel	Zephyrin Engelhardt- The Franciscan Herald Press Chicago, Illinois
Monet: The Late Paintings of Giverny from the Musée Marmottan	Lynn Federle Orr
Onondaga Nation	www.onondaganation.org
Paris: The Secret History	Andrew Hussey; Bloomsburg Press 2006
Pont Neuf	Wikipedia
Porte Saint-Antoine	Wikipedia
Postilion	Wikipedia
Royal Chapel, Versailles	Wikipedia
Science in France in the Revolutionary Era	Maurice P. Crosland; M.I.T. Press
Soapstone	USC Wrigley Marine science Center,

	www.rain.org
Thomas Jefferson and the Storming of the Bastille	www.archives.gov
Tongva canoe	www.keepersofindigenousways.org
	www.CSULB.edu
Tongva People	cobweb.UCLA.edu
Travels in France 1787-1789	Arthur Young
Uninterruptable Power Supply (UPS)	Wikipedia
Valley of the Hahamog'na: Pasadena Through Two Centuries	Pasadena Savings and Loan 1952
Versailles	Wikipedia
	DVD
	The Chateau, the Gardens and Trianon; Christopher Hilbert 1972
Yolande Martine Gabrielle de Polastron, Duchess of Polignac	Wikipedia
Zeeuws Spek	Wikipedia